UNRESTRICTED ACCESS

ALSO BY JAMES ROLLINS

SIGMA FORCE NOVELS

The Last Odyssey
Crucible
The Demon Crown
The Seventh Plague
The Bone Labyrinth
The 6th Extinction
The Eye of God
Bloodline
The Devil Colony
The Doomsday Key
The Last Oracle
The Judas Strain
Black Order
Map of Bones
Sandstorm

INDIVIDUAL ADVENTURES

Altar of Eden
Ice Hunt
Amazonia
Deep Fathom
Excavation
Subterranean

SANGUINES SERIES WITH REBECCA CANTRELL

Blood Infernal
Innocent Blood
Blood Gospel

TUCKER WAYNE SERIES WITH GRANT BLACKWOOD

War Hawk
The Kill Switch

UNRESTRICTED ACCESS

NEW AND CLASSIC SHORT FICTION

JAMES ROLLINS

WM

WILLIAM MORROW

An Imprint of HarperCollins*Publishers*

HarperCollins books may be purchased for educational, business, or sales promotional use. For information, please email the Special Markets Department at SPsales@harpercollins.com.

FIRST EDITION

Library of Congress Cataloging-in-Publication Data has been applied for.

ISBN 978-0-06-268680-0

20 21 22 23 24   LSC   10 9 8 7 6 5 4 3 2 1

To all the Warped Spacers, past and present, who have held my feet to the fire for the past twenty-seven years. You are to blame for this book—and my career.

Contents

UNRESTRICTED ACCESS

How It Began

For the introduction to this collection, let's start at the beginning.

I can succinctly remember a cautionary warning from my ninth-grade English teacher. As she marched before the blackboard, she outlined the skill sets necessary to be a good writer, including comparing the various methods of storytelling.

She explained how a *novelist* had the free range of a nearly unlimited number of words in which to tell a story. Novelists had countless pages to construct a plot, to explore the inner worlds of its characters, to build toward that proverbial darkest hour, and to stick a landing with a satisfying ending. There was even more than enough space for subplots and tangents and trips down blind alleys before backtracking to the main story line.

That was not true when it came to the construction of *short stories*. She described how the amount of elbow room afforded an author became more restricted. To be successful here, a writer had to choose their words more carefully, to pare down a story to its essential parts while still creating the proper impact. To achieve this—and to do it well—took considerably more effort and skill than required of a freewheeling novelist.

But even then, my teacher was not done. She saved the *most* daunting task for last; namely, writing *poetry*. Here the economy of words was even more strangled. Each syllable had to be judged, the rhythm and rhyme metered and tested, each word had to serve multiple purposes. This, of course, took a true genius, a writer of incomparable skill.

I took these various descriptions to heart.

And that is why I became a novelist.

At the beginning of my career, I was self-aware enough to recognize that I was not a person of monastic frugalness when it came to words and stories. I loved reading doorstopper novels, and if those books were a part of a series, all the better. Inevitably, when it came to crafting my first stories, I certainly did not want to be restricted in the number of words or pages in which to tell my tale.

Alas, after writing half a dozen novels, someone asked me to write a short story.

I resisted.

I balked, made excuses, turned my back, ignored such requests.

If you are holding this book, then you know I eventually relented. The first story I wrote was "Kowalski's in Love." It appeared in the International Thriller Writers' first anthology collection, *Thriller: Stories to Keep You Up All Night*, edited by James Patterson. I agreed to write this story for one simple reason: peer pressure. I was on the board of ITW, so how could I refuse? The conceit of this anthology was for each writer to submit a story featuring a character from their respective novels.

By that time, I had been deep into my Sigma Force series. I had been writing about a motley team of former Special Forces soldiers who had been drummed out of the service for various reasons, but because of particular skills or talents, they were secretly recruited by DARPA—the defense department's research-and-development agency—to act as field agents for covert projects and missions. By then, the titular Joseph Kowalski was a member of Sigma, but it was not the first time I had written about him. He debuted in an earlier novel, *Ice Hunt*, but I loved writing about this former navy man—a fellow who was not the brightest of the lot, but who perhaps was special in his own way—so I recruited him into Sigma. Still, I never shared the story of *how* he joined this elite team. So, goaded by peer pressure, I used this opportunity to finally tell the tale of how Kowalski became a member of Sigma.

That is "Kowalski's in Love."

As I wrote this story, I could hear my ninth-grade English teacher whispering in my ear. I sweated each word, pared the story down as much as I could. And while it was hard, I learned that such stories are not without their own particular delights. It allowed me to explore corners and back alleys of my larger work, areas not afforded even within the boundless expanse of a novel.

So let me welcome you all here to those hidden corners, to grant you unrestricted access to those back alleys of my writing. Throughout this collection, I'll pop back in here and there to act as your guide, to let you know how the stories came about—and why.

Still, before we begin, let it be known that I have not forgotten the wisdom and warning of my ninth-grade English teacher. Acknowledging that lesson, I make you all a sincere promise. I'm even willing to set it in print.

I will never write poetry.

Kowalski's in Love

JAMES ROLLINS

He wasn't much to look at . . . even swinging upside down from a hog snare. Pug-nosed, razor-clipped muddy hair, a six-foot slab of beef hooked and hanging naked except for a pair of wet gray boxer shorts. His chest was crisscrossed with old scars, along with one jagged bloody scratch from collarbone to groin. His eyes shone wide and wild.

And with good reason.

Two minutes before, as Dr. Shay Rosauro unhitched her glide-chute on the nearby beach, she had heard his cries in the jungle and come to investigate. She had approached in secret, moving silently, spying from a short distance away, cloaked in shadow and foliage.

"Back off, you furry bastard . . . !"

The man's curses never stopped, a continual flow tinged with a growled Bronx accent. Plainly he was American. Like herself.

She checked her watch.

8:33 A.M.

The island would explode in twenty-seven minutes.

The man would die sooner.

The more immediate threat came from the island's other inhabitants, drawn by the man's shouts. The average adult mandrill baboon weighed over a hundred pounds, most of that muscle and teeth. They were usually found in Africa. Never on a jungle island off the coast of Brazil. The yellow radio collars suggested the pack were once the research subjects belonging to Professor Salazar, shipped to this remote island for his experimental trials. *Mandrillus sphinx* were also considered *frugivorous*, meaning their diet consisted of fruits and nuts.

But not always.

They were also known to be opportunistic carnivores.

One of the baboons stalked around the trapped man: a charcoal-furred male of the species with a broad red snout bordered on both sides by ridges of blue. Such coloration indicated the fellow was the dominant male of the group. Females and subordinate males, all a duller brown, had settled to rumps or hung from neighboring branches. One bystander yawned, exposing a set of three-inch-long eyeteeth and a muzzle full of ripping incisors.

The male sniffed at the prisoner. A meaty fist swung at the inquisitive baboon, missed, and whished through empty air.

The male baboon reared on its hind legs and howled, lips peeling back from its muzzle to expose the full length of its yellow fangs. An impressive and horrifying display. The other baboons edged closer.

Shay stepped into the clearing, drawing all eyes. She lifted her hand and pressed the button on her sonic device, nicknamed a *shrieker*. The siren blast from the device had the desired effect.

Baboons fled into the forest. The male leader bounded up, caught a low branch, and swung into the cloaking darkness of the jungle.

The man, still spinning on the line, spotted her. "Hey . . . how about . . . ?"

Shay already had a machete in her other hand. She jumped atop a boulder and severed the hemp rope with one swipe of her weapon.

The man fell hard, striking the soft loam and rolling to the side. Amid a new string of curses, he struggled with the snare around his ankle. He finally freed the knotted rope.

"Goddamn apes!"

"Baboons," Shay corrected.

"What?"

"They're baboons, not apes. They have stubby tails."

"Whatever. All I saw were their big goddamn teeth."

As the man stood and brushed off his knees, Shay spotted a US Navy anchor tattooed on his right bicep. Ex-military? Maybe he could prove handy. Shay checked the time.

8:35 A.M.

"What are you doing here?" she asked.

"My boat broke down." His gaze traveled up and down her lithe form.

She was not unaccustomed to such attention from the male of her own species . . . even now, when she was unflatteringly dressed in green camouflaged fatigues and sturdy boots. Her shoulder-length black hair had been efficiently bound behind her ears with a black bandanna, and in the tropical swelter, her skin glowed a dark mocha.

Caught staring, he glanced back toward the beach. "I swam here after my boat sank."

"Your boat sank?"

"Okay, it blew up."

She stared at him for further explanation.

"There was a gas leak. I dropped my cigar—"

She waved away the rest of his words with her machete. Her pickup was scheduled at the northern peninsula in under a half hour. On that timetable, she had to reach the compound, break into the safe, and obtain the vials of antidote. She set off into the jungle, noting a trail. The man followed, dragged along in her wake.

"Whoa . . . where are we going?"

She freed a rolled-up rain poncho from her daypack and passed it to him.

He struggled into it as he followed. "Name's Kowalski" he said. He got the poncho on backward and fought to work it around. "Do you have a boat? A way off this friggin' island?"

She didn't have time for subtlety. "In twenty-three minutes, the Brazilian navy is going to firebomb this atoll."

"What?" He checked his own wrist. He had no watch.

She continued, "An evac is scheduled for wheels up at 8:55 A.M. on the northern peninsula. But first I have to retrieve something from the island."

"Wait. Back up. Who's going to firebomb this shithole?"

"The Brazilian navy. In twenty-three minutes."

"Of course they are." He shook his head. "Of all the goddamn islands, I had to shag my ass onto one that's going to blow up."

Shay tuned out his diatribe. At least he kept moving. She had to give him that. He was either very brave or very dumb.

"Oh, look . . . a mango." He reached for the yellow fruit.

"Don't touch that."

"But I haven't eaten in—?"

"All the vegetation on this island has been aerial sprayed with a transgenic rhabdovirus."

He lowered his hand.

"Once ingested, it stimulates the sensory centers of the brain, heightening a victim's senses. Sight, sound, smell, taste, and touch."

"And what's wrong with that?"

"The process also corrupts the reticular apparatus of the cerebral cortex. Triggering manic rages."

A growling yowl echoed through the jungle behind them. It was answered by coughing grunts and howls from either flank.

"The apes . . . ?"

"Baboons. Yes, they're surely infected. Experimental subjects."

"Great. The Island of Rabid Baboons."

Ignoring him, she pointed toward a whitewashed hacienda sprawled atop the next hill, seen through a break in the foliage. "We need to reach that compound."

The terra-cotta-tiled structure had been leased by Professor Salazar for his research, funded by a shadowy organization of terrorist cells. Here on the isolated island, he had conducted the final stages of perfecting his bioweapon. Then two days ago, Sigma Force—a covert US science team specializing in global threats—had captured the doctor in the heart of the Brazilian rain forest, but not before he had infected an entire Indian village outside of Manaus, including an international children's relief hospital.

The disease was already in its early stages, requiring the prompt quarantine of the village by the Brazilian army. The only hope was to obtain Professor Salazar's antidote, locked in the doctor's safe.

Or at least the vials *might* be there.

Salazar claimed to have destroyed his supply.

Upon this assertion, the Brazilian government had decided to take no chances. A storm was due to strike at dusk with hurricane-force winds. They feared the storm surge might carry the virus from the island to the mainland's coastal rain forest. It would take only a single infected leaf to risk the entire equatorial rain forest. So the plan was to firebomb the small island, to burn its vegetation to the bedrock. The assault was set for zero nine hundred. The government could not be convinced that the remote possibility of a cure was worth the risk of a delay. Total annihilation was their plan. That included the Brazilian village. Acceptable losses.

Anger surged through her as she pictured Manuel Garrison, her partner. He had tried to evacuate the children's hospital, but he'd become trapped and subsequently infected. Along with all the children.

Acceptable losses were not in her vocabulary.

Not today.

So Shay had proceeded with her solo op. Parachuting from a high-altitude drop. She had radioed her plans while plummeting in free fall. Sigma command had agreed to send an emergency evac helicopter to the northern end of the island. It would touch down for one minute. Either she was on the chopper at that time . . . or she was dead.

The odds were fine with her.

But now she wasn't alone.

The side of beef tromped loudly behind her. Whistling. He was *whistling*. She turned to him. "Mister Kowalski, do you remember my description of how the virus heightens a victim's sense of hearing?" Her quiet words crackled with irritation.

"Sorry." He glanced at the trail behind him.

"Careful of that tiger trap," she said, stepping around the crudely camouflaged hole.

"What—?" His left foot fell squarely on the trapdoor of woven reeds. His weight shattered through it.

Shay shoulder-blocked the man to the side and landed atop him. It felt like falling on a pile of bricks. Only bricks were smarter.

She pushed up. "After being snared, you'd think you'd watch where you were stepping! The whole place is rigged as one big booby trap."

She stood, straightened her pack, and edged around the spike-lined pit. "Stay behind me. Step where I step."

In her anger, she missed the trip cord.

The only warning was a small *thwang*.

She jumped to the side but was too late. A tethered log swung from the forest and struck her knee. She heard the snap of her tibia, then went flying through the air—right toward the open maw of the tiger trap.

She twisted to avoid the pit's iron spikes. There was no hope.

Then she hit . . . bricks again.

Kowalski had lunged and blocked the hole with his own bulk. She rolled off him. Agony flared up her leg, through her hip, and exploded along her spine. Her vision narrowed to a pinprick, but not enough to miss the angled twist below her knee.

Kowalski gained her side. "Oh, man . . . oh, man . . ."

"Leg's broken," she said, biting back the pain.

"We can splint it."

She checked her watch.

8:39 A.M.

Twenty-one minutes left.

He noted her attention. "I can carry you. We can still make it to the evac site."

She recalculated in her head. She pictured Manuel's shit-eating grin . . . and the many faces of the children. Pain worse than any broken bone coursed through her. She could not fail.

The man read her intent. "You'll never make it to that house," he said. "I don't have any other choice."

"Then let me do it," he blurted out. His words seemed to surprise him as much as it did her, but he didn't retract them. "You make for the beach. I'll get whatever you want out of the goddamn hacienda."

She turned and stared the stranger full in the face. She searched for something to give her hope. Some hidden strength, some underlying fortitude. She found nothing. But she had no other choice.

"There'll be other traps."

"I'll keep my eyes peeled this time."

"And the office safe . . . I can't teach you to crack it in time."

"Do you have an extra radio?"

She nodded.

"So talk me through it once I get there."

She hesitated—but there was no time for even that. She swung her pack around. "Lean down."

She reached to a side pocket of her pack and stripped out two self-adhesive patches. She attached one behind the man's ear and the other over his Adam's apple. "Microreceiver and a subvocal transmitter."

She quickly tested the radio, while explaining the stakes involved.

"So much for my relaxing vacation under the sun," he mumbled.

"One more thing," she said. She pulled out three sections of a weapon from her pack. "A VK rifle. Variable Kinetic." She quickly snapped the pieces together and shoved a fat cylindrical cartridge into place on its underside. It looked like a stubby assault rifle, except the barrel was wider and flattened horizontally.

"Safety release is here." She pointed the weapon at a nearby bush and squeezed the trigger. There was only a tiny whirring cough. A projectile flashed out the barrel and buzzed through the bush, severing leaves and branches. "One-inch razor-disks. You can set the weapon for single shot or automatic strafe." She demonstrated. "Two hundred shots per magazine."

He whistled again and accepted the weapon. "Maybe you should keep this weed-whacker. With your bum leg, you're going to drag ass at a snail's pace." He nodded to the jungle "And the damn apes are still out there."

"They're baboons . . . and I still have my handheld shrieker. Now get going." She checked her watch. She had given Kowalski a second time-piece, calibrated to match. "Nineteen minutes."

He nodded. "I'll see you soon." He moved off the trail, vanishing almost instantly into the dense foliage.

"Where are you going?" she called after him. "The trail—"

"Screw the trail," he responded through the radio. "I'll take my chances in the raw jungle. Less traps. Plus I've got this baby to carve a straight path to the mad doctor's house."

Shay hoped he was right. There would be no time for backtracking or second chances. She quickly dosed herself with a morphine injector and used a broken tree branch for a crutch. As she set off for the beach, she heard the ravenous hunting calls of the baboons.

She hoped Kowalski could outsmart them.

The thought drew a groan that had nothing to do with her broken leg.

Luckily Kowalski had a knife now.

He hung upside down . . . for the second time that day. He bent at the waist, grabbed his trapped ankle, and sawed through the snare's rope. It snapped with a *pop*. He fell, clenched in a ball, and crashed to the jungle floor with a loud *oof*.

"What was that?" Dr. Rosauro asked over the radio.

He straightened his limbs and lay on his back for a breath. "Nothing," he growled. "Just tripped on a rock." He scowled at the swinging rope overhead. He was not about to tell the beautiful woman doctor that he had been strung up again. He did have some pride left.

"Goddamn snare," he mumbled under his breath.

"What?"

"Nothing." He had forgotten about the sensitivity of the subvocal transmitter.

"Snare? You snared yourself again, didn't you?"

He kept silent. His momma once said, *It was better to keep your mouth shut and let people think you a fool than to open it and remove all doubt.*

"You need to watch where you're going," the woman scolded.

Kowalski bit back a retort. He heard the pain in her voice . . . and her fear. So instead he hauled back to his feet and retrieved his gun.

"Seventeen minutes," Dr. Rosauro reminded him.

"I'm just reaching the compound now."

The sun-bleached hacienda appeared like a calm oasis of civilization in a sea of Nature's raw exuberance. It was straight lines and sterile order versus wild overgrowth and tangled fecundity. Three buildings sat on five manicured acres, separated by breezeways, and nestled around a small garden courtyard. A three-tiered Spanish fountain stood in the center, ornate with blue and red glass tiles. No water splashed through its basins.

Kowalski studied the compound, stretching a kink out of his back. The only movement across the cultivated grounds was the swaying fronds of some coconut palms. The winds were already rising with the approaching storm. Clouds stacked on the southern horizon.

"The office is on the main floor, near the back," Rosauro said in his ear. "Careful of the electric perimeter fence. The power may still be on."

He studied the chain-link fencing, almost eight feet tall, topped by a spiral of concertina wire and separated from the jungle by a burned swath about ten yards wide. No-man's-land.

Or rather no-*ape's*-land.

He picked up a broken branch and approached the fence. Wincing, he stretched one end toward the chain links. He was mindful of his bare feet. *Shouldn't I be grounded for this?* He had no idea.

As the tip of his club struck the fence, a strident wail erupted. He jumped back, then realized the noise was not coming from the fence. It wailed off to his left, toward the water.

Dr. Rosauro's shrieker.

"Are you all right?" Kowalski called into his transmitter.

A long stretch of silence had him holding his breath—then whispered words reached him. "The baboons must sense my injury. They're converging on my location. Just get going."

Kowalski poked his stick at the fence a few more times, like a child with a dead rat, making sure it was truly dead. Once satisfied, he snapped the concertina wire with clippers supplied by Dr. Rosauro and scurried over the fence, certain the power was just waiting to surge back with electric-blue death.

He dropped with a relieved sigh onto the mowed lawn, as bright and perfect as any golf course.

"You don't have much time," the doctor stressed needlessly. "If you're successful, the rear gardens lead all the way to the beach. The northern headlands stretch out from there."

Kowalski set out, aiming for the main building. A shift in wind brought the damp waft of rain . . . along with the stench of death, the ripeness of meat left out in the sun. He spotted the body on the far side of the fountain.

He circled the man's form. The guy's face had been gnawed to the bone, clothes shredded, belly slashed open, bloated intestines strung across the ground like festive streamers. It seemed the apes had been having their own party since the good doctor took off.

As he circled, he noted the black pistol clutched in the corpse's hand. The slide had popped open. No more bullets. Not enough firepower to hold off a whole pack of the furry carnivores. Kowalski raised his own weapon to his shoulder. He searched the shadowed corners for any hidden apes. There were not even any bodies. The shooter must either be a poor marksman, or the ruby-assed monkeys had hauled off their brethren's bodies, perhaps to eat later, like so much baboon takeout.

Kowalski made one complete circle. Nothing.

He crossed toward the main building. Something nagged at the edge of his awareness. He scratched his skull in an attempt to dislodge it—but failed.

He climbed atop the full-length wooden porch and tried the door handle. Latched but unlocked. He shoved the door open with one foot, weapon raised, ready for a full-frontal ape assault.

The door swung wide, rebounded, and bounced back closed in his face.

Snorting in irritation, he grabbed the handle again. It wouldn't budge. He tugged harder.

Locked.

"You've got to be kidding."

The collision must have jiggled some bolt into place.

"Are you inside yet?" Rosauro asked.

"Just about," he grumbled.

"What's the hold-up?"

"Well . . . what happened was . . ." He tried sheepishness, but it fit him as well as fleece on a rhino. "I guess someone locked it."

"Try a window."

Kowalski glanced to the large windows that framed either side of the barred doorway. He stepped to the right and peered through. Inside was a rustic kitchen with oak tables, a farmer's sink, and old enamel appliances. Good enough. Maybe they even had a bottle of beer in the fridge. A man could dream. But first there was work to do.

He stepped back, pointed his weapon, and fired a single round. The silver razor-disk shattered through the pane as easily as any bullet. Fractures spattered out from the hole.

He grinned. Happy again.

He retreated another step, careful of the porch edge. He thumbed the switch to automatic fire and strafed out the remaining panes.

He poked his head through the hole. "Anyone home?"

That's when he saw the exposed wire snapping and spitting around a silver disk imbedded in the wall plaster. It had nicked through the electric cord. More disks were impaled across the far wall . . . including one that had punctured the gas line to the stove.

He didn't bother cursing.

He twisted and leaped as the explosion blasted behind him. A wall of superheated air shoved him out of the way, blowing his poncho over his head. He hit the ground rolling as a fireball swirled across of the courtyard overhead. Tangled in his poncho, he tumbled—right into the eviscerated corpse. Limbs fought, heat burned, and scrambling fingers found only a gelid belly wound and things that squished.

Gagging, Kowalski fought his way free and shoved the poncho off his body. He stood, shaking like a wet dog, swiping gore from his arms in disgust. He stared toward the main building.

Flames danced behind the kitchen window. Smoke choked out the shattered pane.

"What happened?" the doctor gasped in his ear.

He only shook his head. Flames spread, flowing out the broken window and lapping at the porch.

"Kowalski?"

"Booby trap. I'm fine."

He collected his weapon from his discarded poncho. Resting it on his shoulder, he intended to circle around to the back. According to Dr. Rosauro, the main office was in the rear.

If he worked quickly—

He checked his watch.

8:45.

It was hero time.

He stepped toward the north side of the hacienda. His bare heel slipped on a loop of intestine, slick as any banana peel. His leg twisted out from under him. He tumbled face-first, striking hard, the weapon slamming to the packed dirt, his finger jamming the trigger.

Silver disks flashed out and struck the figure lumbering into the courtyard, one arm on fire. It howled—not in agony, but in feral rage. The figure wore the tatters of a white butler's attire. His eyes were fever-bright but mucked with pasty matter. Froth speckled and drooled from lips rippled in a snarl. Blood stained the lower half of his face and drenched the front of his once-starched white shirt.

In a flash of insight—a rarity—Kowalski realized what had been nagging him before. The lack of monkey corpses here. He'd assumed they'd been cannibalized—if so, then why leave a perfectly good chunk of meat out here?

The answer: no apes had attacked here.

It seemed the beasts were not the only ones infected on the island.

Not the only cannibals.

The butler, still on fire, lunged toward Kowalski. The first impacts of the silver disks had struck shoulder and neck. Blood sprayed. Not enough to stop the determined maniac.

Kowalski squeezed the trigger, aiming now.

An arc of razored death sliced across the space at knee height.

Tendons snapped, bones shattered. The butler collapsed and fell toward Kowalski, landing almost nose to nose with him. A clawed hand grabbed his throat, nails digging into his flesh. Kowalski raised the muzzle of his VK rifle.

"Sorry, buddy."

Kowalski aimed for the open mouth and pulled the trigger, closing his eyes at the last second.

A gargling yowl erupted—then went immediately silent. His throat was released.

Kowalski opened his eyes to see the butler collapse face-first.

Dead.

Kowalski rolled to the side and gained his legs. He searched around for any other attackers, then ran toward the back of the hacienda. He glanced in each window as he passed: a locker room, a lab with steel animal cages, a billiard room.

Fire roared on the structure's far side, fanned by the growing winds. Smoke churned up into the darkening skies.

Through the next window, Kowalski spotted a room with a massive wooden desk and floor-to-ceiling bookshelves.

It had to be the professor's study.

"Dr. Rosauro," Kowalski whispered.

No answer.

"Dr. Rosauro . . ." he tried a little louder.

He grabbed his throat. His transmitter was gone, ripped away in his scuffle with the butler. He glanced back toward the courtyard. Flames lapped the sky.

He was on his own.

He turned back to the study. A rear door opened into the room. It stood ajar.

Why did that not sit well with him?

With time strangling, Kowalski edged cautiously forward, gun raised. He used the tip of his weapon to nudge the door wider.

He was ready for anything.

Rabid baboons, raving butlers.

But not for the young woman in a skintight charcoal wet suit.

She was crouched before an open floor safe and rose smoothly with the creak of the door, a pack slung over one shoulder. Her hair, loose and damp, flowed as dark as a raven's wing, her skin burnt honey. Eyes, the smoky hue of dark caramel, met his.

Over a silver 9 mm SIG Sauer held in one fist.

Kowalski ducked to the side of the doorway, keeping his weapon pointed inside. "Who the hell are you?"

"My name, *señor*, is *Condeza* Gabriella Salazar. You are trespassing on my husband's property."

Kowalski scowled. The professor's wife. Why did all the pretty ones go for the smart guys?

"What are you doing here?" he called out.

"You are American, *sí*? Sigma Force, no doubt." This last was said with a sneer. "I've come to collect my husband's cure. I will use it to barter for my *marido*'s freedom. You will not stop me."

A blast of her gun chewed a hole through the door. Splinters chased him back.

Something about the easy way she had handled her pistol suggested more than competence. Plus if she married a professor, she probably had a few IQ points on him.

Brains and a body like that.

Life was not fair.

Kowalski backed away, covering the side door. Maybe they'd have to chalk this one up to the bad guys.

A window shattered by his ear. A bullet seared past the back of his neck. He dropped and pressed against the adobe wall.

The bitch had moved out of the office and was stalking him from inside the house.

Body, brains, *and* she knew the lay of the land.

No wonder she'd been able to avoid the monsters here.

Distantly a noise intruded. The *whump-whump* of an approaching helicopter. It was their evac chopper. He glanced to his watch. Of course their ride was early.

"You should run for your friends," the woman called from inside. "While you still have time!"

Kowalski stared at the manicured lawn that spread all the way to the beach. There was no cover. The bitch would surely drop him within a few steps.

It came down to do or die.

He bunched his legs under him, took a deep breath, then sprang up. He crashed back-first through the bullet-weakened window. He kept his rifle tucked to his belly. He landed hard and shoulder-rolled, ignoring the shards of glass cutting him.

He gained a crouched position, rifle up, swiveling.

The room was empty.

Gone again.

So it was to be a cat-and-mouse hunt through the house.

He moved to the doorway that led deeper into the structure. Smoke flowed in rivers across the ceiling. The temperature inside was furnace-hot. He pictured the pack over the woman's shoulder. She had already emptied the safe. She would make for one of the exits. The same constraints on time would be squeezing her.

He edged to the next room.

A sunroom. A wall of windows overlooked the expanse of gardens and lawn. Rattan furniture and floor screens offered a handful of hiding places. He would have to lure her out somehow. Outthink her.

Yeah, right . . .

He edged into the room, keeping close to the back wall.

He crossed the room. There was no attack.

He reached the far archway. It led to a back foyer.

And an open door.

He cursed inwardly. As he made his entrance, she must have made her exit. She was probably halfway to Honduras by now. He rushed the door and out to the back porch. He searched the grounds.

Gone.

So much for outthinking her.

The press of the hot barrel against the back of his skull punctuated how thick that skull actually was. Like he had concluded earlier, she must have realized a sprint across open ground was too risky. So she had waited to ambush him.

She didn't even hesitate for any witty repartee . . . not that he'd be a good sparring partner anyway. Only a single word of consolation was offered. "*Adios.*"

The blast of the gun was drowned by a sudden siren's wail.

Both of them jumped at the shrieking burst.

Luckily, he jumped to the left, she to the right.

The round tore through Kowalski's right ear with a lance of fire.

He spun, pulling the trigger on his weapon. He didn't aim, just clenched the trigger and strafed at waist level. He lost his balance at the edge of the porch, tumbling back.

Another bullet ripped through the air past the tip of his nose.

He hit the cobbled path, and his skull struck with a distinct ring. The rifle was knocked from his fingers.

He searched up and saw the woman step to the edge of the porch.

She pointed her SIG Sauer at him.

Her other arm clutched her stomach. It failed to act as a dam. Abdominal contents spilled from her split belly, pouring out in a flow of dark blood. She lifted her gun, arm trembling—her eyes met his, oddly surprised. Then the gun slipped from her fingers, and she toppled toward him.

Kowalski rolled out of the way in time.

She landed with a wet slap on the stone path.

The bell-beat of the helicopter wafted louder as the winds changed direction. The storm was rolling in fast. He saw the chopper circle the beach once, like a dog settling for a place to sleep, then lower toward the flat rocky expanse.

Kowalski returned to Gabriella Salazar's body and hauled off her pack. He began to sprint for the beach. Then stopped, went back, and retrieved his VK rifle. He wasn't leaving it behind.

As he ran, he realized two things.

One. The siren blast from the neighboring jungle had gone silent. And two. He had heard not a single word from Dr. Rosauro. He checked the taped receiver behind his ear. Still in place.

Why had she gone silent?

The helicopter—a Sikorsky S-76—touched down ahead of him. Sand swirled in the rotorwash. A gunman in military fatigues pointed a rifle at him and bellowed over the roar of the blades.

"Stand down! Now!"

Kowalski stopped. He lowered his rifle, but lifted the pack. "I have the goddamn antidote."

He searched the surrounding beach for Dr. Rosauro, but she was nowhere in sight.

"I'm Seaman Joe Kowalski! US Navy! I'm helping Dr. Rosauro!"

After a moment of consultation with someone inside the chopper, the gunman waved him forward. Ducking under the rotors, Kowalski held out the satchel. A shadowy figure accepted the pack and searched inside. Something was exchanged by radio.

"Where's Dr. Rosauro?" the stranger asked, clearly the one in charge here. Hard blue eyes studied him.

Kowalski shook his head.

"Commander Crowe," the pilot called back. "We must leave now. The Brazilian navy had just ordered the bombardment."

"Get inside," the man ordered Kowalski, the tone unequivocal.

Kowalski stepped toward the open door.

A shrieking wail stopped him. A single short burst. It came from beyond the beach.

In the jungle.

Dr. Shay Rosauro clung to the tangle of branches halfway up the broad-leafed cocoa tree. Baboons gibbered below. She had sustained a deep bite to her calf, lost her radio, and her pack.

Minutes ago, after being chased into the tree, she had found her perch offered a bird's-eye view of the hacienda, good enough to observe Kowalski being led out at gunpoint. Unable to help, she had used the only weapon still at hand—her sonic shrieker.

Unfortunately, the blast had panicked the baboons below her, their sudden flight jostling her branch. She'd lost her balance . . . and the shrieker. As she'd regained her balance, she'd heard the two gunshots.

Hope died inside her.

Below, one of the baboons, the dominant male of the pack, had recovered her sonic device and discovered the siren button. The blast momentarily scattered the pack. But only momentarily. The deterrent was becoming progressively less effective—only making them angrier.

Shay hugged the tree trunk.

She checked her watch, then closed her eyes.

She picture the children's faces . . . her partner's . . .

A noise drew her attention upward. The double *whump* of a passing helicopter. The leaves whipped around her. She lifted an arm—then lowered it.

Too late.

The chopper lifted away. The Brazilian assault would commence in a matter of seconds. Shay let her club, her only remaining weapon, drop from her fingers. What was the use? It tumbled below, doing nothing but drawing the attention of the baboons. The pack renewed its assault, climbing the lowest branches.

She could only watch.

Then a familiar voice intruded.

"Die, you dirty, rabid, motherfucking apes!"

A large figure appeared below, blazing out with a VK rifle.

Baboons screamed. Fur flew. Blood splattered.

Kowalski strode into the fray, back to nothing but his boxers.

And his weapon.

He strafed and fired, spinning, turning, twisting, dropping.

Baboons fled now.

Except for their leader. The male rose up and howled as loudly as Kowalski, baring long fangs. Kowalski matched his expression, showing as many teeth.

"Shut the hell up!"

Kowalski punctuated his declaration with a continuous burst of firepower, turning monkey into mulch. Once finished, he shouldered his rifle and strode forward. Leaning on the trunk, he stared up.

"Ready to come down, Doctor?"

Relieved, Shay half fell out of the tree. Kowalski caught her.

"The antidote . . . ?" she asked.

"In safe hands," he assured her. "On its way to the coast with Commander Crowe. He wanted me to come along, but well . . . I . . . I guess I owed you."

He supported her under one shoulder. They hobbled quickly out of the jungle to the open beach.

"How are we going to get off—?"

"I've got that covered. Seems a nice lady left us a going-away present." He pointed down the strand to a beached Jet Ski. "Lucky for us, Gabriella Salazar loved her husband enough to come out here."

As they hurried to the watercraft's side, he gently helped her onboard, then climbed in front.

She circled her arms around his waist. She noted his bloody ear and weeping lacerations across his back. More scars to add to his collection. She closed her eyes and leaned her cheek against his bare back. Grateful and exhausted.

"And speaking of the love of one's life," he said, igniting the engine and throttling up the watercraft's engine. He glanced back. "I may be falling in love, too . . ."

She lifted her head, startled, then leaned back down.

Relieved.

Kowalski was just staring at his shouldered rifle.

"Oh, yeah," he said. "This baby's a real keeper."

Novel Tie-Ins Become a Novelty

The next five short stories came about due to a trend in publishing, of authors writing stories that dovetailed into their next novels. I'm not sure who first started this, but I do remember cursing that writer—not because of the extra work required, but because of the additional pressure put upon the already constrained art of crafting a short story. After writing "Kowalski's in Love," I knew how painstaking it was to tamp down my natural tendency to write long, complicated doorstoppers and to hone a story to its barest essentials.

Now my publisher needed those stories to tie into an upcoming novel.

After much grumbling, though, I agreed to give it a go. I recall sitting at my desk, pen and paper in hand, trying to figure out this puzzle. I did not want to write a story that ended in a cliffhanger, one that required a reader to buy that upcoming novel to know how the plot ended. I wanted the work to be self-contained with its own arc of character and story.

At that time, my soon-to-be published novel was The Devil Colony. I reviewed the book's plot elements and slowly came to realize three things. First, there was a bit of backstory to the novel—a mystery, if you will—that was never fleshed out in that novel. And second, that mystery was tied to a character who never had a story all of her own. That character was the former-assassin-turned-ally Seichan. Third, I had just returned from Paris where I had a chance to tour the macabre catacombs beneath the City of Lights. Its history and intrigue were bright in my mind. All those elements coalesced into a nasty little story of an assassin on the run that became "The Skeleton Key."

After writing that first tie-in, I quickly learned it was actually fun and challenging to craft such stories. It again allowed me to explore those nooks *and crevices into various character's lives, to link one novel to another, and to write stories that could be swift and brutal. In "Midnight Watch," I was able to send Kowalski on another solo mission. In "Ghost Ship," Commander Gray Pierce and Seichan were granted a little R&R, until their vacation goes wildly awry. In "Crash and Burn," I joined two of Sigma's most unlikely allies, pairing Kowalski with Seichan. And "Tracker" allowed me to introduce two new characters: Captain Tucker Wayne and his military war dog. I'll talk more about that dynamic duo later.*

But until then, I hope you enjoy these short snippets into the secret lives and covert missions of Sigma.

The Skeleton Key

JAMES ROLLINS

She woke with a knife at her throat.

Or so she thought.

Seichan came fully alert but kept her eyes closed, feigning sleep, feeling something sharp slicing into her neck. She instinctively knew not to move. Not yet. Wary, she relied on her senses, but heard no whisper of movement, felt no stirring of air across her bare skin, detected no scent of body or breath that was not her own. She smelled only a hint of roses and disinfectant.

Am I alone?

With the sharp pressure still on her neck, she peeked one eye open and took in her environment in a heartbeat. She lay sprawled in an unknown bed, in a room she'd never seen before. Across the bed, the covers were finely textured brocade; above the headboard, an old tapestry hung; on the mantel over a fireplace, a crystal vase of fresh-cut roses sat beside an eighteenth-century gold clock with a thick marble base. The time read a few minutes past ten, confirmed by a modern clock radio resting atop a walnut bedside table. From the warm tone of the light flowing through the sheer curtains, she assumed it was morning.

She picked out muffled voices, speaking French, a match to the room's decor and appointments, passing down the hall outside the room.

Hotel room, she surmised.

Expensive, elegant, not what she could afford.

She waited several more breaths, making sure she was alone.

She had spent her younger years running the slums of Bangkok and the back alleys of Phnom Penh, half feral, a creature of the street. Back then, she had learned the rudimentary skills of her future profession. Survival on the streets required vigilance, cunning, and brutality. When her former employers found her, and recruited her from those same streets, the transition to *assassin* proved an easy one.

Twelve years later, she wore another face, an evolution that a part of her still fought, leaving her half formed, waiting for that soft clay to harden into its new shape. But what would she become? She had betrayed her former employers, an international criminal organization called the Guild—but even that name wasn't real, only a useful pseudonym. The real identity and purpose of the organization remained shadowy, even to its own operatives.

After her betrayal, she had no home, no country, nothing but a thin allegiance to a covert US agency known as Sigma. She had been recruited to discover the true puppet masters of the Guild. Not that she had much choice. She had to destroy her former masters before they destroyed her.

It was why she had come to Paris, to chase a lead.

She slowly sat up and caught her reflection in a mirror on the armoire. Her black hair was mussed by the pillow, the emerald of her eyes dull, sensitive to the weak morning sunlight.

Drugged.

Someone had stripped her down to her bra and panties, likely to search her for weapons or wires or perhaps purely to intimidate her. Her clothes—black jeans, gray T-shirt, and leather motorcycle jacket—had been folded and placed atop a neighboring antique Louis XV chair. On an Empire-period nightstand, her weapons had been arranged in a neat row, making a mockery of their lethality. Her SIG Sauer pistol was still in its shoulder holster, while her daggers and knives had been unsheathed, shining stingingly bright.

As brilliantly as the new piece of jewelry adorning her neck.

The stainless steel band had been fastened tight and low. A tiny green LED light glowed at the hollow of her throat, where sharp prongs dug deep into that tender flesh.

So this is what woke me up . . .

She reached to the electronic necklace and carefully ran a fingertip along its surface, searching for the mechanism that secured it. Under her right ear, she discovered a tiny pin-sized opening.

A keyhole.

But who holds the key?

Her heart thudded in her throat, pinching against those sharp prongs with every beat. Anger flushed her skin, leaving behind a cold dread at the base of her spine. She dug a finger under the tight band, strangling herself, driving the steel thorns deeper until—

—agony lanced through her body, setting fire to her bones.

She collapsed to the bed, contorted with pain, back arched, chest too constricted to scream. Then darkness . . . *nothingness . . .*

Relief flooded through her as she fell back, but the sensation was short-lived.

Seichan woke again, tasting blood where she had bitten her tongue. A bleary-eyed check of the mantel clock revealed that only a moment had passed.

She rolled back up, still trembling with aftershocks from the near electrocution, and swung her legs off the bed. She kept her hands well away from her neck and crossed to the window, needing to get her bearings. Standing slightly to the side to keep from casting a shadow, she stared below at a plaza at the center of which stood a massive towering bronze column with a statue of Napoleon atop it. An arcade of identical elegant buildings surrounded the square, with archways on the ground floor and tall second-story windows, separated by ornamental pillars and pilasters.

I'm still in Paris . . .

She stepped back. In fact, she knew *exactly* where she was, having crossed that same square at the crack of dawn as the city was just waking.

The plaza below was the Place Vendôme, known for its high-end jewelers
and fashion boutiques. The towering bronze Colonne Vendôme in the
center was a Parisian landmark, made from the melting of twelve hundred
Russian and Austrian cannons collected by Napoleon to commemorate
some battle or other. Across its surface climbed a continuous ribbon of
bas-relief depicting scenes from various Napoleonic wars.

She turned and studied the opulent room, draped in silk and decorated in gold leaf.

I must still be at the Ritz.

She had come to the hotel—the Ritz Paris—for an early-morning
meeting with a historian who was connected to the Guild. Something
major was afoot within the organization, stirring up all her contacts. She
knew that such moments of upheaval, when locked doors were momentarily left open and safeguards loosened, were the perfect time to snatch
what she could. So she had reached in deep, pushed hard, and risked exposing herself perhaps too much.

One hand gently touched the collar—then lowered.

Definitely too much.

One of her trusted contacts had set up this rendezvous. But apparently
money only bought so much trust. She had met with the historian in
the Hemingway Bar downstairs, a wood-paneled and leather-appointed
homage to the American writer. The historian had been seated at a side
table, nursing a Bloody Mary, a drink that had originated at this establish-
ment. Next to his chair rested a black leather briefcase, holding the promise of secrets yet to be revealed.

She had a drink.

Only water.

Still a mistake.

Even now, her mouth remained cottony, her head equally so.

As she moved back into the room, a low groan drew her attention to
the closed bathroom door. She cursed herself for not thoroughly checking the rest of the room upon first waking, blaming it on the fuzziness
of her thinking.

That lack of vigilance ended now.

She stepped silently and swiftly across the room, snatching her holstered pistol off the nightstand. She shook the weapon free as she reached the door, letting the shoulder harness fall silently to the carpet.

She listened at the door. As a second groan—more pained now—erupted, she burst into the bathroom, pistol raised. She swept the small marble-adorned chamber, finding no one at the sink or vanity.

Then a bony arm, sleeved in tattoos, rose from the tub, waving weakly as if the bather were drowning. A hand found the swan-shaped gold faucet and gripped tightly to it.

As she sidled closer, a skinny auburn-haired boy—likely no more than eighteen—used his hold on the spigot to pull himself into view. He looked all ribs, elbows, and knees, but she took no chances, centering her pistol on his bare chest. Dazed, he finally seemed to see her, his eyes widening at both her half-naked state and the obvious threat of the weapon. He scrambled back in the empty tub, palms held up, looking ready to climb the marble walls behind him.

He wore only a pair of boxer briefs—and a stainless steel collar.

A match to hers.

Perhaps sensing the same pinched pressure on his neck as Seichan felt on hers, he clawed at his throat.

"Don't," she warned in French.

Panicked, he tugged. The green light on his collar flashed to red. His entire body jolted, throwing him a foot into the air. He crashed back into the bathtub. She lunged and kept his head from cracking into the hard marble, feeling a snap of electricity sting her palm.

Her actions were not motivated by altruism. The kid plainly shared her predicament. Perhaps he knew more about the situation than she did. He convulsed for another breath—then went slack. She waited until his eyes fluttered back open; then she stood and backed away. She lowered her gun, sensing no threat from him.

He cautiously worked his way into a seated position. She studied him as he breathed heavily, slowly shaking off the shock. He was taller than she'd at first imagined. Maybe six feet, but rail thin—not so much scrawny as wiry. His hair was long to the shoulder, cut ragged with the cool casualness of youth. Tattoos swathed his arms, spilled over his shoulders, and spread into two dark wings of artwork along his back. His chest was clean, still an empty canvas.

"*Comment tu t'appelles?*" Seichan asked, taking a seat on the commode.

He breathed heavily. "*Je m'appelle* Renny . . . Renny MacLeod."

Though he answered in French, his brogue was distinctly Scottish.

"You speak English?" she asked.

He nodded, sagging with relief. "Aye. What is going on? Where am I?"

"You're in trouble."

He looked confused, scared.

"What's the last thing you remember?" she asked.

His voice remained dazed. "I was at a pub. In Montparnasse. Someone bought me a pint. Just the one. I wasn't blottered or anything, but that's the last I remember. Till I woke up here."

So he must have been drugged, too. Brought here and collared, like her. But why? What game was being played?

The phone rang, echoing across the room.

She turned, suspecting the answer was about to be revealed. She stood and exited the bathroom. The padding of bare feet on marble told her that Renny was following. She picked up the phone on the bedside table.

"You're both awake now," the caller said in English. "Good. Time is already running short."

She recognized the voice. It was Dr. Claude Beaupré, the historian from the Panthéon-Sorbonne University in Paris. She pictured the prim, silver-haired Frenchman seated in the Hemingway Bar. He had worn a threadbare tweed jacket, but the true measure of the man was found not in the cut of his cloth, but within the haughty cloak of his aristocratic air and manners. She guessed that somewhere in the past his family had noble titles attached to their names: *baron, marquis, vicomte*. But no longer. Maybe that's why he'd become a historian, an attempt to cling to that once-illustrious past.

When she had met him this morning, she'd hoped to buy documents pertaining to the Guild's true leaders, but circumstances had clearly changed.

Had the man figured out who I am? If so, then why am I still alive?

"I have need of your unique skills," the historian explained, as if reading her thoughts. "I expended much effort to lure you here to Paris, to entice you with the promise of answers. You almost came too late."

"So this is all a ruse."

"*Non*. Not at all, mademoiselle. I have the documents you seek. Like you, I took full advantage of the tumult among our employers—your former, my current—to free the papers you came hunting. You have my solemn word on that. You came to buy them. I am now merely negotiating the price."

"And what is that price?"

"I wish you to find my son, to free him before he is killed."

Seichan struggled to keep pace with these negotiations. "Your son?"

"Gabriel Beaupré. He has fallen under the spell of another compatriot of our organization, one I find most distasteful. The man is the leader of an apocalyptic cult, *l'Ordre du Temple Solaire*."

"The Order of the Solar Temple," she translated aloud.

Renny MacLeod's face hardened at the mention of the name.

"*Oui*," Claude said from the phone. "A decade ago, the cult had been behind a series of mass suicides in two villages in Switzerland and another in Quebec. Members were found poisoned by their own hand or drugged into submitting. One site was firebombed in a final act of purification. Most believed the OTS had dissolved after that—but in fact, they'd only gone underground, serving a new master."

The Guild.

Her former employers often harnessed such madness and honed its violence to serve their own ends.

"But the new leader of OTS—Luc Vennard—has greater ambitions. Like us, he plans to use the momentary loosening of the Guild's reins to exert his own independence, to wreak great havoc on my fair city. For that reason alone, I'd want him stopped, but he has wooed my son with myths of the continuing existence of the Knights Templar, of the cult's holy duty to usher in the reign of a new god-king—likely Vennard himself—a bloody transformation that would require fire and sacrifice. Specifically *human* sacrifice. To use my son's words before he vanished, a *great purging* would herald the new sun-king's birth."

"When is this all supposed to take place?" Seichan asked.

"Noon today, when the sun is at its strongest."

She glanced to the mantel clock. That was in less than two hours.

"That is why I took these extreme measures. To ensure your cooperation. The collars not only punish, but they also kill. Leave the city limits of Paris and you will meet a most agonizing end. Fail to free my son and you will meet the same fate."

"And if I agree . . . if I succeed . . ."

"You will be set free. You have my oath. And as payment for services rendered, the documents I possess will also be yours."

Seichan considered her options. It did not take long. She had only one.

To cooperate.

She also understood why Claude Beaupré had collared her and turned her into his hunting dog. He dared not report what he'd learned from his son to the Guild. The organization could simply let Vennard commit this violent act and turn it to their advantage. Chaos often equaled opportunity to her former masters. Or they would stamp out Vennard and his cult for their hubris and mutiny. In either scenario, Gabriel Beaupré would likely end up dead.

So Claude had sought help outside of regular channels.

"What about the boy?" Seichan asked, staring over at Renny Mac-Leod, unable to fit this one jigsaw piece into the puzzle.

"He is your map and guide."

"What does that mean?"

Renny must have noted her sudden attention on him and grew visibly paler.

"Search his back," Claude commanded. "Ask him about Jolienne."

"Who is Jolienne?"

This time the kid flinched, as if punched in the gut. But rather than going even whiter, his face flushed. He lunged forward, grabbing for the phone.

"What does that bastard know about my Jolie?" Renny cried out.

Seichan easily sidestepped his assault, keeping the phone to her ear and spinning him with one hand. She tossed him facedown on the bed and held him in place with a knee planted at the base of his spine.

He struggled, swearing angrily.

"Stay still," she said, digging in her knee. "Who is Jolie?"

He twisted his head around to glare at her with one eye. "My girlfriend. She disappeared two days ago. Looking for some group called the Solar Temple. I was in that pub last night trying to drum up a search party among the other *cataphiles*."

She didn't know what that last word meant. But before inquiring, her attention focused on the kid's naked back and the sprawl of his tattoo. This was the first chance she'd had to get a good look at it.

In black, yellow, and crimson inks, a strange map had been indelibly etched into his skin—but it was not a chart of streets and avenues. In meticulous detail, the artwork depicted an intricate network of crisscrossing tunnels, widening chambers, and watery pools. It looked like the map for some lost cavern system. It was also clearly an unfinished work: passages faded into obscurity or ended abruptly at the edges of the tattoo.

"What is this?" she asked.

Renny knew what had drawn her attention. "It's where Jolie disappeared."

Claude, still on the phone at her ear, answered her more directly. "It is a map of the Paris catacombs, our city of the dead."

Fifteen minutes later, Seichan was gunning the engine of her motorcycle and speeding over the twelve stone arches of the Pont Neuf, the medieval bridge that spanned the river Seine. She wove wildly around slower traffic, crossing toward the Left Bank of Paris and aiming for the city's Latin Quarter.

Seated behind her, Renny clung to her with both arms. He squeezed tightly as she exited the bridge and made a sharp turn into the maze of streets on the far side. She did not slow down. They were quickly running out of time.

"Take the next right!" Renny yelled in her ear. "Go four blocks. Then we'll have to continue on foot."

Seichan obeyed. She had no other guide.

Moments later, they were both running down the rue Mouffetard, an ancient pedestrian avenue that cut a narrow, winding swath through the Latin Quarter. Buildings to either side dated back centuries. The lower levels had been converted into cafés, bakeries, cheese shops, *crêperies*, and a fresh market that spilled out into the street. All around, merchants hawked their goods while patrons noisily bartered.

Seichan shoved through the bustle, noting the chalkboard menus being filled out, the huge loaves of bread being stacked behind windows. Breathless, winded, she drew in the musky headiness wafting from a tiny *fromagerie* and the fragrant displays of an open-air flower stand.

Still, she remained all too conscious of what lay *beneath* this lively tumult: a moldering necropolis holding the bones of six million Parisians, three times the population above.

Renny led the way with his long legs. His thin form skirted through the crowds with ease. He kept glancing back, making sure he hadn't lost her.

Back at the hotel, he had found his clothes in the hotel closet: ripped jeans, army boots, and a red shirt bearing the likeness of the rebel Che Guevara. Additionally, they'd both put on scarves to hide their steel collars. While they got dressed, Seichan had explained their situation, how their lives depended on searching the catacombs to retrieve the historian's lost son. Renny had listened, asking only a few questions. In his eyes, she noted the gleam of hope behind the glaze of terror. She suspected that the determined pace he set now had little to do with saving his own life and more to do with finding his lost love, Jolie.

Before donning his shirt, he had awkwardly pointed to his lower-right shoulder blade. That corner of the tattooed map was freshly inked, the flesh still red and inflamed. "This is what Jolie had discovered, where she had been headed when she disappeared."

And it was where they were going now, chasing their only lead, preparing to follow in his girlfriend's footsteps.

Claude Beaupré also believed Jolienne's whereabouts were important. Her disappearance had coincided with the last day he'd seen his son. Before vanishing, Gabriel had hinted to his father about where Vennard and the other members of his cult were scheduled to gather for the purge. It was this same neighborhood. So when Claude heard about Renny searching for his lost girlfriend in this area, he began moving his chess pieces together: lowly guide and deadly hunter.

The two were now inextricably bound together, headed toward a secret entrance into the catacombs. Renny had shared all he knew about the subterranean network of crypts and tunnels. How the dark worlds beneath the bright City of Lights were once ancient quarries called *les carrières de Paris*. The ancient excavation burrowed ten stories underground, carving out massive chambers and expanding outward into two hundred miles of tangled tunnels. The quarries had once been at the outskirts of the city, but over time, Paris grew and spread over the top of the old labyrinth, until now half of the metropolis sat atop the mines.

Then in the eighteenth century, city authorities had ordered that the overflowing cemeteries in the center of Paris be dug up. Millions of skeletons—some going back a thousand years—were unceremoniously dumped into the quarries' tunnels, where they were broken down and stacked like cordwood. According to Renny, some of France's most famous historical figures were likely interred below: from Merovingian kings to characters from the French Revolution, from Clovis to the likes of Robespierre and Marie Antoinette.

Seichan's search, though, was not for the dead.

Renny finally turned off the main thoroughfare and ducked down a narrow alley between a coffeehouse and a pastry shop. "This way. The entrance I told ye about is up ahead. Friends—fellow *cataphiles*—should have left us some gear. We always help each other out."

The alley was so tight they had to pass through it single file. It ended at a small courtyard, surrounded by centuries-old buildings. Some of the windows were boarded up; others showed some signs of life: a small dog piping a complaint, a few strings of drying laundry, a small face peering at them through a curtain.

Renny led her to a manhole cover hidden in a shadowed corner of the courtyard. He fished out a crowbar from behind a trash bin, along with two mining helmets with lamps affixed to their front.

He pointed back to the bin. "They left us a couple o' flashlights, too."

"Your *cataphiles*?"

"Aye. My fellow explorers of Paris's underworld," he said, letting a little pride shine forth, his brogue thickening. "We come from every corner of the world, from every walk o' life. Some search the old subways or sewer lines; others go boggin' and diving into water-filled pits that open into flooded rooms far below. But most—like Jolie and me—are drawn to the unmapped corners of the catacombs."

He went silent, worry settling heavily to his shoulders, clearly wondering about the fate of his girlfriend.

"Let's get this open," Seichan said, needing to keep him moving.

She helped pry open the manhole cover and rolled it aside. A metal ladder, bolted to the wall of the shaft, led down into the darkness. Renny strapped on his helmet. Seichan opted for a flashlight.

She cast a bright beam into the depths.

"This leads down to a long-abandoned section of the sewer system, goin' back to the mid-1800s," Renny said, mounting the ladder.

"A sewer? I thought we were going into the catacombs."

"Aye, we are. Sewers, basements, old wells often have secret entrances into the ancient catacombs. C'mon, then, I'll show ye."

He climbed down, and she followed. She expected it to smell foul, ripe with the slough of the city above. But she found it only dank and moldy. They descended at least two stories, until at last she was able to step back onto solid footing. She cast her light around. Mortared blocks lined the old sewer's walls and low ceiling. Her boots sloshed in a thin stream of water along the bottom.

"Over here." Renny led the way along the sewer with the assurance of a well-schooled rat. After thirty yards, a grated gateway opened to the right. He crossed to it and tugged the gate open. Hinges squealed. "Now through here."

Crude steps led deeper into the darkness and down to a room that made Seichan gasp. The walls had been painted in a riotous garden of flowers and trees set among trickling waterways and azure pools. It was like stepping into a Monet painting.

"Welcome to the true entrance of the catacombs," Renny said.

"Who did all of this?" she asked, sweeping her light, noting a few sections marred by graffiti.

He shrugged. "All sorts of dobbers make their way down. Artists, partiers, mushroom farmers. A couple years ago, the *cataflics*—that's our name for the police who patrol down there—discovered a large chamber set up as a movie theater, with a big screen, popcorn maker, and carved-out seats. When police investigators returned a day later, they found it all gone. Only a note remained in the middle of the floor, warning 'Do not try to find us.' That's the underworld of Paris. Large sections still remain unexplored, cut off by cave-ins or simply lost in time. *Cataphiles*, like me and my mates, do our best to fill in those blank spots on the old maps, tracking our discoveries, recording every intricacy."

"Like you've done with your tattoo."

"It was Jolie's idea," he said with a sad smile. "She's a tattoo artist. A dead good one, she is. She wanted to immortalize our journey together underground."

He went silent again, but only for a moment.

"I met her down below, not far from here, both of us all muddy. We exchanged phone numbers by flashlight."

"Tell me about that day she disappeared."

"I had classes to go to. She had the afternoon off and left with another girl, Liesl from Germany. I dinna know her last name. They went down after hearing rumors of some secret group moving through the area."

"The Order of the Solar Temple."

"Aye." He worked the back of his shirt up. "At the base of my neck, you'll see a room marked with a little flower."

She peered closer at his tattoo, shining her flashlight. She found the tiny Celtic rose and touched it with a finger.

Renny shivered. "That's where we are now. We'll follow Jolie's map to the newest piece of my tattoo; that was where she'd been headed. She found an entrance into a forgotten section of the labyrinth, but she'd only just begun to explore it when she heard that rumor about the Solar Temple." He lowered his shirt and pointed to a tunnel leading out. "I know most of the way by heart, but I'll need help once we're closer."

He set off through the dark labyrinth, winding through tunnels and across small rooms and past flooded pits. The walls were raw limestone, sweating and dripping with water. Fossils dotted the surfaces, some polished by previous *cataphiles* to make them stand out, as if the prehistoric past were trying to crawl out of the rock.

The way grew rapidly cooler. Soon Seichan could see her breath. The echoes of their footsteps made it sound as if they were constantly being followed. She stopped frequently, checking warily behind her.

She could see that Renny was growing impatient. "We're not likely to find anyone down here. Even the *cataflics* rarely come to this remote section. Plus there was a gas leak reported near the tourist area of the catacombs. They've been closed for three days."

She nodded and checked his tattoo again. They were not far from the freshly inked section of his map. "If I'm reading this right, your girlfriend's new discovery opens along that passage." She pointed to a narrow tunnel and checked her wristwatch.

Seventy-two minutes left.

Anxious, Seichan led the way. She hurried along, looking for the branching side passage marked on the tattoo.

"Stop!" Renny called behind her.

She turned and found him kneeling beside a tumble of stones. She had walked past the rockfall without giving it a second thought.

Renny pointed his helmet lamp to a rosy arrow chalked above the rock pile. "This is the entrance. Jolie always uses pink chalk."

She joined him and spotted a low tunnel shadowed by the rocks.

Renny crawled on his hands and knees through the opening first. Seichan followed. Within a few yards and a couple of short drops, the way dumped into another tunnel.

As Seichan stood, she saw more shafts and smaller side passages heading off in several directions.

Renny touched a palm against the sweating dampness of the limestone wall. "This is definitely a very old section of the catacombs. And it looks to be a fousty maze from here." He twisted around and fought to raise his shirt. "Check the map."

She did, but the ink of the tattoo stopped at the exact point where they were standing. A cursory exam of the tunnels offered no other chalked clues as to where Jolie might have gone.

From here, it looked like they were on their own.

"What do we do?" Renny asked, fear for his girlfriend frosting his words. "Where do we go?"

Seichan picked a tunnel and headed out.

"Why are we going this way?" he asked, hurrying after her.

"Why not?"

Actually she had a reason for the decision. She had picked the passage because it was the only one that headed *down*. By now, it was clear to her that these tunnel crawlers were drawn to nether regions of the world, driven by curiosity about what lay below. Such snooping always kept them digging *deeper*. Only after reaching the bottom would they begin exploring outward.

She hoped that this was true of Jolienne.

Within a few steps, though, Seichan began to regret her choice. To either side, deep niches had been packed solidly with old human bones, darkened and yellowed to the color of ancient parchment. The skeletons had been disarticulated and separated into their component parts, as if inventoried by some macabre accountant. One niche held only a stack of arms, delicately draped one atop the other; another was full of rib cages. It was the last two niches—one on either side of the passage—that disturbed her the most. Two walls of skulls stared out at the tunnel, seeming to dare them to trespass between their vacant gazes.

Seichan hurried past with a shiver of dread.

The tunnel finally ended at a cavernous chamber. While the roof was no higher than the passageway, it stretched outward into a vast room the length of a football field. Rows and rows of pillars held up the ceiling, like some stone orchard. Each support was composed of stone blocks, one piled on another. Several looked crooked and ready to fall.

"This is the ancient handiwork of Charles Guillaumot," Renny said, speaking in a rushed, nervous tone. "Back in 1774, a major section of the catacombs collapsed, swallowing up several streets and killing lots o' people. After that, King Louis hired himself an architect, Guillaumot, to shore up the catacombs. He became the first true *cataphile*. He mapped and explored most of the tunnels and had these room pillars put in place. Not that collapses don't still happen. In 1961, the ground opened up and swallowed an entire Parisian neighborhood, killing a bunch of people. Even today, cave-ins occur every year. It's a big danger down here."

Seichan only half listened to Renny's story. A glint off one of the pillars had drawn her attention. The reflection was too bright for this dank and dreary place. She approached the pillar and discovered a ring of wires wrapped around the middle of the stack of stones, linking transmitters and blasting caps to fistfuls of yellowish-gray clay.

C-4 explosive.

This was not the handiwork of that eighteenth-century French architect.

She examined the bomb, careful not to disturb it. A small red LED light glowed from the transmitter, awaiting a signal. She cupped a hand over her flashlight and motioned for Renny to do the same with his helmet lamp.

The room plunged into darkness. As her eyes adjusted, she picked out the telltale pinpoints glowing across the room, hundreds of them, coming from pillars throughout the chamber. The entire room had been mined to explode.

"What is all of this?" Renny whispered beside her.

"Vennard's purge," Seichan surmised, picturing the bustling city above.

She wondered how many other chambers across this necropolis were similarly set with explosives. She remembered Renny mentioning a reported gas leak. Such a ruse would be a good way to evacuate the catacombs, leaving the cult free to plant charges throughout this subterranean world.

Renny must have feared the same. His voice grew somber with the implication. "They could bring half of Paris crashing down."

Claude Beaupré had said Vennard wanted human sacrifice, to herald the birth of a new sun-king in fire and blood. Here was that plan about to come to fruition.

As Seichan kept her hand cupped over her flashlight, her eyes acclimated themselves enough to note a wan glow from across the room, marking the entrance to a tunnel on the far side.

She continued across the chamber, heading for that light. She slipped out her pistol and pointed it forward. Keeping her flashlight muffled in her other hand, she allowed just enough illumination to avoid obstacles. Renny kept behind her with his helmet's lamp switched off.

The far tunnel was a mirror to the first one. Bones filled niches; the skeletons again broken down and separated into body parts. Only these bones were bright *white*. There was no patina of age. With growing horror, she realized that what she was looking at were not ancient remains—they were the remains of fresh kills.

One niche, a yard deep, was half full of skulls.

A work in progress.

From their tiny sizes, she could tell that some of the skulls had belonged to children, even infants.

Before Claude had finished his instructions over the phone, he had spoken of a heinous act committed by the former head of the *Ordre du Temple Solaire* in Quebec. The man had sacrificed his own son, stabbing him with wooden stakes, believing the child was the Antichrist. Apparently the order's taste for infanticide was not limited to that single instance.

The tunnel ended after another bend. Voices echoed from there, sounding like they were coming from another cavernous space. Seichan motioned for Renny to hang back. She edged forward, hugging a wall, and peered around the corner.

Another room—smaller, but similarly dotted with pillars—opened ahead. Only the pillars in this room were natural limestone columns, left behind as the miners dug out this chamber, making the space feel more ancient. But like the others, these pillars were similarly decorated with explosive charges.

In the center of the room, Seichan could make out twenty people gathered in a circle, all on their knees—but they were not adorned in ceremonial robes. They wore ordinary street clothes. One couple, arm in arm, had come in formal attire for the momentous occasion. A handful looked drugged, weaving dully where they knelt or with their foreheads lowered to the floor. Three bodies lay sprawled closer to the tunnel where Seichan was hiding: facedown, in pools of blood, as dark as oil against the rock. It looked as if they'd been shot in the back as they tried to flee the coming destruction, likely having had second thoughts about giving up their lives in a suicidal orgy.

A pair of guards, with assault rifles and wearing Kevlar body armor, stood to either side of the gathering, shadowed by pillars, watching the group, ready to discourage any other deserters.

Seichan ignored them for the moment and focused on the two figures standing in the center of the circle. One, with silver hair and Gallic features, wore a cloaked white robe, shining in a spotlight thrown by a nearby sodium lamp. Seichan could hear the soft chug of a generator powering the room. The man smiled beatifically upon his flock, arms raised.

That must be Luc Vennard.

"The time is at hand," he intoned in French. "As the sun reaches its zenith, the destruction wrought here will start. The screams of the dying, the rising souls of the dead, will carry you all upward to the next exultant stage of existence. You will become my dark angels as I claim my solar throne. I promise you: this is not the end, but only the beginning for us all. I must leave you now, but my chosen spiritual right hand will take my place and lead you out of the darkness and into the dawn of a new era."

The man stepped aside, clearly planning to abandon his flock. From the way Vennard cast a glance toward the two armed guards, it seemed he wasn't sticking around for the festivities and had arranged for escorts to guide him out of the catacombs—just in case any of the flock objected to his departure. She suspected the bank accounts of those gathered had been emptied into Vennard's vaults, ready to finance his next venture, to spread more widely the Order of the Solar Temple—or perhaps to buy that new yacht he's had his eye on.

Was he a cultist, a con artist, or merely a glorified serial killer?

From the vacuous sockets of the dead staring out at her from the nearby niche, she suspected the answer was *all of the above.*

Vennard waved the second man forward. In his midthirties, he wore street clothes, his face shining with a sheen of sweat, his eyes glassy from what appeared to be both drugs and adoration. Even without the photo that Claude had left in the hotel room, Seichan would have recognized the historian's son—both from his patrician features and the aristocratic air he shared with his father. Seichan pictured Claude plying his son with tales of past noble titles and lost heritages, instilling in the boy the same sense of bitter entitlement that motivated himself. But while the father had sought solace in the embrace of history, it seemed his son had looked to the future, seeking his own path to that former glory.

And he'd found it here.

"Gabriel—like the angel that is your namesake—you will be transformed by blood and sacrifice into my warrior angel, the most exultant of my new heavenly legion. And your weapon will be a sword of fire." Vennard parted his cloak to reveal a steel short sword. It looked like an antique, a museum piece. "Like you, this steel will soon burn with the energies of the sun's furnace. But first that weapon must be forged, made ready for its transformation. It must be bloodied like all of you. This last death by your hand, this singular sacrifice, will herald the others to come. This honor I give to you, my warrior angel, my Gabriel."

Vennard held up the sword and offered it to the young man.

Gabriel took it and lifted it high—then the two men stepped aside, revealing a low altar behind them. It had its own spotlight, too.

A dark-haired woman was chained naked to the stone, legs spread wide, arms outstretched. A second sacrifice—blond-haired and pale— knelt nearby, shaking in a thin white shift.

On the altar, the woman's head was lolling in a drugged daze. But she must have sensed what was to come and struggled against the chains as Gabriel turned to her with his sword. He stepped far enough aside to reveal the woman's face—but the tattoos across her body were already enough to identify her.

At least for one of them.

"Jolienne!"

Renny's cry shot out of the tunnel like a crossbow's bolt.

All eyes turned in their direction.

Before Seichan could move, a large figure stepped across the mouth of the tunnel—a *third* guard. He'd been hidden to the side, ensuring no one left. She silently cursed Renny. With no time to devise a strategy, she simply had to improvise.

As the guard raised his rifle, Seichan shot him in the knee. The pop of her pistol was explosive in the confined space. The .357 round at such close range blew out his kneecap in a mist of blood and bone.

She leaped as the guard screamed and toppled forward. She caught him up, embracing him with one arm like a long-lost lover, and used her momentum to carry him into the room. She pointed her SIG Sauer past his body and targeted the guard to the right as he stepped clear of the pil- lar. She shot him in the face.

Screams erupted across the room. The flock scattered to all sides, like a flushed covey of quail. The remaining guard fired at her, strafing wildly, but she used her new "lover" as a body shield, bulldozing forward. Rounds pelted into the man's Kevlar armor, but one bullet struck the back of his head. His struggling weight went suddenly limp.

She carried the deadweight another two steps, enough to get a good angle around the pillar. She fired at the exposed man, squeezing the trigger twice. She clipped the guard's ear, knocking his head back. The second shot ripped through his exposed throat, severing his spine. He crashed to floor.

Seichan dropped the guard in her arms and took up a shooter's stance, aiming toward the altar. Vennard had retreated behind it. Gabriel, still dazed and slow to react from the drugs he'd ingested, looked confused. He still held the sword at the throat of the bound woman. A trickle of blood flowed from where the blade's razored edge had already sliced that tender skin.

The other sacrifice, unguarded now, leaped to her feet and fled away. Seichan waved the blond woman toward the exit as she came running at her—only too late did Seichan notice the dagger clutched in the woman's hand.

With a scream of rage, she lunged at Seichan.

Unable to get clear in time, Seichan twisted to the side, ready to take the knife strike to the shoulder, rather than somewhere more vital.

It proved unnecessary.

Before the dagger could hit, something flew past Seichan's shoulder and cracked the woman square in the face. A white human skull bounced to the stone floor and rolled away. From the corner of her eye, she spotted Renny running over, clutching another skull in his fist. He'd clearly grabbed the only weapons at hand from one of the niches.

His attack caused the woman to stumble, long enough for Seichan to get her pistol around and fire point-blank into the woman's chest. The impact knocked her assailant off her feet. She slid across the floor, a bloom of blood brightening the front of her white shift.

Renny came rushing up. He tossed aside the skull and snatched one of the guard's assault rifles from the floor, but from the way he bungled with it, it looked like he'd been better off with the skull. Renny stared down at the dead woman, his face a mask of confusion. The reason for his bewilderment became clear a second later.

From the altar, Gabriel cried out, pain cutting through his drugged haze. "*Liesl!*"

Seichan recognized that name. It was the German girl Renny had mentioned during his recounting of Jolienne's disappearance. The two girls had come down here, exploring together, when Jolienne disappeared. It now seemed that the circumstances surrounding that disappearance weren't as much a matter of accident as it appeared. Renny's girlfriend hadn't stumbled upon the cult's location here—she'd been lured, led by Liesl like a cow to the slaughter, to be the final sacrifice.

"*Non!*" Gabriel wailed, heartbroken. With his eyes fixed on the bloody body, he fell to his knees, the sword clattering to the altar.

Others of the flock began to flee out the tunnel, abandoning their leader. But Vennard was not giving up so easily.

From a pocket of his robe, he pulled out what looked like a transmitter. A green light glowed at the top. He had a finger pressed to a button.

"If I let go of this switch, we all die," he said calmly, his voice resonating with that hypnotic quality that had so easily swayed the gullible. He stepped around the altar. "Let me go. Even follow me out, if you'd like. And we can all still live."

Seichan backed away and waved Renny aside. Despite Vennard's grandiose vision, he was not suicidal. She took him at his word. He would refrain from blowing up the catacombs, at least until he himself got clear.

Vennard studied her, attempting to read her. A good cult leader needed a keen eye to judge people, to predict their actions. He slowly moved forward, step by step, toward the exit, pushing Seichan ahead of him.

"You want to live as much as any of us, Seichan. Yes, it took me a moment, but I recognize you now. From what I've read, you were always reasonable. None of us need to die this—"

A sword burst from the center of his chest, thrust through from behind.

"We must *all* die!" Gabriel yelled as Vennard fell to his knees. "Liesl cannot ascend without the proper sacrifice. Blood and fire. You said so. To become the angels you promised!"

Gabriel shoved the sword deeper as madness, grief, and exaltation glowed in his face. Blood poured from Vennard's mouth.

Seichan dropped her pistol and lunged forward, grabbing for the transmitter with both hands. She got her finger over the trigger before Vennard could let go. Nose to nose, he stared back at her, his eyes shining with disbelief and shock—but also with understanding.

In the end, he had reaped what he had sown.

Gabriel yanked back on the hilt and kicked away Vennard's body to free the blade. Seichan fell to her backside, getting tangled as the cult leader fell on top of her. Gabriel raised his sword high with both hands, ready to plunge it into Seichan.

But Renny stepped behind him and cracked him in the back of the skull with the butt of his rifle. Gabriel's eyes rolled back, and his body crumpled to the floor.

"What a loony bampot," Renny said.

He came forward to help Seichan up, but she waved to the altar. "Go free Jolienne."

He stared down at the transmitter clutched in her hands. "Is it over?"

Seichan caught the glint of steel shining above his scarf.

"Not yet."

With the midday sun cresting high overhead, Seichan waited beside the parked Peugeot 508 sedan in front of the Ritz Paris. The rental had been arranged by Dr. Claude Beaupré to transport them from the Latin Quarter to the rendezvous back at the hotel.

As a precaution, she kept the sedan between her and the doors to the hotel. Additionally, she had Renny retreat to the square of the Place Vendôme. Jolienne was safe at a local hospital, having the cut on her neck treated. He had wanted to stay with her, but Seichan still needed him.

The doors to the Ritz Paris finally opened and discharged a trio of figures. In the center strode Claude, dressed again in tweeds, but he'd donned a rakish hat to shadow his features, clearly as cautious as Seichan about this very public meeting. It would not be good for him to be found associated with a Guild assassin-turned-traitor. He was flanked by two massive men in black suits and long overcoats, surely hiding an arsenal of weapons within those folds.

Claude offered her the barest nod of greeting.

She stepped around to the rear of the sedan to meet him. She kept her hands in the open, offering no threat. Claude motioned for the two men to stay on the curb as he joined her at the back of the car. He carried a black leather Louis Vuitton briefcase.

The historian squinted up into the bright sky, shading his eyes with his free hand. "It is noon, and Paris still stands. I assume that means Luc Vennard's plan failed, his *great purge* quashed."

Seichan shrugged. By now, Renny's *cataflics*, the elite police of that subterranean world, were likely scouring the catacombs, accompanied by the city's *démineurs*, their bomb squads.

"And what of Monsieur Vennard?" Claude asked.

"Dead."

A small smile of satisfaction graced his features. He glanced to the darkened windows of the sedan. "And according to your brief phone call, you rescued my son."

Seichan stepped to the rear of the Peugeot sedan and pressed the zero in the silver 508 emblem beside the taillight. The hidden button popped open the trunk. Within its roomy interior lay Gabriel Beaupré, his limbs bound with duct tape and a ball gag secured in place with her own cashmere scarf. Gabriel winced at the sudden brightness, then struggled when he spotted his father.

Interrupting the family reunion, Seichan slammed the trunk closed. She didn't want anyone passing by to note what was happening. Neither did Claude, who raised no objections to her abrupt gesture. He dared not attempt to free his bound son from the trunk in such a public space.

"As you can see, Gabriel is fine," she said, and held up the sedan's electronic fob. "And here is the key to his freedom."

Claude reached for it—but she pulled her hand away.

Not so fast.

She tugged down her jacket's collar and exposed the steel one beneath it.

"What about this?" She also nodded over to Renny, who still had his scarf in place. "An exchange of keys. Your son's freedom for ours."

"*Oui.* That was the deal. I am a man of my word." He reached into a pocket and removed a hotel keycard. He placed it on the top of the trunk. "Inside your hotel room, you will find what you need to free yourselves."

He must have read the suspicion on her face and smiled sadly.

"Fear not. Your deaths will not serve me. In fact, I plan to pin Vennard's loss upon your traitorous shoulders. With the Guild hunting you, no suspicions will be cast my way. And the faster you run, *ma chére amie,* the better it is for all of us. But, as an additional sign of good faith, I believe I promised you a reward."

He swung the briefcase onto the trunk and ran a hand over the rich leather surface. "Vuitton's finest. The Président Classeur case. It is yours to keep." He smiled over at her with amusement and French pride. "But I suspect what is *inside* is the true price for my son's freedom. A clue to the shadowy leaders of the Guild."

He snapped open the case to reveal a stack of files. On the top folder, imprinted onto the cover, was the image of an eagle with outstretched wings, holding an olive branch in one talon and a bundle of arrows in the other. It was the Great Seal of the United States.

But what does this have to do with the Guild?

He snapped the briefcase closed and slid it toward her.

"What you do with this information—where it will lead—will be very dangerous territory to tread," he warned. "It might serve you better to simply walk away."

Not a chance.

She took the case and the hotel keycard. With the prizes in hand, she placed the sedan's fob on the trunk and backed to the curb, well out of the reach of Claude's guards.

The historian didn't make a move to take the sedan's key. Instead, he placed a palm tenderly on the trunk's lid. His eyes closed in relief as the tension drained from his shoulders. He was no longer a Guild associate, merely a father relieved at the safe return of his prodigal son. Claude took a long breath, then motioned for one of his men to retrieve the key and take the wheel. As his guards climbed into the front seats, Claude ducked into the back, perhaps to be that much closer to his son.

Seichan waited for the sedan to pull away from the curb and head down the street.

As the car vanished out of the square, Renny crossed over to join her. "Did ye get what ye wanted?"

She nodded, picturing the relief Claude must be feeling. For the sake of his son, the historian couldn't risk that Seichan might have searched the papers first. They had to be authentic.

"Do ye think he can be trusted?" Renny asked, reaching to his scarf.

"That remains to be seen."

As they both stared across the plaza, Renny took off his cashmere neckpiece and revealed a close-guarded secret, a secret that Seichan had kept from Claude.

Renny's throat was bare.

He rubbed at the red burn from his earlier shock. "It was good to get that bloody thing off."

Seichan agreed. She reached to her throat and unsnapped her own collar. She stared down at the green LED light. After Vennard's death, she'd found herself with an extra hour before the noon deadline. Taking advantage of the additional time in the catacombs, Seichan had reached out to Renny's network of resources. He'd claimed that his fellow *cataphiles* came from all around the world and from every walk of life.

Upon her instructions, Renny had sent out a clarion call for help. One of the *cataphile* brothers responded, an expert in electrical engineering and microdesign. He was able to get the collars off and removed the shocking mechanism from Seichan's. This was all done underground, where Claude was unlikely to be able to receive any warning signals from the collars.

Once free, Seichan risked making a play for the briefcase.

As she stared at her collar now, Renny's early question played in her head: *Could Claude still be trusted?*

The answer came a moment later.

The green light on her collar flashed to red as it received a transmitted signal, but with the shocking mechanism neutralized, there was no danger.

At least, not for her.

Distantly, a tremendous blast echoed across the city. She searched in the direction of the departed sedan and watched an oily tendril of smoke curl into the bright blue sky.

In the end, it seemed that Claude could *not* be trusted. Apparently, despite his claims otherwise, it was too dangerous to let her live, and he had transmitted the kill order to the collars.

A bad move.

She had given Claude the chance to do the right thing.

He hadn't taken it.

She pictured the scarf securing Gabriel's ball gag. Hidden beneath the cashmere and snapped snugly around the young man's mouth and head was Renny's missing electronic collar. The ball gag was formed out of a molded wad of C4, retrieved from one of the explosive charges in the catacombs. The collar had been wired into a detonator. If and when the electronic collar was jolted, it would set off the C-4. She had calculated the quantity and shaped the explosive to take out the sedan and its occupants with little collateral damage.

She sighed, feeling a twinge of regret.

It was a nice car.

Renny gaped at the smoke signal in the sky, stunned, one hand clutching his throat. He finally tore his eyes away and faced her. "What now?"

She dumped the collar into a curbside trash bin and hefted up the briefcase. She remembered Claude Beaupré's last words to her. *What you do with this information—where it will lead—will be very dangerous territory to tread.*

As she turned away, she answered Renny's question.

What now?

"Now comes the hard part."

Author's Note

What's True, What's Not

At the end of my full-length novels, I love to spell out what's real and what's fiction in my stories. I thought I'd do the same here.

The Ritz Paris. I've never been there, but the details are as accurate as I could make them: from the Hemingway Bar (where the Bloody Mary was invented) to the gold-plated swan faucets in the bathroom.

The Order of the Solar Temple. This is a real apocalyptic cult started in 1984 by Luc Jouret and Joseph Di Mambro. It was originally titled *l'Ordre International Chevaleresque de Tradition Solaire* and eventually simplified to *l'Ordre du Temple Solaire*. The group was notorious for its mass suicides and human sacrifice, including the murder of a founder's infant son in Quebec.

The Paris Catacombs. Every detail about the place is true. They spread for 180 miles in a network of tunnels and rooms beneath the City of Lights, mostly throughout the southern *arrondissements* (districts) that make up the Left Bank of the city. The history of collapses and instability is all real, as are the details of the cat-and-mouse game waged between the *cataphiles* and *cataflics*. And, yes, the catacombs are full of disarticulated skeletons that date back a thousand years. And lots of strange things happen down there: from mushroom-growing to chambers full of elaborate wall art. New entrances, tunnels, and rooms to this subterranean world are continually being discovered by explorers. Even the story of the mysterious movie theater found underground is true.

The Peugeot 508. Yes, that *is* how you open the trunk: by pressing the zero in the 508 emblem. I hated to blow it up.

So that ends this adventure, but a large one is looming ahead as this story continues in *The Devil Colony*. The papers found in that hard-won briefcase will set off a chain of events that will change Sigma forever—and even alter how you view the very founding of America.

The Midnight Watch

A Σ SIGMA FORCE SHORT STORY

JAMES ROLLINS

April 25, 12:21 A.M. EDT
Washington, D.C.

We're under attack.

Jacketless, with his sleeves rolled to his elbows, Painter Crowe paced the length of the communication nest at the heart of Sigma Force's central command. Data streamed across the monitors that covered the curved walls as a single warrior waged a battle against a faceless enemy.

Jason Carter sat at a station, typing with one hand, clutching a Starbucks cup in the other, while studying the screen before him. "It looks like they built their own back door into the Smithsonian Institution's network using a high-level system administrator access. At this point, they literally have the keys to the kingdom."

"But who are *they*?" Painter stopped to stare over Jason's shoulder. The twenty-three-year-old was Sigma's chief intelligence analyst. He had been recruited by Painter after getting kicked out of the navy for hacking into Defense Department servers with nothing more than a BlackBerry and a jury-rigged iPad.

"Could be the Russians, the North Koreans, but I'd place money on the Chinese. This has their fingerprints all over it. A few months back, they hacked into the Office of Personnel Management, stealing information on millions of federal employees. They used a similar back door, giving them administrator privileges to the OPM servers."

Painter nodded. He knew the Chinese government employed an army of hackers, numbering over a hundred thousand, dedicated solely to breaking into US computers. Rumor had it that they had successfully hacked into every major American corporation over the past several years, absconding with blueprints to nuclear plants, appropriating technology from steel factories, even cracking into Lockheed Martin's servers to copy the top-secret schematics for the US military's F-35 fighter jet. If there was any doubt about the latter, one only had to view the new Chinese FC-31. It was almost an exact copy of the American jet.

"If it is Chinese, what are they after?" Painter asked. "Why hack into the Smithsonian servers?"

Jason shrugged his shoulders. "Either data theft or sabotage. That's the end goal of most hacks. But from the code, it looks like they're just blindly grabbing files. I'm not seeing any attempt to install malware into the systems."

"So data theft," Painter said. "Can you stop them?"

In the reflection of a neighboring dark monitor, Painter caught the young man's crooked grin. "Did that a full minute ago," Jason said, "and slammed the door behind them as I kicked them out. They won't be coming in that way again. I'm now attempting to identify which files were taken from which servers."

Painter glanced to the clock.

00:22

The attack had started exactly at midnight, most likely timed to strike when the hack was less liable to be detected. Still, twenty-two minutes was twenty-two minutes too long for an enemy to have unfettered access to the Smithsonian servers. The Institution was home to nine different research centers, encompassing a multitude of programs that spanned the globe.

Still, they were lucky. The only reason this attack had been caught so promptly was that Sigma Force's servers were linked to the Smithsonian's systems—though Sigma's operations were heavily guarded behind multiple firewalls to keep their presence hidden. Painter imagined those towering digital walls. It was a fitting metaphor. Sigma's central command had been covertly established beneath the Smithsonian Castle. He glanced up, picturing the turrets and towers of red sandstone above his head, a true Norman castle perched at the edge of the National Mall.

A fortress that someone had attempted to breach.

Or at least that was Painter's greatest fear: The Smithsonian servers were not the primary target of this attack but, instead, the hackers were sniffing at the walls of Sigma's own digital fortress. Sigma was a covert wing of DARPA, the Defense Department's research-and-development division. The unit recruited former Special Forces soldiers and retrained them in various scientific disciplines to act as field agents for DARPA. It was one of the reasons the Castle had been chosen for Sigma's central command. It was ideally situated within the heart of the political landscape, while allowing Sigma and its operatives to have easy access to the Smithsonian's resources and global reach.

If Sigma was ever compromised, its agents exposed . . .

A small huff drew Painter's attention back to the tangible world.

Jason scooted his chair back from his station, stood up, and stared across the banks of monitors, all still flowing with cryptic data. The young man studied the screens, running fingers through his blond hair, plainly concerned.

Painter stepped to his side. "What is it?"

"The pattern of theft is not random, despite how much they're trying to make it look like it." He pointed to one monitor. "This is no blind smash and grab. There is intent here, masked by all the rest of this noise."

"What intent?"

Jason returned to his station and began typing again, this time with both hands, his nose inches from the screen. "A majority of the files were stolen from one specific research center."

"Which one?"

Jason's voice tightened with plain confusion. "The Smithsonian's Conservation Biology Institute."

Painter understood his consternation. It was a strange target for such a sophisticated and elaborate cyberattack by a foreign enemy.

Jason continued as he typed. "The Smithsonian CBI has labs and facilities both in Virginia and here in D.C., at the National Zoo in Rock Creek Park. In this case, it's the campus at the *zoo* that was being targeted."

"Is there any rhyme or reason to the specific files that were being stolen?"

"Not that it makes any more sense, but a majority of the research material being drained comes from one specific program." Jason looked over his shoulder, displaying a deep frown. "A program titled Ancient DNA."

"Ancient DNA?"

Jason shrugged, just as lost. "The hacked files all belong to a single researcher, a postdoctoral fellow named Dr. Sara Gutierrez."

The young man leaned back from the monitor, revealing a staff identification badge on the screen. The woman on the badge looked no older than Jason, her black hair cut in a short bob, her eyes intent, with a shy grin fixed to her face.

"It looks like they cleaned out half of her files before I slammed the door on them."

"So they failed to get everything . . ." Painter felt a flicker of unease. "What was she working on?"

Jason shook his head. "All I have are the file names, which doesn't tell me much. But if I could access her computer, I might be able to trace the hackers' location. When I cut the connection, some pieces of code might have been left on her terminal, a digital fingerprint that might give us some clue as to *who* was behind this attack."

"You can do that?"

"I can try, but admittedly it's a long shot. Still, the odds would be better if I can get to that computer before anyone else uses it and accidentally wipes away that digital fingerprint."

"Understood. I'll see about arranging that. We'll also want to interview Dr. Gutierrez as soon as possible. Preferably tonight." He glanced to the wall clock. "Let's hope she's a night owl."

"I have her cell number from her records." Jason slipped out his own phone, lifting one eyebrow.

"Call it. Let her know what happened and that we need her help. We should arrange to meet at her office."

As Jason dialed, Painter considered whom to send at this late hour. His usual go-to operative, Commander Gray Pierce, was on a transatlantic flight to Europe to meet Seichan in Paris. Monk and Kat were on their way back from a road trip to Boston with their two young daughters. In his head, he ran through the remaining list of field agents best suited for this investigation.

Jason's voice caught his attention as Dr. Gutierrez answered the call. After some back and forth, the young man sat straighter and placed his cell on speakerphone mode. "And who called you?" Jason asked her.

A small voice whispered from his phone, but the confusion was plain. "They said they were with Zoological Park Police. Claimed someone had broken into my office. They were sending someone over to collect me. But . . ."

Her voice trailed off.

"But what?" Jason asked.

"It's just . . . I don't want to sound racist, but the caller was hard to understand. He had a thick accent. Asian, I think. It's probably nothing, but I got a bad feeling after I hung up."

Jason glanced worriedly in Painter's direction. "Did you tell him your location?" he asked the woman.

"I . . . I did."

"Where are you now?"

"I'm at the National Museum of Natural History. I was collecting

DNA samples from some of the exhibits as part of my program. It's easier after hours. I told the caller I would wait for them outside the museum at the corner of Twelfth and Madison."

"Stay put." Jason looked to Painter for confirmation. "We'll meet you inside the museum."

Painter nodded.

From the small speaker on the phone, a new noise erupted: a sharp and strident ringing.

Alarm bells.

The researcher's voice rose above the din. She sounded spooked. "What do I do?"

Jason eyed Painter while offering the young woman one hope. "Hide."

Painter thought quickly. With an alarm being raised at the museum, he had no time to summon an outside field operative. He momentarily considered going himself, but he knew he was needed here to help hold local law enforcement at bay—at least long enough to safely extract the woman.

That left only one Sigma member to assist Jason—someone still on the premises at this late hour. He pictured the muscled bulk of the former navy seaman, with his shaved head, his crooked nose, and his thick Bronx accent.

Dear god, help us all . . .

Joe Kowalski lay on his back in a puddle of oil. He gave the wrench a final tug to tighten the new filter on the old Jeep. He wiped the surface clean to make sure that the gasket had stopped leaking.

That oughta do it.

He rolled out from beneath the vehicle and shifted over to a cigar resting atop an overturned glass cup. Still on his back, he placed the stub between his lips and drew a couple hard pulls to get the end glowing brightly, then sighed out a long stream of smoke. Maybe it was stupid—

and definitely against the rules—to be smoking in Sigma's motor pool, but who was around to complain at this late hour?

He had the place to himself—which he preferred.

He climbed to his feet and inspected the '79 Jeep CJ7 that he was restoring. He had bought the off-roader three months earlier from a retired Forest Service member who had driven it hard, then let it sit idle for almost a decade. Never a good thing for a beast that loved to tear through a rugged landscape. Kowalski had already done a mild rebuild on the Chevy 400 motor, while troubleshooting issues with the transmission, steering, and drivetrain, but he still wasn't entirely happy with the wiring.

The open-body exterior was a patchwork of Bondo and primer, with some of the original olive-green paint showing. The front seats and rear bench, all original, were ripped and worn. He'd eventually get around to sprucing it all up, but for now, he appreciated his progress.

"You might be an ugly son of a bitch," he mumbled around his cigar, "but you can at least haul ass now."

He stared across the handful of other vehicles in the motor pool, mostly a sleek and polished mix of Land Rovers, German sedans, and a pair of Ducati motorcycles. He ran his palm over the Jeep's quarter panel, feeling the rough texture of Bondo and a small buckle from an old fender bender, all testaments to its hard use and toughness.

He couldn't wait to test this beast off-road, to let her truly loose.

Imagining that, he grabbed the roll bar and climbed behind the wheel—an easy enough maneuver, as both doors were leaning against the neighboring wall, waiting to be reinstalled. He turned the key. The engine coughed twice, belching smoke from the exhaust, then settled into a throaty growl.

He leaned back, allowing a satisfied grin to crack his face.

"Kowalski!"

The sharp voice made him jump. He twisted around to see the lanky form of Sigma's resident computer geek come racing into the garage. A loose navy-blue windbreaker flapped around the kid's thin shoulders, exposing a holster strapped across his chest.

"We have to move!"

Kowalski puffed out a lungful of cigar smoke. "Where?" he growled around the glowing nub.

"Across the Mall. To the National Museum of Natural History."

A twinge of fear spiked down Kowalski's spine—not for himself, but for another. It was a knee-jerk reaction. His girlfriend—or, rather, *ex*-girlfriend—had worked there for the past couple of years, overseeing exhibits on Greek mythology and ancient history. But Elizabeth had left three months ago for Egypt to join an archaeological dig. Their relationship had already taken a rocky turn before that and had been on its last legs. As much as opposites might initially attract, it wasn't necessarily the recipe for a long-term relationship. And though this dig in Egypt had been a great opportunity for her, he knew a large part of her drive to go had been to put some distance between them—less for her sake than his own, he suspected. It was no secret between the two of them that his torch had burned brighter.

And still did.

It was one of the reasons he had purchased the Jeep and undertaken this restoration. He needed something to distract himself with.

Jason pointed to one of the BMW sedans. "Let's go! I'll fill you in along the way!"

Kowalski flicked the nub of his cigar into a nearby pail of water. "Get your ass over here!" he called out, gunning the engine for emphasis. "We'll take my Jeep!"

Jason skidded to a stop and looked skeptically at the vehicle, but he adjusted to the change with the pliability that only came with youth. He ran to the open passenger side and hopped into the seat. He looked for the shoulder strap, but like the doors, the seat belts were also missing.

Kowalski yanked the truck into gear and bucked the vehicle forward. Jason had to grab the edge of the roll cage to keep his seat.

Hmm . . . maybe the tranny needs some further tweaking, too.

Kowalski hauled on the wheel and sent the truck rumbling toward a ramp that spiraled up to a private exit onto Independence Avenue.

Jason spoke rapidly as they climbed, filling Kowalski in on the details of a cyberattack upon the Smithsonian servers—and of a potential asset hiding inside the museum across the Mall. "Director Crowe thinks the enemy has implemented a backup plan. After failing to obtain the information electronically, they're going directly for the source."

For this woman . . .

Once at the top of the ramp, Kowalski pointed toward the glove compartment. "Open that."

Jason obeyed, popping the compartment to reveal a large steel pistol resting inside. He passed the weapon over to Kowalski—using both hands. "What the hell is it?"

Kowalski accepted the huge revolver with a grin. The rubberized grip fit his meaty palm perfectly. "A .50-caliber Desert Eagle."

".50?" Jason said with a whistle. "What's wrong with a .45?"

"Because they make a *.50*," Kowalski said, stating the obvious.

He shoved the large pistol into his belt.

Once out onto Independence Avenue, Jason took a call from Painter as Kowalski wound them in a big circle around the Mall. He ended up behind a massive dump truck trundling and filling his side of the street. Though the National Museum of Natural History was a direct arrow shot across the Mall from the Castle, the circuitous route was further complicated by an ongoing construction project to restore the Mall's ragged turf, which had turned this section of parkland and fields into towering piles of dirt and rock.

Jason hung up. "The director managed to convince DC Metro that it was a false alarm, blaming an electrical surge from the neighboring construction project. But such a ruse will only buy us a narrow window of time."

Kowalski gave a shake of his head. He had to hand it to the director. Painter was a master puppeteer when it came to pulling the strings around Washington.

Jason added, "We've also got clearance to enter the museum through an entrance on the northwest side. It's located—"

Kowalski cut him off. "I know where it's at."

He had sometimes used that entrance to reach Elizabeth's office. It was the most direct route, bypassing the tumult of the main entrance and its flock of tourists. When the dump truck turned onto Madison, Kowalski finally got clear of it and sped up, reaching the parking lot on the western side of the museum.

He raced across the empty lot and skidded to a hard stop near the entrance. They both tumbled out and ran for the door. Jason's head swiveled from side to side, watching for any sign of the enemy. Someone had set off that alarm. But did that mean they were already inside, or had they merely tripped the alarm to flush their quarry out into the open?

Only one way to find out.

Jason reached the entrance first and swiped a black card with a holographic Σ embossed on one side through an electronic reader. The door unlocked with a loud click of its dead bolt. Jason began to open the door, but Kowalski moved him aside and led the way with his Desert Eagle. He entered a nondescript anteroom with a door ahead that opened onto the main levels of the museum. The mouth of a dark stairwell yawned on his left.

"Where is this doctor?" Kowalski asked as Jason followed him inside.

"The alarm was triggered from a first-floor window on the building's north side." He pointed in that general direction. "To keep her well away from that spot, we told her to hole up in Dr. Polk's old office in the basement."

Kowalski glanced sharply back at the kid. "Elizabeth's old place?"

Why send her to my ex's office?

"We knew Dr. Polk's room was empty. The director also chose the rendezvous because you are familiar with the surrounding area. In case we run into trouble."

Great . . . I'm really beginning to hate this place.

With a sigh, Kowalski led Jason to the stairwell and headed down. The steps ended at a maze of narrow passageways that spread under the museum. The way forward was dimly lit with the crimson glow of emergency lights. It was one of the oldest sections of the building, barely touched during the periodic renovations of the public spaces. Beneath their boots, the old marble floors had been honed to a lustrous sheen by decades of shuffling feet. Wooden doors with frosted glass windows lined either side, each pane etched with scholarly enterprises: ENTOMOLOGY, MINERAL SCIENCES, VERTEBRATE ZOOLOGY, BOTANY.

Kowalski knew the path to Elizabeth's office all too well. Memories flickered in the shadows of his mind as he tried to concentrate, to listen for any sign of threat. He remembered picnicking with Elizabeth in her office, hearing her laugh, basking in her smiles. He remembered the two of them stealing away into the old steam tunnels beneath the museum to smoke cigars, which even she partook of on occasion. He also remembered other midnight hours, dozing on her couch while she finished cataloging a new shipment from Greece or Italy, other times when they were engaged in less studious pursuits, wrapped in each other's arms. He felt his blood stirring at those last thoughts and pushed them down—deep down.

Now was not the time.

Still, he could not escape darker memories, of those times when his impatience irritated her, when smiles turned to frowns; when words, spoken on both sides, became painful. They were both hotheaded, both too easy to bruise. Perhaps with time, they would have learned to settle into each other with more care, but all too often he'd been called away on missions abroad, on pursuits he hadn't even been able to talk about upon returning. Likewise, she'd been gone for weeks on end: to dusty digs, to laborious scientific conferences. And while apart, their intimate daily calls, which had previously often lasted for hours, had eventually faded to curt text messages.

And when the end had finally come, it hadn't been any operatic act of betrayal. It had simply been the tide of their relationship ebbing away, until neither of them had been able to dismiss the inevitable. Ever the smarter of the two, Elizabeth had recognized it first and laid out the facts over a long, cold dinner.

Still, it hurt.

At last, a dark door appeared ahead. The frosted glass read Anthro-pology. Below that, hanging on the door from small hooks, was a black metal placard with silver letters that spelled Elizabeth Polk, PhD.

"Here we are," Kowalski said needlessly.

Surprised that she had left the placard, he bent down to unhook it. As he did so, the pane shattered above his head, accompanied by the loud retort of a pistol blast.

Jason dropped to one knee and spun around, cleanly pulling out his side arm, a SIG Sauer P226. He squeezed the trigger twice, shooting blindly down the hall in the direction of the gunshot, hoping to discourage the sniper from firing again. He wasn't entirely successful. A second gunshot blasted from the shadows, splintering wood from the doorframe by his shoulder.

Then a cannon went off by his ear.

A clipped cry rose from down the hall.

Kowalski held his smoking weapon and growled at him. "Get inside!"

Jason dove behind the large man's bulk, grabbed the doorknob—thankfully, the door was unlocked—and shoved the way open with his shoulder. He rolled inside, drawing Kowalski in his wake. Once clear, Jason slammed the office door closed, dislodging a few shattered panes of glass. Though it offered little protection, he thumbed the lock.

"Sara," he called to the dark room, while staying low. "It's Jason Carter."

A small gasp rose from behind the desk. "I'm over here."

He spotted a shadow rising from out of hiding.

"Stay down," he warned.

"They must've tailed us down here," Kowalski grumbled, rising enough to peer out the shattered window.

It made sense. They should have been more cautious. The enemy couldn't have known *where* Dr. Gutierrez had holed up.

Until we led them here, Jason realized.

Either he and Kowalski had been spotted entering the building, or some small expeditionary force had already been inside and had come upon their path down here. Either way, they were trapped.

"This way," Kowalski said and headed away from the door in a hunched crouch. "There's a small storeroom in the back."

Jason followed, collecting Dr. Gutierrez along the way.

Wearing a white lab coat over jeans, she sidled next to him. She clutched a black leather satchel to her chest with one arm. "Thank you," she whispered.

Don't thank us yet.

Jason looked around. The office was large, with shelved walls, a large desk, and an old leather sofa against one wall. But besides a handful of stray papers, it had been thoroughly cleaned out. Kowalski led them to a narrow door on the far side, which stood ajar.

They all piled into the next room, which was twice the size of the office and divided by tall metal shelves. A pair of wooden pallets leaned against one wall. Jason imagined the storeroom had been used as a staging ground for Dr. Polk's work on her antiquities collection.

Kowalski closed the door, which was made of solid pine. Still, it wouldn't give a determined enemy much of a problem, especially since there was no way to lock it from the inside. This didn't seem to bother Kowalski as he headed over to the middle of the room and bent down to a solid grate in the floor. It was sealed with a padlock.

Dropping to a knee and using the light of his cell phone for illumination, Kowalski spun the dial back and forth. Behind them, a tinkle of glass whispered from the neighboring room. Jason pictured a hand reaching through the shattered pane for the lock.

Hurry . . .

Kowalski freed the padlock and hauled up the heavy grate with one arm. A dark opening yawned below. "There's a ladder on the left. It's a short climb down into one of the service tunnels beneath the museum."

Jason didn't question Kowalski's plan or where it might lead. For the moment, the goal was to stay one step ahead of the enemy. He went first, mounting the steel rungs, then helping guide Sara along with him. Rushing, he stumbled as one boot slipped. He ended up sliding the rest of the way down, which luckily was only a couple of yards. He landed roughly, but managed to keep his feet and get Sara safely to the ground.

Overhead, Kowalski closed the grate with a soft clang, then slid down the ladder without a boot touching a rung. He had plainly done this before.

Jason unclipped a penlight and flashed it along the tunnel. The place was sweltering, smelling of wet cement, and echoing with trickles of water. Old pipes, frosted with cobwebs, trailed along the ceiling.

"Where are we?" Sara asked.

Kowalski pushed between them and led the way forward. "Old steam and service tunnels. Elizabeth and I would sometimes sneak down here and smoke." He patted the walls. "It was the safest place without having to climb all the way back outside."

Jason heard a mix of sorrow and wistfulness in his voice.

"Where are we going?" Sara asked, voicing Jason's own concern.

Kowalski coughed to clear his throat a bit. "Place is a maze down here. Some say these tunnels once reached all the way under the White House, but with heightened security, much of it's been partitioned and walled off." He pointed ahead as he turned a corner. "There are stairs this way that lead back up to a service door into the museum."

As they made the corner, a loud clang rang out behind them.

The enemy had discovered their escape route.

Jason flashed his light across the floor of the tunnel. Their footprints in the grime would be easy to follow.

Muffled voices rose behind them.

"Time to haul ass," the big man warned, urging them forward.

Again, Jason didn't question his plan.

Kowalski shoved the Desert Eagle back into his belt and followed the others up the cement stairs. He fumbled with his wallet as he climbed, searching through its contents.

Where the hell are you . . . ?

By now, Jason had reached the stained cement landing at the top of the stairs. A yellow emergency bulb offered meager illumination, enough to reveal a nondescript steel door. It looked like it dated from the museum's opening day, but a modern electronic lock sealed it securely.

Jason tugged on the handle, but it was no use.

Kowalski's fingers finally plucked a card from the many stuffed into a side pocket of his tattered leather billfold. It was an old staff keycard. In one corner, barely discernible under the glow of the lone bulb, was a tiny picture of Elizabeth Polk. Her chestnut hair framed high cheekbones, while a pair of petite eyeglasses balanced on her nose. Elizabeth had given the card to him shortly after they had begun dating, making it easier for him to come and go while visiting her. He should have returned it or cut it up, but he hadn't been able to do either.

The furtive patter of boots on stone echoed up from below.

"Kowalski . . ." Jason hissed to him.

Kowalski hurried forward with the card, praying it was still coded to this service door. He swiped the card down the slit under a red glowing light—it remained red.

Motherfu—

Jason stared at him with huge eyes. Dr. Gutierrez huddled at his shoulder. Beads of sweat pebbled her forehead, while her lips were fixed in a grimace of fear. They were sitting ducks up here.

Kowalski rubbed the keycard's magnetic strip over the sleeve of his jacket. "Sometimes these old readers are finicky."

God, I hope that's it.

A shout rose from below as the enemy abandoned any furtiveness.

Jason swung to the side and used the muzzle of his gun to shatter the lone bulb in its cage. Darkness fell around them, offering some shelter. The kid pulled the woman low, while pointing his gun toward the stairs. He fired once to encourage their pursuers to proceed more cautiously.

Kowalski swiped his card again.

C'mon, Elizabeth, don't let me down.

Despite his silent plea, the tiny light remained red.

What the hell!

He fingered the card, wondering if he didn't deserve this fate. But under his fingertips, he realized the magnetic strip was on the wrong side. In the dark, he had the card turned around the wrong way.

He flipped the card, jammed it through the reader, and watched the light flash to green, accompanied by a gratifying roll of tumblers. He grabbed the handle and shoved the door open.

They all piled into the hallway. Kowalski slammed the door behind them, then leaned against it with relief. Muffled shots rang out from the far side, ricocheting brightly off the steel, reminding them they had no time to relish this small victory.

"We need to keep going," Jason warned. "There's no telling how many more might be out here."

Kowalski nodded. "Follow me."

He pushed off the door and ran down the hall to a stairwell. It was the same one he and Jason had used to reach the basement level. They fled back up to the side exit. Kowalski had his Desert Eagle in hand again, and he waved Jason and Dr. Gutierrez through the door as he propped it open and covered them. He watched the parking lot for any sign of an ambush, while listening with an ear cocked for any sound of pursuit from within the museum.

The Jeep stood only a handful of yards away. Jason got the young woman into the front passenger seat, then hopped onto the rear bench. The kid stood with his back against the roll bar and raised his SIG Sauer, swiveling it to cover the lot.

"Go!" Jason ordered.

Kowalski rolled away from the door, letting it close behind him, and sprinted around the front of the Jeep to reach the driver's side. As he climbed in, he heard a screaming whine rise from behind the museum. He remembered Jason saying that the alarm had been tripped from a broken window back there.

As Kowalski fumbled the key into the ignition, he watched a single headlight come careening around the far corner into the parking lot. It was a motorcycle, bearing two helmeted riders. The one in the rear rose high in his seat, lifting a rifle to his shoulder.

Kowalski twisted the key, and the engine coughed and died.

A rifle blast exploded across the quiet night.

The windshield fractured.

Son of a bitch . . .

Jason returned fire from the back, shooting over the roll bar. Kowalski pumped the accelerator once, then tried the key again, suddenly very worried about his wiring job on the ignition coil. But the engine coughed— then caught with a jolt of the frame, growling roughly.

Good enough.

He yanked them into reverse, then shoved his boot to the floor. The Jeep sped backward, earning a hard *oof* from Jason as the roll bar slammed into his chest. But the kid's assault had succeeded in driving the motorcycle to the side, forcing the enemy to zigzag through a copse of trees flanking Twelfth Street.

Taking advantage of the moment, Kowalski yelled, "Hold tight!" and yanked hard on the wheel.

The Jeep jackknifed around.

Jason hugged the roll bar with one arm to keep his footing.

Dr. Gutierrez slid from her seat into Kowalski's side, but he still managed to shift into first. He sped them away, aiming for Madison Drive, which ran along the front of the museum.

"Kowalski!" Jason hollered.

But he had already spotted the threat. Two more motorcycles converged on their position, coming from opposite directions down Madison: one traveling with traffic, weaving swiftly through the scatter of cars at this hour; the other coming the wrong way down the one-way street.

Gunfire erupted behind them as the first bike took erratic potshots at them.

Rounds pinged off his bumper and back panel.

Jason returned fire just as wildly.

As the Jeep reached the end of the lot, Kowalski thought quickly. He hated to carry this battle to the streets, where innocent bystanders might be caught in the firefight. Plus even if he attempted to take Madison, he would be pinned down on all sides.

That left only one choice.

"Duck low and hold tight!" he ordered his passengers.

He gunned the engine, shifting rapidly up through the three gears, and shot out across Madison. He passed across the path of a late-night bus and between the two converging motorcycles. He hit the far curb, bounced the Jeep high, and crashed through the temporary fencing that surrounded the section of the National Mall that was under construction. He landed hard on all four tires and kept going without slowing.

Ahead, the landscape was a roiled mix of rock piles, towering dunes of soil, and treacherous pits. This phase of the construction project ran the half-mile stretch from Seventh Street almost to the foot of the Washington Monument.

"What're you doing?" Jason called out.

"What the hell does it look like?"

"Looks like you don't know what you're doing!"

"Exactly! It's called improvising!"

As Jason let out a loud groan, Kowalski headed deeper into the tortured terrain at breakneck speed. In the rearview mirror, he saw the three motorcycles close in behind him. The enemy was not giving up that easily.

Kowalski remembered earlier how he had wanted to test this Jeep off-road.

Looks like I'm about to get my chance.

Jason hugged one arm around the roll bar as the Jeep sped deeper into the excavation site. Ahead, the brightly lit spire of the Washington Monument rose into the night sky.

As the Jeep rattled over the uneven ground, he did his best to keep his balance on the rear bench seat, assisted by the fact that one boot had ripped through the worn fabric and sunk into the springs.

A rifle blasted behind him, the round pinging off the back hatch of the vehicle. Still keeping one arm hooked to the bar, he raised his SIG Sauer and fired wildly at the closest motorcycle. It had a good thirty-yard lead on the other two and looked ready to close the distance by itself.

More rifle flashes burst from the cycle. Again all the rounds struck low: into the dirt or ricocheting off the bumper.

Must be trying to take out the back tires . . .

If so, it suggested they were trying to keep Sara alive.

But why?

"Hang on!" Kowalski called out.

What do you think I'm doing back here?

As the lead bike gunned toward them, Kowalski carved a sharp turn around a tall berm of loose dirt. The vehicle tilted precariously. Kowalski expertly downshifted, then punched the accelerator again.

The thick-treaded tires dug into the mound of soil and cast a rooster tail behind the Jeep. The cascading wave of dirt and gravel struck the trailing motorcycle, swamping it and knocking it to the ground.

Kowalski cleared the berm and set off again.

Jason regained his legs, searching behind them.

One down . . .

The two other bikes hit the berm, flew high, landed expertly on their back wheels—and sped after them.

A new barrage of gunfire chased them, coming from both motorcycles.

Jason felt a round whistle past his ear. Two others pelted the top edge of the windshield. Kowalski pushed Sara lower, almost cramming her into the footwell. Jason followed his example and dropped flat to the bench seat.

The sudden change in tactics by the enemy suggested that circumstances had changed, that new orders had been radioed from their superiors.

Shoot to kill.

Kowalski kept one eye on the shadowy terrain ahead of him and another on the rearview mirror. The two angry black hornets gained on his position. The riders had momentarily stopped firing, hunkering down instead, forgoing the attack to race faster.

He understood their plan.

They intended to flank him, to trap the Jeep in cross fire.

Like hell . . . you're on my home turf now.

Though admittedly that turf was long gone. Over the past month, he'd often climbed up to the roof of the Castle and watched the heavy equipment scrape away the old lawn, haul in truckloads of new topsoil, and excavate irrigation trenches and deep pits for future cisterns. He had found the rumble of John Deere motors and the chatter of work crews to be soothing. It was his white noise, his version of the patter of rain or the sonorous calls of whales.

"Where are you going?" Jason called to him, a note of panic in his voice.

Ahead, a mountain of dirt blocked their path, climbing two stories.

"Up," he answered.

He had no doubt the Jeep could tackle this summit, but he needed all the torque he could muster from the Chevy engine. He momentarily slowed, dropping a gear. The two motorcycles narrowed the gap, each swinging wider, preparing to flank him. From the blistering screams of those bikes, he imagined they were stretching their two-stroke engines to their limits.

But was it enough for the steep banks of loose dirt?

Let's find out.

As he reached the foot of the mountain, he pounded the accelerator, while popping into first. The Jeep's wheels momentarily spun—then the treads caught, and the vehicle bolted forward like a spanked horse. It shot up the steep slope, accelerating swiftly, proving how true a thoroughbred the vehicle was deep down.

Dr. Gutierrez gasped, falling back in her seat; Jason swore behind him.

The enemy gave chase, riding up the bank of topsoil. Both riders were plainly skilled, shimmying their rear tires to keep from miring down in the dirt. They soon drew even with Kowalski's rear bumper, their reflections filling either side mirror. The bikers freed pistols from thigh holsters, readying to open fire on the Jeep.

"Kowalski!" Jason moaned.

The crest of the mountain was only yards away. Still, they'd never reach the top before being overtaken.

Just as well.

Kowalski slammed the brakes hard, drawing the Jeep to a swift stop.

The maneuver was too sudden for the enemy to respond. Both bikes blasted past the Jeep's stalled position, then reached the summit and shot high. Kowalski tried to imagine the view from those bikes.

He grinned darkly and edged the Jeep up to the top. From that lofty vantage, he watched the two cycles arc high—then tumble headlong toward a massive pit on the mountain's far side. The hill had been formed as the construction crew had dug out a deep cistern, one that was destined to hold over two hundred thousand gallons of water.

Plus two motorcycles now.

The pair of bikes crashed hard into the muck at the bottom of the pit.

Jason patted Kowalski on the shoulder as he reversed the Jeep down the embankment. "I owe you."

"A dozen hand-rolled Cubans and we'll call it even." Kowalski turned to Dr. Gutierrez, who looked pale and near shock. "So why are you so important?"

Jason let Sara breathe heavily for a couple of minutes before pursuing Kowalski's line of questioning. Once the Jeep cleared out of the restoration site and got back onto Madison Drive, he leaned forward in the back seat. Behind him, he watched the flashing lights of emergency vehicles closing in on the Mall.

It was time to get clear of here—and get some answers.

"Sara, can you tell us what you were working on for the Smithsonian? Why you were at the museum?"

She turned toward him. Her eyes were still huge, but her breathing had calmed. "I'm here on a fellowship, working with the Smithsonian's Ancient DNA program."

Jason had gleaned that much from her staff file. "What sort of work are you doing for them?"

She gave a confused shake of her head. "The goal of our program is to study genetic variability and changes over time in various species. To help achieve that, my colleagues and I extract and analyze DNA from ancient sources."

"Ancient sources?"

"From mineralized bones, archaeological artifacts, or in the case tonight . . ." She retrieved her leather satchel from the footwell and placed it protectively in her lap. "From museum specimens."

Kowalski grimaced at the bag. "What sort of *specimens*?"

"Each of us is assigned a different taxonomic family of species. In my case, I work with all Hominidae. That covers all the great apes. Orangutans, gorillas, chimpanzees, and bonobos."

"But also one other," Jason added. "Hominidae also includes the genus *Homo*, which includes us humans."

She nodded, glancing more intently at him for knowing this. "That's right. I've collected and documented genomic samples from most known hominin species, from the most ancient to modern man." She ticked them off. "*Homo erectus, Homo habilis, Homo neanderthalensis*, and several other obscure ancestors of ours. It's why I was at the museum tonight. To collect DNA samples from a newly acquired set of fossils."

"And you've been storing these results on your lab computer?"

"That's right."

Jason leaned back, struggling to understand what the Chinese might want with such esoteric scientific data. It made no sense. But for the moment that could wait. He remembered the mission assigned to him: secure not only Dr. Gutierrez but also her computer. Beyond safeguarding the files that had not been stolen in the initial cyberattack, he was still hoping there might be some digital evidence left on her computer that might point to the perpetrator.

"Sara, I need to access your computer . . . tonight . . . before anyone corrupts what's there. After we drop you off somewhere safe—"

She swung toward him. "I'll need to go with you."

"Why?"

"My computer is doubly secured, both with an alphanumeric password and an EyeLock myris system."

"What's that?" Kowalski asked.

Jason groaned, knowing the answer. It was a commercially available iris scanner used for identity authentication. "Looks like we're all sticking together awhile longer."

Fifteen minutes later, Kowalski drove the Jeep down a small, winding road through Rock Creek Park. The darkly forested route led toward the rear of the National Zoo property, where a private gate offered easy access to the campus of the Rock Creek Research Labs.

"The gate should be around the next bend," Sara said as she shivered against the gale of cold wind sweeping across the open-air vehicle.

Kowalski had cranked the heater up as high as it would go, but it was like holding your hands around a candle in a blizzard. He found his own teeth beginning to chatter.

"My office is only a short distance past the fence," she promised them.

Jason leaned closer to Kowalski. "The director has the campus locked down by the Zoological Park Police. They should be waiting for us at the gate."

Sara lifted a white staff card. "If not, I have my pass."

As the Jeep rounded the bend, the perimeter fence appeared. A small service gate stood open, lit by a single lamppost. Kowalski spotted no guards or the promised police escort.

He shared a worried look with Jason.

"Maybe the staff left it open for us," the kid offered. "Or maybe they're waiting for us at Sara's office."

And maybe pigs fly out my ass.

As he approached the gate, Kowalski goosed the Jeep faster, just in case anyone tried to ambush them at the fencerow. Neither of his passengers asked him to slow down.

He sped through the gate and onto the zoo grounds. A cluster of office buildings hugged both sides of the road ahead, looking like any business complex. Beyond them, past another fence, the main park beckoned.

"My office is in the second building on the left."

It appeared to be the only one lit up this night. A lone figure stood limned against that glow.

"That's Jill Masterson," Sara said, sighing out her relief, plainly happy to see a familiar face. "She's a lieutenant with the Park Police."

Kowalski drew alongside the officer, still searching for any threat. As he kept the engine idling, he could make out the nighttime cries and calls of the neighboring park's denizens. The breeze carried the scent of cherry blossoms, along with an underlying heavier musk blowing from the grounds.

The lieutenant approached. She appeared to be in her midthirties. She was fit, dressed in a crisp park uniform with her auburn hair tucked into a cap. From the scowl fixed to her face, she was not happy about this midnight assignment.

She introduced herself, then added, "I'm not sure why my boss roused park services to open the gate and secure this building. Everything's been quiet." She offered a brief smile toward Sara. "But it sounds like you've had a rough night, Dr. Gutierrez."

"And I'll be happy when it's over."

They all unloaded and headed toward the office building.

"I thought there would be more boots on the ground here," Jason commented.

Masterson cocked an eyebrow at him. "At this hour? We're not DC Metro. With budget cuts, we barely have enough staff during the day. Still, I managed to corral three officers to canvass the building and make sure everything is secure. I still have a man inside."

"What about the other two?" Kowalski asked.

"Once we had matters in hand, I sent them back into the park. We got a glass-breakage alarm at the front gate's kiosk a few minutes ago. They went to check—" From their expressions, she must have known something was wrong. "What?"

"It's like back at the museum," Sara moaned.

Jason forced them to move faster. "Everyone inside. We need to secure that computer and set up a defense. Radio your man, Lieutenant."

She obeyed, confirming that all remained quiet inside.

Still, Kowalski pulled out his Desert Eagle, which earned a double take from Masterson. Jason took out his cell phone and called Painter, filling him in on the fly. As they entered the front door of the building, Sara guided them in a rush toward her lab offices at the back.

"Help's coming," Jason said as he hung up.

Let's hope they get here in time.

As they crossed the lobby, a loud roar echoed to them.

Kowalski froze, but Sara smiled nervously back at him. "That's Anton, a Siberian tiger caged in the neighboring Reproductive Sciences Department. They've been collecting semen from him this week as part of an endangered tiger breeding program."

Lucky him.

She glanced down a side hall. "Anton's generally a pussycat, but he's notoriously cranky when woken up early."

Me, too.

They hurried to the back of the building and found Masterson's other man waiting inside Sara's office. He introduced himself as John Kress and joined his boss in guarding the hall as Jason followed Sara into the depths of her lab. The small space was cramped with stainless steel equipment, shelves of glassware and pipettes, tall freezers, and a workbench holding a trio of computers.

"Mine's in the center," Sara said.

Jason pulled out a portable thumb drive. "If you can get me access, I need to copy the root directory to capture any malicious executable code and get a record of the night's TCP/IP connections. After that, I'll try to—"

Sara cut him off. "Do anything you have to."

She woke up her computer, typed in the long string of a password, and lifted a wired blue puck toward her face. A small light flashed across her left eye, then the blank login screen cleared, revealing her desktop.

She stepped back. "All yours."

Jason took her place and slipped his drive into a USB port on the side of her keyboard. He began typing rapidly with one hand, while manipulating her wireless mouse with the other.

"Interesting," Jason mumbled.

Sara drew closer. "What?"

"The hackers seemed to have targeted any of your files tagged as *N¬¬_sis*." He glanced back to her. "What does that stand for?"

"It's just my shorthand for *Neanderthalensis*," she answered. "Those are my files comparing Neanderthal sequences with those of modern man, highlighting those genes we obtained from our long-lost ancestor. Most of us carry a small percentage of Neanderthal genes, some of us more than others."

Kowalski waited for someone to glance in his direction at this last statement, but thankfully no one did.

Jason suddenly swore, lifting his hands from the keyboard. Files flashed on the screen, opening and closing on their own, as if there was a ghost in the machine. But it wasn't any *ghost*.

"We're being hacked," Jason realized. "Right now."

Jason kicked himself for being so stupid, so shortsighted. He considered yanking the power cord to the computer, but he knew it was already too late. In just that fraction of inattention, they'd stolen everything.

"What's happening?" Sara asked, watching as he furiously typed.

"As soon as you logged on, the first thing I did was cut your computer off from the Internet, from the world at large, but someone attacked your server through your LAN. Your local area network."

"And that means what?" Kowalski asked.

"The hacker must still be in the area, close enough to have connected to the system locally. Probably in the same building. They must've waited to ambush the system but first needed Sara to unlock it."

No wonder the enemy tried to avoid killing her at the outset. They wanted her to return here and access her computer.

"Even the false alarm must have been used to lure Masterson's forces away," Jason realized aloud, "long enough so that they could get an operative close enough to orchestrate the attack."

"But *where* are they?" Kowalski asked.

Jason continued to type. "That's what I'm trying to figure out, but whoever did this mirrored their trace across *eight* different computers."

Sara clutched her arms across her chest. "That's the number of computers networked in this building," she said, confirming his fear.

"Doesn't matter," Kowalski said, swinging toward the door. "I know where they're at."

Jason looked over a shoulder at him. "How?"

Kowalski collected Lieutenant Masterson and the other officer on his way out the door and down the hall. "One of you, head outside and canvass the perimeter. The other, stay in the lobby and cover the front door."

Just in case I'm wrong.

He had a narrow window to catch the culprits red-handed and retrieve what was stolen. He left Masterson in the lobby as the other officer ran for the front door. He headed to the left, to the hall he had noted Sara glancing down earlier—when the tiger had roared.

He remembered her earlier words: *Anton's generally a pussycat, but he's notoriously cranky when woken up early.*

He hoped she was right on both counts.

He had initially written off the tiger's outburst as a complaint against their arrival, but what if whoever had bothered the tiger was closer at hand, invading the animal's private space? Maybe that was what had made him cranky.

It was a thin lead, but better than nothing.

He reached a set of double doors with a sign that read DEPARTMENT OF REPRODUCTIVE SCIENCES. He hoped Jason was as good as he claimed to be. The kid had said he could hack into the building's security system and unarm all the building's electronic locks, opening a path for Kowalski.

He tested the knob, and it turned freely.

Good job, kid.

Leading with his Desert Eagle, he cracked the door enough to slip inside, then closed it behind him. The hallway ahead was dark, flanked by small offices. The main reproductive lab was directly ahead of him at the end of the hall.

That's where Sara said the department's main server was located. He hoped it was the correct networked computer. He had one in eight odds of being right.

He edged down the hall, sticking to one wall.

His ears strained for any sign of an intruder—then he heard glass break, followed by a shout from outside. A loud gunshot exploded from inside the lab ahead.

Kowalski rushed forward, hit the swinging set of doors, and slid low into the room. Skidding on his knees, he took in the view while bracing his Desert Eagle. The reproductive lab looked more like an operating room, with a pair of stainless steel hydraulic tables, overhead swing-arm lights, and banks of glass cabinets.

Between the tables, a computer rested on a large desk.

At the station, a small, wiry figure was detaching a palm-sized drive from the back of the monitor, while on Kowalski's left, a man who matched him in size and muscle stood bathed in the moonlight flowing through a shattered window. The guy held a smoking pistol in hand—

likely used to fire at the officer outside. The weapon whipped toward Kowalski and fired.

Unable to get clear fast enough, he took the round square to the chest. The impact knocked the air from his lungs and exploded his rib cage with fiery pain. He dropped to his back—and returned fire from under the table on that side. The cannon boomed deafeningly in his hand. The plaster exploded behind the man's legs as the shot went wide. Still, Kowalski took advantage of the moment to roll behind a steel medical cart. The man fired after him, rounds pelting the side of the cart, keeping Kowalski pinned down.

He patted his chest, expecting to find blood, but instead he felt the dented steel plate in his front pocket. It was the nameplate he had unhooked from Elizabeth's office door earlier. He had forgotten he had stolen it, absently slipping it inside his jacket. It had saved his life—at least for the moment.

Sirens sounded in the distance, racing closer.

Must be the reinforcements sent by Director Crowe.

Kowalski gripped his pistol and risked peering past the edge of his shelter.

The small figure by the computer—a young woman—also recognized the approaching threat and called to her partner while pointing to the window.

"*Kwan, zŏu!*"

The man grimaced, clearly being ordered to leave.

With the portable drive in hand, she headed over to her partner's side, ready to make their escape. She had her own pistol out and fixed toward Kowalski's position, as if daring him to show himself.

But Kowalski wasn't the only one irritated by the intruders.

Farther to his left, a tall, shadowy cage door swung open with a creak of heavy steel hinges—and a massive beast stalked into the lab. It seemed Jason's release of *all* the building's electronic locks had included the tiger's cage. A snarling hiss flowed from the cat's throat, and its fur bristled in stripes of black and rust. Paws the size of dinner plates padded across the floor in slow, determined steps, drawn by the figures standing in the moonlight.

The woman backed fearfully from the sight. She tried to pocket the bulky drive, but it slipped from her fingers and clattered to the floor. Clearly panicked, she gripped her pistol with both hands.

Her partner also kept his weapon upon the beast. "*Bù, Shu Wei,*" he whispered to the woman, warning her not to shoot or risk antagonizing the tiger, who was still plainly confused by the noise and commotion.

Instead, he scooped his free arm around the small woman's waist, lifting and drawing her to his side as easily as if she'd been a doll, then the pair fell backward through the open window. The tiger stalked over, drawn by the motion. It sniffed at the breeze, then stretched its neck to a jaw-cracking yawn.

Kowalski used the distraction to back slowly out of hiding—but his knee banged against the corner of the metal cart. The tiger whipped around at the sudden noise, dropping into a hissing crouch. Kowalski dove for the only refuge at hand. He flung himself headlong through the open door of the cage and yanked the gate shut behind him.

The tiger pounced after its prey, slamming into the front of the cage.

Kowalski kept his hands clamped to the bars, holding the door closed.

The tiger rolled to its feet, stalking a bit back and forth, ruffling its fur as if shaking off water. Large brown eyes stared at Kowalski, while hot breath panted through the bars.

"That's a good kitty, Anton," Kowalski said softly, hoping it was true.

A large huff escaped the beast's throat, as if it recognized its name. The tiger stalked back and forth twice more, then settled to the floor, slumping against the bars. After several tense moments, a low rumbling purr flowed from its bulk.

Kowalski swallowed hard—then, knowing he would never have a better chance, he risked reaching through the bars and running his fingers through the warm ruff of the great beast. The purring deepened, proving Sara was right.

You are a pussycat.

As if Anton sensed this thought, the timbre of his purr rattled into a deep, warning grumble. Kowalski retracted his hand.

Okay, maybe not.

Three hours later, Kowalski was back in the motor pool. Painter had debriefed him, and medical had cleared him. Though his rib cage still ached with every breath, he hadn't even broken a rib.

With a smoldering cigar clamped between his molars, Kowalski stared down at the bent length of steel, dimpled in the center from the 9 mm round. He had wanted to dismiss his survival as dumb luck, like something out of a movie, but he knew a part of him had slipped the nameplate inside his jacket on purpose.

Placing it over my heart.

The only luck here was that the Chinese assassin had been such a crack shot.

If he had struck a few inches in any other direction . . .

He ran his fingers over the silver letters, knowing in this moment that their love had saved him this night.

Thanks, Elizabeth . . .

He contemplated repairing the plate, returning it to its pristine condition. Maybe even sending it to her in Egypt with some note, some last attempt at reconciliation. Instead, he exhaled a stream of smoke, recognizing the futility of such an act and accepting the reality of the situation— maybe truly for the first time.

And that was okay.

With a flick of his wrist, he tossed the nameplate into a trash bin, knowing that was where it belonged.

He turned and crossed over to the Jeep. He ran his palm along the front quarter panel, feeling the dimpling of bullet rounds here, too.

He smiled around his cigar.

You, my beautiful girl . . . you I can fix.

Painter Crowe stood inside the communication nest of Sigma command, while Jason Carter once again worked at one of the stations. It had been a long night, with still more meetings scheduled at daybreak. There remained countless unanswered questions, mysteries that would need further investigation in the days ahead.

While Sigma had recovered the drive abandoned by the pair of Chinese spies at the lab—thus safeguarding most of Dr. Sara Gutierrez's research—Jason's forensic analysis of the cyberattack offered no concrete answers as to *who* was actually behind all of this. The Chinese government had already gone into full plausible-deniability mode, and Painter doubted any attempt to identify the three bodies recovered from the Mall's excavation site would trace back to Beijing. The other assailants, along with the two spies at the zoo, had vanished into the wind.

But even more disconcerting was the fact that the *goal* behind all of this remained a complete enigma.

Jason spoke up from his station. "I give up. I can't find any significance to this symbol. Maybe Captain Bryant will be able to use her contacts in the intelligence agencies to offer some further insight once she gets here."

Painter joined Jason, staring at the set of Chinese characters glowing on the screen. The symbols had been found etched on the recovered drive's housing.

方舟

"All I can tell you is that this translates from Mandarin as 'The Ark,'" Jason said. "But beyond that, I have no clue to its significance."

Painter placed a palm on his shoulder. "That'll have to do for now. Why don't you head home and get some well-deserved rest?"

Jason nodded, but he did not look happy.

Neither am I.

Once Painter had the place to himself, he brought up a video file on another screen. It was footage from one of the countless security cams that monitored the nation's capital. In this case, it covered the National Mall.

He watched a small Jeep shoot up the side of a mountain of dirt, coming to an abrupt halt near the top. The pair of pursuing motorcycles shot past the stalled vehicle and went sailing high—before descending in a deadly plunge into a dark pit.

Painter rubbed his chin, appreciating the quick wits and skill involved in pulling off that takedown. He sensed that there remained unplumbed depths to that driver. He even allowed himself to consider an impossible proposition.

Maybe it's high time I gave Kowalski his own mission.

Author's Note

What's True, What's Not

At the end of my full-length novels, I love to spell out what's real and what's fiction. I thought I'd briefly do the same here.

Smithsonian's Conservation Biology Institute. This research station's main facility encompasses thirty-two hundred acres in Fort Royal, Virginia, but it also has a campus at the Rock Creek Research Labs at the National Zoo. One of the programs mentioned here—the "Ancient DNA" project—is an ongoing endeavor. The researchers seek to study changing patterns of genetic variation over time by analyzing DNA collected from museum specimens and archaeological artifacts. Where this might lead—as well as the implication for our species—is fascinating. And it leaves lots of room for further exploration on an even grander scale.

National Mall Turf and Soil Restoration. This is indeed an active project to restore the thirteen acres of heavily trafficked lawns. Since the current phase of this project has ripped up the acres that lie between the Smithsonian Castle and the National Museum of Natural History, I thought what better chance for an off-road chase scene, especially with the site's towering piles of dirt and deep excavations, including the digging of a 250,000-gallon cistern to collect stormwater.

Chinese Hackers. It seems like seldom a week goes by that we don't hear of a new cyberattack by Chinese agents, whether it's the infiltration of the Office of Personnel Management or the theft of fighter jet schematics. But these incursions are not only to steal intellectual property; they're also to compromise systems. Chinese cyberforces—which do number into the hundreds of thousands—have damaged systems aboard commercial ships and even an airline used by the United States. And they have grown bolder of late, even sending operatives onto US shores in an attempt to nab Chinese defectors, as reported by the president recently. As to the next level of attack, I believe it's coming—soon.

So that ends this tale—but as you might imagine, it's only the beginning of a much larger story, *The Bone Labyrinth,* an epic adventure like no other, one that will reveal a real-life archaeological mystery tied to Neil Armstrong, one that masks a monumental secret about the moon itself . . . all that, and also the introduction of a new character, unlike any seen in print before.

Ghost Ship

A SIGMA FORCE SHORT STORY

JAMES ROLLINS

January 21, 9:07 A.M.
Queensland, Australia

Now, you don't see that every day . . .

From the vantage of his horse's saddle, Commander Gray Pierce watched the twelve-foot saltwater crocodile amble across the beach. A moment ago, it had appeared out of the rain forest and aimed for the neighboring sea, completely ignoring the trio of horses standing nearby.

Amused and awed, Gray studied its passage. Yellow fangs glinted in the morning sun; a thick-armored tail balanced its swaying bulk. Its presence was a reminder that the prehistoric past of this remote stretch of northern Australia was still very much alive. Even the rain forest behind them was the last vestige of a jungle that once stretched across the continent, a fragment dating back some 140 million years, all but untouched by the passage of time.

As the crocodile finally slipped into the waves and vanished, Seichan frowned at Gray from atop her own horse. "And *you* still want to go diving in those waters?"

The final member of their group—who was acting as their guide—dismissed her concern with a wave of a darkly tanned hand. "No worries. *That* particular salty bloke is a mere ankle biter. Quite small."

"Small?" Seichan lifted an eyebrow skeptically.

The Aussie grinned. "Some of the males can grow to be seven meters or more, topping off at over a thousand kilos." He nudged his horse and led them across the beach. "But like I said, not much to fret about. Salties generally only kill two people a year."

Seichan cast a withering look at Gray, her emerald eyes flashing in the sunlight. She plainly did not want to fill that particular quota today. She tossed the length of her black ponytail over a shoulder in obvious irritation as she set off after their guide.

Gray watched her depart for a breath, appreciating the grace of her movements. The sight of her almond skin glistening in the sweltering heat drew him after her.

As he joined her, she glanced to the rain forest. "We could still turn back. Spend the day in the lodge's spa, like we'd planned."

Gray smiled at her. "What? After we came all this way?"

He wasn't just referring to the trail ride to reach this isolated stretch of beach.

For the past half year, the two of them had been slowly circumnavigating the globe, part of a sabbatical from their work with Sigma Force. They had been moving place to place with no itinerary in mind. After leaving D.C., they had spent a month in a medieval village in France, then flew on to Kenya, where they drifted from tent camp to tent camp, moving with the timeless flow of animal life found there. Eventually, they found themselves amid the teeming sprawl of Mumbai, India, enjoying humanity at its most riotous. Then over the past three weeks, they had driven across the breadth of Australia, starting in Perth to the east, traversing the dusty roads through the Outback, until finally reaching Port Douglas on Australia's tropical northeast coast.

Seichan nodded to their guide. "Who knows where this guy is really taking us?"

"I think we can trust him."

Though the two of them had been traveling the globe under false papers, Gray had never doubted that Sigma was covertly keeping track of their whereabouts. This became self-evident last night, when upon returning from a day hike into the Daintree Rainforest, they had stumbled upon a familiar figure holed up in their hotel's lounge, belting down a whiskey, trying to act inconspicuous.

Gray eyed the broad back of their rugged Aussie guide. The man's name was Benjamin Brust. The fifty-year-old Australian happened to be the stepfather of Sigma's young intelligence analyst, Jason Carter. The Aussie had also helped Sigma resolve a situation a year or so ago in Antarctica.

So to find the man seated in their hotel bar . . .

Ben had tried to dismiss the chance encounter as mere coincidence, quoting *Casablanca* at the time. "*Of all the gin joints in all the towns in all the world . . .*"

Gray hadn't bought it.

Ben had recognized this and simply shrugged it off, as if to say, *Okay, you caught me.*

From Ben's presence, Gray realized that Sigma's director must have leaned on former colleagues and associates to keep an eye on the pair during their half-year sojourn.

Accepting this reality, Gray hadn't pressed Ben on his subterfuge. Exposed and apparently apologetic for agreeing to spy on them, the man had offered to take them on a guided tour to a few of the region's highlights, spots known only to the locals.

Judging by the scuba gear they carried with them, Gray expected they were likely headed to some remote dive spot. Ben had refused to offer any further details, but from the mischievous gleam in his blue eyes, he had some surprise in store for them.

"We can tie the horses in the shade over there." Ben pointed an arm toward a tumble of rocks amid a copse of palm trees.

Gray leaned toward Seichan. "See, we're already here."

She grumbled under her breath, while maintaining a wary watch on the beach and forest. He recognized the tension in her back. Even after months on the road, she refused to let her guard down. He had come to accept it. Trained from a young age to be an assassin, she'd had paranoia and suspicion incorporated into her DNA.

In fact, Gray shared some of that same genetic code, courtesy of his stint with the US Army Rangers and his years with Sigma Force, which operated under the auspices of DARPA, the Defense Department's research-and-development agency. Members of Sigma Force acted as covert field agents for DARPA, protecting the globe against various burgeoning threats.

In such a line of work, paranoia was a survival skill.

Still . . .

"Let's just try to enjoy this adventure," Gray said.

Seichan shrugged. "A hot stone massage would've been enough of an adventure for me."

They reached the tumble of boulders and dismounted. In short order, they had their horses secured.

Ben stretched a kink from his back with a rattling sigh, then pointed to a forested promontory jutting into the blue sea. "Welcome to Cape Tribulation. Where the rain forest meets the reef."

"It is stunning," Seichan admitted with some clear reluctance.

"Only place in the world where *two* UNESCO World Heritage Sites butt up against each other." Ben pointed to the forest. "You got the Wet Tropics of Queensland over there." He then squinted out to sea. "And the Great Barrier Reef stretching way out there."

Seichan kicked off her sandals and wandered farther along the beach, her gaze taking in the sight of the jungle-shrouded cliffs tumbling into the crashing waves. Birdcalls echoed across the beach, while the perfume of the fragrant forest mixed with the bitter salt of the Coral Sea.

Gray stared appreciatively after her, which Ben noted.

"Quite the sight," he said with a big grin. "You should put a ring on that finger before you lose your chance."

Gray scowled at him and waved to the laden horses. "Let's unpack our gear."

As they worked, Gray nodded to the promontory. "How'd this place get the name Tribulation?" he asked. "Looks pretty damned peaceful to me."

"Ah, you can blame that on the poor navigation skills of Captain James Cook. Back in the eighteenth century, he ran his ship aground on Endeavour Reef." Ben pointed out to sea. "Tore out a section of the keel and almost lost his boat. Only through some desperate measures were they able to keep her afloat and manage repairs. Cook named the place Cape Tribulation, writing in his logbook '*here begun all our troubles.*'"

"And not just for Captain Cook," Seichan called back to them, plainly overhearing Ben's explanation. She pointed down the beach, drawing both men toward her.

As Gray cleared the rock pile, he spotted a mound half buried in the sand and draped in strands of seaweed. A pale, outstretched arm rested atop the beach.

A body.

They hurried over. The dead man lay on his back, his eyes open and glazed. His legs were covered by wet sand but his exposed chest was striped with blackened marks, as if he'd been lashed with a flaming whip.

Ben dropped to his knees with a sharp curse. "Simon . . ."

Gray crinkled his brow. "You know this man?"

"He's the reason we're all here." Ben gazed out to sea, plainly searching the waters. "He was a biologist working for the Australian Research Council. Part of the Coral Reef Study. He was out here monitoring the spread of coral bleaching. It's knocked out two-thirds of the reef. A bloody international disaster. One Simon was trying to prevent from spreading."

Seichan frowned at the blackened stripes across his body. "What happened to him?"

Ben spat into the sand as he stood. "*Chironex fleckeri.*"

"And that would be *what*?" Gray pressed.

"The Australian box jellyfish. One of the most venomous creatures on the planet They're as big as basketballs with three-meter-long tentacles full of stinging cells. It's why we call them sea wasps. You get stung by one of those and you can die an agonizing death before you reach shore." Ben shook his head, continuing to stare out to sea. "They've multiplied like crazy since the bleaching, thriving on these oxygen-deprived waters."

Gray studied the ravaged body, noting the rictus of pain frozen on the dead man's face. Seichan gently picked up his outstretched hand, examining the pliability of the fingers. She glanced significantly at Gray.

At these warm temperatures, with his body baking in the sun, rigor mortis would have set in within four hours. Which meant he'd died recently.

"Makes no sense," Ben muttered as he stepped away, rubbing the stubble across his chin and cheek.

Gray followed him, hearing the worry behind his words. "What makes no sense?"

Ben waved to their gear spread over the sand. "It's why I hauled in full wet suits. While the seas around here might be plenty warm enough to go skinny-dipping in, you don't go diving in these waters without covering yourself up."

While unpacking the gear, Gray had noted the set of Ocean Reef Neptune masks, meant to cover a diver's face and head. They even had integrated comm units to allow them to communicate with each other underwater.

"Simon would've known better than to go swimming in these waters without proper protection." Ben gave another shake of his head. "Something's bloody wrong here. Where's his catamaran? Where are the others?"

"Others?" Gray asked.

"He was working with a small team from ANFOG." Ben noted Gray's confusion. "The Australian National Facility for Ocean Gliders. They're a group of oceanographers that deploy underwater gliders, unmanned drones that patrol the reefs. The devices can continuously sample water, monitoring temperature, salinity, light levels."

"To help study the coral bleaching," Gray said.

"There were four scientists from the University of Western Australia aboard his boat, along with a graduate student." Ben glanced with concern at Gray. "Simon's daughter, Kelly."

Gray understood.

The others wouldn't have abandoned the dead man, especially his daughter.

Seichan joined him, her brows pinched with suspicion. "You said the dead man was the reason we're here. Why?"

"Simon knew I was up in the Queensland area. He wanted to see if I might help him solve a mystery. One suited to my particular skill set."

Gray frowned. "What skill set?"

"At mapping and traversing tricky cavern systems."

Gray knew the man's history. He was formerly with the Australian army, specializing in infiltration and extractions. He had been recruited from a military prison to help with an operation in Antarctica two decades ago, one involving an unexplored cavern system and a missing team of scientists.

"What did Simon want with your skills here?" Gray asked.

"Three days ago, one of the group's gliders revealed the opening to an underwater cave, likely exposed from the cyclone that swept this coast last month."

Seichan crossed her arms. "And he wanted you to help explore it. Why?"

"Because of what he found in the sand at its entrance. A set of old manacles and a half-buried ship's bell. They recovered the objects and found a name inscribed on the bell. The *Trident.*"

Ben glanced between them to see if they recognized the name.

Gray shrugged.

"The *Trident* was a convict ship that transported prisoners from Great Britain to Australia. While docked in Melbourne in 1852, a group of prisoners teamed up with a handful of the ship's mutinous crew. They commandeered the *Trident,* absconding with several crates of gold mined from the Victorian goldfields. After that, the ship vanished into history."

"Until now," Seichan commented drily.

Gray stared out at the promontory jutting into the sea. "Perhaps Captain Cook wasn't the only one who had trouble navigating these waters."

"That's certainly true. You can find plenty of shipwrecks out there. Like the ruins of S.S. *Yongala* farther south. It sank during a cyclone a century ago."

Seichan sighed. "So you brought us to the edge of a graveyard of ships."

"I thought you might like to do a little treasure hunting with us. I never thought . . ." His words died away as he glanced at the remains of his friend.

"If this is truly foul play," Gray said, "then someone else must have caught wind of Simon's discovery. What else did your friend tell you?"

"Only to meet him here, and if he was delayed, to head to the coordinates of the glider's discovery."

Gray frowned. "And where is that?"

Ben pointed to the promontory of Cape Tribulation. "On the far side of that ridge."

Before he could drop his arm, a sharp chatter of gunfire echoed from that direction. A startled flock of birds took flight from the forest near there.

Knowing what this implied, Gray cursed himself for leaving his satellite phone back in D.C., but the device was Sigma property.

"With no cell signal and no radio," Gray said, "we have no way of alerting authorities."

"So what do we do?" Ben asked.

Gray turned his back on the sea and stalked toward their gear. "We suit up and get to work."

9:51 A.M.

As Seichan swam from the shallows to the deeper water, her body shed the dulling months of relaxation. With each stroke and kick, an icy coldness suffused her limbs. It sharpened her senses, honing her reflexes. The weeks of leisure faded into a dream, proving how illusory those months had been.

She settled into that cold center of her being. Her true nature was as cold-blooded as any shark in these warm waters, predators that needed to keep moving to survive.

It was a lesson she knew all too well.

She followed behind Gray and Ben as they glided over the bright reefs. She studied Gray's physique, the kick of muscular legs, the sweep of his arms. She remembered the glint in his eyes as he turned from the seas to prepare for this dive.

Like her, he was in his element.

After recent events back in the States, the two of them had attempted to flee, to vanish for a spell, to use the time to heal, to discover each other in new ways. And they had. But they both seemed to sense that such a sojourn could not last.

Not forever.

It wasn't who they were.

She felt that even more keenly now.

Accepting this, she took in her surroundings. Life stirred all around her, as rich as the densest jungle. The trio whisked through a school of sleek black-and-silver barracuda, scattering them like a flock of birds. Sea turtles hung motionless in the water, watching them pass with unblinking eyes, while gorgonian sea fans waved from ridges of hard coral. Elsewhere, eagle and manta rays glided out of their way with an unearthly elegance. For several yards, a googly-eyed grouper as large as a Volkswagen van paced alongside them before losing interest and lumbering away.

Across this wonderland, they slowly made their way along the promontory, intending to circle past its tip to reach the far side. Their only weapons were the element of surprise and one dive knife each. Seichan regretted their lack of firepower, especially after hearing those earlier rifle blasts.

"Slow up," Ben radioed through their comm units.

As they bunched together, Seichan reached a gloved hand to the sandy bottom to steady herself. Before she could touch the seabed, Ben knocked her arm away.

"Watch yourself," he warned.

The sand where she had been about to place her palm suddenly sprouted spines. A creature burst from beneath the silt—and swam away.

"Stonefish," Ben explained. "Most venomous fish in the world. Get stung badly enough by those spines, you can die in seconds. Sometimes just from the sheer pain. Only safe place to grab them is by the tail."

She retracted her hand to her chest.

I'll pass.

"We've cleared the promontory," Ben informed them, while checking a wrist GPS. "I'll take the lead from here as we head back along the far side toward Simon's coordinates."

The coordinates of a dead man.

If that thought wasn't ominous enough, the terrain around them quickly changed—from multicolored splendor to gray desert. They had reached a section of the bleached reef. Sea life appeared to have fled the desolation.

"My god . . ." Gray mumbled.

Ben explained as they worked back toward shore, using the distraction to temper the tension. "It's not as hopeless as it appears. The bleached coral is still alive. It's just been stressed by the higher temperatures to expel the symbiotic algae that give the reef its vibrant colors. If left unchecked, the coral polyps will eventually die. But if the stressors can be eliminated in time, the reefs can return to life. Unfortunately, the Great Barrier Reef has suffered back-to-back bleaching events. If this continues, by some estimates, the entire reef could vanish in the next couple decades."

"Solving that particular danger will have to wait for the moment," Gray said, and pointed ahead.

Thirty yards away, two large shadows hovered above, linked to the seafloor by taut anchor cables. One boat had a single keel. The twin hulls of the other marked it as the scientific team's catamaran.

Ben eyed the larger single-hulled craft. "Definitely unwanted company."

Gray drew closer to him. "How far off are we from Simon's coordinates to the sea cave?"

Ben pointed toward the promontory coastline. "Fifty meters farther along."

Gray nodded and turned his attention toward the surface.

Seichan could guess the question plaguing him. With no knowledge of the situation above, they faced a troubling choice.

Which boat should they attempt to board first?

The answer was taken from them—suddenly and violently.

The dark shadows beneath the catamaran suddenly erupted with a fiery explosion. The ship lifted out of the water for a breath, then crashed back down. Its shattered hulls crumbled in on themselves, then slowly sank as the sea flooded its compartments.

Seichan shook her head, expelling a breath.

The concussion of the blast ached in her ears and chest.

If we'd been any closer . . .

Ben swore as he gaped at the sinking wreck.

Seichan spotted a body rising off the broken deck, trailing blood.

One of the oceanographers.

The earlier gunfire echoed in her head. She pictured the ravaged body of Ben's friend. Whoever these pirates were, they had moved beyond executing their prisoners. They were cleaning house.

But what did that mean? Were any of the other scientists still alive? And what about Simon's daughter?

Are we already too late?

Only one way to know for sure.

"Let's go," Gray said coldly.

10:10 A.M.

Gray hung in the shadow of the boat with Ben. The craft appeared to be an old fishing charter with a wide open rear deck, a small raised wheelhouse, and a cubby cabin beneath the bow.

He and Ben had taken up position under the steel dive deck at the stern. Across the length of the twenty-foot hull, Seichan hovered near the bow. She clutched one hand to the anchor cable. Over her head, the line rose out of the water and up to a bow roller and a winch. She would use the cable like a rope to board the boat from that side.

At the moment, they dared not even use their radios, fearing that in such close quarters the enemy might hear them. He couldn't risk losing their best weapon.

The element of surprise.

He rose up until his palm rested against the starboard side of the dive deck. Ben followed him, taking a position on the port side.

Once ready, Gray eyed Seichan—then sliced his free arm through the water.

They all moved at once.

Gray grabbed the edge of the dive deck and smoothly pulled himself out of the water and twisted around to land his backside on the steel. He kept his head below the stern rail. Ben mirrored his maneuver on the far side. With no alarm raised, they shifted to get their legs under them and freed their dive knives.

As he crouched, he heard low, furtive voices, one deep chuckle, and someone softly crying. All the sounds seemed to be coming from the open rear deck—but was anyone in the ship's wheelhouse or in the lower cabin?

Only one way to find out.

He waited for the right moment—and it came with a shout of surprise from the deck. Upon that signal, both he and Ben burst up and hurdled the stern rail. Across the boat, a figure stood exposed atop the bow deck.

While still underwater, Seichan had unzipped and stripped down the top half of her wet suit. She stood now in her bikini top, leaning nonchalantly with her hips cocked, a hand leaning on the neighboring rail. With her bottom half still encased in her black wet suit, she looked like a mermaid stranded atop the deck.

Her sudden appearance—along with her bored expression—momentarily baffled the two armed men guarding a pair of kneeling prisoners. Even before they could shift their weapons toward her, Gray came up behind and knifed the first man in the side of the throat. Ben was less lethal and clubbed his target with the hilt of his weapon, striking him expertly behind the left ear. Bone cracked, and the man crumpled limply to the deck.

Gray grabbed the Desert Eagle pistol carried by his target and focused on the empty wheelhouse, where a closed door led down to the cubby cabin. He collected the other weapon and tossed it to Seichan, who caught it one-handed.

She quickly crossed to the door to the cubby cabin, kicked it open, and surveilled the cramped space below. "All clear," she called as she retreated to join them.

The two prisoners were a red-haired young man and a woman in her late forties.

Ben knelt before them as they stared wide-eyed and stunned at the sudden assault. "We're friends of Simon," he assured them. "I'm guessing you're part of the ANFOG team working with him."

The woman took a shuddering breath, wiped tears from her cheeks, and nodded.

"What happened here?" Gray asked.

The story unfolded in stuttering bits and pieces, told by the pair of survivors, Maggie and Wendell. Three hours ago, the assailants had pretended to be a fishing charter. The ruse lasted long enough for the armed men to assault the catamaran. Simon had tried to fight them, but he was overpowered, stripped, and tossed overboard.

"Why?" Ben asked. "Why not simply shoot him?"

Maggie looked near shock with the retelling. "They were trying to get his daughter to cooperate."

"Kelly?"

She nodded. "Only Kelly knew the coordinates where the *Trident*'s artifacts had been found. We were all on a dive that day, leaving her, as our lowly student, aboard the ship to monitor a routine glider survey. It's mind-numbing work. While watching the feed, she happened to spot the bell and shackle. Excited, she free-dove down to collect the trophies. But when she recognized the name on the bell—and what such a discovery implied—she erased the glider's record. Though she told us about the discovery, she kept its exact location secret."

"But not from her father," Ben added.

Wendell looked startled. "What?"

"Kelly told Simon," Ben said. "Then he told me."

Gray suspected Simon shared this information with Ben for selfish reasons. He likely wanted to recruit Ben before his daughter tried doing anything even more foolhardy, like attempting to search those caves on her own.

"Kelly eventually broke and told the gunmen the coordinates," Maggie explained. "But before they could pull Simon out of the water . . ."

Ben grimaced. "He ran afoul of a box jelly."

She nodded. "Kelly witnessed it all. That poor girl."

"Where is she now?" Seichan asked.

The woman stared out toward the forested cliffs. "They forced her to go along with them. When she initially refused, they shot Tyler and threatened us."

Gray pictured the dead man floating amid the wreckage. "How many went with her?"

"Six, including Dr. Hoffmeister."

Ben frowned. "Dr. Hoffmeister?"

"Our team leader," Wendell elaborated with a bitter scowl. "He was the one who betrayed us to those murderous bastards."

Seichan snorted. "So much for the purity of scientific research."

Maggie looked down. "We'd all heard rumors he had a gambling problem, but I never imagined he could be so callous. Especially with those he worked alongside."

Gray was not as surprised. All too often greed trumped friendship or loyalty.

"You have to do something," Wendell said. "They'll kill Kelly once they find what they're looking for."

Gray knew he was right. And from the despair in the kid's voice, his interest in Kelly was more than merely collegial.

Seichan glanced toward the coast and shrugged. "Three against six. Not bad odds."

"And we still have the element of surprise," Ben added.

Gray began to nod when a crackling noise drew his attention to the dead assailant on the deck. The noise rose from a radio headpiece.

He quickly snatched it free and lifted the radio to his ear and lips. A trail of words reached him.

"... *late in reporting in. What's your status?*"

Gray had to take the chance. "All quiet here," he said gruffly.

There was a long pause before the voice on the line returned, angry and suspicious. "*Who the hell is this?*"

Seichan stared at him as he lowered the radio.

He shook his head.

So much for the element of surprise.

10:25 A.M.

"Let's give those blokes a wide berth," Ben radioed to them.

Seichan didn't argue as she followed the two men. A trio of bull sharks circled the wreck of the catamaran, likely drawn by the blood of the murdered oceanographer. Their group steered well clear of that wreckage and headed for the coast.

Earlier, before going overboard, they had briefly searched the guards for the boat's keys but had no luck. They also found the ship's radio disabled, requiring a digital code to unlock it. So as a precaution, they had ordered Maggie and Wendell to suit up and swim to shore, sending the pair out of harm's way with instructions to get word to someone in authority and let them know the situation.

Seichan knew better than to expect any help in time.

We're on our own.

Before leaving, Maggie had also informed them what they'd be facing. The crew had departed with spear guns and carried satchels of demolition charges.

Seichan glanced to the ruins of the catamaran, recognizing the handiwork of those explosives. The thieves plainly had come prepared in case they had to blow their way into that cavern system in order to search for the cache of gold.

She pictured the mutinous crew back in 1852 rowing into those same sea caves to hide their loot, perhaps fearing the *Trident* might be recaptured by British forces. But was the gold still here after so long?

As they neared Simon's coordinates, Ben waved for them to spread wider, making their group less of a target. They proceeded with great caution, using the ridges of reefs as cover. If the assailants suspected treachery after the aborted radio call, the enemy would likely have a guard hidden near the entrance to the cavern system. If any of their team flushed him out, the other two would still have a chance to take him down.

Unfortunately, once they drew closer to the coordinates, they realized the guard at the entrance was not what they expected. They almost missed it as the waters grew murkier, clouded by sand and silt stirred up by the waves crashing into the towering coastal cliffs.

Through the gloom, a yellow torpedo-shaped tube with fins hovered a couple yards in front of the black eye of a tunnel. Its nose cone pointed out toward the sea, its buoyant length gently bobbing in the current.

"One of ANFOG's gliders," Ben hissed.

The thieves must have left this electronic guard dog to watch the entrance to the cavern system. Someone was likely monitoring its feed from inside the sea caves.

"No way we can sneak past that glider's sensors," Ben said. "If we get too close, the enemy will know we're on our way inside."

"Then we find a way to blind it," Gray said.

"How?"

Gray reached to a webbed bag hanging from his weight belt. He pulled out one of the two demolition charges they had found aboard the boat during their search.

"If you try to blow the glider up," Ben warned, "it'll be as good as being spotted. They'll still know we're coming."

"That's not my plan."

Gray swam back several yards, then used his dive knife to remove three-quarters of the charge's load of plastic explosive, weakening its potential blast. He then quickly buried it a foot into the sand at the base of a ridge of bleached, brittle coral.

"Move well back." He waved them farther from the shoreline. "I set the timer for thirty seconds. Be ready to go on my mark."

With the charge buried, they retreated.

Seichan counted down in her head as she swam. When she reached zero, a muffled *whump* thudded into her ears and rib cage. She twisted back around as the section of the seabed where Gray had buried the charge belched upward with a massive flume of sand and shattered coral. The current immediately swept the cloud toward shore.

"Now!" Gray radioed. "Get into the debris field and stick close together."

Seichan understood. She swam with the others into the dense cloud of sediment. They quickly lost sight of one another, even when clutching an elbow or the edge of a neighbor's fin. Still, Ben guided them unerringly forward, swimming by instruments alone, following his wrist GPS. He skirted them to the side of the blinded electronic guard dog, then along the rocks.

Moments later, the Aussie was pulling them into the mouth of tunnel. Even from here, Seichan could not spot the glider through the stirred-up silt. It was as if the entire world had vanished beyond the tunnel.

Ben took her hand and drew her fingers to a length of rope staked along the seabed. It led deeper into the tunnel.

She understood.

Follow the line.

She set off behind Ben, with Gray behind her. She was soon grateful the enemy had left this path to follow. With each kick and paddle, their motion stirred up more silt in the tunnel. Not only could she barely see Ben's fins ahead of her, but being weightless in her gear added to her disorientation. It was almost impossible to tell up from down.

Once far enough away from the glider's sensors, Ben risked switching on a pair of small lights flanking his mask. "Okay, I love caving and I love scuba diving, but when you combine the two into *cave diving*," he groused, "it turns into bloody death sport. And even more so now."

Ben slowed and pointed to a blinking red light fixed to one side of the tunnel. It was one of the demolition charges. The enemy must be planning to blow the entrance on their way out once they secured the treasure.

As Seichan continued, following the staked line of rope, she oriented herself enough to realize the tunnel was less a passage drilled through solid rock than a winding, torturous path through and around a jumble of boulders and broken slabs.

"It's an old rock slide," Ben confirmed, scanning his lights around as he wriggled between two blocks of granite leaning against each other.

As Seichan followed, she sensed the precarious nature of this pile, suspecting it wouldn't take much of a blast to bring this all crashing down.

After another minute of kicking and squirming, Ben's voice dropped to a hissed whisper. "Got lights ahead."

He doused his own lamps and slowed to a crawl. The passage widened enough for the three to cluster together. The way opened directly ahead, illuminated by a figure floating weightless in scuba gear beyond the tunnel. The man's attention was on the glowing device he held in his hands. Its screen was as bright as a lamp in the dark waters.

Ben glanced significantly at them.

It must be the monitoring device and control unit for the glider outside.

Gray held up a palm, indicating the other two should hang back.

He then pushed off the tunnel floor and glided toward the man's back. Some warning eddy of current must have alerted his target.

The diver spun around, fumbling for his shouldered spear gun—but Gray was already atop him.

He plunged his knife under the man's chin and clutched him with his other arm. The body writhed for several seconds, then went slack. Gray deflated the man's buoyancy vest and let his weighted form sink into the dark depths, but not before relieving him of his spear gun and glider's control unit.

Ben and Seichan joined Gray as he doused the device, returning the waters to a stygian darkness—or at least, it should have.

They all turned their faces upward.

Through the waters overhead, a soft, shimmering glow beckoned to them. The diffuse light gave dimension to the flooded cavern around them. It had to be half the size of a football stadium. The glow also revealed the surface of the lake inside here. It stretched about ten meters overhead.

They slowly rose toward the shine.

With great caution, they risked peeking the edges of their masks above the water.

Ben gasped next to Seichan. "Holy Mother of God . . ."

10:42 A.M.

Gray understood the Aussie's stunned shock.

The roof of the cavern glowed with what appeared to be swaths of stars, shining in hues from a deep blue-green to a bright silver. The glow revealed long filaments hanging from the roof, each lined by rows of pearlescent droplets.

"Glowworms," Ben explained.

Gray had heard of caves in Australia and New Zealand that harbored these bioluminescent larvae, but he had never imagined they could produce such a brilliant display. There had to be millions glowing throughout here, attempting to lure prey with their shine into their sticky traps.

But the true wonder was not found across the roof.

The glowworms had found a more convenient purchase.

The wreck of the *Trident*.

The three-masted sailing ship listed crookedly in the cavern, having run aground into a sandbar on the far side. The entire surface of the ship was draped in glowworms and their fine silk nets. It was as if the wreck of *Trident* had risen from ghostly seas, still draped in bioluminescent kelp and algae.

Despite the wonder of the sight, movement—both on the sandbar and atop the deck—drove Gray back underwater, drawing the others with him.

"Did you notice the ship's sails were furled and tied?" Ben said as he joined Gray. "At one time, this cavern must've been open to the sea. The crew likely sought to shelter here during a storm. Maybe even hiding from a cyclone."

Gray pictured the rockslide they had traversed to get here. "And in doing so, the bastards got themselves trapped here."

"Let's not suffer the same fate," Seichan reminded them.

Gray nodded. "We need to find Simon's daughter, secure her, and get the hell out of here."

"I spotted a blond woman with the group on the sandbar," Seichan said.

"That'd be Kelly," Ben confirmed.

Gray set off toward shore. "Then let's go get her."

As they traversed the lake, they kept deep. The lake bed slowly rose up under them as they neared the far side. Even here, life thrived. Centuries-old coral fluttered with sea fans. Brightly colored fish darted from their path, while albino lobsters as long as Gray's forearm stalked the reefs.

Seichan swam beside him, carefully eyeing the sand and rocks for threats. Something caught her eye, drawing her to the side.

Before he could inquire about her interest, they reached the *Trident*. From here, they would have to work swiftly. At any moment, someone might try to radio the man they had taken out earlier. Gray knew they had only a narrow window before their presence in the cavern was exposed.

Hidden in the shadow of the wreck's hull, he worked quickly with the others, making sure everyone was prepared. Once satisfied, they set off again. They circled the bulk of the *Trident* and approached the sandbar, hugging the lake bed. Gray was counting on the gleam of the glowworms reflecting off the lake's dark surface to keep their group hidden for as long as possible.

As they reached the shallows, Gray could make out figures atop the sand, not far from where the *Trident* had run aground. The ship loomed above the small group, revealing a huge crack in its hull. A trio of wooden chests stood nearby. From the drag marks in the sand, it appeared the boxes had been hauled from the ship's broken hold.

Gray didn't doubt what they contained.

The *Trident's* lost treasure.

Ignoring the wealth stored in those chests, he concentrated on the watery image of the three mercenaries standing guard over the treasure—and one lone girl.

Kelly knelt in the sand, her shoulders slumped, her face despondent.

One of the men had a pistol casually pointed at the back of her head, clearly awaiting the order to dispatch this witness. The other two were similarly armed. Their abandoned spear guns were propped on boulders behind them. It seemed the crew must have packed in additional weapons in waterproof cases.

Gray cursed their preparedness, but there was nothing he could do about it. His team was committed now. He curled his body and got his legs under him. He glanced right and left to make sure the others were ready.

In his head, a countdown had been running, matching the timer he had set on the demolition charge. Moments ago, he'd attached his remaining device to the far side of the *Trident's* hull. He even added the leftover plastic explosive from the earlier charge.

As the countdown reached zero, he burst out of the water.

At the same time, the explosion rocked the cavern with a deafening blast. Water and broken planks flumed high into the air behind him.

Gray already had his stolen spear gun at his shoulder. He fixed his aim and squeezed the trigger. The steel spear shot through the air and struck the gunman looming over Kelly in the eye. The bolt pierced his skull and threw his body backward.

To his left, Seichan whipped her arm and deftly sent her dive knife flying from her fingertips. No one was deadlier with a blade than her. Her dagger impaled her target in his Adam's apple, dropping him into a gurgling heap.

With a knife in hand, Ben barreled out of the water to Gray's right. He aimed for the third assailant, who stood closest to the water's edge. The enemy—stunned by the blast and the sudden attack—still managed to swing his pistol toward Ben.

Before he could fire, Kelly lunged up from the sand and knocked his arm high. The pistol cracked brightly, but the shot went wild. Ben crashed hard into the gunman, which threw off his attack. His initial knife jab was blocked by an elbow.

Still, Ben was not done.

With a hard shove, the Aussie sent his target stumbling backward— straight into one of the spear guns propped against a boulder behind the man. The impact drove the loaded bolt through his back and out his chest. The man sank to his rear, his mouth opening and closing, gasping like a beached fish, before he finally sagged and fell on his side.

Before anyone could speak, a thunderous groan drew all their attentions to the lake. In slow motion, the glowing bulk of the *Trident* tipped sideways, falling toward the water, collapsing on the side blown out by Gray's charge. Its masts shook and its deck canted.

"Look!" Kelly yelled.

Two figures—one thin-limbed and spry, the other bulky with muscle—leaped over the rails on the far side and dove toward the lake. They hit the water together and vanished into the dark depths. Gray imagined these last two men must've been scouring the *Trident* for any last treasures.

"No, no, no . . ." Kelly said.

Gray turned to her, noting the bright terror in her face.

"That was the leader of these bastards," she explained. "And Dr. Hoffmeister."

The traitor.

"They won't get far," Ben assured her. "We'll find them."

"No, you don't understand," Kelly said. "Hoffmeister has the transmitter for the demolition charges."

Gray understood. "He'll blow this place behind him once he's safely clear."

Ben pointed to where a few brighter lines of sunlight pierced the glowing roof, marking the presence of cracks. "It could bring this whole place crashing down."

Knowing this to be true and with no time to spare, Gray stripped his body of nonessential weight, grabbed one of the spear guns, and sprinted into the water.

Seichan followed his example and dove alongside him.

They swam in tandem after the fleeing men. With the enemy already having a significant lead, it was likely a futile chase. Still, Gray refused to give up.

He glanced over to Seichan.

Behind her shoulders, the *Trident* sank into the depths, its bulk still aglow as it finally met its doom.

As he turned back around, something silvery flashed past his nose.

A spear.

The bolt shot between the two of them.

Ahead, a shadow rose from behind a ridge of a reef. It was the mercenary leader. He was already raising a second spear gun. Beyond the man, a small iota of light bobbled in the darkness.

Hoffmeister.

He was getting away.

10:55 A.M.

Seichan knew they had only one chance.

She lifted her spear gun with one arm and kicked hard. As she passed Gray, she shoved her free hand into his shoulder. "Go! I'll deal with this bastard."

Gray didn't hesitate or balk. It was one of the reasons she loved him. As exasperating as he could be at times, he trusted her fully. He did not suffer from some overinflated conceit of male bravado. Instead, they were a team. They knew each other's strengths and weaknesses—and Gray was the better swimmer.

Proving this, he twisted to the side and swam off. He vanished almost immediately as he circled around the threat.

Seichan continued on a straight path.

She lifted her spear gun.

The enemy did the same.

Let's do this.

When only yards separated them, they both fired. Spears flashed through the dark waters. Seichan twisted to the side, but the bolt grazed the length of her thigh, slicing her wet suit and leaving a line of fire down her leg.

Her aim was better. But at the last moment, the mercenary leader deflected the bolt with the steel butt of his gun, sending the spear careening to the side.

So be it.

She closed the distance between them. She had suspected all along this battle would end in a knife fight.

She reached for the sheath at her waist—but her fingers came up empty.

Cursing silently, she pictured the blade impaled in the throat of her target on the beach. In her haste to depart, she had never collected it.

Her enemy was not so ill prepared.

He bared a foot-long dagger.

10:58 A.M.

Across the lake, Gray continued his chase after the fleeing light. It was a beacon in the darkness and became his sole focus as he kicked and swept his arms. He used it to distract him from his worry about Seichan.

Slowly the luminous speck grew before him, offering both encouragement and hope. He still had his spear gun over one shoulder.

If I can get close enough . . .

Then suddenly the light vanished ahead of him, blinking out entirely. Caught by surprise, he momentarily slowed—then realized what the loss implied.

Hoffmeister had reached the tunnel.

I'm out of time.

11:01 A.M.

Unarmed, Seichan fled from her assailant.

Like Gray, she was practical. She knew her limitations and recognized the skill of her adversary. Her only hope was to keep ahead of his muscular bulk. With that goal in mind, she headed back toward the sandbar, following the path the team had used earlier.

Her brutal training as an assassin had taught her always to memorize her surroundings, to weigh every variable at hand.

So she headed unerringly along their prior path.

She pictured the dive knife abandoned on the sandbar.

It was a stupid lapse.

One I'll not make again.

But first she had to live.

She was already slowing, both from exhaustion and from the blood trailing from her sliced leg. It was becoming harder to kick with her wounded limb. Still, if nothing else, her injury drew her attacker onward, like a dog after a wounded bird.

A glance over her shoulder revealed the man was almost on top of her.

Good.

She slowed even further as she neared the location fixed in her mind's eye, a spot that had drawn her attention earlier on the way to the sandbar, enough to draw her away from Gray briefly.

She crested over a coral ridge and dove down to a stretch of bare sand.

She had noted a weapon here earlier.

One of those many variables.

With her gloved fingers, she reached for it—just as a shadow loomed over her.

Following Ben's warning from earlier in the day, she grabbed the weapon by its tail. She whipped around as the mercenary plunged his dagger toward her back. She easily avoided the strike, taking advantage of the man's overconfidence.

She swung and struck the stonefish into the man's neck. Spines pierced his flesh. Venom pumped. The effect was instantaneous. His body stiffened. He dropped his dagger and pawed at his neck, knocking the impaled fish away—but the damage was done.

His body thrashed in the water. The pain so maddened him that he ripped off his mask and regulator. Fingernails clawed at his face. Then his limbs slackened, falling away leadenly. He hung in the water. His blind eyes stared back at her. She didn't know if the pain had killed him, or the poison, or if he'd simply drowned.

She knew only one certainty, picturing the ravaged body of Kelly's father.

Good riddance.

11:05 A.M.

Gray scrambled along the rope as it wound a serpentine course through the old rockslide. He hauled with arms and kicked off purchases with his feet. His shoulders remained hunched by his ears. At any moment, he expected the charges hidden along the passageway to explode, to send the pile crashing down atop him.

His only hope was that Hoffmeister would wait until he was well clear of the coastal cliffs before he risked using his transmitter. The oceanographer must know the blasts could cast off massive boulders that would pound into the water around him.

But would the panicked bastard be that cautious?

Gray grabbed the rope with both hands and yanked his body around another turn in the tunnel. As he continued, the line suddenly went slack. The next pull only drew the rope toward him.

Gray cursed, knowing what this meant.

Hoffmeister had cut the safety line.

Gray took care not to pull on the rope. He needed its draped length to lead him out of here. Still, the stirred-up silt made it hard to see the line. He had to proceed with greater care—which slowed him down considerably.

I'll never make it now.

But then, impossibly, a light appeared out of the murk ahead.

Daylight.

He hurried again, rushing the last of the distance. As he burst out of the tunnel, he found Hoffmeister only ten yards away. He was crouched low to the seabed.

Gray was shocked to find the man so near. He quickly hauled the spear gun from his shoulder.

Hoffmeister had nowhere to flee.

Gray was wrong.

From the seabed, a yellow torpedo shot upward, jetting away from the oceanographer.

It was the ANFOG glider.

Suddenly, Hoffmeister was torn off his feet. His body flew after the glider, dragged in its wake. The man had clipped and tethered himself to the glider by a length of cable. He plainly intended to escape using his own tool, likely manually setting the glider's motor to maximum power a moment ago.

Gray fired after his retreating form, but his shot didn't come close.

He even tried to swim after the bastard but quickly recognized the futility. In less than a minute, Hoffmeister would be far enough out into open water to use his detonator.

It's over.

But as Gray watched, the yellow torpedo suddenly made a sharp left turn, banking quickly. It rolled Hoffmeister like a rag doll through the water.

Confused, Gray swam out farther to follow its trajectory.

The glider aimed for the wreck of the catamaran—and the frenzy of bull sharks drawn by the blood of Hoffmeister's murdered colleague. The oceanographer must have sensed the threat, even more so when the glider began to slow as it neared the wreckage.

Hoffmeister frantically tried to unclip his line from the glider before it dragged him into the sharks. As the torpedo decelerated, the oceanographer finally broke free and fought his way from the danger.

But sharks were not the only predators hunting these waters.

From the wreck below, a dark shape shot upward, jaws impossibly wide. Yellow teeth clamped on Hoffmeister's left arm and shoulder. A thick armored tail whipped in a circle, sending the crocodile's half-ton mass into a wrenching spiral.

Hoffmeister's body went flying away—minus his entire left arm.

Still, the man lived. With blood pouring from his shoulder, he kicked and pawed with his one arm. Then a bull shark swept down, snatched him up, and with a whisk of its powerful tail, vanished into the sea.

Aghast, Gray retreated toward the sea tunnel. He glanced to the passageway. He suddenly suspected the source for the glider's deadly turn.

Hoffmeister wasn't the only one who knew how to operate the glider.

So did a certain lowly graduate student.

11:11 A.M.

Poor girl . . .

Seichan watched Kelly drop the glider's control unit to the sand. Gray had left the device here before diving into the waters after Hoffmeister. It was Ben who had suggested the girl use her past experience with the underwater drones to monitor the seas beyond the cave.

Little did the Aussie know how fortuitous such a suggestion would prove to be.

Kelly remained on her knees. Ben was beside her. He hooked an arm around her shoulders and pulled her to his chest.

"Nicely done, Kelly . . . nicely done."

The only response from the girl was the shaking of her thin shoulders as she sobbed silently into Ben's chest. Though Kelly had exacted her revenge, it would not bring back her father.

Seichan stepped toward the water, leaving the girl to her mourning, knowing there were no words to ease that pain.

Instead, she stared up at the glowing stars, trying to find meaning. Long ago, greed had led a mutinous crew to a tragic end here in this cavern. And centuries later, it was greed again that led to more bloodshed and death.

Were some places simply cursed?

She remembered Captain Cook's name for this corner of the world.

Cape Tribulation.

She shook her head.

Maybe this place wasn't cursed, but it had certainly lived up to that name.

7:56 P.M.

A low groan drew Gray's attention to the left. He lifted his face from the padded doughnut of the massage table and stared over at the source of the complaint.

Seichan lay on the neighboring table. She was naked, covered only by a modesty towel over her buttocks and a row of steaming stones along her spine. He stared at the line of Steri-Strips closing the shallow laceration down her upper thigh.

"You okay?"

"More than okay," she said with contented sigh. "Like I said earlier, this is more than enough of an adventure for me."

He grinned and settled back to his table.

A heated stone was gently placed on the center of his lower back.

It was his turn to groan.

He allowed himself to drift in the pleasure of the attention. Earlier, Ben had facilitated their escape from Cape Tribulation, keeping them out of the ensuing limelight. Ben had also promised to protect Kelly in the weeks ahead, determined that the recognition for the discovery of the *Trident* go to her and her father—along with the gold.

In turn, Kelly intended that the treasure be used to finance her father's passion.

Protecting the reefs.

It would be the perfect way to honor the man's sacrifice.

Seichan made another noise—this time more thoughtful.

He glanced over again. "What now?"

She rested her cheek on the table, staring back at him. "I was just thinking about where we should go next."

"Any ideas?"

"Somewhere that's still warm and tropical." She lifted her cheek, staring pointedly at him. "But *without* box jellyfish, saltwater crocodiles, or stonefish."

"Like where."

"I was thinking Hawaii . . . maybe Maui."

"Really? Aren't those islands too tame and boring for you?"

She shrugged. "I've never been there. And right about now, boring sounds perfect."

"Then a Hawaiian vacation it is." He settled his face back into his doughnut. "Surely nothing can go wrong there."

Author's Note

What's True, What's Not

At the end of my full-length novels, I love to spell out what's real and what's fiction in my stories. I thought I'd briefly do the same here.

Cape Tribulation. I was lucky enough to spend some time in this area near Port Douglas in Queensland and always wanted to set a story here. It's truly a magical place, where the rain forest meets the Coral Sea. I also took a horseback ride to the beach featured in this story, where I watched a huge saltwater crocodile saunter across the sand and into the surf. While there, I also became enamored with the history of the region. The site was indeed named by Captain Cook after his fateful accident on the nearby reefs. So I thought it would be fun to tell a story of a ship that suffered a similar, if more tragic, fate.

The *Trident*. While the ship featured in this short story is purely fictional, I based its fateful tale on the histories of two real convict ships: the *Success* and the *Hive*. Their combined stories involved mutiny, gold, and lost shipwrecks. So I borrowed their tales for this adventure.

The Great Barrier Reef. As I was setting this story here, I couldn't help but mention the tragic bleaching that is currently affecting two-thirds of the reef's coral, covering a swath almost nine hundred miles long. The reef is home to many endangered species, along with four hundred types of coral and fifteen hundred species of fish. It's an invaluable habitat, one that three hundred million people rely on for food, employment, and livelihood. So let's not lose it.

ANFOG Gliders. Yep, those yellow research torpedoes are real . . . though I may have stretched their capabilities a bit. But not by much!

WHAT'S NEXT?

At this story's conclusion, Seichan makes a fateful decision to head to Hawaii, specifically Maui. Gray has, of course, cursed them by declaring *nothing can go wrong*. Their sabbatical from Sigma Force is about to come to a crashing end—and nothing will ever be the same for the two of them. Already forces are in motion, fueled by an ancient horror known only as *The Demon Crown*. So hold tight, and I hope you enjoy the wild ride to come!

Crash and Burn

A SIGMA FORCE SHORT STORY

JAMES ROLLINS

April 17, 7:48 P.M.
Airborne over the North Atlantic

You've got to be kidding me.

A wolf whistle of appreciation drew Seichan's attention across the plush cabin of the Gulfstream G150. The configuration of the private jet allowed for four passengers, but at the moment she shared this flight from D.C. to Marrakesh with only one other traveler, but his size and bulk filled most of the plane's starboard side.

Joe Kowalski stood well over six feet, most of it muscles and scars. His legs stretched from one chair to the other, his boots propped on the leather seat. He cradled a long case open on his lap. He rubbed a finger along his lower lip, his craggy brows pinched in concentration as he studied the contents cushioned in the box. His other hand traced the contours of the snub-nosed shotgun resting there.

"Nice," he muttered.

Seichan frowned at him. "How about *not* playing with a gun at thirty-five thousand feet."

Talk about the wrong time, wrong place.

He scowled at her concern and picked up the weapon, turning it one way, then the other. "It's not like it's loaded." He cracked the action open, exposing the double chambers—along with the two shells resting there. He quickly removed them and cleared his throat. "At least, not *now.*"

The case also held a belt of extra rounds. While the gun's side-by-side double barrels looked like something out of the Old West, Seichan knew there was nothing old-fashioned about the weapon. The label stamped inside the case confirmed this:

PROPERTY OF HOMELAND SECURITY ADVANCED RESEARCH PROJECT

The military prototype was called the Piezer. The stock of the weapon housed a powerful battery. Each 12-gauge shell—rather than being filled with buckshot or rock salt—was packed with piezoelectric crystals capable of holding an electric charge. Once powered up, the weapon would electrify the load, and with a pull of a trigger, the fired shell would explode in midair, blasting out a shower of shocking crystals, each carrying the voltage equivalent of a Taser. With no need to trail wires, the nonlethal weapon had a range of fifty yards, perfect for crowd control situations.

"I thought we agreed to keep your new toy locked up until we landed," she said.

Per mission protocol, their weapons—including her sheathed daggers—were stored in a camouflaged crate, one engineered to withstand most scrutiny.

He shrugged sheepishly. Plainly he must have gotten bored and decided to break those rules, wanting something to play with during the long flight.

"Pack it back up," she told him. "Crowe said you could field-test the weapon in your spare time, but he meant on the ground."

And preferably well away from me.

They would be going their separate ways once they reached Morocco.

She had been sent by Director Painter Crowe to investigate the black-market trafficking of stolen antiquities in Marrakesh. The funds financed various terrorist groups, and with her own past ties to such organizations, Seichan was perfectly suited to infiltrate and expose the operation.

Kowalski, on the other hand, was hitching a ride, about to begin an extended leave of absence from Sigma Force. Once they landed in Marrakesh, he would continue on to Germany, to visit his girlfriend in Leipzig, where the woman was working at a genetics lab.

Besides sharing this flight, Seichan and Kowalski also shared the dubious honor of being the black sheep of Sigma Force. The covert group was part of DARPA, the Defense Department's research-and-development administration. Its members were former Special Forces soldiers who had been retrained in various scientific disciplines to act as field agents for DARPA, to protect US interests against various global threats.

She and Kowalski did not fit that mold.

Seichan was a former assassin, now employed off the books by Sigma. Kowalski had been a navy seaman who happened to be at the wrong place and wrong time, but who proved adept enough at blowing things up to serve as extra muscle and support for the group.

And while she and Kowalski shared this outsider status, the two could not be more different. He was all-American, loud and brash, rough around the edges, with a pronounced Bronx accent. She was Eurasian, svelte and nimble, trained for the shadows.

Still, despite their differences, she recognized a commonality. She had overheard him talking to his girlfriend, Maria, on the phone before their jet had lifted off. The relationship was new, untested, full of possibility. He smiled broadly when he talked, laughed with his entire body. In his voice, she heard the familiar undertones of longing and desire—some physical, some rising from deeper wellsprings.

Likewise, she had found someone, a man of remarkable ability and unfathomable depths of patience. He seemed to know when to draw close and when to pull back. It was a necessary skill to love someone like her. After decades in the shadows, to commit the acts she had done, she'd had to let that darkness inside.

Even now, she remained haunted, discovering her new life with Sigma was not all that different from her past. She still had to linger in the dark.

Not that I have any other choice.

After she'd betrayed her former employers, enemies now surrounded her on all sides. Her only refuge was within Sigma, but even there, she was a ghost, with only a handful of personnel aware of her presence or her past.

She turned to the window, to the sun sinking toward the ocean. Its brightness pained her, but she did not blink, trying to let that light deep inside her, to get it to chase away her black thoughts and dispel those shadows. But she knew better. It would be nightfall before much longer. Even the sun could not hold back the darkness forever.

The pilot called over the radio. "We'll be touching down at Ponta Delgada in another fifteen minutes."

Seichan stared below the wings, toward the archipelago of volcanic islands stretching ahead of them. The Azores were an autonomous region of Portugal. Their jet would be landing on São Miguel, the largest of the archipelago's nine islands—but only long enough to refuel. The Gulfstream's range was not far enough to make the transatlantic trip in a single hop.

As the plane began its descent, she studied the sweep of the Azores, noting the tiny silvery lakes glinting from the basins of green calderas. Most of the populace clustered in small towns or the main city of Ponta Delgada. The bulk of those islands remained untouched.

The pilot came back on. "Secure the cabin for final—"

His words ended with a loud screech from the radio. At the same time, Seichan's body was set on fire. Blinded by pain, she gasped as her skin burned. Kowalski howled from across the cabin. As she breathed flames, the entire plane bobbled. The jet rolled into a nose dive. Still on fire, Seichan felt herself rise from her seat, restrained by her lap belt.

Then it all ended.

Her sight returned, and the searing pain in her skin dulled to the smolder of a sunburn. Kowalski sat in a shocked hunch, his large mitts clamped to his armrests.

What the hell . . .

Though the agony had ended, the jet continued to plummet. Seichan took a breath to collect herself and to see if the pilot regained control of the aircraft. When nothing happened, she snapped off her seat belt and fell toward the small cockpit. She forced the door open and hung from the threshold. Their pilot—a sixty-two-year-old air force veteran named Fitzgerald—slumped leadenly in his chair, held up by his restraints, but clearly unconscious—if not dead.

She dropped into the empty copilot seat and switched controls to her side. She grabbed the yoke with both hands and pulled back hard. Past the windshield, blue ocean filled the world, rising quickly toward her. She fought to haul the nose up.

C'mon, c'mon . . .

As the front of the plane slowly lifted, the view shifted, showing a line of . . . then a fringe green forest . . . and finally the sheer flank of a volcano.

Though she had pulled out of the dive, their descent remained steep, their speed too fast. She had neither the time nor the clearance to sweep back into the air. A quick eye flick across the instrument panel—showing a plummeting altimeter and a map of a doomed glide path—confirmed her grim assessment.

We're going down.

Knowing this, she cut the throttle.

She hollered to Kowalski. "Crash position! Now!"

One-handed, she pulled her own restraints over her shoulders and snapped her belt in place. As the jet raced for the water, she continued to hold the yoke to her belly. She trimmed the flaps, struggling to keep the aircraft's wings even.

Still, at the end, she had to abandon the high-tech instruments and go by the seat of her pants. She stared out the window, eyeballing the ocean rushing toward her, noting the curved line of a beach ahead. Beyond it, a stretch of forest lined the base of a towering wall of black cliffs. But between the beach and the forested cliffs, a large resort shone in the last rays of the sun. Its dozen stories of white walls and windows glowed brightly, like the pearly gates of some tropical heaven.

And we're about to go crashing into them.

To avoid such a fiery end, Seichan had to attempt a hard water landing. As the ocean swept up, she waited until the last moment and timed her move as best she could. Just before they struck the water, she dropped the flaps and hit the throttle hard. Goosed by the sudden power, the plane flared up, nose lifting. The tail end hit the waves first. On that signal, she cut the engines. The rest of aircraft belly-slammed into the water.

Thrown forward into her restraints, she could do nothing more as the jet's momentum sent the craft skipping and spinning across the water like a flat stone. The tip of a wing struck a wave, sending the jet cartwheeling the last thirty yards, until it finally ground into sand, coming to a stop in the shallows.

She sagged in her own restraints, breathing hard, trying to force her heart out of her throat.

"Still in one piece back here!" Kowalski called from the cabin. "Not so sure about the plane."

Of course, Kowalski was okay. The man had too few marbles to be truly rattled by anything.

"Help me with Fitzgerald," she ordered.

The pilot remained unconscious, but at least he appeared to be breathing. She unbuckled herself, then freed Fitzgerald, catching his weight as he fell forward.

Kowalski joined her and grabbed the pilot under his arms and hauled his prone body out of the cockpit. "What happened to him?"

"We'll figure it out later." She remembered the blast of fiery pain, but she had no clue as to its source or what it meant.

One problem at a time.

Seichan wiggled past the pair and shouldered the cabin door open. A breeze blew in, bringing the scent of salt water, along with the smell of burning oil. A glance forward showed smoke rising from the crumpled engine cowling. Though they had been flying on a nearly empty fuel tank, the risk of an explosion remained.

She hopped into the thigh-deep water, soaking her boots and jeans. She hiked her jacket higher to keep it dry as waves washed over her legs.

She pointed to the beach. "Hurry!"

Kowalski jumped out, not bothering to keep his knee-length leather duster dry. He hauled Fitzgerald by his armpits and dragged the pilot behind him.

The group waded stiffly away from the side of the plane and climbed out onto the dry sand. By now, the sun had sunk into the ocean, leaving the skies aglow behind them, but ahead, the dark volcanic peak loomed, framed by the first sweep of stars.

She guessed they had crashed into one of the outer islands of the Azores.

But where exactly?

She stared down the beach. A hundred yards away, the resort she had spotted from the air appeared to be the only habitation. It rose from a dense forest of palms and dark trees. Flickering torches illuminated the hotel's many terraces. The faint strains of music wafted over to them.

Seichan knew any help lay in that direction, but she remained on edge since the crash. *Something's not right here.*

Even Kowalski acknowledged this. "How come no one's running over here to check on us?"

A groan drew their attention to the sand. The pilot was finally stirring, shivering from being dragged through the cold water.

Kowalski dropped to a knee, helping Fitzgerald sit up. "Hey, man, you're okay."

But the man wasn't.

His eyes snapped toward Kowalski, the groan turning into a low growl. Shocked, Kowalski leaned away. Fitzgerald's face contorted into a mask of rage, and he shoved Kowalski back, forcefully enough to knock the large man on his rear. The pilot leaped to his feet, but he remained leaning on the knuckles of one hand.

Fitzgerald's eyes swung between the two of them, his lips snarling, baring his teeth.

Then without warning, he leaped toward Seichan, likely going for the smaller target. Seichan caught him and used his momentum to toss his weight over her hip. Or that was the plan. He hooked an arm around her waist, moving far faster than she expected from a sixty-year-old. Trapped together, they both fell hard to the sand. She landed on her back and twisted her head to the side as he snapped at her face, coming close to taking off her ear.

They grappled for several long breaths, rolling across the sand. She fought to break free, but the man's muscles were iron hard, his reflexes cunning. She finally got her legs bunched under her and kicked him in the stomach, hard enough to finally break his hold and send him flying back.

Before she could even regain her feet, Fitzgerald landed in a crouch, skidding in the sand but staying impossibly upright. He lunged again for her.

But a blast sounded behind her. A scintillating blue cascade shot over her head and struck the pilot in the chest. A few shards of the brilliance shattered past his form and danced over the dark sand.

Fitzgerald sprawled across the beach, his limbs jerking and twitching. His wet clothes ran with fiery spiderwebs of electricity. As the dazzling effect faded, his body went slack and limp, out cold again.

Seichan looked back to see Kowalski standing with his new toy at his shoulder. One muzzle of the Piezer's double barrels still glowed softly from the discharged energy. Clearly, the man had refused to abandon the weapon and hidden it under his duster. The gun's ammunition belt was already hooked around his waist.

Thank god for the man's love of his toys.

Kowalski lowered his shotgun, eyeing it appreciatively. "Guess it works."

She glanced down at the unconscious pilot.

It certainly does.

She studied the smoking jet, wondering if she should risk going for her own weapons.

"Company's coming," Kowalski said, drawing her attention down the beach.

Past the resort property, a pair of headlamps had blinked on and shone brightly along the dark curve of sand. The rumble of an engine echoed over the water, as a large truck started in their direction.

"Looks like someone's finally checking for survivors," Kowalski said.

After all this strangeness, she suspected the opposite was more likely true. She pointed to Fitzgerald. "Drag him into the forest."

"Why are we—?"

"Just do it. Now!"

As Kowalski obeyed, she rushed over and grabbed a dry palm frond. She did her best to erase their path into the woods, or at least obscure the number of footprints. Once under the bower, she tossed her makeshift broom aside.

"Keep moving. Find a place to hide Fitzgerald."

"Then what are we going to do?"

She stared through the trees toward the flickering torches. "Let's go inquire about a late check-in."

8:38 P.M.

Hidden behind a fragrant hedgerow of blue-flowering hydrangeas, Seichan studied the shadowy grounds behind the resort. Nothing stirred across the acres of manicured lawns, and garden paths. The only noise came from a few small fountains burbling from decorative ponds. Higher up, a group of candlelit tables illuminated a second-story dining terrace, all deserted.

Definitely something wrong here.

Closer now, she could tell the resort property was a new construction. It still showed signs of ongoing work: scaffolding along one side, tilled but unplanted garden beds, rows of sapling trees waiting in buckets.

Still, from the faint strains of music and the flaming torches, it was clear the place was open for business, even if it was only a soft opening to test staff and facilities.

Beside her, Kowalski swatted as something dark swept past his cheek. "What's with all these friggin' bats?"

She had noted the same while crossing through the woods. Scores of leathery wings had flitted among the branches, accompanied by an ultrasonic chorus that set her teeth on edge. Across the grounds, smoky clouds of bats swirled in bands, rising low and sweeping high. More and more seemed to be flowing down from the dark flank of the volcano behind them, rising out of caves and rocky roosts to hunt the night.

But the bats weren't her true concern at the moment.

She glanced to her left. Off by the beach, lights glowed through the trees, marking the location of the truck and whoever had been drawn to the crashed jet. Occasional louder voices reached them, the words too muffled to make out clearly. She knew searchers were probably already combing the woods after finding the aircraft empty. She and Kowalski needed to get under cover quickly, and the hotel offered them a multitude of hiding places.

Kowalski nudged her and pointed. "By that ATV. Are those legs sticking out from behind it?"

She peered in that direction and saw he was right. "Let's check it out."

She shifted over to an opening in the hedgerow and entered the rear grounds, staying low and avoiding the occasional torch burning along the periphery. The small Kawasaki ATV had a trailer attached to it, loaded with trays of potted flowers. It was parked beside an empty garden bed. A man lay facedown in the grass next to the trailer. From the looks of his green overalls, he was part of a landscaping crew.

She saw his chest rise and fall.

Unconscious.

Kowalski leaned down, his finger reaching to check a pulse.

Seichan pulled him back, picturing Fitzgerald's snarling countenance. "Don't." She motioned to the tall patio doors under the dining terrace. "Let's get inside, out of the open."

She headed straight across, hurrying faster as flashlights bobbled through the forest to her left. She reached the doors and tugged. *Locked.* She shifted along the back of the building, testing each door until finally one gave way. She tugged it open and pushed into a dark hallway with Kowalski shadowing her.

"What now?" he whispered.

"Weapons."

She headed down the carpeted hallway, picturing the dining terrace outside. *There must be a kitchen nearby.* Halfway along the empty hall, she found a door marked EMPREGADOS APENAS. Her Portuguese was rusty, but the sign was easily translatable as *Employees Only.*

She tested the knob, found the door unlocked, and headed through it. Past the threshold, a narrow staircase led up. She mounted the steps.

"C'mon."

The spaces back here were more utilitarian. The walls were unpainted, further evidence that the hotel was a work in progress. At the next landing, she followed the smell of frying grease and spices to a set of swinging stainless steel doors.

She peeked one side open and discovered a large commercial kitchen, with stacks of ovens and rows of gas burners. Several pots bubbled and steamed; a few had boiled over. A set of four pans smoked with what might have been fish fillets, now charred into blackened crisps.

The reason for the mess was clear. A dozen or more bodies in white aprons were sprawled across the floor, limbs tangled, some atop one another. Like the gardener, they looked like they were still breathing.

"Careful," Seichan whispered. "Watch where you step."

She headed in first and worked her way across the space, placing each foot gingerly so as not to disturb those on the floor. She did not want a repeat of the incident with Fitzgerald.

Though uncertain of what was going on, she had begun to get an inkling. She remembered the flare of fiery pain aboard the jet. Seated in front, the pilot must have taken the full brunt of that unknown force. Insulated in back, she and Kowalski were less impacted.

She stepped over the fat belly of a man whose chef's hat lay deflated next to his head. He snored loudly. Whatever blow was struck here did not appear fatal. Still, from Fitzgerald's heightened aggression and adrenaline-fueled strength, there was lasting damage, some violent alteration of personality.

She reached a row of cutting utensils and grabbed a long butcher's knife and a smaller boning blade. Kowalski picked up a big meat cleaver. He still had his shotgun clutched in one hand, but clearly he wanted something more lethal if it came down to hand-to-hand combat.

"This is more like it," he said, stepping back.

His heel struck a sleeping dishwasher in the nose. A sharp snort of pain alerted them to the misstep. They turned to find a pair of narrowed eyes glaring up at them. The worker jerked his limbs under him, again moving with shocking speed. He leaped up—only to be met with the thick wooden handle of Kowalski's cleaver coming down. The impact sounded like a hammer hitting a coconut. The dishwasher seemed to hang in the air for a beat, then his body collapsed back to the floor.

"That's right," Kowalski said. "Go back to sleep."

Seichan bent down. The man's eyes had rolled white, but he should be all right, except for the goose egg he'd find behind his left ear later. She straightened and scowled at Kowalski.

"I know, I know." He waved her on. "Watch my step."

She led the way out of the kitchen but noted a tall cake on a serving trolley near the door. It was frosted with pink flowers and displayed a cartoonish red dog saying *Parabéns, Amelia! Feliz aniversário!* Clearly someone was celebrating a birthday. Though the presence of only nine candles made her blood run cold.

"Let's go," she said, and hurried out of the kitchen and down a short hall.

Another set of double doors opened into a four-story lobby. To her left was the torch-lit dining terrace. Seichan headed right, wanting to get a view out to the grounds bordering the beach. She pictured the child's birthday cake and rushed faster. Ahead, a series of tall patio doors had been rolled open. A gentle sea breeze wafted into the marble interior— carrying with it a smattering of bats that swept in diving arcs through the crystal chandeliers.

Closer by, other bodies dotted the lobby's tile floor or were slumped in chairs. She headed for a cocktail lounge opposite the reception desk. Its bar abutted the floor-to-ceiling glass wall that overlooked the ocean. They could shelter behind the counter and still spy upon the grounds outside.

She wound through the tables, avoiding a nicely dressed woman collapsed on the floor next to a shattered martini glass.

Circling behind the bar, Seichan drew Kowalski alongside her.

"Stay low," she warned.

The space behind the counter was occupied by the crumpled figure of a man in a pressed black suit. He had fallen to his rear, his back leaning against a tall, glass-fronted wine refrigerator. His head lolled to the side, with a rope of drool hanging from his lips.

She pointed to the bartender, but before she could say a word Kowalski waved her on.

"Watch my step," he said. "I know."

They crossed over the obstacle and hunkered down at the far end, where a window offered an expansive view across a hedge-lined terrace that surrounded a midnight blue pool.

Kowalski settled with a sigh. He had nabbed a bottle of whiskey from a shelf and cracked the seal with his teeth. As she frowned at him, he mumbled around the cap. "What? I'm thirsty." He spat out the lid and cocked his head toward the window. "Besides, it's a party."

She returned her attention to the poolside terrace. Tables had been set up across the space, each bearing centerpieces of pink balloons. As elsewhere, bodies were strewn all around. Torsos were draped across dishes; chairs had toppled over. Servers lay amid platters of broken dishes and glasses. Most of the figures appeared to be adults.

Except for the table in the center.

A triple set of balloon bouquets decorated that spread. To the side, a wide bench supported a stack of gaily wrapped presents. All around, small bodies—like a flock of felled sparrows—dotted the tiled pavement. At the head, a tiny figure lay slumped to the table, her face turned to the side, as if too exhausted to hold up her head, burdened by the paper crown she wore.

Here must be the reason for this celebration.

Seichan remembered the child's name, written in pink icing.

Amelia.

The girl was clearly loved, likely the child of one of the staff or management. The family was probably taking advantage of the resort's soft opening to throw the girl this private party.

Seichan wondered what it would be like to be that girl, to have grown up with such all-encompassing love, to have your life celebrated under the sun. She found it nearly incomprehensible to imagine, having spent her early years in the alleys of Bangkok and Phnom Penh, then later in the stygian folds of the Guild. She stared at that bright paper crown and felt the shadows within her grow darker by contrast.

"Truck's coming back," Kowalski said.

She shifted her attention to the stretch of beach on the far side of the pool. Unlit and gloomy, washed by black waves, the sands grew brighter as the large truck trundled over from the crash site. Its headlamps speared across the tiny bay, revealing an unpaved gravel road on its far side, cutting through the forest, likely heading to some small town or village.

She willed the truck to keep heading that way.

Instead, the truck braked to a stop, its lights shining across a marble staircase that climbed from the beach to the terrace. The vehicle had a double cab with an open bed. Men with rifles and flashlights hopped out of the back, and doors popped open, but it was what was braced in the bed that drew Seichan's full attention.

Before evacuating the vehicle, the crew's flashlights revealed a refrigerator-sized steel box with thick cables running to a row of car batteries. Topping the device was a meter-wide metal dish, swiveled halfway up, pointing toward the sky.

That's gotta be the cause for whatever happened here.

Kowalski nodded toward the group climbing the steps. "Fitzgerald."

The pilot was on his feet, his hands tied behind his back. He looked dazed, stumbling along the steps, but a giant dressed in black commando gear had Fitzgerald's elbow clamped in a firm grip and held him up, forcing him to climb the stairs. Still, the pilot seemed to have come to his senses. Though cowed, he searched around, plainly trying to comprehend what was happening.

Seichan studied the pilot. Was Fitzgerald's recovery just a matter of time or had they given him some agent to counteract his mania?

Her gaze returned to Amelia.

But a sharp voice drew her attention back to the group as they reached the pool deck. The words echoed across the terrace and through the open patio doors.

"Fear not, gents. Noises won't wake them." The silver-haired speaker wore a crisp white suit, his accent distinctly British. He waved an arm over the tables as they drew closer. "From our preliminary studies, they're deaf in this comatose state. But take care not to otherwise disturb their slumber. They will attack anything that moves."

He was accompanied by a younger bearded man in a beige uniform, clearly Persian, likely Iranian. He spoke as the group drew nearer to the hotel. "Dr. Balchor, this alteration in the victims' mental status, tell me more. If we are to continue financing your research, the army will want full details of your progress."

"Of course, Colonel Rouhani. What you're seeing here is a side effect of Colossus." He motioned toward the device aboard the truck. "One we had not anticipated. My initial research goals were to build your army a new *active denial system*, a nonlethal defensive energy weapon. Typical systems used by current police and military forces employ microwave beams that penetrate the top layers of the skin to trigger an excruciatingly painful experience. But today's systems have limited range and scope."

"And Colossus?"

Balchor smiled proudly. "I wanted to create a system that could do the same, but with a scope capable of taking down entire city blocks, even penetrating buildings."

Rouhani looked around. "And you achieved this how?"

"It's technical, but basically I discovered that by crossing a high-powered microwave beam with an electromagnetic pulse, I could produce a unique resonance wave. The resulting beam is capable of passing through most solid objects in order to strike its intended targets. Again, I thought the beam would only act as a *deterrent*, triggering intense, debilitating pain in those caught in its path."

Seichan remembered that effect. Her skin still ached from that phantom burn.

Balchor continued, "But upon modulating that wave, I discovered it could penetrate *deeper* than just the outer layers of the skin. The electromagnetic component of the beam could reach the brain. Now, normally an electromagnetic pulse—an EMP—has no deleterious effects on living tissue, so you can imagine my shock to see victims collapse and have their behavior altered."

Rouhani frowned. "So then what is happening?"

"To answer that very question, it took further investigation. Eventually I came across research being conducted in China, where scientists had discovered that a certain frequency of an EMP could cause an increase in vascular permeability in the cerebral cortex. In other words, it makes a brain's blood vessels more *leaky*. My device was doing something similar, only affecting the permeability of *neurons* directly."

"I don't understand," Rouhani said. "Why is that significant?"

"Because leaky neurons *can't* conduct electricity properly. The result is that Colossus shuts down a target's cerebral cortex, knocking them out. If woken, the subjects react at a primitive level. It's all that still functions. Pure fight or flight—though mostly *fight*, as it turns out. Spiked on adrenaline, the subjects have proven to be inordinately strong and aggressive."

Rouhani nodded. "That is why you claimed that Colossus was the first *biological* EMP."

"Indeed. A typical EMP knocks out electronic circuits without harming humans or other biological life. But when modulated and crossed with a high-powered microwave—an HPM—the result is the opposite. Colossus targets living subjects, those with an advanced cerebral cortex, while leaving anything electronic untouched."

"So such a weapon could incapacitate an enemy, yet leave the infrastructure intact for an invading force to utilize."

"Precisely. And as you can see, we've made good progress. But I'd still like to understand this effect in more detail. It is one of the reasons for today's test firing, both as a demonstration for you and to further my own studies." Balchor turned to the steroid-bulked giant holding Fitzgerald hostage. "Dmitry, have your men pick out seven or eight subjects for further examination at the lab. I'll want a sampling of all ages for a proper assessment."

Dmitry nodded and yelled orders in Russian to his other men. From the giant's razor-cropped hair, he was clearly ex-military, probably acting as a security detachment for the field test of this weapon.

His men readied long-barreled handguns, loading in feathered darts, plainly intending to tranquilize their targets prior to hauling them away. His seven-man team spread out, calling to one another, searching for the best subjects.

A pair approached the children's table. The two eyed Amelia and nodded a confirmation to each other. One man lifted his gun and fired into the child's neck. The girl jerked, rolled slightly to the side as if about to wake, then slumped back down as the fast-acting sedative kicked in.

Seichan's hands balled into tight fists.

Motherfu—

The shooter stood guard over the girl as other subjects were picked out. One target—a twentysomething young man—reacted more vigorously to the dart's impact. He swatted blindly and flew to his feet, stumbling in a circle. A second feathered dart bloomed on his chest, but by then, he had trampled over two others. One lunged up and went for the groggy young man, clawing at his face. The other scrabbled low across the tiles, going for the shooter.

Before the matter escalated out of hand, another gunman stepped forward with a regular pistol and fired twice—making two clean head shots—and bloodily ended the threat.

The young troublemaker, now doubly sedated, slumped heavily to the ground.

As the remainder of the crew worked through the partygoers, making their selections, Balchor led the Iranian colonel toward the patio doors. "Let's head inside. I'll buy you a drink while Dmitry's men finish up here."

"Just water." Rouhani looked shaken up by the violent episode. He cast a worried eye at the remaining thirty or forty bodies still strewn across the terrace.

"Ah, yes, sorry. I forgot your faith forbids the use of alcohol. Luckily my religion is *science*, and a glass of champagne is well deserved under the circumstances."

Rouhani suddenly ducked and batted at his head. A small black shape fluttered away. "Why are there so many bats?"

Balchor searched up at the dark clouds winging and spiraling above the terrace. Occasional streams shot lower, dive-bombing and cartwheeling, casting off individual bats that glided through the assembly outside.

"I believe the wave must have agitated them from their caves, stirring them up. With their keen sonic senses, they might have been drawn here, zeroing in on the source of the beam." Balchor shrugged and headed toward the patio door. "It's interesting—and one of the reasons we run field tests. To see how such a weapon performs in real-world scenarios. That includes bats and all."

Seichan lost sight of them as they entered the lobby, but she heard their footsteps approaching across the hard marble. She glanced up at the wall of bottles over the bar, suddenly questioning her choice of hiding place.

Kowalski must have realized the same and firmed his grip on his shotgun. He shifted to her side of the bar, both their backs now pressed against the counter.

Dmitry had accompanied the pair, still holding Fitzgerald. "What about the man we find in woods?" he asked, his English stilted and heavily accented.

The footsteps stopped, and Balchor answered, "The man claims to have been the only one aboard the plane. So we may be fine."

Seichan shared a look with Kowalski.

Good going, Fitzgerald.

"But, Dmitry, I think a more vigorous interrogation of the pilot is in order before we vacate the island. I'll leave you and your men to handle that once they finish up here."

"Still, what about his plane?" Rouhani asked. "*Why* did it crash? I thought Colossus didn't affect electronic systems."

"Indeed it doesn't. I suspect the beam we aimed from the parking lot toward the hotel must have reflected off the building—or off the cliffs behind it—and struck the aircraft by accident."

Seichan bit back a groan at their bad luck.

Definitely wrong place, wrong time.

Balchor continued, "The backwash must have been painful enough to make the pilot lose control but not strong enough for the full neurological impact."

Seichan knew the good doctor was wrong about that last part, which made her wonder again about Fitzgerald's recovery. Clearly Balchor's team hadn't administered any counteragent to help Fitzgerald return to his senses. She glanced over to the weapon in Kowalski's hand, remembering the doctor's description of Colossus's effect, how it could turn off the electrical flow through the cerebral cortex.

Had the shock delivered by Kowalski's weapon restarted that flow, like some defibrillator for the brain?

The footsteps continued again, heading toward the bar.

Off to the side, she watched Amelia being lifted from her chair, her paper crown fluttering to the tabletop. The gunman hauled her over his shoulder like a sack of flour and headed toward the truck on the beach.

"What will you do with the rest of the people out there?" Rouhani asked as the pair reached the counter, speaking directly over where she and Kowalski hid.

Balchor sighed heavily. "I'll blast another wave as we leave. Prior tests show that a second insult to such afflicted individuals results in total brain death. They won't be telling any stories." He clapped his hands, changing the subject. "It looks as if this bar is self-service at the moment, so I'll have to go around and fetch my own champagne."

We're out of time.

Seichan lifted a fist in front of Kowalski, signaling him.

Don't move.

After getting a nod from him, she turned to her other side and kicked the man sharing their hiding place. The bartender's head snapped up, throwing a rope of drool that struck Seichan in the cheek. She remained a statue, not even blinking, recalling Balchor's earlier warning about the newly awakened.

They will attack anything that moves.

Rouhani leaned over the counter, his head turned, calling over to Balchor. "Maybe I will take a small drink after all."

The bartender was happy to assist.

The man burst to his feet and dove at the Iranian. Caught off guard, Rouhani failed to react in time. The bartender's fingers latched on to the colonel's throat. Rouhani tried to push off the bar to escape.

Not so fast.

Seichan leaped up and twisted around. She swung her arm down and stabbed the stolen butcher's knife through the back of the colonel's hand, pinning it to the mahogany bar. Without waiting, she rolled over the countertop and landed in a crouch on the far side.

Balchor was already running for the patio doors, shouting for help.

Before she could give chase, she had another obstacle to address.

Across the cocktail lounge, Dmitry shoved Fitzgerald to the floor and reached for a holstered sidearm.

Not good.

Kowalski had their only gun.

She glanced to her right, hoping her partner saw the threat, but Kowalski was focused elsewhere. At the bar, Rouhani struggled and gurgled. The bartender's teeth were sunk deep into the man's neck, ripping his throat open. Kowalski fired his Piezer—but not at the Russian. The scintillating blue flare struck the bartender, sending him flying and hopefully back to sleep.

Still, the dazzling blast succeeded in startling Dmitry. The Russian fell back several steps, but unfortunately, he had freed his sidearm by now.

Using the momentary distraction, Seichan flipped the boning knife in her fingers and flung it across the lounge. Dmitry easily dodged the blade—but the Russian wasn't her target.

The knife struck the thigh of the woman behind Dmitry. She was the bar patron sprawled on the floor next to a shattered martini glass. The pain of the impaled blade drove the woman to her feet with a furious cry. She looked for the nearest person to blame.

Caught off guard, Dmitry could not turn in time. The woman hit him broadside, taking him to the floor. But the Russian was no amateur. He tossed the woman away and rolled back to his feet, but the sudden blow had knocked his pistol from his grip.

It lay under a table next to him.

He made a move in that direction, but Kowalski fired at him. A fiery blue blast exploded over the tabletop, sparing the Russian sheltered below from the brunt of the electrifying charge. Still, several crystals managed to hit him and drove him away, his face tight with pain. Dmitry twisted around, dug in his toes, and dove toward the patio door.

"Have to reload," Kowalski called out.

Seichan rushed forward, diving across the floor. She scooped up the abandoned handgun, a .50-caliber Desert Eagle, and fired at Dmitry. But the Russian, running low, pursuing his employer, had made it out to the terrace, where a storm was brewing.

In his hurry to escape, Balchor must have stepped on a few comatose patrons, rousing them in his wake. They in turn disturbed others. Cries and screams rose out there, accompanied by the breaking of furniture.

Kowalski's weapon blasted again. Seichan ducked and turned in time to see the sharply dressed madwoman go flying backward, her chest dancing with blue fire.

Almost forgot about her.

Out on the terrace, Dmitry fled through the escalating riot, punching and elbowing his way forward. Across the pool, Balchor tripped and fell down the far steps, landing near the bumper of the truck. One of Dmitry's men helped him up, guiding him toward the cab as the engine growled louder, preparing to leave.

Kowalski skidded up next to her, the muzzle of his weapon glowing. "All set. What now?"

She ignored him for the moment and picked up the boning blade that had knocked free during the scuffle and crossed to Fitzgerald. "How're you feeling?"

The pilot sat up, looking stunned, but nodded. "O . . . okay. Better."

Good.

He had clearly returned to his senses, and she could guess why.

As she sliced the man's bonds and freed him, she finally answered Kowalski's question. She nodded to his weapon. "That seems to shock them out of their madness." She pointed out to the patio. "So you're on crowd control."

She swung around and headed in the opposite direction.

"Where are you going?" Kowalski shouted after her.

She pictured Amelia. The girl was already aboard the truck with the others. "Making sure somebody has a happy birthday."

9:09 P.M.

Standing beside the unplanted garden bed, Seichan yanked the pin connecting the flower-laden trailer from the Kawasaki ATV and hopped onto the seat. Earlier she had noted the sleeping gardener's keys were still in the ignition.

She started the engine and gunned the throttle, bucking the vehicle up on its back wheels. Then the front tires slammed down, and she shot forward. She cut across the newly planted lawn and over gravel paths, aiming for the dark wing still under construction.

No lights shone there, but such places were where she worked best.

In the shadows.

She wasn't the only one. The air was full of bats, swooping and keening in ultrasonic fury. The winged horde had grown tenfold thicker in just the short time she had been inside the hotel. A stray bat struck Seichan's face and fluttered off, leaving a welt of pain. She ignored it and sped faster, her knobby tires chewing through the terrain. She dared not slow.

A minute ago, as she had exited the back of the resort, she had heard the truck engine's roar settle into a steady growl.

The others were already leaving.

With Balchor's team having a head start, she refused to lose any more ground. She reached the far corner of the resort and sped around the turn, lifting up on two tires, challenging the limits of the ATV. As she cleared the bend, she had to dodge through an array of construction equipment and supplies: piles of concrete pavers, stacks of lumber, a parked backhoe.

She cursed the obstacle course, trying not to slow down. In her haste, her front bumper clipped a crated statue. The ATV skidded sideways. Instead of braking, she let it spin a bit further, then gunned the engine and sent the vehicle racing for a slab of granite that had slipped off its stack and fallen crookedly in front of her. She shot up the makeshift ramp, caught air, and flew several yards. She landed with a crunch and a bounce in the gravel of a parking lot.

Finally clear of the construction zone, she sped toward the road that led into the forest. Distantly through the trees, she spotted the rear lights of the trucks. The fleeing vehicle was even farther ahead than she had feared.

Behind her, the occasional shotgun blast echoed, continuing proof that Kowalski was still alive and doing his best to manage crowd control. She left him to his work and raced to the road and into the forest. She kept her lights off and followed the glow through the trees.

The road paralleled the curves and bends of the island's coast, allowing her to stay out of direct sight, but eventually the path straightened. Fearing she would be spotted, she guided her ATV to the edge of the trees, doing her best to stay in the darker shadows under the canopy, hiding from the moon and stars.

The truck suddenly veered to the left, leaving the road, which continued following the coastline. Seichan hurried to close the distance. As she reached the corner, she discovered the turnoff led to a long pier, where a floatplane—a Cessna Caravan—waited at its end. A large cargo hatch was open on one side, its lighted interior shining in the darkness.

Fifty yards ahead, the truck had pulled alongside the base of the pier. Men busied themselves around it.

She could've abandoned the ATV and gone on foot, using the cover of the forest, but she heard Balchor shout.

"Get Colossus onto the plane! Then the test subjects!"

Seichan pictured the paper crown falling from Amelia's bowed head and made a sharp turn onto the side road and headed straight for the truck. She raised her huge pistol—the stolen Desert Eagle—and fired over the hood of the truck. She struck a man in the shoulder, sending him spinning from the impact of the large-caliber slug. The recoil almost tore the pistol from her grip, but she tightened her fingers and kept her aim high, away from the back bed and cab, fearing she might hit one of those "test subjects."

Return fire sparked toward her, but the shots were wild as the crew was caught by surprise. She crouched low, balancing her wrist on the ATV's short windshield, and fired back.

Four men managed to lug the dish device out of the bed and ran with it down the dock, dragging cables. Balchor fled alongside them, guarded by Dmitry. The bulk of the truck blocked her from shooting after them. Still, she dropped another Russian by the back bumper. The rest of the crew finally abandoned the vehicle and followed the others—especially as the floatplane's engine roared louder, readying to depart. Its propellers spun faster.

As Seichan reached the truck, coming in fast, she braked hard and skidded the ATV sideways, slamming broadside into it. She hopped out of the seat and quickly checked the rear cab and back bed. Sedated bodies were tossed inside both compartments like so much firewood. She spotted the thin limbs of a child.

Amelia . . .

Seichan shifted to the front of the truck, leveling her big pistol across the hood of the vehicle. Balchor was already aboard the plane, waving for the others to haul Colossus into the cargo hold with him. Dmitry helped, looking as if he could pick up the unwieldy contraption all by himself.

She held off shooting, afraid of drawing return fire toward the truck, where a stray round could injure or kill those sleeping inside. Plus, if her count was right, she was down to a single round. Still, such restraint made her grit her teeth in frustration.

Even before the final man was aboard, the plane headed across the water. The last straggler tossed the dock lines and dove into the hold. Seichan watched the plane gain speed and rise off the water, skimming the waves, then climbing higher. She imagined Balchor's research lab must be hidden on one of the many tiny islands that dotted the North Atlantic. She would leave it to Painter to discover where the doctor might be holed up.

Impotent and angry, she watched the Cessna continue upward—but then the wings tilted. The aircraft swung in a wide, low turn, coming back around. Seichan glanced over her shoulder toward the resort. Distantly a shotgun blast echoed to her. She faced the floatplane again as it circled in her direction. The cargo hatch was still open. The interior cabin lights revealed men clustered around Colossus, positioning the dish to face the door.

Apparently the bastards weren't leaving without first saying good-bye. They must intend to deliver a parting shot before they fled home. She remembered Balchor's description of the effect of a second wave striking those already afflicted.

Total brain death.

She retreated several steps, watching the Cessna complete its slow turn, the open hatch coming around. Men fled back into the hold. She spotted a large bulk standing behind Colossus.

Dmitry.

The Russian loosened the dish and swiveled it down. He pointed toward the forest ahead of her—but that was not the true objective. As the plane turned, the device's wave would soon sweep over her and the truck.

Though there was no sound, no visible sign, she *felt* Colossus activate. It was like a sunburst in the forest, the heat burning her face and arms— and she knew this was just the weapon's backwash. Her skin grew steadily hotter as the plane continued to turn, swinging the beam's full force toward her.

Still, she kept her position, determined to guard the truck and its occupants.

She planted her legs, cradling the Desert Eagle in both hands. She lifted her arms and aimed toward the cargo hold, toward Dmitry. Her skin burned, her eyes wept, but she held steady. The rising pain made her want to scream—so she did as she fired.

The big gun blasted, the recoil driving her arms up.

She failed to hit Dmitry.

But again he wasn't her target.

The large-caliber slug sparked off the upper lip of the dish; the impact kicked the loosened dish up, pointing it toward the roof of the cargo hold. Sharp screams of agony cut through the engine's low roar as the searing wave washed over the passengers.

The plane canted wildly. Then the nose lifted, shooting the plane higher and away, as if the pilot were trying to escape the fire in the rear cabin. Then it dipped down, wings bobbling back and forth. But as it fled toward the resort, its path began to straighten.

Seichan scowled.

Someone must have managed to switch Colossus off.

The aircraft steadied and banked over the resort, turning toward the volcanic cliffs—but would it continue away or would the bastards come around and try again to blast the resort with Colossus's beam?

Seichan held her breath.

In the end, the decision was taken from them.

The large dark cloud that swirled above the hotel suddenly gusted higher, spiraling toward the source of the ultrasonic blast. The plane was quickly lost in a mass of furious bats.

Again the aircraft wobbled wildly, as if its wings were trying to swat away the bats. Its engine coughed, likely inhaling some of the horde. Blinded and assaulted, the Cessna dipped and dove faster over the treetops, still out of control, canting madly—then slammed into the nearby volcanic cliffs and exploded.

A fireball lit up the black rock, then rolled higher, trailing smoke.

Seichan let out the breath she had been holding.

But another distant shotgun blast reminded her that there was still work to do.

She crossed over to the truck, discovered the keys were still in the ignition after the team's hasty departure, and climbed inside. In short order, she had the truck turned around and was trundling back to the resort.

As she reached the beach, she parked the vehicle at the foot of the wide staircase that led up to the terrace. The truck's headlights revealed dazed figures seated on the steps, some crying, others holding their heads in their hands.

She climbed out, wary at first, but it was soon clear that the men and women here had recovered from their madness, the same as Fitzgerald. The likely source of their "cure" called out from the upper deck.

"Is that the last of them?" Kowalski yelled.

"Think so!" Fitzgerald answered. "At least out here!"

Seichan hurried up the steps. She reached the top in time to see Kowalski grab a middle-aged woman by the face and shove her into the pool. Five other figures splashed and howled in the waters, teeth gnashing, hands clawing.

Kowalski noted her arrival. "Check this out."

He stepped back, aimed his Piezer at the pool, and fired.

A flash of blue fire shot into the water. Electricity danced outward in sparks and skittering lines across the surface. The half-dozen bodies— trapped in the pool and caught in that shocking wake—shook and twitched in the water. But as the effect faded, the figures slumped and stumbled around in bewilderment, still conscious, but plainly returning to their senses.

Fitzgerald called and waved to them, ready to help them out. Other recovered patrons came forward to assist him.

Seichan glanced to Kowalski as he hiked his weapon to his shoulder. A lit cigar was clamped between his back molars.

When did he have time to—

Never mind.

She shook her head, having to at least respect the man's resourcefulness at coming up with this economical way of using his ammunition.

Kowalski crossed to her and sighed heavily. "So *now* can I go on vacation?"

April 18, 7:09 A.M.

By the next morning, order was mostly restored.

As the sun rose on a new day, Seichan stood at the edge of the shadowy forest. A borrowed motorcycle was parked behind her. She stared out at the sprawl of the resort, the curve of sand, the bright pool.

Out in the bay, a Portuguese military cruiser bobbed in the water. A pair of ambulances sat on the beach. Overnight, medical crews had turned one floor of the hotel into a makeshift hospital, attending to the injured, trying their best to mitigate the physical and psychological damage inflicted here. The more critically wounded had already been evacuated by helicopter to Ponta Delgada.

Seichan had also reached Painter Crowe last night. He was already working with Portuguese intelligence services to locate Dr. Balchor's lab. The director had also managed to cover her involvement in events here, along with that of Kowalski and Fitzgerald.

The two men were already en route to a small town on the island's far side, where a new plane waited to evacuate them. From there, Seichan would continue to Morocco, while Kowalski headed to Germany to enjoy his vacation.

We're back on schedule . . . as if nothing had happened.

But before she mounted her motorcycle and headed after Kowalski and Fitzgerald, she wanted this moment alone, to take measure of all that *had* happened.

She had crashed here, struck down by blind chance. And while it was easier to dismiss such a mishap as bad luck, she knew better. She knew exactly *why* she had crashed on this island. It wasn't a matter of being at the *wrong place, wrong time.*

Instead, she was at the *right place, right time.*

So this could happen.

From the shadows, Seichan watched a small girl run across the sunlit terrace, her bright pink dress blooming behind her. She ran into her father and hugged his legs with both arms. He lowered a fresh paper crown to her head, lifted her in his arms, and kissed her on the forehead.

Satisfied, Seichan turned away, drawing deeper into the shadows. She now understood it was darkness where she needed to be, so others could play in the sun.

Happy birthday, Amelia.

Author's Note

What's True, What's Not

At the end of my full-length novels, I love to spell out what's real and what's fiction in my stories. I thought I'd briefly do the same here.

First, I thought I'd share the genesis for this story. I blame it on the season. When I began writing this, October was just around the corner, so I thought what better way to celebrate that spooky month than to craft a Sigma story featuring a haunted hotel, hordes of bats, and rampaging zombies—then throw Kowalski into the mix with a new toy. Speaking of which . . .

Piezer. Kowalski's new toy is based on a true concept being explored by HSARPA—Homeland Security Advanced Research Project. It's a double-barrel shotgun that can fire showers of shocking piezo-electric crystals, with a range of one hundred and fifty feet, all without those pesky Taser wires. So, of course, Sigma Force would be perfect to field-test such a prototype, and who else but Kowalski is best suited for this gun? You see more of this innovative weapon as it's put through its paces—in ways only Kowalski would think to employ—in *The Seventh Plague*, the Sigma novel that follows.

Colossus. The other weapon showcased in this story is based on a Boeing patent for a new HPM (high-powered microwave) deterrent. Like the device featured in the story, Boeing is exploring *crossing* two such beams and modulating the frequency and resonance to produce a unique and powerful effect. Has anyone thought of crossing an HPM with an EMP? So far only me—but I wouldn't put it past someone to explore this possibility. Especially since researchers at the Natural Science Foundation of China have published a paper on how certain wavelengths of an electromagnetic pulse (an EMP) *do* have an effect on the brains of rats, causing an increase in cerebral vascular permeability. Could it create zombies? Am I wrong to hope it does?

The Azores. I've never been to this Portuguese archipelago in the North Atlantic, but with their verdant grottos, steaming hot springs, crater lakes, and stunning beaches, I'm ready to go when you all are. Let's just not visit a certain resort that's about to have its grand opening.

WHAT'S NEXT?

At this story's conclusion, Seichan is headed on assignment to Marrakesh, and Kowalski is off to visit his girlfriend in Leipzig, Germany, but alas, neither of them will get to enjoy their time apart for very long. Soon the pair will be summoned to join forces yet again, to thwart an ancient peril ripped from the pages of the Bible in *The Seventh Plague.* I hope you enjoy the mayhem to come!

Tracker

JAMES ROLLINS

March 4, 5:32 P.M.
Budapest, Hungary

He knew she was being hunted.

Seated at a chilly bistro table, wrapped in a woolen jacket, Tucker Wayne watched the woman hurry across the icy medieval plaza known as *Szentháromság tér*, or Trinity Square. The blonde, early twenties, glanced over her shoulder one too many times. She wore sunglasses even though most of the plaza was already thick with shadows as the sun set. Her crimson silk scarf had been tugged too high over her chin, not because she was cold; such thin material offered little practical protection against the chilly gusts that swept the plaza. Also, she walked too fast compared with the others ambling around the heart of the city's Royal Castle District, a major tourist hub for Budapest.

The army had trained him to maintain such diligence, to watch for the unusual amid the ordinary. When he'd been a captain with the US Army Rangers, he and his partner had served as the unit's trackers through two tours in Afghanistan—for search-and-rescue operations, for extraction, for hunting down targets of acquisition. In the outlying districts and villages of Afghanistan, the difference between life and death was not so much about rifles, Kevlar, and the latest risk assessments as it was about noting the rhythms of the environment, the normal ebb and flow of life, and watching for anything out of the ordinary.

Like now.

The woman didn't belong here. Even the brightness of her clothing was out of place: the ivory knee-length coat, the red shoes that matched her scarf and hat. Among a winter crowd dressed in browns and blacks or tans and grays, she stood out.

Not wise when you were being hunted.

As he watched her nervous progress across the square, he cradled the cup of hot coffee between his palms. He wore a pair of gloves with the fingertips cut out of them. Other patrons of the pastry shop gathered inside the small space, where it was warm and crowded at this hour. They were bellied up to the counter or perched at small window-side tables. He was the only one banished to the outdoor patio at the edge of the cold square.

He and his partner.

The compact shepherd, known as a Belgian Malinois, lay at his feet, the dog's muzzle resting on the tip of his boot, ready for any command. Kane had served alongside him through two tours in Afghanistan. They'd worked together, eaten together, even bunked together.

Kane was as much a part of his body as his own arm or leg.

When Tucker left the service, he took Kane with him.

Since then Tucker had been adrift in the world, intending to stay lost, taking the occasional odd job to support himself—and then moving on. He liked it that way. After all he had seen in Afghanistan, he needed new horizons, new vistas, but mostly, he had a drive to keep moving.

With no family attachments in the States, he no longer needed a home.

It came with him.

He reached down and ran his fingers through the dog's dense black-

and-tan fur. Kane's muzzle lifted. Dark brown eyes, flecked with gold, stared up at him. It was one of the unique features of domesticated dogs—*they studied us as much as we studied them.*

He matched that gaze and gave a small nod—then flicked his eyes to the square. He wanted his partner to be ready as the woman crossed toward them, about to skirt past the outdoor patio.

Tucker scanned the flow of humanity into and out of the plaza as it wound around the towering statue in the center of the square. Its baroque façade was covered in marble figures, climbing skyward, toward a brilliant gold star. It represented those in the city who had escaped the Black Plague during the eighteenth century.

As the woman neared, he kept a close eye on anyone staring toward her. There were a few. She was a woman who naturally turned heads: slender, curvaceous, with a fall of blond hair to the middle of her back.

At last, across the plaza, he spotted her hunter—or rather, *hunters.*

A mountain of a man, flanked by two smaller figures, entered from a street to the north. They were all dressed in trench coats. The leader was black-haired, well over six feet, hugely muscled, and, from the prominent pocking over his face, a chronic abuser of anabolic steroids.

Tucker noted bulges under the trench coats that suggested concealed weapons.

The woman didn't notice the group, her eyes glancing right over them.

So she knew someone might be looking for her, but she didn't have the skill or knowledge to pick them out. Yet she had the instinct to stay around other people.

She hurried past his location, a whiff of jasmine left in her wake.

Kane tilted his nose up to her scent.

She headed toward the doors of the massive Matthias Church, with its towering stone-laced gothic spire and fourteenth-century reliefs depicting the Virgin Mary's death. The doors were still open, waiting for the last of the day's tourists to straggle out. She headed inside, casting a final look around before ducking past the threshold.

Tucker finished his coffee, left a tip, and stood. He grabbed Kane's leash and exited just as the trio of hunters swept past. As he followed them, bundled in his jacket and coat, he heard the tallest of the three give quick orders in Hungarian.

Local thugs.

Tucker shadowed the group as they moved toward the church. One of the three glanced back at him, but Tucker knew what he would see.

A man in his late twenties, taller than average, sandy blond hair worn a little shaggy, walking a dog outfitted in a brown sweater. Tucker hid some of his muscled height by slumping his shoulders and hunching down. His clothing was already nondescript: worn jeans, a battered olive green coat, a wool cap tugged low. He knew *not* to avoid eye contact—that raised as much suspicion as staring. So he merely nodded politely back and showed disinterest.

As the other turned around, Tucker touched his nose and ticked his finger toward the mountain of a man in the middle.

Acquire that one's scent.

Kane had a vocabulary of a thousand words, understood a hundred hand gestures, making the dog an extension of himself. The shepherd trotted forward, sniffing behind the man, close to his heels, nose near the edge of the trench coat.

Tucker pretended to ignore his partner's efforts, staring off across the square.

Once Kane secured what he needed, the dog dropped back and waited for the next command. His ears remained stiff, his tail high, expressing his alertness.

As the trio reached the church, more orders were passed brusquely in Hungarian, and the group split up, spreading out to cover the exits.

Tucker stepped over to a park bench, crouched down next to Kane, and tied the end of the leash loosely around its iron leg but unclipped the other end. He merely tucked it in place behind Kane's collar, making it look as if the dog were secured there.

Next, he slid his fingers under the brown sweater to the camouflaged K9 Storm tactical vest. It was waterproof and Kevlar reinforced. His fingers flicked on the built-in camera and snaked up its fiber-optic lens, smaller than a pencil eraser, hiding it between the dog's pricked ears.

"Stay," he ordered.

Kane sat in the deep shadows of the church, just another dog waiting for the return of its master.

With a final scratch at his partner's ear, ensuring the Bluetooth ear-piece was secure, Tucker leaned forward, bringing his face close to his dog's. It was a ritual of theirs.

"Who's a good boy?"

Kane reached his cold nose forward and touched his.

That's right. You are.

A tail thumped good-bye as Tucker straightened. Turning, he watched the huge man stride toward the church's main entrance with the full confidence of a hunter whose prey had been trapped.

He followed, freeing his modified cell phone—courtesy of the military, as was the tactical vest, both stolen when he had left the service. For that matter, so was Kane. But after what had happened at that village outside Kabul . . .

He shied from that painful memory.

Never again . . .

His whole unit had helped him escape with the dog.

But that was another story.

He switched on the phone, tapped a few icons on the screen. Then a video appeared: of his backside, walking away, the feed coming from Kane's camera.

All was in order.

Tucker pocketed the phone and followed the tall hunter through the doors of the church. Inside, massive spiral pillars held up a cavernous space. All around, the plastered walls displayed a frenzy of brilliant golden frescoes depicting the deaths of Hungarian saints, brought to life by the flickering of candles throughout the nave. Farther down, a series of chapels opened off to the sides, containing a few sarcophagi and a museum of medieval carvings. The entire place smelled vaguely of incense and mildew.

Tucker easily spotted the target, again standing out in her ivory coat. She sat in a pew halfway down the length of the nave, her head bowed.

The hulk of a man took a post near the entrance, leaning against the wall, preparing to wait her out. Clearly, the group was afraid to nab her in front of witnesses and was biding its time before making a move. With the sun almost down and the church emptying out, it would not be a long wait.

Unless Tucker did something about it.

He slipped past the wide bulk of the man, noting the earpiece in his left ear, then continued into the main church. He moved down to the pew where the woman had parked herself and slipped in next to her. She moved a few inches farther down the bench, barely glancing his way. She had taken off her hat and sunglasses in respect for the church. He reached up and did the same with his cap.

Her hair shone like gold in the candlelight. Her eyes, as she glanced at him, were a watery blue. In her hands, she fondled a cell phone, as if unsure whom to call—or maybe she was hoping for a call.

"Do you speak English?" he asked softly.

Even the whisper made her flinch, but after a long pause, she answered curtly, "Yes, but I prefer not to be bothered."

She spoke the words as if she had said them countless times before. Her accent was distinctly British, as was her reserve as she slid a full foot away from him.

He knelt down in the pew, offering a less intimidating pose, bowing his head to his hands as he spoke. "I wanted to warn you that three men are following you."

She tensed, looking ready to bolt.

"I think you should pray," he said, motioning her down.

"I'm Jewish."

"And I'm only here to help you. If you want it."

Again that calculating pause, but she slipped gently to her knees.

He whispered without facing her. "They are watching each door out of here." When she tried to glance back, he tightened his voice. "Don't."

She bowed her forehead to her hands. "Who are you?"

"Nobody. I saw those armed men following you. I saw how scared you looked—"

"I don't need your help."

He sighed. "Okay. I offered."

He began to stand up, knowing he had done as much as his conscience demanded. He couldn't help those who were too proud or stubborn to accept it.

She reached low and pinched the sleeve of his jacket. "Wait." When he settled back to his knees next to her, she asked, "How do I know I can trust you?"

"You can't know for sure." He shrugged. "Either you do or you don't."

She stared at him, and he met her gaze. "I remember you. You were sitting at that patio with a dog."

"*That* you noticed. Not the armed thugs trailing you."

She turned away. "I like dogs. She was pretty."

He smiled into his raised palms, warming up to this woman. "His name is Kane."

"Sorry. Then *he* was handsome." She moved a little closer, sounding calmer. "But what can *you* do?"

"I can get you out of here. Away from them. What you want to do from there is up to you." That was one of his specialties.

Extraction.

She glanced over to him, swallowing hard. "Then please, help me."

He held out his hand. "Then let's get out of here."

"How?" she asked, surprised. "What about—?"

His hand closed over hers, silencing her. Her palm burned like an ember in his. "Just stay close to me."

He drew her back out of the pew, letting go of her hand but motioning her to stay behind him. In his other hand, he held a black KA-BAR fighting knife hidden alongside his leg. He had slipped the blade out of its ankle sheath as he knelt. He hoped he wouldn't have to use it.

He led her away from the main entrance toward a smaller exit on the south side of the church. He glanced sidelong toward the tall man. The hunter was already swinging away, touching his ear, plainly alerting the man guarding this door. Then his hulking form vanished out of sight as he swung around the church to join his comrade. They were likely planning on ambushing her once she stepped outside.

Once he was gone, Tucker abruptly turned, caught the woman around the waist, and swung her around.

"What are you—?"

"Change of plans," he said. "We're going out the other way."

Without letting go of her waist, he hurried her toward the north-facing portal, hoping that the radioed message from the big man was drawing all eyes to the south, expecting her to exit there.

Once at the door, he paused. He held her back and checked his cell phone. Video bloomed to light on the tiny screen. Though the sun had set by now, the view through the night-vision camera was grainy but bright. It showed the plaza and the main entrance to the church as Kane stared toward where his partner had vanished, waiting patiently.

Good boy.

Satisfied, he stepped toward the exit, hoping the guard posted out there had been tricked into retreating to the other side of the church, along with their leader.

And apparently his ruse worked, unfortunately not to his benefit.

The door swung open as Tucker reached for it. The third hunter barged inside, plainly intending to take a shortcut *across* the church rather than *around* it, planning to bring up the rear behind his fleeing quarry.

Both Tucker and the man were equally caught off guard.

Tucker reacted first as the hunter's eyes spotted the woman in the ivory coat and struggled to comprehend how she could be there.

Using that momentary confusion, Tucker lunged and barreled into the man with his shoulder, driving him back out the door and into a narrow dark alley. He slammed him against the brick wall on the far side, driving an elbow into his solar plexus, hard enough for the air to burst from his chest.

The man gasped and slumped, but he had enough wits to paw for a hidden weapon. Tucker spun, swinging his arm with all the strength in his shoulder. He struck the hilt of his KA-BAR dagger against the man's temple—and drove him to his knees, where he fell limply on his face.

Tucker quickly searched him. The woman stepped out, too, smartly closing the door to the church, looking terrified.

For the moment, with the church mostly deserted, no one seemed to note the attack. He confiscated a FÉG PA-63 semiautomatic pistol, used commonly by the Hungarian police and military. He also found an I.D. folder topped with a badge and flipped it open, recognizing the man's face, but not the badge, though it looked official. Across the top it read *Nemzet-biztonsági Szakszolgálat*, and at the bottom were three letters: NSZ.

The woman gasped upon seeing it, recognizing it.

That can't be good.

He stared up at her.

"He's with the Hungarian national security service," she said.

Tucker took a deep breath and stood. He had just coldcocked a member of the Hungarian FBI. What had he gotten himself into? Right now, the only answers lay with this woman.

He knew he didn't want to be found crouched over this unconscious form, especially by the guy's teammates. People still had a tendency to disappear in this former Soviet Bloc country, where corruption continued to run rampant.

And, at the moment, was he on the *right* side of the law or the *wrong*?

As he stood, he studied the scared eyes of the woman. Her fear seemed genuine, based on confusion and panic. He remembered how she had crossed the plaza, offering so open a target. Whoever she was, she wasn't some criminal mastermind.

He had to trust his instincts. One of the reasons he had been paired with Kane was his high empathy scores. Military war dog handlers had a saying—*It runs down the lead*—describing how emotions of the pair became shared over time, binding them together as firmly as any leash. The same skill allowed him to read people, to pick up nuances of body language and expression that others might miss.

He stared at the woman and recognized she was in real trouble.

Whatever was happening was not her fault.

Committed now, he took her hand and headed quickly for a back alley. His hotel was not far off—the Hilton Budapest, right around the corner. Once he got her stashed somewhere safe, he could figure out what was really going on and do something to end it.

But first, he needed more information. He needed ears and eyes in the field—and in this case, a nose, too.

He recovered his cell phone, tapped a button, and radioed a command.

Kane hears the word in his ear, spoken with authority.

"TRACK."

He stands and tugs free of the leash, ignoring the clatter of the clasp on the pavement behind him. He slinks behind the bench to where the shadows will hide him. He lifts his nose to the night, senses swelling outward, filling in the world around him with information beyond mere sight, which is keen enough in the dark.

The ripeness of garbage rises from a pail . . .

The tang of old urine wafts from the stone wall . . .

The smoky exhaust of cars tries to wash through it all . . .

But he stays focused, picking out the one scent he was told to follow. It is a blazing trail through all else: the smell of leather and sweat, the salt of skin, the musky dampness held trapped beneath the long coat as the man walked in front of him.

He follows that trail now through the air as it hangs like a lighted beacon through the miasma of other scents. He hunts along it from the bench to the stone corner, staying to shadows. He watches the prey come running, circling back into view.

He slinks low.

The prey and another man rush past him, blind to him. He waits, waits, waits—only then does he follow.

Belly near the ground, he moves from shadow to shadow until he spots

the prey bent over another man. They pick him up, search around, then head
away.

He flows after them, a ghost upon their trail.

Tucker hurried the woman through the main entrance to the Hilton Budapest. The historic structure was just steps away from the Matthias Church. They had no trouble reaching it unseen.

He rushed her into the lobby, struck again by the mix of modern and ancient that typified this city. The hotel incorporated sections of a thirteenth-century Dominican monastery, integrating a pointed church tower, a restored abbey, and gothic cellars. The entire place was half modern hotel and half museum. Even the entrance they passed through was once the original façade of a Jesuit college, dating back to 1688.

He was allowed a room here with Kane because of a special international military passport that declared the dog to be a working animal. Kane even had his own rank—major, one station higher than Tucker. All military war dogs were ranked higher than their handlers. It allowed any abuse of the dogs to be a court-martial offense: *for striking a superior officer.*

And Kane deserved every bit of his rank and special treatment. He had saved hundreds of lives over the course of his tours of duty. They both had.

But now they had another duty: to protect this woman and discover what they had stumbled into.

Tucker led her across the lobby and up to his guest room: a single with a queen-sized bed. The room was small, but the view looked off to the Danube River that split the city into its two halves: Buda here and Pest across the river.

He pulled out the chair by the desk and offered her a seat, while he perched on the edge of the bed. He glanced to the video feed and saw that Kane continued to track the two men, now carrying their third teammate, groggy and slung between them. The group threaded through a series of narrow winding streets.

He kept the phone on his knee as he faced her. "So maybe now you can tell me how much trouble I'm in, Miss—?"

She tried to smile but failed. "Barta. Aliza Barta." Tears suddenly welled, as the breadth of events finally struck her. She looked away. "I don't know what's going on. I came from London to meet my father—or rather *look for him*. He is a professor at the Budapest University of Jewish Studies."

Aliza glanced back at him to see if he knew the university.

When he could only give her a blank expression, she continued, some family pride breaking through her tears. "It's one of the most distinguished universities of rabbinical studies, going back to the mid-1800s. It's the oldest institution in the world for training and graduating rabbis."

"Is your father a rabbi?"

"No. He is a historian, specifically researching Nazi atrocities, with a special emphasis on the looting of Jewish treasures and wealth."

"I've heard about attempts to find and return what was stolen."

She nodded. "A task that will take decades. To give you some scale, the British Ministry that I work for in London estimates that the Nazis looted $27 trillion from the nations they conquered. And Hungary was no exception."

"And your father was investigating these crimes on Hungarian soil?" Tucker began to get an inkling of the problem here: missing historian, lost Nazi treasures, and now the Hungarian national security service involved.

Someone had found something.

"For the past decade he had been researching one specific theft. The looting of the Hungarian National Bank near the end of the war. A Nazi SS officer—*Oberführer* Erhard Bock—and his team absconded with thirty-six cases of gold bullion and gems valued today at $92 million. According to reports at the time, it was all loaded onto a freighter steaming up the Danube, headed to Vienna, but the party was bombed by fighter planes, and the treasure was jettisoned overboard, near where the Morava River joins the Danube."

"And this treasure was never found."

"Which struck my father as odd, since this theft was so well known, as was its fate. And the mouth of the Morava River is quite shallow that time of year, made even shallower by a two-year-old drought at the time. To my father, it seemed like *someone* would have found those heavy crates before the river mud claimed them."

"But your father had another theory, didn't he?"

Her bright eyes found his. "He thinks the treasure was never removed but hidden somewhere here in Budapest, stashed away until Erhard Bock considered it safe to return. Of course, that never happened, and on his deathbed, Bock hinted that the treasure was still here, claiming it was *buried below where even the claws of the Jewish dead could reach it*."

Tucker sighed. "Like they say, once a Nazi, always a Nazi."

"Then, two days ago, my father left me a cryptic message on my answering machine. Claimed he had made a breakthrough, from a clue he had discovered in some newly restored archive of the university's library, something from the Prague cave."

"The Prague cave?"

A nod, then Aliza explained, "The university library here contains the largest collection of Jewish theological and historical literature outside of Israel. But when German troops marched into the city, they immediately closed the rabbinical university and turned it into a prison. However, just before that happened, the most valuable manuscripts were hidden in an underground safe. But a significant number of important documents—three thousand books—were sent to Prague, where Adolf Eichmann planned the construction of a *Museum of an Extinct Race* in the old Jewish Quarter."

"What a nice guy."

"It took until the eighties for that cache of books to be found in a cave beneath Prague. They were restored to the library here after the fall of communism in 1989."

"And your father discovered something in one of those recovered books."

She faced him, scrunching up her face. "In a *geology* text, of all places.

On the message, he asked for my help with the British Ministry to obtain satellite data. Something my father in Hungary couldn't easily access."

"What sort of data?"

"Ground-penetrating radar information from a US geophysical satellite. He needed a deep-earth scan of the district of Pest on the far side of the Danube."

She glanced out the window toward the river as the spread of the city glowed against the coming night. "After I got that message, I tried calling him for more details, but I never heard back. After twenty-four hours, I got concerned and asked a friend to check his apartment. She reported that his flat had been ransacked, torn apart, and my father was missing. So I caught the first flight down here. I spent the day with the Hungarian police, but they had barely made any headway and promised to keep me informed. When I got back to my hotel room, I found the door broken open, and all my luggage searched, the room turned over."

She glanced at him. "I didn't know what else to do, didn't know who to trust, so I fled and ended up at the square. I was sure someone was watching me, following me, but I thought maybe I was being paranoid. What could anyone want with me? What were they looking for?"

"Did you ever get that satellite information your father asked about?"

Her eyes widened, and her fingers went to the pocket of her coat. She removed a tiny USB flash drive. "Is this what they were looking for?"

"That, and possibly *you*. To use you as leverage against your father."

"But why? Where could my father be?"

Tucker stared down at the cell phone on his knee. The party that Kane tracked had reached a parked sedan beyond the historical district. He saw Kane slow to a stop and slink back into the shadows nearby. The leader was easy to spot, leaning against the hood, a cell phone pressed to his ear.

"Maybe these guys can tell us," he said. "Do you speak Hungarian?"

"I do. My family is from here. We lost most everyone following the deportation of Hungarian Jews to Auschwitz. But a few survived."

He patted the bed next to him. "Then listen to this."

She joined him and stared at the live feed on the screen. "Who is film-ing this?" She leaned closer. "Aren't those the men who were following me?"

"Yes."

She squinted up at him. "How—?"

"I had my dog track them. He's outfitted with a full surveillance pack-age."

His explanation only deepened that pinched look. Rather than elabo-rating in more detail, he simply turned up the speakerphone so the audio from the video feed could be heard. Traffic noises and a whisper of wind ate most of the big man's words, but a few coarse phrases came through clearly.

Aliza cocked her head to the side, listening.

Tucker appreciated the long curve of her neck, the way her lips pursed ever so slightly as she concentrated.

"What are they saying?" he asked.

She spoke haltingly, listening and speaking at the same time. "Some-thing about a cemetery. A *lost* Jewish cemetery." She shook her head as the man ended his call and vanished into the sedan. "He mentioned some-thing at the end. A street. *Salgótarjáni.*"

As the car pulled away, Tucker lifted the phone and pressed the but-ton, radioing to Kane. "Return home. Good boy, Kane."

Lowering the phone, he watched Kane swing around and begin back-tracking his way to the hotel. Satisfied, he turned to Aliza.

"I'm guessing that trio went rogue. Some faction heard about your father's inquiry, about his possible breakthrough in discovering that lost treasure trove. And they're trying to loot what was already looted."

"So what do we do? Go to the police?"

"I'm not sure that's the wisest plan, especially if you want your father back alive."

She paled at his words, but he didn't regret saying them. She had to know the stakes.

"Now that they've lost your trail, they'll run scared." He saw it even on that grainy footage. "The police are already investigating the disappearance of your father. Since they came after you, to use as leverage, that suggests he's still alive at the moment. But now with the police closing in and you nowhere to be found, they'll act rashly. I fear that if they can't get what they want by tonight, they'll kill your father to cover their tracks. Likewise, if he gives them what they want, the end result may be the same."

"So there's no hope."

"There's always hope. They're scared and will be more apt to make a mistake."

And be more dangerous, he added silently. "Then what do we do?"

"We find out where they took your father. That street you mentioned. Do you know where that's located?"

"No. I don't know the city that well."

"I've got a map."

He retrieved it and spread it on the bed.

She leaned next to him, shoulder to shoulder, her jasmine perfume distracting. "Here it is," she said. "*Salgótarjáni* Street."

He ran a finger along the dead-end street. "It lies near the center of Pest, and it looks like it runs adjacent to . . ." He read the name and looked at her.

"Kerepesi Cemetery. Could that be the lost Jewish burial site you heard them talking about?"

"No. I don't see how. Kerepesi is the oldest cemetery in all of Hungary." She shifted her finger closer to the Danube. "This is the Jewish Quarter, where you'll find most of our burial plots. It's a good three miles away from Kerepesi Cemetery."

"Then I'll have to take Kane and check out that street myself."

"It's too dangerous." She touched his arm. "I can't ask you to do that."

"You don't have to ask. If I don't end this, they'll come after me, too. That guy I knocked down in the alley will know you weren't alone. I'd rather not spend the rest of my life looking over my shoulder for a rogue agent from the Hungarian NSZ."

"Then I'm coming with you."

"Sorry. Kane and I work alone. You'll be safer here."

She blocked him when he made a move toward the door. "You don't speak the language. You don't know what my father looks like. And you don't know anything about the city. It's my father's life that's in danger. I'm not going to sit idly by, hoping for the best. That didn't work so well for my people in the past."

She was ready to argue, but Tucker shrugged. "You had me at *You don't speak the language.* Let's go."

Tucker shared the back seat with Aliza as the taxi swept along the arched magnificence of the Chain Bridge as it spanned the Danube. She sat in the middle, between him and Kane. The shepherd spent most of the ride with his nose pushed out the crack in the window, his tail thumping happily.

Beside him, Aliza stroked Kane's shoulder, which probably contributed to much of the tail thumping. At least the presence of the dog had helped calm her. The tension in her body, while still there, had softened a bit. Still, she clutched an old sweater of her father's in her lap, her knuckles pale.

Upon exiting the hotel, they had stopped long enough to collect Kane, who had been dutifully waiting for them outside the entrance to the Hilton. They had also stopped along the way out of Buda to meet with a friend of Aliza's father, one who was willing to sneak into the taped-off apartment and steal an article of clothing from the hamper in the closet. They needed her father's scent. It was a risky move, but apparently no one was watching the place. Still, Tucker kept an eye out for any tail as they left the bridge and headed into Pest, leaving Buda behind.

In another fifteen minutes, they reached the heart of this half of Budapest and skirted past the rolling-park-like setting of Kerepesi Cemetery, with its massive mausoleums, acres of statuary, and hillsides of gravestones.

The taxi rolled to a stop at Salgótarjáni Street, on the border of the cemetery. Aliza spoke a few words of Hungarian with the driver, who'd spent most of the cab ride eyeing Kane with suspicion. Aliza paid him, handing over a couple extra bills for his trouble.

They all piled out and waited for the taxi to leave.

As it pulled away, Aliza turned to him. "What do we do now?"

"We will let Kane take point from here, but first I need to prep him."

Tucker pointed to a dark park bench, well hidden and shadowed by an ancient oak. The entire street ahead looked overgrown and forgotten, densely forested with beech and birch, thick with broad-leaf bushes and tangles of wild roses. A few homes dotted the way, evident from a scatter of lights glowing through the trees. The road itself was crumbled and pitted, long forgotten.

He led her to the bench, and they sat down.

Kane came trotting up to them after lifting his leg on an old stump, claiming this street for himself. Tucker scuffled his scruff and shook the hidden tactical vest, making sure nothing rattled to give the dog away. From here, they needed as much stealth as possible. He thumbed on the camera, raised the lens, and checked the dog's earpiece.

"All suited up, buddy," Tucker said, nuzzling close. "Ready to hunt?"

A savage swipe of his tail answered that. His dark eyes shone in the shadows.

Aliza passed Tucker the wool sweater. Kane had already taken a good whiff of her father's scent, but it never hurt to reinforce it.

"Target," Tucker said as Kane snuffled deep into the woolen garment. As the dog lifted his nose free again, Tucker pointed down the tree-shrouded street. "Track and find."

The dog twisted and took off. In seconds, he vanished into the shadows as if he were never there.

Tucker stood, freeing his cell phone. He had donned his own earpiece and taped on a throat mike to communicate hands-free with the shepherd. In his ear, he heard the dog sniffing and softly panting, the sounds amplified by the sensitive microphones of the surveillance gear.

Trying one last time, Tucker turned to Aliza. "You could wait here. If we find anything—"

She looked tempted but stood up. "I'm right behind you."

He nodded and checked on the stolen FÉG PA-63 pistol tucked into the back of his belt. "Let's see what Kane can find."

They set off down the road. He kept them to the deeper shadows of the overgrown lane, avoiding the pools of light cast by the occasional brick houses. Not that such caution was overly necessary. He heard Kane, and with the aid of the camera, saw through the shepherd's eyes. The dog was as much an extension of his senses as he was a partner.

As they continued, other dogs barked in the distance, perhaps scenting the arrival of Kane. While humans had on average six million olfactory receptors in their noses, hunting dogs like Kane had three hundred million, which heightened their sense of smell a thousandfold, allowing them to scent a target from two football fields away.

Tucker kept one eye on the road ahead and an ear out for any noise behind him. All the while, he monitored Kane's progress as he crisscrossed and pursued any evidence of a scent trail through here. Tucker felt his perception widening, stretching to match that of his dog, blurring the line between them.

He became more keenly aware of Aliza: the smell of her skin, the tread of her heels, the whisper of her breath as it wheezed. He even felt the heat of her body on his back when she hovered close.

On the screen, Kane ran low across the street one more time, circling toward what appeared to be a dead end. There were no homes back here, and the forest seemed to grow thicker and taller, the trees even older. A brick archway appeared, half buried in the woods, its façade cracked and gap-toothed. A rusted black iron gate blocked the way through that archway.

What lay beyond it?

As Kane approached, he swept the edge of the turnaround, staying hidden. A small caretaker's house abutted the archway, evident from the dark windows to one side. When Kane reached the gate, he sniffed along the lower edge—then his body stiffened, nose out, tail back.

The pointed posture silently heralded his partner's success.

Tucker turned and touched Aliza's arm. "Kane found your father's scent up ahead."

Her eyes widened with hope. She stepped forward, ready to move faster, but he held her in check, his fingers tightening on her arm.

"Just stay behind me." He touched his throat mike and subvocalized to Kane. "Good boy. Stand down. Hide."

On the screen, he watched Kane break from his position, wheel away, and slip into the shadows to the right of the archway.

Tucker led Aliza forward. As they reached the end of the road, all seemed quiet. He maneuvered her under a beech tree.

"I'm going to check on the gate," he said. "See if it's locked. You stay hidden until I give you the all-clear."

She nodded, one hand rising nervously to her throat.

He then took Kane's example and edged along the periphery of the turnaround versus going straight across, sticking to the deepest shadows. The moon was bright overhead, casting too much light.

He dropped low and kept out of direct sight of the windows of the cottage that merged with the bricked archway. Without raising any alarm, he reached the gate. He saw no chain and risked reaching out to push one side of the gate, but before he could do so, a twin set of lights—headlamps—blazed from beyond the gate, spotlighting and blinding him.

A familiar gruff voice called out of the darkness; unfortunately, it was in Hungarian. So Tucker decided to ignore it. He whipped to the side, yanking out the FÉG PA-63 pistol, and fired at the headlamps.

Return fire pinged off the gate and chewed into the bricks.

One headlamp blacked out in a shattering *pop* of glass.

Then the car came jamming forward.

Crap.

Tucker danced back out of the archway, diving to the side as the sedan came charging toward him. He shoulder-rolled clear, the gates banging open behind him as the huge black beast came blasting into the turnaround. Gunfire chased him into the forest's edge. He ducked behind the bole of an old oak and caught his breath.

He subvocalized a command to Kane. "Stay hidden."

He planned on doing the same.

Then that Hungarian voice yelled to him, heard above the growl of the idling engine. He risked a glance to the street. The back passenger door was ajar. He saw Aliza being dragged into the glow of the headlamp. The burst of the sedan must have caught her by surprise, the light reaching her hiding spot, exposing her.

The gruff Hungarian with the pocked face held her by the throat, a pistol at her temple. The man tried English this time. "You come now or woman dead!"

With no choice, Tucker stepped into the open, his hands high, the pistol hanging loosely from one finger.

"Toss gun!" he was ordered.

Tucker underhanded it toward the sedan. It skidded under the car.

"Come now!"

Now this should get interesting . . . which was never a good thing.

He joined Aliza, who cast him an apologetic look. He shook his head. Not your fault.

After his body was given a cursory search, he and Aliza were forced at gunpoint toward the archway and the gate, now broken and hanging askew. The sedan backed up behind them, pushing them all forward.

Beyond the brick span, the forest grew even denser, overgrown with ivy and thick ferns. Graves and mausoleums looked tossed about like children's blocks. Many looked broken into, leaving gaping holes in the ground. Other markers had been toppled or leaned drunkenly against one another. Moss and lichen etched the white marble and stone. Mounds of leaf matter and broken deadfall obscured many of the rest.

Tucker glanced to Aliza.

He saw the recognition in her eyes.

The closest gravestone bore a deeply inscribed Star of David.

Here was the lost Jewish cemetery.

They were forced to the side, toward the caretaker's cottage. A small room in back glowed feebly with light seeping past heavy drapes.

As they neared it, a door opened and allowed that blaze to sweep over them.

A stranger stood there, a tall man with a skeletal frame and thick black-rimmed glasses. His eyes swept past Tucker and focused on Aliza.

She stumbled forward, then restrained herself. "Professor Csorba."

So she knew this man.

"*Jó estét*, Miss Barta," he greeted her. "I'm sorry this reunion is under such poor circumstances."

He stepped clear of the doorway.

"Domonkos, bring our two guests inside." The professor's eyes finally found Tucker's face. "I did not imagine the independent Miss Barta would hire a bodyguard. An oversight of mine, but no harm done in the end."

The pock-faced hulk named Domonkos shoved Tucker toward the steps and through the door.

Inside, the cottage room was quaint, with a raw-hewn plank floor covered in thick but worn rugs, heavy wood beams strapped to a low ceiling, and a small hearth glowing with embers.

Tucker was forced against one wall, guarded over by Domonkos. One of the other two thugs took a post by a nearby window. The last vanished down a hall, likely to watch the street outside, ready to respond if the brief firefight drew any unwanted attention.

As he settled against the wall, Tucker smelled a familiar sourness to the air, coming from those shadowy spaces beyond this room. Somewhere back there, a body or two moldered and had begun to stink. Likely the original caretakers.

But not all the bloodshed here was old.

Tied to a chair was an elderly man with a full head of gray hair. His face was bruised, one eye swollen, dried blood running in trails from both nostrils. When Tucker first stepped inside, that remaining eye had blazed with defiance—but no longer, not after the slim figure followed Tucker inside.

"Aliza!" he croaked out.

"Papa!" She rushed forward, collapsing on her knees at his side. Tears were already running down her face. She turned to the man who had greeted her. "How could you?"

"I'm afraid I have ninety-two million reasons why, my dear."

"But you worked with my father for thirty years."

"Yes, ten of those years under communist rule, while your father spent that time in London, raising a family, enjoying the freedom of such a life." The man's voice rang with jealousy and pent-up fury. "You have no understanding of what life was like here, if you could call it that. I lost my Marja because they didn't have enough antibiotics. Then my brave little Lujza, living up to her name as *warrior*, was shot during a protest. I will not see this treasure handed back to the Hungarian government, one little better than before, with many of the same players in power. *Never!*"

"So you will take it for yourself?" Aliza asked, not backing down from his vehemence.

"And I will use it for good, to help the oppressed, to heal the sick."

"And what of my father?" she sobbed. "Will you heal him?"

"I will let him live. If he cooperates, if you do the same."

Fat chance, Tucker thought.

The same doubt shone from Aliza's face.

Csorba held out his palm. "I have contacts enough to know, Aliza, that you have obtained what your father asked. The satellite feed from the Americans."

"Don't do it . . ." her father forced out, though each syllable pained him.

She glanced over to her father, then looked at Tucker.

He recognized she had no choice. They'd search her, punish her, and in the end, they'd get what they wanted.

He lowered his chin, passing on his opinion—but also hiding his throat mike. They had taken his phone, his knife, but hadn't noticed the earpiece shoved deep in his left ear or the thin sensors of the radio microphone taped over his larynx. It was sensitive enough to pick up the slightest subvocalized whisper.

As Aliza handed over the USB flash drive, stirring up excitement in the room, Tucker covered his mouth and whispered quiet commands.

Kane hides in shadow, his heart thunders, his breathing pants quietly.

He remembers the aching blasts, the screech of tires, the spew of oily exhaust. He wanted to run to his partner, to bark and howl and bite.

But he stays in shadow because that was what he was told. Now new purpose fills his ear.

"RETRIEVE MY GUN. HIDE UNDER CAR."

He stares out of the darkness to the moonlit pavement, to the gun out there. He knows guns. He watched it slide under the car when his partner threw it. Then the car left. The gun stayed.

Kane shoots out of the darkness, gliding low. He scoops up the gun, smelling smoke and fire and the whisper of his partner's sweat. He rushes back into darkness, into hiding, but he does not stop. He swerves on silent paws, diving back around. He races through the archway, drawn to the soft putter of a cooling engine, to the reek of burned oil—ready to slide beneath and wait.

But a growl comes from the left.

Shadows break out of the forest, the largest before him. He has smelled the other dogs, along the road, upon the bushes, in the air. They marked this place as their own. He lowers the gun to the dirt. He recognizes the leader by his stiff-legged movements as he stalks forward in the slink of the shadows that share this space. This was their wild land, and they claimed it for themselves.

To help his partner, Kane must make it his own—if only for the night.

With a low growl, he leaps for the largest shadow.

The howl and wails of a savage dogfight echoed eerily through to the cottage. It sounded like something from a prehistoric epoch, full of blood, anger, and survival.

Tucker heard it through his earpiece, too. Kane.

His heart clutched in fear.

Domonkos smiled, drawn by that chorus. He said something in Hungarian that made the one at the window laugh.

Csorba did not lift his face from a laptop he had pulled out of a brief-case. "Wild dogs," he explained as he worked. "They make their home in this forgotten cemetery."

No wonder no one had reacted to Kane's earlier canvass of the place. To those here, he was just another shadowy cur skulking about.

"Dogs!" Csorba continued. "*That* is who you want to hand that great treasure over to, Jakob."

Aliza's father lifted his head enough to glare at the man. Father and daughter clutched hands together. Neither was deceived that they would survive.

"But men in power are more savage than dogs," Csorba continued. "Give them that much gold, and it will fuel a firestorm of corruption and abuse. Many will die. It is better this way."

Tucker had a hard time concentrating through the ongoing chorus of growls and snarling barks—then suddenly the dogfight ended, as swiftly as it started. Holding his breath, he strained to listen for the outcome of that fight, but he heard nothing.

No panted breath, no snuffle, no soft pad of paw.

The continuous and reassuring presence of his dog had gone silent. Had the camera's audio gotten damaged or accidentally switched off dur-ing the fight?

Or was it something worse?

His heart pounded in his throat.

Kane . . .

Csorba rubbed his hands. "At last."

The screen of his laptop filled with an old map of this cemetery, one drawn by hand, even showing the brick archway.

The professor pointed to the screen. "Jakob discovered this map amid old papers that described an interment back in 1888. How gravediggers broke into a cave beneath this cemetery. The Hungarian landscape is full of such natural cavern systems. Even here under Budapest, over two hundred caves—big and small—are found right under our capital, most formed by the natural geothermic activity of this region."

Aliza stirred, her eyes widening. "The dying words of *Oberführer* Erhard Bock. That the stolen gold was *buried below where even the claws of
the Jewish dead could reach it.* He was being literal, referring to a Jewish
cemetery. *Below* a Jewish cemetery."

"How like a Nazi to bury his looted treasure in a Jewish cemetery,"
Csorba said. "Erhard Bock must have heard the stories about this small
cemetery, one well away from the Jewish Quarter, and learned about the
cave beneath it. After burying his treasure, he likely slew anyone who
knew about it, removed all references to it, ensuring the secret would die
with him if he wasn't able to retrieve it later."

Jakob lifted his head, speaking to his daughter. "But he never thought
one of those old books would survive and make its way back to Budapest.
Evil never thinks of everything."

Those last words were directed at Csorba, but they fell on deaf ears.

"Here we go," the professor said.

On the screen, modern satellite data began overlaying the old hand-
drawn map. The ground-penetrating radar was capable of discerning
pockets deep beneath the earth: hidden cellars, bunkers, caves, even entire
cavern systems. Upon the screen, topographic lines revealed the contour
of the cemetery's surface, while darker splotches revealed hidden pockets
below. In the upper left quadrant, an oily blotch grew distinct, underlying
one of the graves marked on the map.

Csorba turned, his face glowing with excitement. "That's it!"

His eyes turned to Domonkos. "Gather your two men, along with
hammers, crowbars, and flashlights. If the treasure is here, we'll have one
night to empty it all into a truck and get it out of Budapest before anyone
grows suspicious."

The big man pointed to Tucker, speaking in Hungarian.

Csorba nodded and answered. Tucker turned to Aliza.

She explained, looking scared. "He says you look strong. That they
might need extra muscle to break open the grave."

And likely it would become his own grave.

Csorba pointed to Aliza. "Tie her down. We will deal with them once
we confirm that the treasure is here."

Aliza's wrists and ankles were quickly bound with plastic ties.

Once she was secure, Csorba lifted a small case, placed it on the desk, and opened it, revealing blocks of yellow-gray C-4 wired with blasting caps. He flicked a switch, and green lights lit up in a row. Csorba turned, speaking in English, plainly for his prisoners' benefit. "This comes courtesy of colleagues of Domonkos at the Hungarian national security service." He lifted a wireless transmitter. "A small gift to help erase our handiwork here, while creating enough chaos to aid our escape out of Hungary."

His gaze fixed to Tucker as he pocketed the transmitter. "And for now, I believe, it shall serve as extra insurance in case you decide to try something foolish. With the press of a button, Aliza and Jakob will make this cemetery their final resting place."

Tucker was shoved toward the door and out into the night. After the brightness inside, the shrouded cemetery seemed infinitely darker. He searched around for Kane.

Had he made it under the sedan with the gun? There was no way of knowing without looking.

He tripped himself and went sprawling flat on his belly, raising a guffaw from Domonkos. On the ground, Tucker searched beneath the sedan's undercarriage. It was dark, but he saw nothing there.

No sign of Kane.

A meaty hand grabbed him and hauled him up. "There are hidden grave markers and stones littered across these fifteen acres," Csorba warned. "It would be easy to crack your head open. So you should best watch your step."

Tucker heard the veiled threat.

Csorba headed out, taking the lead, holding a flashlight in one hand and a handheld GPS in the other.

Tucker followed, trailed by the other men, across the overgrown cemetery. Ivy scrabbled over every surface. Corkscrewed tendrils snagged at his jacket. Broken branches snapped like brittle bones underfoot.

All around, the flashlights danced over shadows and revealed greater threats than old markers on the ground. Yawning black pits began to open around them, half hidden by foliage or stripped over by vines, revealing collapsed or ransacked old tombs.

Threat or not, Tucker decided to take Csorba's words to heart and watched where he placed each foot.

The men chattered excitedly behind him in their native tongue, likely planning how to spend their share of $92 million. The professor moved silently, contemplatively.

Tucker used the distraction to touch his throat mike and try radioing Kane.

Can you hear me, buddy?

Kane crouches amid the shadowy pack.

He bleeds, pants, and stares the others down.

None come forward to challenge. The one who first did slinks forward on his belly with a low whine of submission. His throat still bears the mark of Kane's fangs, but he lives, having known to submit to an opponent who outmatched him. He still reeks of urine and defeat.

Kane allows him to come forward now. They lick muzzles, and Kane permits him to stand, to take his place in the pack.

Afterward, Kane turns. The battle has carried him far from the car, from the gun. As he stares, pondering what to do, a new command fills his ear.

"TRACK ME. BRING GUN. STAY HIDDEN."

With this wild land now his, Kane heads back to where the fight began. He rushes silently through the woods, whispering through bushes, leaping darkness, dodging stone.

But it is not only the land that is his now. Shadows ghost behind him.

He is not alone.

Csorba called out in Hungarian, holding out his GPS.

He had stopped near a flat-topped crypt raised a foot above the ground. Its surface was mostly obscured under a thick mat of leaf detritus and mulch, as if the earth were trying to swallow the tomb up.

Tucker was handed a hammer and a crowbar. He considered how

best to use them to his advantage, but now the professor had a pistol in hand, pointed his way, plainly not planning on getting his own hands dirty. Plus the man still had the wireless transmitter in his pocket. Tucker remembered the frightened look on Aliza's face, the grief shining from her father's.

He could not fail them.

With no choice but to cooperate, Tucker worked with the others. Using hammers, they managed to loosen the lid. Once done, they all jammed crowbars into one side and cranked together on the slab of thick marble, as if trying to pry open a stubborn manhole cover. It seemed an impossible task—then, with a grating *pop* of stone, the lid suddenly lifted. An exhalation of sulfurous air escaped, like the brimstone breath of the devil.

One of the trio made a sign of the cross on his forehead, in some superstitious warding against evil. The others made fun of this action, but only halfheartedly.

Afterward, with some effort, they pushed and shoved and worked the lid off the base of the crypt. Csorba came forward with his flashlight and pointed the beam down. He swore happily in Hungarian. Cheers rose from the others.

Stone stairs led from the lip of the tomb and vanished into darkness below.

They'd found the right tomb. Orders were quickly made.

Tucker was forced to sit on the edge of another crypt, guarded at gunpoint by two of the men. Domonkos and Csorba, both with flashlights in hand, climbed down together to see what lay below, vanishing away, leaving only the glow of their lights shining eerily out of the open tomb.

With nothing to lose, Tucker sat with his arms behind his back, feigning full cooperation. As if mumbling to himself or praying, he subvocalized into the throat mike. "Kane. Keep hidden. Bring gun."

He held his palms open behind him and waited.

He breathed deeply to keep himself calm. He let his eyes drift closed. *C'mon, Kane . . .*

One of the men yelped. He saw the man twirl pointing his pistol toward the woods. A low growl flowed from the forest, a shadow shifted to the left, twigs cracked. Other throats rumbled in the darkness, noise rising from all sides. More shadows shifted.

The two men spoke rapidly in Hungarian, their eyes huge.

It was the cemetery's pack of wild dogs.

Then Tucker felt something cold and wet touch the fingers behind his back. He jumped, startled. He hadn't heard a thing. He reached back there and found fur. Then something heavy was dropped into his palms.

The pistol.

"Good boy," he whispered under his breath. "Stay."

It seemed Kane had won over some friends.

Tucker gently placed the pistol on the tomb behind him. Using the ongoing distraction, he reached blindly back to Kane to investigate the audio glitch. He didn't want to be cut off from his partner any longer.

Especially not now.

He needed this link more than ever.

He toggled the camera off, then on again, rebooting it, praying that was enough.

A moment later, a satisfying squelch of static in his left ear meant all was right with the world.

"All done, Kane. Go back and hide with your friends."

All he heard as Kane retreated was the softest scrape of nail on marble. Within another minute, the forest went quiet again, the pack vanishing into the night.

The two guards shook off their fear, laughing brusquely now that the threat seemed to have backed off, sure they had intimidated the pack away. As Tucker listened to the soft pant of Kane in his ear, he slipped the pistol into his belt and hid it under the fall of his jacket.

And not a moment too soon.

A shout rose from the open crypt. The light grew brighter. Then Domonkos's pocked face appeared and barked new orders, smiling broadly. Tucker could almost see the sheen of gold in his eyes.

Had they actually found the stolen treasure? Tucker was forced to his feet and made to follow Domonkos down into the crypt. He guessed they needed as many able-bodied men as possible to haul up the treasure from below. Tucker mounted the steps, trailed by the other two men.

The narrow stairs descended from walls made of brick to a tunnel chiseled out of natural stone. He lost count at a hundred steps. Conversation had died down as they descended, stifled by the weight of stone above and the dreams of riches below. Soon all Tucker heard was the men breathing around him, their echoing footfalls, and somewhere far below the drip of water.

Good.

At last, the end of the staircase appeared, lit by the glow from Csorba's flashlight.

Reaching the cavern, Domonkos entered ahead of them, sweeping his arm to encompass the space as if welcoming them to his home. He found his voice again and chattered happily to his comrades.

Tucker took a few steps into the space, awed by the natural vault, dripping with water, feathered with thick capes of flowstone and spiked above by stalactites. Tucker wondered how many Jewish slaves *Oberführer* Erhard Bock had worked to death to tunnel into this secret cavern, how many others had died to keep its secret—and as he stared over at Csorba, he wondered how this Jewish scholar could so blithely discount his own heritage and prepare to steal gold soaked in his ancestors' own blood.

Csorba stood next to a stack of crates, each a cubic foot in size and emblazoned with a swastika burned into the wood. He had broken one open, pulled down from the top of the pile. Hundreds of gold ingots, each the size of a stick of butter, spilled across the floor.

Csorba turned, wide-eyed.

He spoke to the others, who all cheered. He even shared the news with Tucker.

"Erhard Bock lied," he said, awe filling his voice. "There are not thirty-six crates here. There are over *eighty*!"

Tucker calculated in his head. That equaled over $200 million.

Not a bad haul if you don't mind murdering some innocent cemetery care-takers, a kindly university professor, his daughter—not to mention yours truly. And who knows how many more.

He'd heard and seen enough.

He slipped out his pistol, raised it, and shot three times.

Three head shots.

Three bodies fell. The last was Domonkos, who sank with the most bewildered expression on his face.

He couldn't bring all four back to the surface by himself.

Too risky.

But he could bring one, the man behind all this.

Csorba stumbled into the crate and yanked his wireless detonator out of his pocket. "Another step and I'll press it."

To see if he'd actually do it, Tucker took that step and another. He saw the man's thumb tremble on the button.

Then, with a wince, Csorba finally pressed it. "I . . . I warned you."

"I didn't hear any explosion," Tucker said. "Did you?"

Csorba pressed it several more times.

Tucker closed the distance, plucked the useless detonator out of his grip, turned it off, and pocketed it. He waved his pistol toward the steps.

"I don't understand . . ." the professor mumbled as he obeyed.

Tucker didn't bother to explain. Once he got hold of the pistol from Kane, he could have shot Domonkos and his two cronies up top, but he feared that if Csorba heard gunfire he might panic and do what he just did—press the transmitter.

So Tucker had to come down here to be certain.

A quarter of the way along the steps, he had lost his wireless connection to Kane. That panting in his ear had died away again. So he was confident Csorba's transmitter, buried four times deeper, would be equally useless—only after knowing that for sure by coming down here did he feel it safe enough to act.

They finally reached the top of the crypt. Csorba tried to bolt for the forest. "Kane, stop him."

Folding out of the woods, a shadow blocked the professor's path, growling, eyes shining in the dark. Others materialized, closing in from all sides, filling the night with a low rumble, like thunder beyond the horizon.

Csorba backpedaled in fright, tripped over a stone, and fell headlong into one of the open graves. A loud *thud* followed, accompanied by a worrisome *snap*.

Tucker hurried forward and stared into the hole. The professor lay six feet down, his neck twisted askew, unmoving. Tucker shook his head. It seemed the ghosts of this place weren't going to let this man escape so easily.

Around him, the dark shadows faded back into the forest, vanishing upon some unspoken signal, until only the whisper of leaves in the wind remained.

Kane came slinking up, fearful he had done wrong.

Tucker knelt and brought his friend's face close to his. "Who's a good boy?"

Kane reached and touched a cold nose against his.

"That's right. You are."

Half an hour later, Tucker sat in the sedan with the broken headlamp, the engine idling. He had freed Aliza and her father and told them all that had happened. He was going to leave it to them to explain as best they could to the authorities, leaving his name out.

Aliza leaned her face through the open window. "Thank you." She kissed him lightly on the cheek. "Are you sure you don't want to stay? If only for another night."

He heard the offer behind her words, but he knew how complicated things would become if he did stay. He had two hundred million reasons why it was time for him to go.

"What about a reward?" she asked.

He pictured Csorba falling into his own grave, snapping his neck.

"There's too much blood on that gold," he said. "But if there's any spare change, I know of some hungry dogs that share this forest. They could use food, a warm place to lay their head at night, a family to love them."

"I'll make it happen," she promised. "But aren't those things what we all want?"

Tucker looked at the stretch of open road beyond the brick archway.

Maybe some day, but not today.

"Good-bye, Aliza." He revved the engine.

Kane's tail thumped heavily on the seat next to him, his head stuck full out the window. As Tucker gunned the engine, a howl burst from his partner, an earsplitting call, singing to his own blood.

The sedan shot forward and barreled out the archway.

Behind them, the forest erupted with a chorus of yowls and wails, echoing up into the night and chasing them out into the world.

As they raced away, the wind blew brochures around the car's interior. It seemed the prior owner had been dreaming of faraway trips, too, ways to spend that gold.

One landed against the windshield and became plastered there crookedly.

The photo depicted palm trees and sandy white beaches.

Its exotic name conjured up another time, a land of mystery and mythology.

Zanzibar.

Tucker grinned, and Kane wagged his tail. Yeah, that'll do.

No Good Deed Goes Unpunished

Igave the New York Times *bestseller Steve Berry one of his first blurbs. He came to me with hat in hand and extolled how much he liked my first novel,* Subterranean, *and asked if I'd read his debut novel for a potential blurb. Now I had been in his same position myself at the start of my career and discovered that authors are a generous lot. Clive Cussler, Doug Preston, and many others had written nice reviews for my early books, so, of course, I happily read Mr. Berry's first novel,* The Amber Room, *and wrote a few glowing words about it.*

Unbeknownst to me, Steve had already sought a review from another author, someone few people had heard about at the time, a guy named Dan Brown, who was about to come out with a book called The Da Vinci Code. *Well, you can guess what happened next. By the time* The Amber Room *was published, Dan Brown's quote was emblazoned across the cover of Steve's book. My blurb was relegated to small print on the back cover, something along the lines of "I like it, too!"*

Since then we've been the best of friends.

Steve and I have even featured each other's characters in our respective novels. So much so, in fact, that for a while people thought we were the same person writing under two different pen names. We eventually had to go on a book tour together to disprove this myth. Since then, at every book-signing event, we've both been asked, "When are you two going to write a story together?"

So, to (somewhat) quiet this clamor, we eventually did just that. For the first time ever, we cowrote a story together, pairing up the main character from Steve's book—Cotton Malone—with the team leader of Sigma, Commander Gray Pierce.

That became "The Devil's Bones."

And yes, even after this pairing, we're still friends.

The Devil's Bones

JAMES ROLLINS AND STEVE BERRY

Commander Gray Pierce stood on the balcony of his suite aboard the luxury riverboat and took stock of his surroundings.

Time to get this show on the road.

He was two days upriver from Belém, the bustling Brazilian port city that served as the gateway to the Amazon—one hour from the boat's last stop at a busy river village. The ship was headed for Manaus, a township deep in the rain forest, where his target was supposed to meet his buyers.

Which Gray couldn't allow to happen.

The long riverboat, the MV *Fawcett*, glided along the black waterway, its surface mirroring the surrounding jungle. From the forest howler monkeys screamed at its passage. Scarlet and gold flashes fluttering through shadowy branches marked the flight of parrots and macaws. Twilight in the jungle was approaching, and fishing bats were already hunting under the overhanging bowers, diving and darting among a tangle of black roots, forcing frogs from their roosts, the soft *plop*s of their bodies into the water announcing a strategic retreat.

He wondered what Seichan was doing. He'd left her in Rio de Janeiro, his last sight of her as she donned a pair of khaki shorts and a black T-shirt, not bothering with a bra. Fine by him. Less the better on her.

He'd watched as she tugged on her boots, the cascade of dark hair, how it brushed against her cheeks and shrouded her emerald eyes. He found himself of late thinking about her more and more.

Which was both good and bad.

A ringing echoed throughout the boat.

Dinner bell.

He checked his watch. The meal would begin in ten minutes and usually lasted an hour. He'd have to be in and out of the room before his target finished eating. He checked the knot on the rope he'd tied to the rail and tossed the line over the side. He'd cut just enough length to reach the balcony directly below, which led into the suite belonging to his target.

Edward Trask. An ethnobotanist from Oxford University.

Gray had been provided a full dossier. The thirty-two-year-old researcher disappeared into the Brazilian jungle three years ago, only to return five months back—sunburnt and gaunt, with a tale of adventures, deprivation, lost tribes, and enlightenment. He became an instant celebrity, his rugged face gracing the pages of *Time* and *Rolling Stone*. His British accent and charming self-deprecation seemed crafted for television and he'd appeared on a slew of national programs, from *Good Morning America* to the *Daily Show*. He quickly sold his story to a New York publisher for seven figures. But one aspect of Trask's story would never see print, a detail uncovered a week ago.

Trask was a fraud.

And a dangerous fraud.

Gray gripped the rope and quickly shimmied down. He found the balcony below and climbed on, taking a position to one side of the glass doors.

He peered through the parted curtain and tested the door.

Unlocked.

He eased the panel open and slipped inside the cabin. The layout was identical to his suite above. Except Trask seemed a slob. Discarded clothes were piled across the floor. Wet towels lay scattered on an unmade bed. The remains of some meal cluttered the table. The one saving grace? It wouldn't be hard to hide his search.

First, he'd check the obvious. The room safe. But he had to be quiet, so as not to alert the guard posted outside. That security measure had necessitated his improvised point of entry.

He found the safe in the bedroom closet and slipped a keycard, wired to an electronic decoder, into the release mechanism. He'd already tested and calibrated the unit on the safe in his cabin. The combination was found and the lock opened. But the safe contained only Trask's wallet, some cash, and a passport.

None of which Gray was after.

He closed the safe and began a systematic exam of the room's hidden corners and cubbies, keeping his movements slow and silent. He'd already reconnoitered his own suite in search of any place that might hide something small.

And there were many possibilities.

In the bathroom he checked the hollows beneath the sink, the underside of drawers, the service hatch beneath the whirlpool tub.

Nothing.

He took a moment and surveyed the tight space, making sure he didn't miss anything. The bathroom's marble vanity top seemed a collage of dried toothpaste, balled-up wet tissues, and assorted creams and gels. From his observations over the past three days he knew Trask only allowed the maid and butler into the room once a day, and even then, they were accompanied by the guard, a burly fellow with a shaved scalp and a perpetual scowl.

He left the bathroom.

The bedroom was next.

A loud *oomph* reverberated from the cabin door, which startled him.

He froze.

Was Trask back? So soon?

What sounded like something heavy slid down the door and thumped to the floor outside.

The dead bolt released and the doorknob turned.

Crap.

He had company.

———

Cotton Malone crouched over the slumped guard. He held a finger to the man's thick neck and ensured the presence of a pulse. Faint, but there. He'd managed to surprise the sentry in a choke hold that took far longer than he expected. Now that the big man was down he needed get him out of the hallway. He'd just arrived on the boat an hour ago at its last stop, so everything was being improvised. Which was fine. He was good at making things up.

He opened the door to Trask's cabin and hauled the limp body by the armpits. He noted a shoulder holster under the guard's jacket and quickly relieved the man of his weapon. He'd not had time to secure a side arm due to the foreshortened nature of this mission. Yesterday, he'd been attending an antiquities auction in Buenos Aires, on the hunt for some rare first editions for his Danish bookshop. Cassiopeia Vitt was with him. It was supposed to be a fun trip. Some time together in Brazil. Sun and beaches. But a call from Stephanie Nelle, his old employer at the Magellan Billet, had changed those plans.

Five months ago, Dr. Edward Trask had returned from the Brazilian rain forest, after three years missing, toting a slew of rare botanical specimens—roots, flowers, leaves, and bark—all for the pharmaceutical company that had funded his journey. He claimed his discoveries held great potential, holding the hope for the next cancer drug, cardiac medicine, or impotency pill. He'd also returned with anecdotal stories for each of his samples, tales supposedly told to him by remote shamans and local tribespeople. Over the intervening months, though, word had seeped from the company that the samples were worthless. Most were nothing new. A researcher for the pharmaceutical firm had privately described the much publicized bounty best. *It was like the bastard just grabbed whatever he could find.* To both save face and protect the price of its stock, the company clamped a gag order on its employees and hoped the matter would just go away.

But it hadn't.

In fact, darker tales reached the US government, as it seemed Trask had not come out of the forest entirely empty-handed. Folded amid his specimens—like a single wheat kernel amid much chaff—lay the real botanical jackpot. A rare flower, still unclassified, of the orchid family, that proved to hold an organic neurotoxin a hundredfold deadlier than sarin.

Talk about a jackpot.

Trask had been smart enough to both recognize and appreciate the value of his discovery. He'd analyzed and purified the toxin at a private lab, paid for out of his own pocket, his book deal and television appearances lucrative enough to fund the project. Part P. T. Barnum, part monster, last week Trask secretly offered his discovery for auction, posting its chemical analysis, its potential, and a demonstration video of a room full of caged chimpanzees, all bleeding from eyes and noses, gasping, then falling dead, the air clogged with a yellow vapor. The infomercial had gained the full attention of terrorist organizations around the world, along with US intelligence services. Malone's old haunt, the Magellan Billet, had been tasked by the White House to stop the sale and retrieve the sample. His mistake had come when he'd mentioned to Stephanie Nelle last week, during a casual conversation between old friends, that he and Cassiopeia were headed to Brazil.

"*The sale will happen in Manaus,*" Stephanie told him yesterday on the phone.

He knew the place.

"*Trask is there with a video crew from the Discovery Channel, aboard a luxury riverboat. They're touring the neighboring rain forest and preparing for a television special about his lost years in the jungle. His real purpose for being there, though, is to sell his purified sample. We have to get it from him, and you're the closest asset there.*"

"*I'm retired.*"

"*I'll make it worth your while.*"

"*How will I know if I found it?*" he'd asked.

"*It's stored in a small metal case, in vials, about the size of a deck of cards.*"

"*I assume you want me to do this alone?*"

"Preferably. This is highly classified. Tell Cassiopeia you'll only be gone a few days."

She'd not liked it, but Cassiopeia had understood Stephanie's condition. *Call, if you need me,* had been her last words as he left for the airport.

Cotton hauled the guard over the cabin threshold, closed the door, and secured the dead bolt.

Time to find those vials.

Movement disturbed the silence.

He whirled and saw a form in the dim light, raising a weapon. Trask was gone. In the dining room. He'd made sure of that before his assault on the sentry.

So who was this?

He still held the gun just retrieved from the guard, which he aimed at the threat.

"I wouldn't do that," a gruff voice flavored with slight a Texas twang said.

He knew that voice.

"Gray friggin' Pierce."

Gray kept his pistol firmly aimed and recognized the southern drawl. "Cotton Malone. How about that? A blast from the past."

He took stock of the former agent in the dim light. Midforties. Still fit. Light brown hair with not all that much gray. He knew Malone was retired, living in Copenhagen, owning a rare bookshop. He'd even visited him there once a couple of years ago. There were stories that Malone occasionally moonlighted for his former boss, Stephanie Nelle. Malone had been one of her original twelve agents at the Magellan Billet, until he opted out early. Gray knew the unit. Highly specialized. Worked out of the Justice Department. Reported only to the attorney general and the president.

He lowered his gun. "Just what we need, a damn lawyer."

"About as bad as having Mr. Wizard on the job," Malone said, lowering his gun too.

Gray got the connection. Sigma Force, his employer, was part of DARPA, the Defense Advanced Research Projects Agency. Sigma comprised a clandestine group of former Special Forces soldiers, retrained in scientific disciplines, who served as field operatives. Where Sigma dealt with a lot of science and a little history, the Magellan Billet handled global threats that delved more into history and little science.

"Let me guess," he said to Malone. "You know about Trask's neurotoxin?"

"That's what I'm here to get."

"Seems we have an interagency failure to communicate. The coaches sent two quarterbacks onto the field."

"Nothing new. How about I go back to Buenos Aires and you handle this?"

Gray caught the real meaning. "Got a girl there?"

"That I do."

An explosion rocked the boat—from the stern, heaving the hull high, tossing them both against the wall. Gray tangled with Malone, hitting something solid, but managed to keep hold of his gun. The blast faded and screams filled the air, echoing throughout the ship.

The riverboat listed to starboard.

"That sounded like someone took this ship out," Malone said as they both regained their balance.

"You think."

The boat continued to list, tilting farther starboard, confirming the hull was taking on water. A glance past the balcony revealed a pall of black smoke wafting skyward.

Something was on fire.

A pounding of boots sounded from beyond the cabin door. A shotgun blast tore through the dead bolt and the door crashed open. Both he and Malone swung their guns toward the smoky threshold. Two men barged inside, dressed in paramilitary uniforms, their faces obscured by black scarves. One carried a shotgun, the other an assault rifle. Gray shot the man with the double-barrel, while Malone took down the other.

"Okay, this is interesting," Malone muttered, as Gray quickly checked the hallway and confirmed only the two gunmen. "Seems we're not the only ones looking for Trask's poison. Were you able to find it?"

He shook his head. "I only had a chance to search half the suite. But it shouldn't take long to—"

Gun blasts popped in the distance.

He cocked an ear. "That came from the dining hall."

"Our visitors must be going after Trask," Malone said. "In case he's got it on him."

Which was a real possibility. He'd already considered that option, which was why he'd gone to great lengths to keep his search of the cabin under the radar. If the effort proved futile, he didn't want to alert Trask and make him extra guarded.

"Finish your search here," Malone said. "I'll get Trask."

Gray had no choice. Things were happening fast and off script. Lawyer, or no lawyer, he needed the help.

"Do it."

Malone raced down the canted passageway, a hand on the wall to keep his balance. He'd not seen Gray Pierce since that day in his bookshop a couple of years ago. He actually liked the guy. There were a lot of similarities between them. Both were former soldiers. Both recruited into intelligence services. Each seemed to have taken care of themselves physically. The big difference came with age, Pierce was at least ten years younger and that made a difference. Particularly in this business. The other contrast was that Pierce was still in the game, while Malone was merely an occasional player.

And he wasn't foolish enough not to realize that also mattered.

He skidded to a stop as he approached the stairs that led down to the riverboat's dining hall. Take it slow from here in. Through a window he surveyed the river outside. The boat sat askew, foundering in the swift current. Past a roil of smoke he spotted a gunmetal gray craft prowling into view. A uniformed man, whose features were obscured by a wrap of black cloth, stood at its stern, the long tube of a rocket-propelled-grenade launcher resting on his shoulder.

Which apparently was how they'd scuttled the boat.

He rounded the landing and double doors appeared below. A body lay at the threshold in a pool of blood, the man dressed as a maître d'. Malone slowed his pace and negotiated the steps with care, approaching the door from one side, and snuck a quick peek into the room.

More bodies lay strewn among overturned tables and chairs.

At least two dozen.

A large clutch of passengers huddled to one side of the spacious room, held at gunpoint by a pair of men. Another two men stalked through bodies, searching. One held a photograph, likely looking for someone who matched Trask's face. Amid the captives Malone spotted the good doctor. Stephanie had provided him an image by email. Trask kept his back to the gunmen, hunching into his dinner jacket, a hand half covering his face, trying to be one among many.

That ruse wouldn't last long.

Trask was strikingly handsome in a roguish way, with unruly auburn hair and sharp planes marring his face. Easy to see how he became a media darling. But those distinct looks should get him flushed out of the crowd and into the assault force's custody in no time.

Malone couldn't let that happen.

So he bent down and patted his palm into the maître d's blood. Not the most hygienic thing in the world, but it had to be done. He painted his face with the bloody palm, then slipped the pistol into the waistband of his pants, at the small of his back, and tugged the edge of his shirt over it.

Why he did stuff like this he'd never know.

He stumbled into view, limping, holding a bloody hand to his fouled face.

"Help me," he called out in a plaintive tone, as he wove a path deeper into the room—only to be accosted by one of the gunman holding the passengers at bay.

Orders in Portuguese were barked at him.

He feigned surprise and confusion though he understood every word—a benefit of the eidetic memory that made languages easy for him. He allowed the man to drive him toward the clutch of passengers. He was shoved into the crowd, bouncing off a matronly woman who was held close by her husband. He shifted deeper into the mass, bobbling his way through until he reached Trask's side. Once there, he slipped the pistol out and jabbed it into botanist's side.

"Stay nice and still," he whispered. "I'm here to save your sorry ass."

Trask flinched and it looked like he was about to speak.

"Don't open you mouth," Malone breathed. "I'm your only hope of getting out of here alive. So don't look a gift horse in the mouth."

Trask stood still and asked, his lips not moving, "What do you want me to do?"

"Where's the biotoxin?"

"Get me out of here, and I'll bloody well make it worth your while."

Typical opportunist, quickly adapting.

"I'm not telling you a thing until you have me somewhere safe."

Clearly the guy sensed a momentary advantage.

"I could just identify you to these gentlemen," Malone made clear.

"I have the vials on me. If even a single one breaks, it'll kill anything and everything within a hundred yards. Trust me, there's no stopping it, short of incineration." Trask threw him a glorious smile of victory. "So I suggest you hurry."

Malone took stock of the four gunmen. The two searchers had about completed their path through the corpses. To better the odds of success he needed them all grouped together. As he waited for that to happen, he decided to press his own advantage.

"Where did you find the orchid?"

The doctor gently shook his head.

"You'll tell me that much, or I'll shoot my way out of here and leave you to them—making sure I'm a hundred yards away fast."

Trask clenched his jaw and seemed to get the point.

They both continued to stare out at the macabre scene.

"Six months into the jungle I heard a rumor of a plant called *Huesos del Diablo*," Trask said, keeping his lips still.

He silently translated.

The devil's bones.

"It took another year to find a tribe that knew about it. I embedded myself into their village, apprenticed myself to the shaman. Eventually he took me to a set of ruins buried in the upper Amazon basin, revealing a vast complex of temple foundations that stretched for miles. The shaman told me that tens of thousands of people once lived there. A vast unrecorded civilization."

Malone had heard of similar ruins, identified via satellite imaging, found deep in the hinterlands of the Amazon, where no one thought people lived. Each discovery defied the conventional wisdom that deemed the rain forest incapable of supporting civilization. Estimates put the number living there at over sixty thousand. The fate of those people remained unknown, though it was theorized starvation and disease were the main culprits of their demise.

But maybe there was another explanation.

The searchers across the dining hall checked the last of the bodies. The two armed men closest to them alternated their attention from their colleagues to their captives.

"Among the ruins I found piles of bones, many of them burned. Other bodies looked like they died where they dropped. The shaman told me the story of a great plague that killed in seconds and wilted flesh from bones. He showed me an unusual dark orchid growing nearby. I didn't know then if the orchid was the source of the plague, but the shaman claimed the plant was death itself. Even to touch it could kill. The shaman taught me how to gather it safely and how to wring the poison from its petals."

"And once you learned how to gather this toxin?"

Trask finally glanced at him. "I had to test it, of course. First on the shaman. Then, on his village."

Malone's blood went cold at the matter-of-fact admission of mass murder.

Trask turned back. "Afterward, to ensure I had the only source, I burned all pockets of the orchids I could find. So you see, my rescuer, I hold the key to it all."

He'd heard enough.

Stick to my side, he mouthed.

He eased toward the edge of the crowd, towing Trask in his wake. Once there, Malone knew he had to incapacitate the four armed men as quickly as possible. There'd only be a few seconds of indecision. The men were finally gathered in a group. Seven rounds remained in his gun's magazine. Not much room for error. He eyed an overturned table with a marble top that should offer decent cover. But he needed to be away from the civilians before the shooting started.

He gripped Trask by the elbow and motioned to the table. "Go with me. On my mark."

He did a fast three count, then sprinted toward the table, swinging his gun into view—only to have the floor beneath his feet jolt, throwing him high. He flew past the table, crashing hard, losing his grip on the gun, which skittered across the floor out of reach. He rolled to see the front of the dining hall tear away, glass exploding, the walls splintering open.

Dark jungle burst inside.

Then he realized.

The boat had hit shore and run aground.

Everybody had been knocked off their feet, even the gunmen. He searched for Trask. The botanist had been tossed amid the assault team. Trask straightened up and even the blood gushing from a broken nose failed to hide his features. Surprised voices erupted from the four gunmen. Rifles were pointed and Trask lifted his arms in surrender.

Malonee searched for the pistol, but it was gone.

Trask glanced in his direction, the fear and plea plain in his face.

The man's thoughts clear. *Help me. Or else.* Malone shook his head and brought a finger to his lips, signaling silence, the hope being that the doctor would realize selling him out was not a good idea.

One of them had to be free to act.

Trask hesitated, was jerked to his feet, but said nothing.

A parrot screamed across the ruins of the dining hall, cawing, seemingly voicing Malone's frustration.

And he could only stare as Trask and his captors vanished into the dark bower of the jungle.

Gray stared across the ruins of the dining hall, studying the dark jungle beyond a gash in the walls. "So you lost him."

"Not much I could do," Malone said, on his knees, searching amid a tumble of chairs and tossed tables. "Especially after the boat ran aground."

Trask's cabin had come up empty. But Gray now knew that the doctor had the sample hidden on him. He'd also listened as Malone reported everything else Trask had said.

Malone reached under a tablecloth and came up with a pistol he'd lost earlier. "Lot of good it does me now. What's our next move?"

"You don't have to stay on this. You're retired. Go back to your lady in Buenos Aires."

"I wish I could. But Stephanie Nelle would have my ass. I'm afraid you're stuck with me. I'll try, though, not to get in the way."

He caught the sarcasm.

So far, this brief partnership between Justice and Defense had proved fruitless. But with Trask captured by a guerrilla force, as much as Gray hated to admit it, he could use the help.

Malone picked his way across the dining hall to the demolished wall of the ship. Gray watched as the former agent bent down and examined something. All the other passengers were gone, being off loaded to other boats.

"Got a blood trail here."

He hustled over.

"Has to be Trask," Malone said. "He broke his nose when the ship crashed. It was bleeding badly."

"Then we follow it."

"I saw a patrol boat earlier. They could have offloaded him by river."

"I spotted that craft, too, from the cabin. But it took off shortly after we went aground. The attack, the fire, the crash . . . It's drawn lots of river traffic."

"You think the ground team and the boat are planning a rendezvous farther along the Amazon? Where there are fewer eyes to see them?"

"It makes sense. And that gives us a window of opportunity."

"A small one, which is shrinking fast." Malone pointed to the drops of blood, scuffed by the boot of one of the guerrillas. "Once in the jungle, it'll be hard to track in the dark."

"But they're in a hurry," Gray said. "Not expecting anyone to follow. And they'll have to stay close to the riverbank, waiting for their ride. With four men and a prisoner in tow, they should leave an easy trail."

Which proved true.

Minutes later, slogging across the muddy bank, Gray saw that it wasn't difficult to spot where the guerrillas had pushed into the forest. He glanced back at the beached riverboat, its bulk angled in the river, the stern still billowing black smoke into the twilight sky. Other watercraft had now come to its rescue. Passengers were being ferried away as the fires aboard spread.

He turned from the smoking ruins of the MV *Fawcett*.

The boat had surely been named after the doomed British explorer, Percy Fawcett, who vanished in the Amazon searching for a mythical lost city. Gray faced the dense jungle, hoping the same fate didn't await them.

"Let's go," he said, leading the way.

Less than ten feet into the dense vegetation the forest snuffed what little light remained. Night shrouded them. He limited any illumination to a single penlight, which he shone ahead, picking out boot prints in the muddy mulch and broken stems on the bushes. The trail was easy to track but hard to traverse. Every vine was armed with thorns. Branches hung low. Thickets were as convoluted as woven steel.

They forged onward, moving as quietly as possible. A growing raucous of the night forest helped mask their advance. All around them were screams, buzzes, howls, and croaking. The shine of the tiny light also caught eyes staring back at them. Monkeys huddled in trees. Parrots nesting atop branches. A pair of larger pupils—like yellow marbles with black dots—glowed.

Maybe a jaguar or a panther.

Which wasn't good.

After forty minutes of careful advancing, Malone whispered, "To the left. Is that a fire?"

Gray stopped and shaded his penlight with his palm. In the blackness, he spotted a flickering crimson glow through the trees.

"They made camp?" Malone whispered.

"Maybe waiting for full night before making a break for the river and their boat."

"If it's them at all."

Only one way to find out.

He flicked his flashlight off and continued toward the glow, noting that the path they were following led in that direction, too. Twenty minutes of careful prodding were needed to close the distance. They halted in a copse of vine-laden trees, which offered cover and a vantage point to spy upon the camp.

Gray surveyed the clearing.

Mud-and-thatch huts indicated a native village. He spotted a clutch of children and a handful of men and women, including a wizened elder who cradled an injured arm. All were held at gunpoint by one of the guerrillas from the boat. The campfire must have attracted their attention, too. He spotted Trask, on his knees, by the flames. One of the guerrillas leaned over him, clearly shouting, but the words could not be heard. Trask shook his head, then was backhanded for his stubbornness, sprawling the doctor to the ground. Another of the assailants came forward, balancing a small metal case on his open palm. His captors must have searched Trask and found the vials. The faint glow of LED lights could be seen on the case.

"Locked with an electronic code," Malone said.

Gray agreed. "Which they're trying to learn from Trask."

"And I can tell you, from our little conversation, he's going to drive a hard bargain."

He counted the same four guerrillas, each heavily armed. The odds weren't good. Two to one. And any firefight risked harming or killing the villagers.

A new group appeared at the village's western edge, filing out of a worn trail that likely led to the river.

They numbered another six, along with a seventh who stood taller than the others and unwrapped the black cloth from his face. A deep scar ran down his left cheek, splitting his chin. He barked out orders, which were instantly obey.

This one was in charge.

"That's not good," Malone said.

No, it wasn't. Two to one just became five to one.

The newcomers were also heavily armed with assault rifles, grenade launchers, and shotguns.

Gray realized the futility of their situation.

But Malone seemed unaffected. "We can do this."

Malone watched as the assault force leader yanked Trask to his feet and pointed west, toward the river, where the boat was likely waiting.

"We can't let them get to the water," he said. "Once they've cleared the village, we can use the jungle to our advantage."

"Guerrilla warfare against guerrillas." Pierce shrugged. "I like it. They teach you that in law school?"

"The navy."

Pierce smiled. "With any luck, maybe in the confusion we can grab Trask and the vials."

"I'll settle for the vials."

Their targets left the village.

They kept low, running parallel. Interesting how their quarry was making no effort to move quietly. Orders were barked in loud voices, the crunch of boots and snap of branches clearly announcing a retreat toward the river. The entourage moved as if in total command of their surroundings— which, in a sense, they were. This was home field for them. But that didn't mean the visiting team couldn't score a few points every once in awhile.

They neared the village clearing and Malone noted two of the gunmen had remained behind, assault rifles still trained on villagers.

A problem.

It seemed the guerrillas intended to leave no witnesses behind. He caught Pierce's attention, pantomimed what they should do, and received a nod of acknowledgment. They closed the last of the distance at a run, bursting into the clearing, appearing in an instant behind the two gunmen.

A shot to the chest and Malone dropped one.

Pierce killed the other.

The pistol blasts were loud, echoing into the forest.

Malone skidded on his knees and caught the assault rifle as his target collapsed. Pointing it toward the sky he strafed a fierce blast at the stars. He hoped the initial pistol shots accompanied by the rifle fire would be taken by the retreating guerrillas as the village's bloody cleanup.

Pierce motioned for the locals to stay calm and not spoil the ruse. The elder nodded, seeming to understand, and waved the others down, ensuring that mothers kept frightened children quiet, signaling the men to gather what they could in preparation to flee.

Pierce holstered his SIG Sauer and gripped one of the guerrilla's rifle. Malone followed that example. He spotted a grenade launcher resting on the ground near one of the bodies. He considered taking it, too, but it would likely only burden him in the confines of the jungle. The rifle and his pistol would have to do.

They fled toward the trail taken by the guerrillas.

Thirty yards in the shadowy form of a guerrilla blocked their path. Someone must have been sent back to make sure the village was secure. Before they could react, the man opened fire, shredding leaves and sending them diving into the vegetation.

Malone rolled behind the bole of a tree and twisted in time to see the muzzle flash of Pierce's returned fire.

Not bad. Fast response.

The guerrilla was thrown backward, his chest blown out as bullets bit into flesh.

The body thudded to the ground.

"Keep going," Pierce said. "Let's try to stay on their flanks."

Malone bit back a groan of complaint from his sore knees. Jungle warfare was definitely a younger man's game.

But he could handle it.

He plunged ahead.

Gray kept track of Malone's progress, matching the pace. What they needed was any boat waiting for the group to be out of commission. Unfortunately, they were a little shorthanded and would have to handle the situation once there.

He continued through the forest, paralleling the path taken by the guerrilla force. He to one side of the trail, Malone to the other, out of sight. A slight wind coursed through the trees. Its direction appeared away from the river, inland. Shouts from ahead brought him to a stop. First in Portuguese, then English.

"Show yourself, or I kill your man."

Gray edged forward and crouched low.

A deadfall opened ahead, where one of the canopy trees had recently fallen tearing a hole in the forest. Starlight bathed the open wound, revealing the leader of the guerrillas. He held aloft the small steel case, its LED display still glowing. Another of the guerrillas nestled the muzzle of an assault rifle to the back of Trask's skull. Gray cared nothing for the doctor's life. Malone had shared what he'd learned as to how Trask had obtained his prize and at what cost. All that mattered was securing the toxin before it escaped to some foreign enemy's manufacturing lab, where it could be mass-produced.

"Come out now, or I kill him," the leader shouted.

From the edge of the deadfall, another pair of gunmen appeared.

Only then did Gray realize his mistake.

Your man.

Prodded at gunpoint, a second prisoner was thrust into view, gagged, his face bloody.

Malone.

Malone kept his fingers folded atop his head. He'd been ambushed shortly after parting company with Pierce. A shadow had loomed behind him, clamping a hand over his mouth, an arm around his throat. Then a second figure slammed the butt of a rifle into his gut, dropping him to the ground. Dazed, he'd been gagged with one of their face scarves and thrust forward at gunpoint. He now stared out at the dark forest, willing Pierce not to show himself.

Unfortunately his silent plea was not answered.

Twenty yards away Pierce appeared, rifle high over his head, surrendering.

One of his captors shoved Malone forward.

Pierce caught his gaze as he staggered near and mouthed, *Be ready to run.*

Gray stepped past Malone and shouted, "I surrender," which gained the guerrilla leader's full attention.

He tossed the assault rifle away, twisting slightly. As expected, all eyes followed the weapon's trajectory across the deadfall. He quickly dropped an arm to his waist, yanked out his SIG Sauer, and shot from the hip, taking out the two closest gunmen.

Now for the real prize.

He aimed at the leader and fired.

Instead of a clean kill, the round pierced the man's outstretched hand, smacking into the steel case, then penetrated the chest. A yellowish mist burst instantly outward, swamping those nearby. He remembered Malone's relating the botanist's warning. *If even a single vial breaks, it'll kill anything within a hundred yards.*

The cloud spread.

Screaming began.

He backpedaled as the breeze caught the cloud and blew it toward him. Malone, still gagged, didn't have to be told twice and bolted for the trailhead. Gray turned to follow—only to see a figure emerge from the toxic cloud.

Trask.

His face appeared parboiled, eyes weeping and blind. Another few steps and a convulsion jackknifed through every muscle, throwing the body off balance and to the ground.

Couldn't happen to a nicer guy.

Gray turned and sprinted after Malone. The windblown danger rolled after him. He glanced back at the spreading devastation. Monkeys fell from tree limbs. Birds took flight only to cartwheel to the ground. Anything that crawled, slithered, or flew seemed to instantly succumb. He caught up with Malone and together they fled down the last of the trail and burst into the village clearing.

Which unfortunately wasn't empty.

The locals were still there, having not yet evacuated. Children darted behind mothers' legs, frightened by their sudden reappearance, thinking perhaps the guerrillas had returned. Matters weren't helped by the fact that Malone was bloody and gagged. Gray drew to a halt and swung around to face the trail. Above the canopy, a flurry of bats spun and darted, beginning their nightly forage for insects. Then they began to drop from the sky—at first, farther out, then closer.

Death swept toward them, carried by the wind.

He turned to the villagers and saw frightened faces. None of them, himself included, would ever be able to run fast enough to escape the cloud.

His errant shot had doomed them all.

Malone searched for their only hope, again skidding to his knees and snatching up the RPG launcher.

A quick check confirmed the weapon was loaded.

Thank god.

"What are you doing?" Pierce yelled.

No time to explain.

He hoisted the tube to his shoulder, aimed for the trailhead, and fired. The weapon jolted against his face, spitting out smoke behind him. A grenade whistled in a tight arc then blasted down the throat of the trail.

A fiery explosion lit the night.

Trees erupted in a smoldering rain of limbs and leaves.

Heat washed over him. Was it enough? Trask's words echoed in his head. *When it comes to this toxin, there is no cure, no decontamination. Except incineration.*

Malone tugged the gag free.

Fire spread outward from the blast site. Flames danced high into the night. Smoke billowed upward, masking the stars, consuming all the air around it, which hopefully included the toxin. He held his breath, not that it would save him if the cloud reached here. Then, from the edge of the forest, a dark shape burst into view, a shred of a living shadow. A panther. Yellowed claws dug deep into the dirt. Dark eyes reflected the campfire's glow. The big cat hissed, showing fangs—then burst to the side, diving back into the dark bower.

Alive.

A good omen.

He waited another minute. Then another.

Death never came.

Pierce joined him, patting his shoulder. "Nice tag team on that one. And damn quick thinking, old man."

Malone lowered the weapon.

"Who you callin' old?"

Two Heads Are Better Than One

The prior story was not my first attempt at cowriting a project. That disputable honor went to an author of indisputable talent, Rebecca Cantrell.

I had first met Rebecca at a writers' retreat associated with the Maui Writers Conference. I was leading a small group of authors during that week-long retreat and encountered a young writer who was plainly skilled and was already about to be published. She was clearly so talented that I even leaned on her as I taught that class. Afterward we stayed in contact, and the first book in her Hannah Vogel mystery series (A Trace of Smoke) was shortly published to great acclaim.

Years passed, and as I was wont to do, I discovered a new story while staring at Rembrandt's painting The Raising of Lazarus. It was a new take on vampirism and the Catholic Church. The idea became stuck in my head, and I could not shake it loose. Eventually, I did some research, built a whole mythology, along with a pantheon of characters. The only problem: I didn't think this was a story that I could do true justice to by myself. It wasn't entirely in my wheelhouse. I felt confident I could bring the creatures to life on the page, even build a roller coaster of a plot full of sudden drops and unexpected twists, but this story also needed a rich, gothic quality that would be difficult to manage on my own.

Recognizing this, I called Rebecca. I knew she had the skill set to help bring this story to its best light and asked her if she would be willing to work on this project with me.

She asked, "What's it about?"

I said, "Vampires."

She responded, "Absolutely not."

Then I slowly stated my case, sharing the history—both canonical and supernatural—along with its cast of characters. She was slowly won over, and we began working on this series together. Neither of us had cowritten a book before, so it was a learning curve on both our parts. We quickly realized that one of the best aspects of a joint project was that you had two minds to draw upon. We could challenge each other, solve problems that confounded the other, commiserate together in the trenches. It was hard, but magical in its own way. I believe the end result was something better than either of us could have produced on our own.

To give you a taste of that collaboration, the next two stories tie into the first two novels in that vampiric series. "City of Screams" is a ghostly tale that precedes the first book in the Sanguines series, The Blood Gospel. The short story introduces one of the series' main characters in a solo adventure set amid the haunted ruins of war-torn Afghanistan. The second story—"Blood Brothers"—more directly introduces vampires and delves into how the past haunts the present.

City of Screams

JAMES ROLLINS AND REBECCA CANTRELL

October 23, 2:09 P.M.
Kabul, Afghanistan

It started with the screams.

Sergeant Jordan Stone listened again to the snippet of an SOS that had reached the military command in Kabul at 4:32 that morning. He rested his elbows on the battered gray table, his palms pressing the oversize headphones against his ears, trying to draw out every clue the recording might offer.

A lunch of lamb kebabs and local lavash bread sat forgotten, though the smell of curry and cardamom still permeated the air, contributing to the nausea he felt as he listened. He sat alone in a small, windowless room at the Afghan Criminal Techniques Academy, a one-story nondescript building at the edge of Bagram airport outside Kabul.

But his mind was out there, lost in that firefight recorded on tape.

He strained, his eyes closed, listening for the fourteenth time.

First screams, then a spatter of words:

They're coming again . . . helpushelpushelpus . . . !

The sound faded in and out, but that did nothing to hide the terror and panic of those simple words.

Next came gunfire—frantic, sporadic, uncontrolled, echoing around—interspersed by more chilling screams. But what raised the small hairs on the back of his neck was the silence that followed, dead air as the radio continued to transmit. After a full two minutes, a single phrase rasped forth, distorted, unintelligible, as if the speaker's lips were pressed close enough to brush the microphone. That intimacy more than anything set his teeth on edge.

Jordan rubbed his eyes, then pulled the headphones from his ears. Plainly the situation out there had ended badly in the wee hours of the morning. Hence the need for Jordan's team to be summoned. He and his men worked for JEFF, the Joint Expeditionary Forensic Facility, out of Kabul. His team served as crime scene investigators for the military: gathering evidence from insurgent suspects, examining and testing homemade bombs, tearing down mobile phones found at battlefield sites or ambushes. If there was a mystery, it was their job to solve it.

And they were good at what they did. They'd solve this one, too.

"I've got more intel," Specialist Paul McKay said as he entered and plopped down into a metal chair. It squeaked under his weight. The man stood a head taller and a belly wider than Jordan, and he knew his business, recruited out of an Explosive Ordnance Division. Smart and unflappable. "That recording came from an archaeological team up at Bamiyan Valley. Four men and a woman. All Americans. Command sent a team of rangers to secure the scene. We've got an hour to figure out what we can here, then we're supposed to follow them out into the field."

Jordan nodded. He was used to the pressure, liked it even. It kept him running, kept him from thinking too much. "I'm going to work on this message. You and Cooper get a full murder kit together and meet me at the chopper."

"You got it, Sarge." McKay tossed him a quick salute and hurried out.

Jordan listened to the mysterious phrase at the end of the message again, then called in translators. That didn't help. None of them could even tell him what language it might be; not even the local Afghanis recognized it. A few claimed that it wasn't human at all, but some kind of animal.

Someone quickly tracked down a British historian and archaeologist, Professor Thomas Atherton, who had been working with the team in Bamiyan, and brought him to Jordan. A fit and sturdy scholar in his early sixties, the archaeologist had come to Kabul two days before to have a broken arm set. As the historian listened to the screams, he grew pale. He ran one hand through his well-trimmed gray hair.

"I think that's my team, but I can't be certain. I've never heard them scream like that." He shuddered. "What could make them scream like that?"

Jordan handed him a Styrofoam cup of water. "We have a chopper full of rangers on their way to help them."

The professor looked like he knew such aid would arrive too late. He adjusted his wire-rimmed glasses on his narrow nose and said nothing. When he lifted the cup, his hand trembled so much that water spilled onto the desk. He set the cup back down, his cast clunking against the table.

Jordan gave him a minute to pull himself together. Listening to his colleagues' deaths had hit him hard, a natural reaction.

"That last phrase." Jordan rewound the recording to that final whispery phrase. "Do you know what language it is?"

He played it again for Atherton.

A muscle under the professor's eye twitched. "It can't be."

He gripped the edge of the table with both hands, as if he expected it to fly away. Whatever it was, it unnerved him more than the screams had.

"Can't be what?" Jordan prompted.

"Bactrian." The professor whispered the word. His knuckles whitened as he tightened his grip on the table.

"Bactrian?" Jordan had heard of Bactrian camels, but never a Bactrian language. "Professor?"

"Bactrian." The professor stared at the headphones as if they were lying to him. "A lost language of Northern Afghanistan, one of the least known of the Middle Iranian dialects. It hasn't been spoken since . . . for centuries."

Strange.

So someone had attacked a group of archaeologists—then left a message in an ancient language. Or had the message come from a survivor? Regardless, to Jordan, that didn't sound like a standard insurgent attack. "Can you tell me what it means?"

The professor didn't lift his eyes from the table when he answered. "The girl. It means the girl is ours."

Even stranger.

Jordan shifted in his chair, anxious. Were those final words a threat? Did they indicate that one of the archaeology team—a woman—was still alive, maybe being held hostage or tortured? A few years ago he might have wondered who would do such a thing, but now he knew. When it came to dealing with Taliban forces or the isolated tribesmen, nothing surprised Jordan anymore.

And that worried him.

How had a farm boy from Iowa ended up in Afghanistan investigating murders? He knew he still looked the part, with his wheat-blond hair, clear blue eyes, his square-jawed face. No one needed to see the Stars and Stripes sewn onto the shoulder of his fatigues to know he was American. But if you looked closer—at the scars on his body, at what his men called his thousand-yard stare—you'd see another side of him. He wondered how well he would fit in those cornfields of his former home. If he could ever go back.

"How many women were there at the site?" Jordan asked.

The door opened and McKay poked his head in, a finger pointed at his wrist.

Time to go.

Jordan held up one hand, telling him to wait. "Professor Atherton, how many women were at the site?"

The professor stared at him a long second before answering. "Three.

Charlotte. I mean, Dr. Bernstein, from the University of Chicago; a local woman who cooked for us; and her daughter. A little girl. Perhaps ten?"

Jordan's stomach churned, upset at the thought of a little girl caught in what sounded like a massacre. He should have felt outrage, too. He searched for it, but found only disillusionment and resignation.

Am I that hardened?

October 23, 4:31 P.M.
Bamiyan Valley, Afghanistan

Jordan stared out the chopper's window at the bowl-shaped valley below. Framed by snow-dusted mountain ranges to the north and south, the entire valley stretched thirty miles long, an oasis of farmlands and sheep ranches nestled between the tall, stony peaks of the Hindu Kush. Though only a short hop by helicopter over the mountains, the city of Kabul seemed a million miles from this isolated valley.

They circled the empty village where the archaeologists had set up their camp. The village was little more than a small cluster of a dozen mud-brick buildings, some with thatched roofs, others topped by rusted metal, a few open to the snowy sky. It didn't look as if anyone had lived there for a long time before the archaeologists moved in.

Snow fell around them, thick, fluffy flakes that were collecting on the ground and obscuring any evidence. Jordan shifted impatiently in his seat. If they didn't get there soon, he might not be able to do any good. Plus with the sun to set in the next half hour, they were about to run out of daylight.

They landed, and he and his team, now including Professor Atherton, hiked to the location identified by the rangers as the murder site. Jordan had brought the professor along in case they needed a Bactrian translator.

Or someone to identify the archaeologists' bodies. He hoped the professor was up to the task. The guy had been getting twitchier the closer they got to the site. He'd started picking at the rim of his cast.

Jordan paced carefully around the edges of the gruesome crime scene.

Thickening snow and careless feet had already disturbed the details of the crime, but they failed to hide the blood.

There was too much of it: splashed against crumbling stone walls on either side of the hard-packed dirt street, dragged into a rusty-red path out of the village. The wide smear looked like the thumbprint from a bloody god. It seemed that same god had stolen the bodies, too, leaving only evidence of a recent massacre.

But where were the victims taken? And why?

And how?

He stared at the heavy flakes that fell from a darkening gray sky. They had only scraps of daylight left.

"Treat the entire village as a crime scene," he instructed his two teammates. "I want it all secured. And I don't want anyone else setting foot in here until we're done."

"Closing the barn door after the horse is out?" McKay stamped his feet against the cold and tugged his cold-weather gear more tightly over his wide shoulders. He pointed to a boot print that marred a pool of blood. "Looks like someone forgot to take their shoes off."

Jordan recognized the tread mark of a US-military-issue boot. This unfortunate contamination of the crime scene must be the result of the ranger team who had locked down this valley in the preceding hours, securing the area for the arrival of Jordan's team.

"Then let's take a lesson and keep our own steps light from here," Jordan warned.

"Got it. Light as a feather," his second teammate acknowledged. Specialist Madison "Mad Dog" Cooper clapped a large black hand atop McKay's shoulder and patted his friend's ample stomach with the other. "But that might be a problem for McKay here. Back in Kabul, he's been spending more time in the chow line than at the gym."

McKay shoved him away. "It's not about weight. It's about technique."

Cooper snorted. "I'll take the north side. You cover the south."

McKay nodded, hiking his pack higher on his shoulder and freeing his digital Nikon camera, ready to begin photographing the site. "First one back with a real clue buys the next round when we hit stateside."

"Like you need another beer in that gut of yours," Cooper said, waving him off.

Jordan watched them head off in different directions, following protocol, preparing to canvass the periphery of the town for tire tracks, footprints, abandoned weapons, anything that could identify the perpetrators of the attack. His two men were each trailed by an Afghani police officer—one was named Azar; the other, Farshad—both trainees from the Afghan Criminal Techniques Academy.

Jordan knew the banter of his two teammates masked their uneasiness. He read it in their eyes. They didn't like this situation any better than he did. A bloody crime scene with no bodies smack in the middle of nowhere.

"Why would anyone live up here?" he mumbled, not expecting an answer but getting one.

"It may be that very isolation that first drew the Buddhist monks to this valley," Professor Atherton said behind him. Jordan had practically forgotten that he was there.

"What do you mean?" Jordan unpacked his video camera. If the snow kept up, these pictures might be all they had to go on later. He drew a grid in his head and walked to the edge. He took off his gloves so he could work the camera. "Stay behind me, please, and out of the crime scene area."

Atherton took a long draw of breath through his pinched nose, eyes darting from side to side as if afraid to settle on a single detail. When he spoke, his voice came out in a high-pitched rush. "This entire valley was revered by the Buddhists. They developed a vast monastic complex, digging out meditative caves and tunnels in the cliffs. Some of the world's first oil paintings still decorate those cave walls."

"Mmm-hmm." Jordan switched the camera to low light. He wanted to get every detail he could.

The professor turned from the valley to the cliffs and continued with what sounded like an oft-delivered speech, slipping into a monotone. "Monks sculpted colossal statues of Buddha out of the cliff faces centuries ago. If you squint, you can still see the niches that once housed them."

Jordan stared at the distant yellow cliffs and could make out the dark pocks marking tunnel and cave openings, along with giant archways, the niches of which the professor spoke.

"The Buddhas the Taliban destroyed back in 2001," Jordan said, remembering the international outcry.

"Sadly true. They came with tanks and bombs and blew up the famous statues, declaring them an insult to Islam." The professor kept his eyes fixed to the faraway cliffs, clearly trying not to look at the blood surrounding him. Blood that could have been his. He talked more, his voice never changing from its even pitch. Jordan was starting to find it a little creepy. "All that's left of the former colossi are those empty niches, holding rubble. It's as if this valley is cursed."

Jordan noted the professor's attention had turned from the cliffs to a tall hill that overlooked the tiny village and shadowed this crime scene. He could make out bits of stone walls, pieces of ancient parapets, and sections of towers. It reminded him of a child's sand castle that had been kicked over and left to the elements. The surface had been worn down by rain and wind and snow, until the entire edifice had dissolved into a misshapen version of itself, crumbled back to sand and rock, with only hints of its past still showing.

"If this valley is indeed cursed," Atherton continued, "there's the source. The Muslims named this set of ruins Mao Balegh, which means Cursed City." Curiosity piqued in Jordan at his words, along with a trickle of dread. Something about the place unnerved him—and few things made him uneasy. "What happened to it?" He kept filming. He might as well get more background information from the professor while he was at it.

"Betrayal and massacre. But, like many such stories, it started with a tragic pair of young lovers." The professor paused, as if waiting for a response from Jordan.

Jordan didn't have time to humor him. He tried to move a little faster. The valley was losing light fast, and by tomorrow the snow would have covered everything. He hated the thought of having to finish their investigation in the dark, where they might miss something key.

"This city was once one of the richest in all of Afghanistan." The professor gestured toward the ruins with his casted arm. "It served not only as a monastic center but also as a major trading post for caravans traveling along the Silk Road from Central Asia to India. To protect that wealth, a Shansabani king named Jalaludin built this citadel. For a full century, it was considered impregnable, growing to house over a hundred thousand people. Stories say it was riddled with secret passageways to help defenders attack their enemies. It even had its own underground spring to make it easier to withstand prolonged sieges."

"So how did it end up like this?" The ruins had clearly fallen a long way since their glory days. Jordan zoomed in on a blood splash, trying to get a clean shot in the bad light.

"Genghis Khan. A Mongol by descent, he wanted to control this valley. So he sent his favorite grandson to negotiate a peaceful takeover, but the young man was killed instead. Then Khan moved his forces into the valley, swearing to slay every living thing in retribution. But once here, even his vast forces couldn't find a way to breach the citadel."

Still filming, Jordan took another careful step forward. "He must have found a way. You mentioned something about a betrayal . . ."

The inflectionless voice continued. "And a love story. The king's only daughter had fallen in love during the months prior to the siege. But her father had refused her desired suitor, decapitating him when they tried to elope. Heartbroken and angry, she left the citadel and went to Genghis Khan under the cloak of darkness. To avenge her love, she showed the Mongols the secret passages, told Genghis Khan where the king's forces were hiding at the underground spring."

Jordan listened to the story with half an ear, concentrating on his work, finishing one side. His efforts weren't as careful as he would have liked, but conditions were worsening. He crossed to the other side of the street, wiped a melted snowflake off the lens, and filmed his way along.

Atherton stood silent for a breath, then suddenly spoke again, as if he had never stopped. "And once Genghis Khan breached those walls, he did as he had promised. He killed everyone in the city, over a hundred thousand people. But he didn't stop there. It is said he slaughtered every beast of the field, too. It was those dark acts that earned the city the name it bears today." The professor shuddered. "Shahr-e-Gholghola. The City of Screams."

"And what happened to the daughter?" Jordan could tell that the professor was a nervous talker. He needed an ancient story to distract him from the reality of what had happened to his colleagues.

"Genghis put her to the sword, for betraying her father. It is said that her bones, along with the bones of the other dead, both man and beast, are still buried within that hill. To this day, they've never been found." Atherton glanced up the bloody trail to a cleft in the mountain a few hundred yards away, and his eye twitched. His voice dropped to an imploring whisper. "But we were close. We had to get as much work done before this winter as we could. We had to. We had to get any historical artifacts unearthed and secured before they risked succumbing to the same fate as the Buddha statues. We had to work fast to get artifacts out. To save them."

"Could the team have been attacked because of what they found over the last couple of days while you were gone? Maybe some sort of treasure?"

"Impossible," the professor said. "If the stories are true about this place, Genghis Khan cleared out anything of value before destroying this city. We've never found anything valuable enough to kill for. But superstitious tribesmen did not want us to disturb this mountain-size tomb of their ancestors. Stories abound around here of ghosts, djinns, and curses, and they were afraid that we would awaken something evil. Perhaps we did."

Jordan let out a soft snort. "I'm less worried about dead enemies than I am about live ones."

He was glad to have the rangers at their backs. He didn't trust the professor or the locals here, not even the Afghani trainees under his care. Out here, loyalties shifted in less than a second. Hell, that Shansabani king had lost his kingdom because he couldn't even trust his own daughter.

He turned from the ruins and stared at a pair of CH–47 Chinook helicopters that sat a kilometer away, snow collecting on their blades, positioned at the edge of the neighboring town of Bamiyan. They had a team of investigators questioning the townspeople. They were all fighting the night.

Jordan turned off the camera. He'd study the video later, but for now he wanted to think, to feel the scene.

What could he tell by the setting? Someone had attacked the archae-ologists with a brutality he'd rarely seen. Blood was everywhere. It looked like a knife fight, not a gunfight, blood arcing out in thin spatters from a flurry of cuts, not single blotches as from a bullet wound. But the sheer amount of blood made it hard to be sure.

Who had done this . . . and why?

Had the Taliban taken some religious affront to the work here? Or maybe opportunists in town grabbed the researchers as a part of a ran-som scheme that got out of hand? Or maybe the professor was correct—superstitious tribesmen had killed them because they feared what the researchers might disturb here. He hoped the rangers were having more success than his team, because he didn't like any of these answers.

By now, the ice mist had grown thicker, the snowfall heavier, slowly erasing the world around them. Jordan lost sight of the choppers, of the distant town of Bamiyan. Even the neighboring ruins of Shahr-e-Gholghola had almost vanished, offering mere peeks of rubble and ruin.

It was as if the world had shrunk to this small village.

And its bloody secrets.

The professor took off his glove and bent to pick something up.

"Stop!" Jordan called. "This is still a crime scene." The professor pointed to a scrap of sea-green fabric frozen in a pool of blood. His voice shook. "That's Charlotte's. From her jacket."

Jordan winced. There were so many senseless, savage ways to die. "I'm sorry, Professor Atherton." Jordan looked from the professor's anguished face down at his own hands. His right hand was twisting his gold wed-ding band around and around on his ring finger. A nervous habit. He let the ring go.

Heavy footfalls, rushed and determined, sounded from his left. He swung around, freeing his weapon—a compact Heckler & Koch MP7 machine pistol.

The shadowy form of McKay appeared out of the mists, trailed by Azar, his Afghan trainee.

"Sarge, look at this."

Jordan shouldered his weapon and waved McKay forward.

The corporal closed in and used the bulk of his body to shield his Nikon camera from the blowing snow. "I took pictures of some tracks I found."

"Footprints?"

"No. Look."

Jordan stared down at the tiny digital screen. It showed a trail of bloody tracks across a snow-crusted stretch of rock. "Are those paw prints?"

McKay scrolled through a few more shots, showing a close-up of one of the prints. "Definitely an animal of some sort. Maybe a wolf?"

"Not wolf," Azar interjected in stilted English. "Leopard."

"Leopard?" McKay asked.

Azar huddled next to them and nodded. "Snow leopards have lived here for thousands of years. Long time ago they were a royal symbol for this place. But now, not so many are left. Maybe a few hundred. They attack farmers' sheep and goats. Not people." He scratched his beard. "Not enough rain this year and early winter. Maybe they came down here to look for food."

That wasn't even a threat Jordan had considered before now. He felt better thinking that animals had attacked the archaeologists. Animals could be dealt with. Leopards didn't have weapons, and they weren't likely to be sheltered by the locals. It also explained the ferocity of the attack, the firefight, and the blood. But could it be that easy?

Jordan straightened with a shake of his head. "We don't know that the cats killed them. They might have come to scavenge afterward. Maybe that's why we didn't find any bodies. They were dragged to wherever this pride of leopards—"

"*Leap* of leopards," McKay corrected, ever the stickler for details. "Lions come in prides."

Atherton hunched in on himself. "If the cats have taken the bodies, they are close." He pointed his cast toward the ruins. "This place is riddled with hiding places. And also land mines from the many decades of war up here. You have to be careful where you step among those ruins."

"Great," McKay grumbled, "like we don't have enough problems with man-eating leopards. We get land mines, too."

Jordan had maps of the area with the land mines marked on them, but he didn't look forward to hunting through that maze to recover the bodies—especially in the dark—but he knew that might become necessary. Any clues to who killed the archaeologists might still lie with those mauled corpses. It couldn't have been leopards, he realized. Leopards didn't whisper in ancient languages. So the words must have come either from a survivor or a murderer. They had to go now. The longer they waited, the less likely the survivor would still be alive, or the murderer would be brought to justice.

"How big are these cats?" Jordan asked.

Azar shrugged. "Big. I've heard of males as big as eighty kilos."

Jordan did the math. "That's about a hundred seventy-five pounds."

Scary, but not too bad.

McKay chuffed his disagreement. "Then you'd better look at this."

He flicked to another picture and showed a paw print with a shiny quarter next to it, using the coin to reveal the perspective of its size.

Jordan felt a deep-seated cold fear, a primal reaction to when his ancestors huddled in caves against what hunted the night. The paw print looked to be eight inches wide, the size of a small dinner plate.

"I found another line of tracks, too." McKay showed them on his camera.

He ended on another paw print, again photographed with a quarter, only this one was smaller—not by much, but clearly different.

"So there are at least *two* cats hunting here," Jordan said.

"And *both* a lot larger than a hundred and seventy-five pounds,"

McKay added. "I'd estimate twice that, maybe more. The size of African lions."

Jordan stared over at the misty ruins, remembering the tale of two African lions, nicknamed The Ghost and The Darkness, who terrorized Kenya for almost a year during the turn of the century. The two lions were said to have killed over a hundred people, often pulling them out of their tents in the middle of the night.

"We're going to need more firepower," McKay said, as if reading Jordan's mind.

Unfortunately, his team had traveled here light, one weapon each. They had expected to come and go before dark. Plus, with the ranger unit standing nearby, it had seemed like plenty of protection.

That is, until now.

A crackle from the radio caused both Jordan and McKay to wince and grab for their earpieces. It was Cooper.

"I've got movement over here," Cooper radioed in. "Inside the village. Spotted a flicker through one of the windows."

"Stay put," Jordan ordered. "We'll join you. And be on the lookout for leopards. We may not be alone out here."

"Got it." Cooper's voice sounded more annoyed than frightened. But he hadn't seen the tracks.

After Cooper passed on his location, Jordan led the others to the far side of the village. He found Cooper crouched with Farshad by a jumble of boulders at the edge of the village. The ruins of Shahr-e-Gholghola rose behind their position. Jordan felt uneasy turning his back on that mountainous graveyard to face the village.

"Over there," Cooper said, and pointed his rifle at a small mud-brick house with a snow-dusted thatched roof. The door was closed, but a window faced them. "Someone's in there."

"Or maybe you're jumping at shadows," McKay said. "The rangers cleared every building. They found nothing."

"Doesn't mean someone didn't sneak back here when we weren't looking." Cooper turned to Jordan. "I swear I saw a flash of something pale pass by that window. It wasn't a gust of snow or a trail of mist. Something solid."

McKay showed Cooper the pictures of the giant paw prints.

Cooper crouched lower and swore. "I didn't sign up to be a big game hunter. If that's some big lion in there—"

"Leopard," McKay corrected.

"I don't give a flying fart what it is. If it's got teeth and likes to eat people, I'll let McKay's big ass take point."

"Fine by me," McKay said. "Especially since we know there are at least *two* of them and the professor here thinks they're holed up in that craggy hill behind you."

Cooper glanced over his shoulder and swore again.

Jordan settled the matter. "Cooper and Farshad, stay here with the professor. I'll take McKay and Azar and check out that house."

With his H&K pistol in hand, Jordan led his two men toward the targeted house, feet silent in the newly fallen snow. He was confident his weapon had enough firepower for whatever hid in this house. Still, he kept looking over his shoulder, wishing he had more ammunition.

As Azar kept his weapon fixed on the window, he and McKay approached the door. They slipped to either side and readied themselves. Jordan glanced over and got a silent confirmation from his teammate.

Upon Jordan's signal, McKay stepped up and kicked the door in.

It burst open with a loud crack of wood.

Jordan ran low inside, weapon at his shoulder. McKay kept post, standing higher, sweeping the room with his own gun.

The home was a single room with a small table, a corner stone oven, and a pair of straw beds, one large and one small. Empty. Just as the ranger search team reported. Cooper had been wrong, which both surprised and relieved Jordan. He should have known—

"Don't move, Sarge," McKay said from the doorway.

He obeyed, hearing the urgency in his teammate's voice.

"Look slowly up. At your eight o'clock."

Jordan shifted his eyes in the direction indicated, barely moving his head. He followed the mud-brick wall to where it met the thatched roof. Half hidden by a rafter, a pair of eyes shone back at him, as if lit by an inner fire. A rustling of straw whispered in the quiet room as the hidden watcher slipped deeper into the nest of thatch, a perfect hiding place, using the musty, stale straw to mask any scent.

Smart.

Jordan slung his weapon back and lifted his empty arms.

"It's okay," he said softly, gently, as if he were encouraging a skittish colt. "You're safe. Come on down."

He didn't know if his words could be understood, but he hoped his tone and mannerisms made his intent plain.

"Why don't you—"

The attack came suddenly. The shadowy lurker leaped from the rafters, coming down with a rain of dry thatch. McKay's weapon twitched up.

"Don't!" Jordan warned.

He caught the diving shape in his arms, recognizing the simple need in that falling form. He had been raised with a passel of brothers and sisters, and now nieces and nephews. Though he had no children of his own, he knew that plain desire. It went beyond language and country and borders.

A child needing comfort and reassurance.

Small arms clasped around his neck, a soft fiery cheek pressed against his own. Thin legs wrapped around his waist.

"It's a little girl," McKay said. A *terrified* little girl.

She quaked in his arms, shivering with fear. "You're safe," he assured her, while silently hoping that was true. He turned to McKay. "Bring Cooper and the others inside."

McKay dashed out, leaving Jordan alone with the child. Jordan guessed the girl was no more than ten. He crossed to the table and sat down. He unzipped his coat and wrapped it around her, cradling her thin form against his chest. Her small body burned against him, feverish through the pajamalike garment she wore. He read raw terror in her every twitch and soft sob as she hovered at the edge of shock.

What had she seen?

He hated to treat this small child as a witness, especially in this state, but she might have the only answers to what really happened here.

The other men crowded into the small room, which only made the girl cling more tightly to him, her eyes huge upon the newcomers. He squeezed as much reassurance as he could. Her small round face, framed by black hair parted down the middle, constantly glanced at him, as if making sure he didn't vanish.

"Leopard tracks all around the house, Sarge," Cooper said. "It's like they had a dance party out there."

Atherton spoke from the door. "She's the cook's daughter. I don't know her name."

The girl looked at Atherton as if she recognized him, then shrank back against Jordan.

"Can you ask her questions?" Jordan asked. "Find out what happened?"

Atherton kept his distance from the girl. He rapped out questions as if he wanted to get through them as quickly as possible. His eye twitched madly. She answered in monosyllables, her eyes never leaving Jordan's face.

Holding the girl gently, Jordan noted the two Afghanis standing by the smaller of the two beds. One man knelt down and picked up a pinch of white powder from the dirt floor and brought it to his lips. It looked like salt and from the squint and spit probably tasted like it, too.

Jordan noted that a whitish ring circled the bed, and a cut rope hung from one bedpost.

The two Afghanis kept their heads bowed together, looking from the circle of salt to the girl. Their eyes shone with suspicion—and not a small amount of fear.

"What's that about?" McKay whispered to Jordan.

"I don't know."

Atherton answered their question. "According to folklore, ghosts or djinn often attack someone as they sleep, and the salt holds them at bay. The mother probably believed she had to protect her child, what with them working within the shadow of Shahr-e-Gholghola. And perhaps she did. Things happen out here in the mountains that you cannot believe when you are safe in the city."

Jordan kept himself from rolling his eyes. The last thing he needed was for the professor to start spouting nonsense. "What did the girl say happened here?"

"She said the team had a breakthrough yesterday." He tapped his cast and grimaced. "I missed it. Anyway, the tunnel they had been digging had broken into a cache of bones. Both human and animal. They were to begin removing them in the coming days."

"And what about last night?" Jordan asked.

"I was just getting to that," Atherton said with a pique of irritation.

He returned to questioning the girl, but Jordan felt her body stiffen. She shook her head, covered her face, and refused to say more. Her breathing grew more rapid and shallow. The heat of her body now burned through his coat.

"Better leave it for now," Jordan said, sensing the girl retreating into shock.

Ignoring him, Atherton grasped her arm roughly. Jordan noticed a loop of rope dangling from her slender wrist. Had she been tied to the bed?

Atherton's words grew harsher, more insistent. "Professor." Jordan pulled his hand off her. "She's a sick and traumatized little girl. Leave her alone."

McKay drew Atherton away. The professor retreated from the girl until his back was flat against the mud wall and then stared at her as if he, too, were afraid of her. But why? She was just a scared little girl.

The girl glanced up at Jordan, her body burning up in his arms. Even her eyes glowed with that inner fire. She spoke to Jordan, pleadingly, faintly, before slipping away.

How long had it been since she had eaten or drunk anything?

"That's enough for now," Jordan said to McKay. "Let's get her to medical help."

He took out his water bottle and coaxed her to take a sip.

The girl whispered something so softly that Jordan couldn't make out the words, if they were words and not just a sigh.

The professor's face blanched. Atherton glanced to the two Afghanis, as if to verify they had heard her words, too. Azar backed toward the door. Farshad to the bed, stepping within the ring of salt, bending to fix the area where he'd picked up the salt a moment before.

"What?" Jordan asked.

"What the hell's going on?" McKay echoed. Atherton spoke. "That last bit the girl just said. It wasn't Hazara dialect. It was Bactrian. Like from the recording."

Was it? Jordan wasn't so sure. He wasn't sure she'd said anything and, if she had, that the professor would have been able to hear it. He had listened over and over again to that taped SOS. The words at the end certainly hadn't sounded like what the girl had just said. He remembered those words, deep, guttural, sounding angry: *The girl is ours.*

The voice had reeked of possessiveness.

Maybe it was her father . . .

"What did she say just then?" Jordan asked. He felt a rising skepticism toward the professor. How could a ten-year-old girl speak a language that had been dead for hundreds of years?

"She said, *Don't let him take me back.*"

From beyond the mud-brick walls of the home, a ululating yowl pierced the mists.

A moment later, it was answered by another. The leopards.

Jordan glanced toward the window, noting that the sun had set during the last half hour, falling away suddenly as it did in the mountains. And with the sun now down, the leopards had come out again to hunt.

Azar darted for the open door, panicked. Farshad called after him, clearly imploring him to come back, but he was ignored. The man vanished into the snowy darkness. A long stretch of silence followed. Jordan heard only the soft *hush* of falling snow.

Then, after a minute, gunfire burst out, followed by a piercing scream. The cry sounded both distant and as close as the dark doorway. It rang of blood and pain and raw terror. Then silence again.

"McKay, secure the entrance," Jordan barked out.

McKay hurried forward and shouldered the wooden door closed again.

"Cooper, try to reach that ranger battalion parked over at Bamiyan. Tell them we need assistance. Pronto."

As McKay trained his weapon toward the door, Jordan shifted away from the table, to the floor, drawing the girl with him. She clung to his side, breathing hard. He freed his machine pistol and kept his sights on the window, waiting for the cats to come through.

"What now, Sarge?" McKay asked.

"We wait for the cavalry," he answered. "It shouldn't take them too long to get those birds in the air."

Cooper shook his head and lifted their radio unit in his hand. "I'm getting no pickup. Just dead air. Makes no sense, not even with this storm."

Atherton looked at the little girl as if she had knocked out their radios. Jordan tightened his grip on her.

"Does anyone hear that?" McKay asked, cocking his head slightly.

Jordan strained, then heard it, too. He waved everyone to stay quiet. Out of the darkness, through the fall of snow, a whispering reached them. Again it sounded both close and distant at the same time. No words could be made out, but it set his teeth on edge, like a poorly tuned radio station. He remembered thinking earlier that nothing surprised him anymore. He'd have to revise that. This whole situation had him surprised right out of his comfort zone.

"I think it's Bactrian, too," Atherton said, his voice taking a keening, panicked edge. He crouched like a frightened rabbit near the stone oven. "But I can't make anything out."

It didn't sound like a language at all to Jordan. Maybe the shock of the day had caught up to the professor. Or maybe it wasn't even Bactrian on the tape.

Farshad crouched beside the salt-ringed bed. He stared daggers at the child, as if she were to blame for all of this.

"Remember what I translated from that desperate radio call?" Atherton's glassy eyes stared past Jordan's shoulder at nothing. "Those last words. *The girl is ours.* They clearly want *her.*"

The professor pointed a trembling finger at the child.

Whispers out in the night grew louder, taking on a gibbering sound, a chorus of madness just beyond the edge of hearing. It felt as if the words ate through his ears, scratching to get inside his skull. But maybe those were just normal leopard noises. Jordan had no idea what a leopard was supposed to sound like.

Atherton clamped his hands over his ears and crouched lower to the floor.

Farshad barked out words in Pashto, his native language, and raised his rifle at Jordan, at the girl. He motioned toward the door with the tip of his weapon. Between the pantomime and the bit of Pashto that Jordan understood, the message was clear.

Send the girl outside.

"Not happening," Jordan said grimly, staring him down.

Farshad had gone red-faced by now, his dark eyes wild. He shouted again in Pashto. Jordan made out the word *djinn* and something like *petra*. He kept repeating the word over and over again, shoving his weapon belligerently toward Jordan each time. Then a round fired and blasted dirt near Jordan's knee.

That was enough for his men.

Defending him, Cooper and McKay fired their weapons at the same time.

Farshad fell back across the bed, dead before he hit the girl's straw mattress.

The child cried out and buried her face in Jordan's chest.

Atherton moaned.

"What was Farshad yelling at the end?" Jordan asked. "That word *petra.*"

Atherton rocked slightly, never lifting his face. "An old Sanskrit word, used by both Buddhists and local tribespeople of this region. It translates as *gone forth and departed,* but it usually means demonic ghosts, those still craving something, unsettled spirits."

Jordan wanted to scoff at such a thing, but he couldn't find the words.

"Farshad believed the girl is possessed by an escaped djinn and that the ghosts of the mists want her back."

"What I photographed out there," McKay said, "those looked like *leopard* prints, not *ghost* prints."

"I . . . I don't know." Atherton kept rocking. "But perhaps he was right. Maybe we should send the girl out there. Then they'll leave us alone. Maybe she's all they want."

"Who wants?" Jordan spat back. He wasn't going to send the girl to her death.

As answer, a heavy weight hit the thatched roof overhead, raining down dry straw. Jordan swung his machine pistol up and fired through the roof. His men followed suit, the blasts deafening in the small space.

A screeched yowl—not pained, just angry—met their efforts, followed by a scrambling retreat. It didn't sound injured—just pissed. Was the creature out there attempting to draw their fire, to lure them into wasting ammunition?

Jordan checked his weapon. He caught the matching frowns as his teammates did the same. Not good. They were going to run out fast.

Another feline scream came from near the door. Cooper and McKay swung around, training their weapons there. Jordan returned his sights to the window, staring out at the mist-shrouded ruins. "If you see them, shoot. But be cautious with your ammo."

"Got it," Cooper said. "Wait till you see the whites of their eyes."

"That roof isn't going to withstand many more attacks like that," McKay said. "A few more poundings, and those leopards will come crashing on top of us."

McKay was right. Jordan recognized the futility of staying holed up here. They didn't have enough weapons to hold off a pair of three-hundred-pound monsters, especially in such cramped quarters. They were as likely to shoot each other as the animals.

Jordan regained his feet, scooping the girl in his arms.

"Do you have a plan?" Cooper asked.

Jordan stared at the door. "But it's not a good one."

"What are you going to do?" McKay asked, looking worried.

"I'm going to give them what they want."

5:18 P.M.

Jordan ran through the snow, through the night, staying low but carrying the burden over one shoulder, limp and silent. The girl's sleeve brushed his cheek, smelling of sweat and fear. He didn't know if she was the source of all this, if the leopards were fixed on her scent. He didn't know if those whispers in the mists were echoes from far away or something else.

Right now, it didn't matter.

If they wanted the girl, let them follow his trail, his movements.

He fled *away* from the distant glow of Bamiyan and *toward* the ruins of Shahr-e-Gholghola. He followed instructions given to him by Atherton, pointing him to the archaeology team's excavation site. It was only a fast fifty-yard sprint away.

That graveyard offered the only hope now.

He and his men had just a few weapons and a limited amount of ammunition left. And these beasts had proven themselves to be crafty, experienced hunters, definitely hard to kill, plainly wary of guns. His best hope was to lure the beasts away and trap them.

After he was done with them, he'd deal with whoever was out there whispering in the mists.

Or at least that was his plan.

As he raced, McKay kept to his heels.

They'd left Cooper back at the house, covering their flight from the window. Maybe the cats would get into his sights, and Cooper would bring them down and solve all their problems.

Jordan crossed the last of the way, dodging through a maze of wheelbarrows, mounds of excavated gravel and sand, and stacks of abandoned tools to reach the entrance to the archaeological dig site. Cold wind cut through his shirt. He missed his coat. As he skidded up to the mouth of the tunnel, he shifted his burden higher on his shoulder, making sure his weapon wasn't compromised.

McKay panted beside him. The exertion didn't make him short-winded, nor the elevation here. It was simple fear.

"You know what you have to do," Jordan said.

"I'll see what I can dig up—literally."

Jordan grinned, appreciating his friend's levity, while still knowing the fear it hid. "If I'm not back in ten minutes—"

"I heard you the first time. Now get going." A screaming howl punctuated that order.

McKay slapped Jordan on the shoulder, then disappeared with a map fluttering in his hand. Jordan clicked on the xenon tactical flashlight mounted to his weapon and pointed it down the tunnel that had been excavated into the heart of the ruins.

Now to set the trap . . .

He ducked low to keep the girl's clothing from ripping on the rough-hewn walls and set off into the tunnel. He needed the cats to follow him, luring them with his bouncing light, his frantic flight, and the scent of the child's fever-damp clothes. The low ceiling required him to run in a crouch, his shoulders bumping the walls to either side.

As he chased his beam of light down into the depths of the dark ruins, he noted a warmer breeze wafting up from below, as if trying to blow him back outside. It smelled of damp rock along with a chemical sting, like burning oil. He was grateful for the warmth, until his eyes began to water, and his head spun.

He knew some natural caves *breathed*, exhaling or inhaling depending on surface pressures and temperatures. Was that how the archaeologists knew where to dig? Had they noted a section of the Shahr-e-Gholghola sighing out, revealing its inner secrets, and dug toward it?

Within a few more yards, he had his answer. The excavated walls turned to natural stone. He discovered steps carved into the rock under-foot. The archaeologists must have broken into a section of the secret passages that once riddled the ancient citadel.

But what had they found?

A scream of fury chased him, echoed by another. He pictured the two cats crouched at the entrance, sensing their quarry was trapped. He breathed a sigh of relief for McKay.

They're still coming after me . . .

Spurred by that thought, Jordan rushed deeper, knowing where he must reach, a place roughly described to him by Atherton, even though the professor had never been there himself.

Within a few steps, the tunnel ended at a large cavern, a dead end. He slid slightly on damp stone, coming to rest at a pile of bones, a deadfall of limbs, skulls, and rib cages. The scatter of bones covered the stone floor of the cavern, forming a macabre beach at the edge of a pool of black water. More bones glowed up through the shallows.

Jordan remembered Atherton's story of the citadel's subterranean spring—and the slaughter that took place here centuries ago.

But the deaths here weren't all ancient.

Resting atop the bones, at the water's edge, were the bloody bodies of fresh kills. The corpses were torn, gutted, and broken-limbed. Here lay the remains of the archaeology team, and what appeared to be the girl's mother. From the gnawed state of their bodies, Jordan knew he had found the lair of the leopards. They hadn't waited long to take over the newly opened cave.

As if sensing his violation, a yowl echoed down to him, sounding much closer than before. Or maybe it was his fear accentuating his senses. His head also continued to spin from the fumes that filled the space. By now, his eyes wept, and his nose burned.

He had to work fast.

He stepped to the edge of the boneyard and tossed his burden far. The girl's clothes fluttered open, scattering straw that he'd stolen from the mattress and stuffed inside. If the beasts hunted by scent or sight, he'd wanted to do his best to convince the hunters that the girl was with him.

Or maybe it didn't matter.

Maybe, as with Azar earlier, it merely took his own flight to draw the beasts.

Cats hunted things that ran from them.

And if he had failed to draw them after him, he had left Cooper back at the mud-brick house with the girl and the professor. It was the best plan he could muster to keep them safe with their meager resources.

Jordan unhooked the flashlight from his gun and flipped it to the opposite side of the cavern. The beam flipped end over end, a dizzying effect with his head already spinning. The light landed near the far side of the underground spring, glowing like a beacon.

Jordan fled away from it, to a cluster of boulders at the right of the tunnel entrance. He crouched down, drew his weapon, and waited. It didn't take long.

He smelled the muskiness of the leopards before the first brute stalked into the cavern. It was a sinewy monster, nine feet long, all fiery furred and marked with black rosettes, a male. It flowed like a tide into the space, silent, purposeful, unstoppable. A second beast followed, smaller, a female.

He caught a glimpse of its dark eyes as it surveyed the room. They burned with an inner fire, much as the girl's eyes had earlier.

Jordan held his breath.

The world turned watery, his head more muzzy. Movement became smudging blurs.

The male rushed to the discarded clothing, snuffling deeply, intent on its focus.

The second animal slid past its mate, drawn to the light, stalking low toward it.

A rippling of the water drew his attention to the spring-fed pool. He watched the male cat's reflection shimmer, wavering. For the briefest flicker, he thought he saw another image hidden beyond the fiery fur, something pallid and sickly, hairless and hunched. Jordan blinked his burning eyes, and it disappeared.

He shook his head and tore his gaze away. He dared not wait any longer.

He slipped as quietly as possible out of hiding and toward the open tunnel, sneaking back the way he had come. He had to steady himself with one hand on the wall to keep upright.

Then sudden movement made him freeze. The male leopard, its back still to Jordan, lifted its head from the mound of discarded clothes and yowled its frustration at the roof, knowing it had been tricked.

Under its paws, the bones began to shift.

To Jordan's addled senses, they seemed to stir on their own—scraping against one another, knocking hollowly. He gaped, trying to convince himself the movement was merely the massive beast shifting its weight.

He failed.

Numb with primal terror, he stumbled backward toward the mouth of the tunnel. The shaking of the bones grew worse. He watched one of the archaeologists' bodies rise, belly up, back broken.

He wanted to look away, but horror transfixed him.

As he stared, the carcass lifted up on limbs twisted the wrong direction. It scuttled across the bone field like a crab. Its head hung askew, mouth open. From that gullet, gibbering whispers flowed. Words in the same archaic language as on the recording.

A second corpse stirred, missing a lower jaw, throat bared open.

It added to the chorus of madness.

Can't be . . . I'm seeing things.

Grasping at this thin hope, he turned and fled up the tunnel, rebounding off the walls every few feet. The world continued to churn around him, betraying his steps. He fumbled for the penlight in his pocket.

He found it, flicked it on, and lost it as it slipped from his fingertips.

It bounced away behind him.

Still, the glow offered enough light from behind to help illuminate the way up.

He ran—while a howl arose behind him.

As it echoed away, he heard a faint whispering in his ear.

". . . hurry. All done here . . ."

McKay.

Jordan forced himself upward: buffeted by that foul wind, chased by howls, pursued by things that scratched rock with rotted nails and bone.

Shadows cast up from below danced on the walls around him, ahead of him, capering up from the fires of Hell.

Heavy footfalls rushed up the tunnel behind him. No more howls now. Just the silent hunt.

Jordan ran his palms along the wall to keep his legs under him. He tore his skin on the coarse stone, but he didn't care. The pain meant he had abandoned the smooth natural cavern walls below for the excavated sharp edges of man-made work.

Behind him, a harsh panting echoed. The penlight's glow vanished.

Darkness collapsed around him as the beasts closed in.

He ran faster, his lungs burning.

He smelled the creatures now, the stench blown up to him by the foul breath of the cave: stinking of meat and blood and horror.

Then light shone ahead. The exit.

He fled toward it, diving through it from a yard away to freedom, landing hard, almost forgetting to make that last leap to save his life.

McKay caught him in his arms and rolled him to the side.

A howl burst forth from the tunnel, full of frustration and the promise of bloody vengeance.

As Jordan tumbled away, he caught sight of the male leopard stepping to the mouth of the tunnel—then the world exploded.

Fire. Smoke.

Pelting rocks and stinging grit.

Jordan shook free of McKay's embrace but stayed on his knees.

He took in deep gulps of fresh air, trying to clear his head.

He watched for any sign of the leopards through the smoke, but the tunnel had completely collapsed. As he stared, an avalanche of rock continued to flow down from above, further sealing the passageway, reburying those bones along with the two leopards inside.

"How many land mines did you use?" Jordan gasped out, his ears still ringing from the blast.

"Just one. Didn't have time to dig up more than that. Plus, it was enough."

Before him, the mass of Shahr-e-Gholghola steamed and shuddered. Jordan pictured the subterranean cavern collapsing into stony ruin below. More explosions ripped through the ruins, blasting smoke and rock.

"The quaking is triggering other land mines to blow," McKay said. "We'd better haul ass out of the way."

Jordan didn't argue, but he kept a wary eye on the ruins.

They retreated to the thatched-roof house. Cooper came stumbling out to meet them. Blood ran down one side of his face.

"What happened?" Jordan asked.

But before Cooper could answer, Jordan hurried past his teammate to find the home empty.

What the hell . . .

Concern for the girl spiked through him.

Cooper explained. "As soon as you went into the cave, the girl dove through the window. I tried to go after her, but that damned professor clubbed me, screaming, 'Let her go! Let the demons take her.' That guy was a whack job from the beginning."

"Where are they now?"

"I don't know. I just woke back up."

Jordan sprinted out of the hut. Falling snow filled in their tracks but he could see that the girl's tiny feet pointed west, the professor's east. They'd gone in opposite directions.

McKay caught up to him.

A *thump-thump*ing beat echoed in the distance.

A helicopter, ablaze with light, came sweeping toward them from Bamiyan, drawn like moths to a flame. The rangers had heard the explosions.

"Great," McKay said. "*Now* the cavalry comes."

"What's next, Sarge?" Cooper asked.

"We let someone else get the professor," Jordan said, rediscovering his outrage. It flowed through him, warming him, telling him what he must do, centering him again at long last. "We go get that little girl."

Three days later, I sit in my nice warm office at the Afghan Criminal Techniques Academy. All the paperwork has been filed; the case is closed.

The events surrounding that night were blamed on a single unusual finding at the ruins of Shahr-e-Gholghola: a gas signature emanating from deep underground. The gas was a hydrocarbon compound called ethylene, known to cause hallucinations and trancelike states.

I remember my own confusion, the things I thought I saw, the things I wished I hadn't. But they weren't real. They couldn't have been. It was the gas.

The scientific explanation works for me. Or at least I want it to.

The reports also attribute the leopards' strange and aggressive behavior to the same hydrocarbon toxification.

Other loose ends are also resolving.

Professor Atherton was found a mile from the ruins of Shahr-e-Gholghola—barefoot, raving, and suffering from hypothermia. He ended up losing most of his toes.

McKay, Cooper, and I had searched through the night for the little girl, and eventually I found her nestled in a shallow cave, unharmed and warm as toast in my coat. I'd been grateful to find her, relieved that I had cared enough to keep searching. Maybe I'd find my way back to those innocent Iowa cornfields someday after all.

The girl had no memory of the events at the ruins, likely a blessing. I'd taken her to a doctor, then turned her over to her relatives in Bamiyan, thinking that was the end of it.

But the cave where I found her, not far from the ruins, revealed itself to be the entrance to a small crypt. Inside rested the remains of a young man, entombed with the weapons and finery of a Mongol noble. Genetic studies are under way to determine if the body might not be that of Genghis Khan's grandson, the emissary the king of Shahr-e-Gholghola had murdered centuries ago that set in motion the events that would lead to the citadel's downfall.

But it was the manner of that young man's death that keeps me sitting at my desk this winter morning staring at the neatly filled out report and wondering.

According to Atherton's stories, the Shansabani king had slain his daughter's suitor by decapitating him after he discovered their planned elopement. And the Mongolian body in the tomb had no head.

Could the emissary and the lover have been the same man? Had the king's daughter fallen in love with the Khan's grandson? Had that tragic love triggered the massacre that followed? Everyone always said that love led to good things, but it didn't always. I find myself playing with my wedding ring again and make myself stop.

I don't know, but as I sit here, stuffing the reports in a folder, I remember more details. How Azar told me that leopards were the royal symbol of the Shansabani kings. How Farshad screamed about the girl being possessed by a djinn and hunted by ghosts.

Was he right after all?

With the opening of the tombs, had something escaped?

Had the wisp of a long-dead princess slipped into the girl, seeking another to help carry her to her lost love?

Had her father, still mired in anger and vengeance, possessed those two leopards, the royal sigils of his family, and tried to drag her back to the horrors hidden under Shahr-e-Gholghola?

And in the end, had the explosions that resealed that tomb reburied his grave along with the bones of the leopards, ending the angry king's ghostly pursuit of his daughter?

Or were the pair of hunters merely leopards, not possessed by anything more than hunger, their aggression fueled by the toxic gas in their new den?

And those voices. *Had it just been the cats? I hadn't been able to track down another Bactrian scholar, so no one but the professor had translated those eerie sounds into words. Maybe he was unhinged by his colleagues' deaths or already affected by the gas from his earlier work at the dig site.*

I shake my head, trying to decide between the logical explanation and the supernatural one. Usually, I'm a logical guy.

These crazy thoughts must be the aftereffects of all the gas I breathed in the cavern. But when I think back to the professor's words, I can't be so sure: Things happen out here in the mountains that you cannot believe when you are safe in the city.

A knock at the door interrupts my train of thought, and I'm grateful for it.

McKay comes in, steps to the desk. He carries a paper in hand. "New orders, Sarge. Looks like we're shipping out."

"Where?"

"Masada, Israel. Some strange deaths reported following an earthquake out there."

I reach to the folder on my desk and close it, ending the matter.

"I bet this assignment will be easier than the last one." McKay frowns. "What's the fun of that?"

Blood Brothers

JAMES ROLLINS AND REBECCA CANTRELL

Summer, Present Day
San Francisco, California

Arthur Crane woke to the smell of gardenias. Panic set in even before he opened his eyes. He lay still, frozen by fear, testing the heavy fragrance, picking out the underlying notes of frangipani and honeysuckle.

It can't be . . .

Throughout his childhood, he had spent countless hours reading in the greenhouse of his family's estate in Cheshire, England. Even now, he remembered the hard cement bench in a shaded corner, the ache in his lower back as he hunched over a novel by Dickens or Doyle. It was so easy to lose himself in the worlds within those pages, to shut out his mother's rampages and threatening silences. Still, no matter how lost he was in a story, that scent always surrounded him.

It had been his childhood, his security, his peace of mind.

No longer.

Now it meant only one thing. Death.

He opened his eyes and turned his nose toward that scent. It came from the empty pillow next to him. Morning sunlight slanted through his bedroom window, illuminating a white *Brassocattleya* orchid. It rested in an indentation in the middle of the neighboring pillow. Delicate frilled petals brushed the top of his pillowcase, and a faded purple line ran up the orchid's lip.

His breathing grew heavier, weighted by dread. His heart thumped hard against his rib cage, reminding him of his heart attack last year, a surprise gift for his sixty-eighth birthday.

He studied the orchid. When he'd last spotted such a flower, he'd been a much younger man, barely into his twenties. It had been floating in a crimson puddle, its heavy scent interwoven with the hard iron smell of his own blood.

Why again now . . . after so many years?

Arthur sat up and searched his apartment's small bedroom. Nothing seemed disturbed. The window was sealed, his clothes were where he'd left them, even his wallet still lay on the bureau.

Steeling himself, he plucked the orchid from his pillow and held its cool form in his palm. For years he'd lived in dread of receiving such a flower again. He fought out of the bedsheets and hurried to the window. His apartment was on the third story of an old Victorian. He picked the place because the stately structure reminded him of the gatehouse to his family's estate, where he'd often found refuge with the gardeners and maids when the storms grew too fierce at the main house.

He searched the street below. Empty.

Whoever had left the flower was long gone.

He took a steadying breath and gazed at the blue line of the bay on the horizon, knowing that he might not see it again. Decades ago, he had reported on a series of grisly murders, all heralded by the arrival of such an orchid. Victims found the bloom left for them in the morning, only to die that same night, their bloody bodies adorned with a second orchid.

He turned from the window, knowing the flower's arrival was not pure happenstance. Two days ago, he had received a call from a man who claimed to have answers about a mystery that had been plaguing Arthur for decades. The caller said he was connected to a powerful underground organization, a group who called themselves the *Belial*. That name had come up during Arthur's research into the past orchid murders, but he could never pin down the connection. All he knew was that the word *belial* came from the Hebrew Bible, loosely translated as *demonic*.

But did that mean the past murders were some form of a satanic ritual? How was his brother involved? "Christian . . ."

He whispered his brother's name, hearing again his boyish laughter, picturing the flash of his green eyes, the mane of his dark hair that he always let grow overly long and carefree.

Though decades had passed, he still did not know what had happened to his brother. But the caller had said that he could reveal the truth to Arthur.

Tonight.

He glanced at the orchid still in his hand.

But will I live long enough to hear it?

As he stood there, memories overwhelmed him.

Summer 1968
San Francisco, California

Another funeral.

Morning light from the stained-glass windows painted grotesque patterns on the faces of the young choir at St. Patrick's Cathedral. But their ethereal voices soared to heaven—clear, beautiful, and tinged with grief.

Such grace should have brought comfort, but Arthur didn't need comfort. He wasn't grieving. He had come as an interloper, a foreigner, a young reporter for the *Times* of London.

He studied the large lily-draped photo of the deceased mounted on an easel next to a carved mahogany coffin. Like most of the people in the church, he hadn't really known the dead man, although everyone in the world knew his name: Jackie Jake, the famous British folk singer who had taken the United States by storm.

But that tempest was over.

Ten days ago, Jackie Jake had been found murdered in an alley off San Francisco's Mission Street. Arthur's newspaper had flown him from London to cover the death—both because he was their youngest reporter and because he was the only one who admitted to having listened to Jake's music. But the last was a lie. He had never heard of Jackie Jake until this assignment, but the ruse got him on the plane to California.

He had come to San Francisco for another reason. A hope, a chance . . . to right a terrible wrong.

As the funeral Mass continued, the crowd shuffled restlessly in the pews. The smell of their unwashed bodies rose in a cloud around them. He'd assessed them when he came in earlier, taking stock of Jake's fans. They were mostly young women in long skirts and blousy white shirts, many with flowers in their hair. They leaned in postures of utter grief against men with the beards of ascetic hermits.

Unlike most of the crowd, Arthur had worn a black suit, polished shoes, something that befit a funeral. Despite his desire to shake the iron rule of his childhood household, he could not escape the importance of correct attire. He also wanted to present a professional demeanor for the policemen investigating Jake's murder. Arthur sensed that their sympathies would not lie with this hippie crowd.

As the service ended and the mourners began to file out, Arthur spotted his target near the back of the nave, a figure wearing a black uniform with a badge on the front. Arthur contrived to bump against him as he exited.

"I'm very sorry, Officer," Arthur said. "I didn't see you standing there."

"Not a problem." The man had the broad American accent that Arthur associated with California from films and television programs.

Arthur glanced with a heavy sigh back into the church. "I can't believe he's gone . . ."

The police officer followed his gaze. "Were you close to the deceased?"

"Childhood friends, in fact." Arthur held out his hand to cover his lie. "I'm Arthur Crane."

The man shook Arthur's hand with a too-firm grip. "Officer Miller."

The officer kept an eye on the exiting crowd, his face pinched with distaste. A man wearing jeans and sandals swept past, leaving a strong smell of marijuana in his wake. The officer tightened his jaw, but did not move after him.

Arthur played along with his obvious disdain, hoping to tease information out of the officer. "Jackie and I were friends before he came here and got involved with"—he waved his hand at the crowd of hippies— "that lot. I wouldn't be surprised if one of these flower children had killed him. From my experience, it's a fine line between fan and fanatic." Officer Miller shrugged, his eyes still on the mourners. "Maybe. The killer did leave a flower near his body . . . some type of orchid."

And that was how Arthur first found out about the orchids.

Before Arthur could inquire further, Miller lunged to the side as a rake-thin man grabbed an easel near the door, clearly intending to steal the blown-up photo of the folksinger. The thief's dark eyes looked wild under his unkempt hair, his dirty hands gaunt as a skeleton's.

As the officer interceded, the man abandoned the photo, grabbed the easel, and swung it like a club.

Miller tried to dodge, but his hip crashed against a neighboring pew. The easel struck the officer on the shoulder, driving him to his knees. The thief raised the easel again, high above the head of the dazed officer.

Before Arthur could consider otherwise, he rushed forward. It was the kind of foolhardy action his brother, Christian, would take in such a circumstance—but it was out of character for the normally reserved Arthur.

Still, he found himself barging between the two men as the crowd hung back. He grabbed the attacker's arm before he could deal a fatal blow to the fallen police officer. He struggled with the assailant, giving Miller time to scramble to his feet. The officer then manhandled the attacker away from Arthur and quickly secured the man's wrists behind his back with handcuffs. The man glared all around. His pupils filled his entire irises, making his eyes look black. He was definitely under the influence of some kind of drug.

Miller caught Arthur's gaze. "Thanks. I owe you one."

Breathing hard, his heart thumping in his ears, Arthur could barely manage a nod and pushed back toward the exit.

What was I thinking . . .

As he reached the streets, the bright City by the Bay seemed suddenly a darker place, full of shadows. Even the morning light failed to dispel them. He fetched up against a light pole and stood there for a moment, trying to slow his breath, when a flash of white caught his eye.

A paper flyer had been pasted onto the pole. The title drew his attention.

Have you seen this man?

But it was what was beneath those hand-scrawled words that sucked the air from his lungs and turned his blood to ice. It was a black-and-white photo of a handsome young man in his midtwenties, with dark hair and light eyes. Though the photo had no color, Arthur knew those eyes were a piercing green.

They belonged to his brother. Christian.

The flyer contained no further details except a phone number. With trembling fingers, Arthur wrote the number on the bottom of his notebook. He hurried down the crowded street, searching for an empty phone box. When he found one, he slotted his money into it and waited. The phone burred in his ear, once, twice, five times. But he couldn't put it down.

He let it ring, balanced between disbelief and hope.

Finally, a man answered, his voice spiked with irritation. "What the hell, man? I was sleeping."

"I'm sorry," Arthur apologized. "I saw your flyer on the street. About Christian Crane?"

"Have you found him?" The man's tone sharpened, annoyance replaced with hope. "Where is he?"

"I don't know," Arthur said, fumbling for his words. "But I'm his brother. I had hoped—"

"Damn," the voice cut him off. "You're the Brit? His foster brother. I'm Wayne . . . Wayne Grantham."

From the man's tone, he clearly thought Arthur would recognize him, that Christian might have spoken to Arthur about him—but Arthur hadn't shared a word with Christian for over two years, not after the way they had left matters in England, after their fight. It was why Arthur had come to San Francisco, to mend fences and start anew.

Arthur pushed all that aside. "How long has Christian been gone?"

"Eleven days."

That was one day before Jake was killed. It was a ridiculous time to peg it to, but the folk singer's murder was fresh in his mind.

"Have you called the police?" Arthur asked.

A snort answered him. "Like they give a damn about a grown-up man gone missing in San Francisco. Happens all the time, they said. City of Love, and all that. Said he'd probably turn up."

"But you don't believe that?"

"No." Wayne hesitated. "He wouldn't have left without telling me. Not Christian. He wouldn't leave me not knowing."

Arthur cleared his throat. "He left without telling *me*."

"But he had his reasons back then, didn't he?" Guilt spiked through Arthur.

"He did."

Wayne had nothing else to add, and Arthur reluctantly gave up without asking the most important question of all. There were some questions he still had difficulty asking, stifled by prejudice and made uncomfortable by his ingrained formal upbringing.

Instead, he went back to the hotel and filed his story, burying the new detail of the orchid a few paragraphs in. For good measure, he also reported Christian missing to the police.

As Wayne had said, they did not care.

The next day, Arthur woke to the screaming headline of a second murder. He read the paper standing at his kitchen counter, a mug of coffee growing cold in his hand. As with Jackie Jake, the victim's throat had been torn out. The body of the young man—a law clerk—had been found only a few blocks away from St. Patrick's Cathedral—where Jackie Jake's memorial service had been held. The article hinted that the murders were connected, but they didn't elaborate.

Two hours later, Arthur sat at a diner across from Officer Miller, calling in his favor, admitting that he was a reporter for the *Times*.

"Can't tell you much more than was in the *Chronicle* here," Miller admitted, tapping the local newspaper. "But there was a flower—another orchid—found at this crime scene, too. According to a roommate, the victim found the orchid in his bedroom the morning he was killed, like the murderer left it as a calling card."

"Were there any witnesses? Did anyone see someone at the crime scene . . . or see whoever left that orchid?"

"Nothing concrete. Someone said they saw a skinny, dark-haired man lurking around the church at the time of the murder, taking pictures, but it could be a tourist."

Arthur could glean nothing else from what the officer told him. The mysterious photographer did add a good detail for the report Arthur intended to file, but the fact was certainly not as juicy as the detail about the second orchid.

That afternoon, Arthur composed and wired in the story. He dubbed the murderer "the Orchid Killer." By the next day, the name was plastered across every newspaper in the city and across the nation, and his reputation as a journalist grew.

His editor at the *Times* extended his assignment to cover the murders. He even convinced the paper to give him enough of a stipend to rent a dilapidated room in the Haight-Ashbury district—where both victims spent most of their time. Arthur used the little money left over to buy a radio and tuned it to the police band.

Over the next days, he worked and ate with the radio on. Most of the chatter was dull, but four nights later, a frantic call came over the band. A dead body had been discovered, just blocks from Arthur's rented room, a possible third victim of the Orchid Killer.

He hailed a cab to get there quickly, but the police had already cordoned off the area to keep the press away.

Standing at the yellow strip, Arthur lifted his Nikon camera. It was outfitted with a zoom lens. Christian had given it to Arthur as a present when he finished school, telling him that he could use the extra eye. Arthur still wasn't very good with the camera—he preferred to tell stories with words rather than pictures—but without a photographer assigned to him, he would have to manage on his own.

To get a better vantage point, he shifted away from the police cordon and climbed a few steps onto the porch of a neighboring Victorian home. He leaned against a brightly painted column to steady himself and examined the crime scene through the lens of the camera. It took some fine-tuning of the zoom to draw out a clear picture.

The victim lay flat on his back on the sidewalk. A dark stain marred his throat and spread over the stone. One arm was outstretched toward the street as if beckoning for help that would never come. In that open palm lay a white object.

Arthur zoomed in and tried to identify it, finally discerning the details of its frilled petals and subtle hues. It was an orchid, but not *any* orchid. Arthur's stomach knotted with recognition.

It was a *Brassocattleya* orchid.

Such orchids were common enough, used as corsage flowers because of their powerful scent and their durable beauty. His mother had raised that particular breed because she adored the scent.

Arthur remembered another detail. Christian had always loved them, too.

His mind's eye flashed to the poster, to the still life of Christian printed there, his brother's smile frozen, his eyes so alive even in the photo.

As he stared at the orchid in the dead man's palm, the sweet smell seemed to drift across the street to him, although that couldn't be true. He was too far away, but even the imagined scent was enough to dredge up a long-buried memory.

Arthur sat on the stone bench in the corner of his mother's greenhouse holding a pruning knife. The familiar scents of orchids and bark surrounded him, as the afternoon sunlight, trapped under all that glass, turned the winter outside into a steamy summer inside.

He stared at the long tables filled with exotic plants. Some of the orchids he'd known for years, watching them flower over and over again throughout his lonely childhood.

Since he was a little boy he had come here to watch his mother work with the orchids, crooning to them, misting them gently, stroking their leaves, giving them the love that she did not give to him. They were special and rare and beautiful—and he was not.

He'd had a secret dream that when he grew up he would do something so wonderful that she would look up from her pots and notice him.

But now that would never happen.

She had died two days ago, taking her own life in one of her fits of black melancholy. Today she had been planted in the earth like one of her beloved orchids.

He ran his thumb across the sharp knife.

He'd overheard the staff talking about the value of his mother's orchid collection. She had spent a lifetime accumulating it—buying each plant from a funny little man dressed all in black with a bowler hat. He gathered them from botanical gardens around the world, from other collectors, and even from men who traveled into the distant rain forests and brought the specimens out in burlap sacks.

Now all her precious orchids would die or be sold.

A light winter rain began to patter on the glass roof and ran down the sides in streaks. Arthur laid the cold knife blade against the warm softness of his forearm.

This is how she did it . . .

Before he could act, the greenhouse door slammed open, and Arthur jumped.

The knife clattered to the tile floor.

Only one person dared to crash around the estate like that. Christian had come to the London house when both boys were fourteen. Christian's parents had died in a car crash outside of San Francisco. Arthur's father was second cousin to the boy's father and took the teenager into their home. Though the two boys were related, it was only in blood—not in demeanor.

"Arty?" he called brashly. "I know you're in here."

Arthur stirred on the bench, and Christian spotted him, crossing over to join him. Christian's brown hair was slicked flat from the rain, and his bright green eyes were puffy and rimmed in red. Unlike Arthur, Christian could let himself cry when he was hurt. It was an American trait. Something Arthur's father and mother would never tolerate.

Reaching the bench, Christian pulled the dark lens cap off his camera. He carried the thing everywhere. He took pictures all day and spent half the night in a makeshift darkroom developing them. Arthur's mother said that he had real talent, and she would not have said that if it weren't true.

Christian planned to become a photojournalist. He wanted to travel to the world's war zones, taking pictures—using his art to change the world. He'd even convinced Arthur that he could come along, too, as a journalist. They'd be a team. Arthur wasn't sure that he had the talent for such a career, but he liked to be drawn into Christian's whimsies. The other boy had a reserve of boundless optimism that Arthur often warmed himself against.

But today even that wasn't enough.

Christian snapped a picture of the abandoned pruning knife on the tiles, then turned toward the rows of specimen tables. He headed to his favorite orchid: the Brassocattleya *cross.*

First, he took a close-up shot of the blossom, then he pinched off a dead leaf and felt its edges to see if it was moist, just as their mother used to.

"She'll miss these flowers," Christian commented. Certainly more than me, *Arthur thought dourly. Christian plucked the flower, and Arthur gasped.* Mother would never have allowed that.

Christian dropped the flower on Arthur's lap and picked up the pruning knife from the floor.

Arthur watched the blade. He imagined how it would feel if it cut into his wrists, how the blood would well out and drop onto the floor. His mother would know. She'd used a long knife from the kitchens to slit her wrists in the bath. When Arthur found her, the water was such a deep red that it looked as if the whole tub had been filled with blood.

Christian touched the inside of Arthur's wrist. His fingers slid back and forth along the same spot where his mother had used the kitchen knife.

"Do you think it hurt much?" Christian asked, not shying from the harder questions. His fingers still rested on Arthur's wrist.

Arthur shrugged, suddenly nervous—not at the subject matter but at the intimacy.

Christian moved his fingers aside, replacing his touch with that of the cold edge of the pruning knife.

Arthur stayed very still, hoping.

Christian took a deep breath, then sliced into Arthur's wrist—but not too deep. It didn't hurt as much as he had anticipated. No more than a sting really.

Blood welled out.

Both boys stared at the shiny scarlet line on Arthur's white skin.

"She left me, too," Christian said and put the flower into Arthur's hand.

Arthur clenched his fist, crushing the orchid, and more blood flowed out of his wound. "I know."

"My turn now." Christian drew the bloody blade across his own wrist.

"Why?" Arthur asked, surprised.

Christian turned his arm over and dropped his wounded wrist on top of Arthur's. Their warm commingled blood ran down their arms and dripped onto the clean-swept floor.

With his other arm, Christian took several snapshots: of the crimson drops on the white stone tile, of the bloody flower crumpled on the bench. Last, Christian angled the camera up to take a picture of the two of them together, their arms linked.

"I will never leave you," Christian whispered to him. "We're blood brothers, now and forever."

For the first time since Arthur had found his mother in the crimson water—her stained blond hair floating on the surface, her head tilted back to stare at the plaster ceiling—he broke down and wept.

Arthur felt a hand shove him from behind, stumbling him back to the present.

"Get off my porch!"

He turned to discover a middle-aged woman standing there—about the same age his mother would have been if she'd lived. She scolded him and herded him off her home's stoop, her flannel nightgown billowing in the night breeze.

Arthur's reporter instincts came back. "Did you see anything?"

"None of your business what I saw." She crossed her arms over her chest and sized him up. "But I can say that I don't like how this Summer of Love has turned out."

Later, when Arthur filed his story, the headline read *Summer of Death follows the Summer of Love*.

"I still haven't heard any word from Christian," Wayne said over the phone three days later. "Our friends in the city haven't either."

Arthur frowned, cradling the phone to his ear as he sifted through piles of police reports and forensic exams from the latest murder, a *third* victim. The young man was named Louis May, recently arrived from Kansas City. Like Christian, the man had likely been drawn by the promise of California, a modern-day gold rush of free love and openness, only to die on the sidewalk, his throat torn open and a flower in his hand.

Had the same happened to Christian? Was his body yet undiscovered?

"But something strange happened this morning," Wayne said, interrupting Arthur's line of worry.

"What?" He sat straighter and let the papers settle to the tabletop.

"A Catholic priest came by, knocking at my door at an ungodly early hour."

"A priest? What did he want?"

"He asked if I knew where Christian might be, where he hung out, especially at night. Strange, huh?"

Strange barely fit that description. Despite his brother's name, Christian had no religious affiliation. In fact, he only had disdain for those who piously bent their knees to an uncaring god, like Arthur's parents had. So why would a priest be interested in his brother?

As if hearing Arthur's silent question, Wayne explained. "The priest said it was important that he find your brother and talk to him. Said Christian's immortal soul hung in the balance. He told me to tell Christian that he could turn his back on what he'd become and accept Christ into his heart and find salvation. Those were his exact words."

Arthur swallowed, hearing an echo of his own words to Christian on that last night, words that could not be easily taken back. He had called Christian names, demanded he change, telling him that the path Christian had chosen would only lead to a lonely death. Their argument had grown more and more heated until the brothers fled from each other.

The next day, Christian was gone.

"You should have seen that guy's eyes," Wayne continued. "Scared the hell out of me, I have to say. Never met a priest like that. What do you think he really wanted?"

"I have no idea."

After that call, Arthur sat in his tiny rented room, studying pictures and news clippings taped to the walls. Like Christian, all the victims were men in their twenties. They were dark-haired and handsome.

Arthur stared at a publicity photo of Jackie Jake. The folk singer's black hair flopped over his eyes, reminding Arthur acutely of Christian. Jake even had the same bright green eyes.

It was at that moment that Arthur realized he didn't have a single picture of his brother. After their quarrel, in a fit of pique, Arthur had destroyed them all. In many ways, he was as volatile and temperamental as his mother—and in the end, just as judgmental.

Arthur had been a fool back then. He knew it now. He wanted only to find Christian and apologize, but he worried that he might never get that chance. He could never make it right.

Over the following three days, he buried himself in the case, sensing Christian was linked to the murders. But how? Was he a victim, or somehow involved? The latter seemed impossible. Still, he remembered the madman at the memorial service. Could Christian have been drugged, maybe brainwashed by some murderous cult, and turned into a monster?

Needing answers, Arthur started his investigation with the orchids, but too many of the city's flower shops sold them. He showed around the picture of Christian from Wayne's flyer, but none of the shopkeepers remembered any particular customers buying those orchids around the times of the murders. It was no surprise. It was summer, and orchids were in demand for the dances of the upper class, those lofty creatures of wealth far removed from the men who lived on the streets or in squat houses or died holding one in their hands.

He touched base with Officer Miller every day, hoping for any news. All the while, the city held its breath for the next murder. Arthur learned from Miller that the latest victim, like the others, had also received his orchid on the morning of his death. It had been delivered to Louis May's stoop, and twelve hours later the young man was dead.

With morning coffee in hand, Arthur contemplated this cruelty, this promise of death delivered to a doorstep. He climbed to his rented room and returned to his cluttered workspace.

There, resting on the keys of his typewriter, was a single white bloom.

A *Brassocattleya* orchid.

"Look, Mr. Crane," Officer Miller said. "I can imagine you're spooked, but folks around here think this might be a publicity stunt. To sell more papers."

Arthur stared dumbfounded across Miller's desk into the crowded squad room. He had come straight here after finding the orchid. Right now it lay on the battered metal desk in front of him. "You can't think—"

Miller held up a beefy hand. "I don't. I trust you plenty, but I can't help you. My hands are tied."

Arthur's stomach sank. He'd been fighting the police for hours, hoping for some kind of protection, but no one took him seriously. "How about I just sit in the police station then? Just for twenty-four hours?"

"I can't allow you to do that." Miller's freckled face looked concerned, but his chin was firm. He wouldn't give in.

"Then arrest me."

Officer Miller laughed at him. "On what charge?" Arthur punched him right in his freckled face.

It took three days for the *Times* to bail Arthur out. In the interim, a fourth victim had received an orchid and had been murdered. The new death further convinced the police that Arthur either had been lying about the orchid or someone had played a cruel prank on the British reporter.

Arthur knew better.

Still, what did it mean? Had the killer passed him by? Or was he just biding his time to make the kill? Not knowing for sure, Arthur spent his first night of freedom in Sparky's twenty-four-hour diner, afraid to go home. He brought a giant pile of notes and used the time to outline a book, a treatise about the murders. Truman Capote's *In Cold Blood* had come out two years ago, and the narrative of those killers had mesmerized him. He wanted to do something similar, to find some way of making sense of these deaths, to nail them down between the cold, dispassionate pages of a book.

Seated at a corner table of the diner, with a clear view to all the exits, he nibbled on his third piece of apple pie and downed his umpteenth cup of coffee. All night long, he had refused to give up his table, despite the jaundiced glances from the waitress.

But now the sky had pearled to a pale gray, and he knew it was time to move on. He could not live inside the diner forever. So he packed up his things, left a generous tip for the waitress, and trudged toward his apartment. As he walked, he rubbed the grit from his exhausted eyes. He squinted at the sun breaking over a boarded-up and abandoned storefront ahead. The five-story building had become the home of squatters. It was regularly raided, emptied, only to fill again.

As he crossed along it, he hefted his satchel of notes. He knew he could get a book out of these murders, something dark and fascinating and significant, the kind of thing that could make his career.

A few meters away, a figure stepped out of the door of the dilapidated store, sticking to the shadows. Even though he was barely visible in the gloom, Arthur recognized him and stopped, stunned and incredulous.

"Christian . . . ?"

Before he could react, his brother was upon him, pulling him tightly in an embrace that was both intimate and frightening. Fingers dug into his shoulders, his elbow, hard enough to find bone.

Arthur gasped, tried to pull away, but it was like trying to unbend iron. Pain weakened him further, forcing him to drop his bag.

Lips moved to ear. "Come with me."

The breath was icy, smelling of sour meat and rot. The tone was not one of invitation but of demand.

Arthur was lifted off his feet and dragged away, as easily as a mother with an errant child.

In a moment, they were through the doorway and up a flight of rickety stairs to an upper room. Refuse littered the floor. Old ratty blankets bunched along the walls, abandoned by their former dwellers. The only place of order was a thick oak table in the center, its surface polished to a high sheen, so out of place here.

As was the smell.

Past the reek of sweat, waste, and urine came the wafting sweetness of honeysuckle and gardenia. The scent rose from a spray of white orchids, all *Brassocattleya*.

If Arthur had any doubts as to the role Christian played in the recent murders, they were dispelled at this sight. The table looked like a shrine or an altar to some dark god.

Arthur tried to struggle out of that iron grip, but he could not escape the hand clamped to his forearm. For his efforts, he was slammed against a wall, hard enough to bruise his shoulder, and pinned there. Fearing for his life, he searched for his only weapon, the same weapon that once drove the two brothers apart in the past.

His words.

But what could he say?

Arthur looked at his attacker, dismayed by what he found there. Christian looked exactly the same—yet completely changed. His face and bearing were as they always had been, but now he moved with a speed and strength that defied reason. Worst of all, his gentle expression had turned hard and angry.

Malice shone in eyes that were once bright and full of joy.

Arthur knew this dreadful condition must be secondary to some kind of drug. He remembered the madman in the church, recalled the horror stories he had read of addicts on a new pharmaceutical called PCP. The drug had arrived in the Haight-Ashbury district just last year.

Was that the explanation here?

"You can stop this," Arthur tried. "I can get you help. Get you clean."

"Clean?" Christian pushed his lips up into a ghastly grimace and laughed, a mocking rendition of his usual playful mirth.

Changing tactics, Arthur tried reaching him through their shared past, to draw him out, to make him remember who he once was. "*Brassocattleya,*" he said, nodding to the table. "Like Mother grew and loved."

"They were for you," Christian said.

"The orchids?"

"The murders." Christian faced him, showing too many teeth. "The orchids were merely to lure you here. I knew you were at the *Times* and hoped word of the orchids would draw you here. That's why I took that singer first, the one from London."

Arthur went cold, picturing Jackie Jake's face. He had contributed to the poor man's death.

"You came sooner than I expected," his brother said. "I had hoped to leave a longer trail of invitation before entertaining you here."

"I'm here now." Arthur's shoulder throbbed, aching even his teeth. "Whatever is wrong between us, we can fix it together."

Christian exposed his arm, turning it to reveal the pale scar on his wrist. Arthur had a matching scar.

"That's right," Arthur said. "We're blood brothers."

"Forever . . ." Christian sounded momentarily lost.

Arthur hoped this was a sign of him finally coming out of his dark, drug-fueled fugue. "We can be brothers again."

"But only in blood." Christian faced him, his eyes hard and cold. "Isn't that right?"

Before Arthur could answer, Christian threw him to the floor, riding his body down and straddling atop him. His brother's white face hovered inches above his, those eyes reading his features like a book.

Arthur tried to throw him off, but his brother was too strong.

Christian leaned closer, as if to kiss him. Cold breath brushed against Arthur's cheeks. His brother used a thumb to turn Arthur's chin, to expose his neck.

Arthur pictured the morgue photos of Christian's victims, their throats ripped out.

No . . .

He struggled anew, bucking under Christian, but there was no escaping his brother. Impossibly sharp teeth tore into the soft skin of his throat.

Blood drowned Arthur's scream.

He wrestled against his death, struggled, cried, but in a matter of moments, the fight bled out of him. He lay there now as waves of pain and impossible bliss throbbed through his wounded body, borne aloft by each fading heartbeat. His arms and legs grew heavy, and his eyes drifted closed. He was weakening, maybe dying, but he didn't care.

In this bloody moment, he discovered the connection people sought through love, drugs, religion. He had it now.

With Christian . . . It was right.

Suddenly, that moment was severed, coldly interrupted.

Arthur opened his eyes to find Christian staring down at him, blood dripping from his brother's chin.

In Christian's eyes, Arthur read horror—and sorrow—as if the blood had succeeded where Arthur's words had failed. Christian put an ice-cold hand against the wound on Arthur's throat, as if he could stop the warm blood flowing out of it.

"Too late . . ." Arthur said hoarsely.

Christian pressed harder, tears welling. "I'm sorry. I'm sorry. I'm sorry."

His brother stared down, clearly struggling to hold in check the evil inside him, to hold on to himself. Arthur saw his nostrils flare, likely scenting the spilled blood. Christian moaned with the need of it, but Arthur heard an undertone of defiance.

Arthur wished he could help, to take away that pain, that struggle.

He let that desire show in his face, that love of brother for brother.

A tear rolled down Christian's cheek. "I can't . . . not you . . ."

With both arms, he picked up Arthur, crossed to a window, and threw his body out into the sunlight. As he flew amid a cascade of broken glass, he stared back, seeing Christian withdraw from the sun, back into shadows, forever lost.

Then Arthur crashed to the street.

Still, darkness found him in that sunlight, swallowing him away. But not before he saw an orchid land on the pavement near his head, floating in a pool of his blood. The sweet scent of it filled his nostrils. He knew it would be the last thing he ever smelled.

His mother would have been happy about that.

An unknown number of days later, Arthur woke to pain. He lay in a bed—a hospital bed. It took him several breaths to work out that his legs were suspended in front of him, encased in plaster. Turning his head took all his effort. Through his window, he saw weak afternoon sunlight.

"I see that you're awake," said a familiar voice.

Officer Miller was seated on his other side. The police officer reached to a table, retrieved a water glass with a straw, and offered it. Arthur allowed the man to slip the straw between his lips. He drank the lukewarm water until it was all gone.

Once done, Arthur leaned back. Even the short drink had left him exhausted. Still, he noted the purplish bruises ringing Miller's eyes, courtesy of Arthur's earlier sucker punch.

Miller fingered the same. "Sorry we didn't take you more seriously, Mr. Crane."

"Me, too," he croaked out.

"I have to ask . . . did you recognize the man who attacked you?"

Arthur closed his eyes. In truth, he didn't recognize the creature who had attacked him, but he did recognize the man who had flung him into the sunlight, away from the monster trying to claw back into control. In the end, Arthur knew Christian had saved his life. Could he condemn him now?

"Mr. Crane?"

Behind Arthur's eyelids, he saw the face of Jackie Jake and the broken body of the man on the sidewalk. Even if he could forgive Christian's attack on himself, he could not let that monster inside him continue to kill.

Arthur opened his eyes and talked until he drifted off to sleep.

When he awoke, it was night. He was terribly thirsty, and his legs still hung in front of him like a bizarre sculpture. A quiet murmuring off to the left must be the nurses' station. He reached for the bell to summon—

He was on the street, looking through eyes that were not his own. A brick tower loomed ahead of him. A church. In the middle of the tower was a door. A spill of light fell onto the dark front steps.

Weeping, he ran toward the light, moving with a speed beyond imagining. Traffic droned next to him, and far away a siren sounded. None of that mattered. He had to reach that tower. He had to get through that door.

But as he neared the church, a figure stepped into view, bathed in that warm glow from inside. It was a priest. Though the distance was great, whispered words reached his ear. "This is hallowed ground. Be warned, it is inimical to the curse within you. If you come, you will have but one choice. To join us or die."

The strange priest's words proved true. With each step, the strength of his limbs faded. It was as if the ground itself drew energy away from him. Heat rose through his feet. For a second it was wonderful, because he was so cold. But then it burned him cruelly.

Still, he did not stop. He lifted first one leaden leg and then another, fighting the heat and the weakness. He must reach that door, that priest. All depended on it.

He was now close enough to note the gothic design, etched in verdigris, on the tall doors. He spotted the priest's Roman collar, made of old linen, not modern plastic. He staggered now toward that man. Despite his weakness, he knew this one was like him, cursed but somehow enduring.

How?

The priest stepped back, beckoning him inside.

He fell across the threshold and into a vast nave. Pillars and arches rose on either side of him, and far ahead candles burned on an altar.

On his knees now, he burned within the holiness found here.

Fire raged through his body.

The priest spoke behind him. "Be welcome, Christian."

Arthur thrashed in his bed, still burning from his waking dream. A rope broke and dropped one of his legs. This new pain centered him, drawing him out of the flames.

A nurse in a white cap rushed into the room. Seconds later, a needle pricked his arm, and everything blessedly went dark.

Days later, Arthur awoke again. His head was clear, but he felt terribly weak. The nurses tried to convince him that his vision of burning in the church was a side effect of the morphine or a fever dream secondary to shock. He believed neither explanation. Instead, he carried those last words inside him, knowing they'd be etched there forever.

Be welcome, Christian.

Arthur knew somehow he had been connected to his brother for that brief, agonizing moment, perhaps a gift born of the blood they shared. He also remembered Wayne's description of the priest who had come looking for Christian. Was that the same priest, offering some form of salvation for Christian, a path he might yet follow?

Or was it all *a bad trip*, to use the vernacular of the youth thronging into San Francisco?

Either way, Arthur slowly healed. Bedridden for most of it, he used his downtime to dictate his new book to an assistant hired by the newspaper. Her name was Marnie, and he would marry her as soon as he could stand.

Following Arthur's attack, the murders had suddenly stopped, but public interest had not waned. A year later, his book, *The Orchid Killer*, became an international bestseller. As far as the world was concerned, he had solved the case, even if the police had never apprehended Christian.

His brother had simply vanished off the face of the earth. Most believed he was dead or had possibly even killed himself. But Arthur never forgot his dream of crawling on his knees into a church, burning in that holiness.

He clung to his hopes that Christian yet lived.

But if he was right, which one had survived that church?

His brother or that monster?

Summer, present day
San Francisco, California

As the sun sank toward the horizon, Arthur brought the orchid to his face and breathed in its fragrance. The petals tickled his cheeks. He carried the blossom into his study. Books lined the walls, and papers covered his oak rolltop desk.

In the years after Christian's disappearance, Arthur had spent most of his life traveling, reporting, and chasing down leads about savage killings and mysterious priests, trying to find his brother, or at least to understand what had happened to him. It was a passion that he had shared with

Marnie, until her death six months ago. Now he wanted only to finish the work and be done with it.

With everything.

At last, at the end of things, he was close.

Several years ago, Arthur had uncovered rumors of a secret order buried deep within the Catholic Church, one that traced its roots to its most ancient days—a blood cult known as the Order of the Sanguines. He crossed to his desk and picked up a leaf from an old notebook, the edges ripped and curling.

A photo had been taped to it. Someone had sent the picture anonymously to Arthur two years ago, with a short note hinting at its importance. It showed Rembrandt's *The Raising of Lazarus*, portraying Christ's resurrection of a dead man. Arthur had marked it up, annotating his many questions about this dark order, of the rumors he had heard.

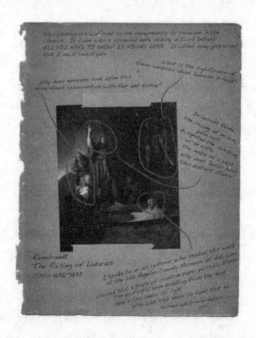

He let the sheet slip from his fingers, remembering the dream of a burning church.

Had his brother joined this order in the past? He glanced at the orchid.

If so, why come for me now, Christian?

Arthur suspected the reason. It was stacked on his desk in a neat pile. Over the past decades, Arthur had gathered further evidence, enough to be believed, about this Sanguines cult within the Church. Tonight, his source—a representative of a group called the Belial—was scheduled to come and deliver the final piece of proof, something so explosive that the truth could not be denied.

Arthur picked at one of the soft petals of the orchid.

He recognized it as a threat, a warning, an attempt to silence him.

Arthur would not be intimidated. As the day wore on, he tried repeatedly to reach his Belial source—a man named Simeon—to move up their evening meeting, but he could never reach the man. By that afternoon, Arthur considered simply fleeing, but he realized that there was no point in trying to hide. He was already in too deep. Besides, a recklessness had settled over him since Marnie's death—he just didn't care anymore.

So he waited for the night, enjoying his favorite meal from an Italian restaurant down the street, complementing it with a bottle of his finest pinot noir. He saw no reason to skimp. If this was to be his last meal, he might as well enjoy it. He ate it in his kitchen while watching the sky turn orange behind the Golden Gate Bridge.

Finally, a knock sounded at his apartment door. Arthur crossed from his study and peeked through the peephole. A man dressed in a navy blue suit stood out in the hall. His face and shorn black hair were familiar from a grainy photograph passed to Arthur at a bar in Berlin. It was Simeon.

Arthur opened the door.

"Mr. Crane?" The man's voice was low and hoarse, with a Slavic accent that Arthur couldn't quite place. Maybe Czech.

"Yes," Arthur said, stepping aside. "You should come inside, quickly now. It might not be safe."

This earned a soft smile from the man, possibly amused by Arthur's caution. But the man did not know about Christian or the orchid.

As his guest entered, Arthur checked the hall outside and the stairs leading down to the old Victorian's stoop. All clear.

Still, a chill ran up Arthur's back, a prickling of the fine hairs on the nape of his neck, a sense of immediate danger. He quickly followed Simeon inside and closed the door behind him, locking the dead bolt.

Simeon waited in the foyer.

"Let's go to my study." Arthur led the way.

Simeon followed him and stepped to Arthur's desk, staring around the room. His gaze settled upon the marked-up page showing *The Raising of Lazarus*. He motioned to that sheet.

"So I see you already know of the bloody origins of the Sanguinists," Simeon said. "That Lazarus was the first of them."

"I've heard fantastical rumors," Arthur said. "Dark stories of monsters and creatures of the night. None of it to be believed, of course. I suspect the stories are there to scare people away from the truth."

Arthur stared expectantly at Simeon, hoping to hear that truth.

Instead, Simeon touched Christ's face on the page with one curiously long fingernail. "There is much about the Sanguinists that defies belief."

Arthur did not know what to say to that, so he kept quiet.

Simeon scratched his nail down the notebook page. "Show me what you already know."

Arthur handed him a folder of the manuscript he was working on, with notes scribbled to indicate where documents and pictures should be inserted.

The man riffled through the pages swiftly, too fast to truly read it. "You have passed this along to no one?"

"Not yet."

Simeon met his eyes for the first time. His eyes were brown and fringed by thick lashes, handsome eyes, but what struck Arthur most about them was that they did not blink. The hair rose on his arms, and he took a step backward from the man, suddenly realizing the prickling danger he had sensed earlier had come from this man, not from some hidden threat beyond his apartment.

"You are close to the truth," Simeon said, no longer hiding the menace in his presence, looming taller. "Closer than you know. Too close for *our* comfort."

Arthur took another step back. "The Belial . . ."

"The Sanguinists defy us at every step, but that war must be kept secret." Simeon stepped after him. "Our darkness cannot thrive in the light."

The buzz of a motorcycle on the street distracted Arthur. He glanced toward the sound—and Simeon was upon him.

Arthur crashed painfully to the floor. Simeon pinned him there. Arthur struggled against him, but Simeon had an implacable strength that Arthur had only experienced once in his life—on the day Christian nearly killed him.

"You want the truth," Simeon said. "Here it is." The man's lips split to reveal sharpened teeth, impossibly long.

He flashed to that moment with Christian, suddenly remembering what he blanked out, what his mind would not allow him to fully see.

Until now.

There *were* monsters in the world.

Arthur redoubled his struggles, but he knew he was at his end.

Then a crash of shattered wood and glass rose from his bedroom. He pictured his window exploding. But he was on the third story.

Simeon turned as a dark shadow flew into the room, tackling the monster off Arthur. Gasping, Arthur crabbed on his hands and feet away from the fighting, backing into his study's cold hearth.

The war raged across the tight room, too fast to follow, a blur of shadows, accompanied by flashes of silver, like lightning in a thundercloud. The battle smashed across his desk and crashed into his bookshelf, scattering volumes across the floor.

Then a feral scream, full of blood and fury.

A moment later, a head bounced across his wooden floor, spilling black blood.

Simeon.

From beyond Arthur's desk, a shadow rose and shed its darkness.

The figure wore a black leather motorcycle jacket, open, revealing the Roman collar of the priesthood. He stepped around the desk, his pale face scratched, bleeding. He carried two short swords in his hands, shining like liquid silver, marred with the same black blood as seeped across the golden hardwood floor.

Impossibly, the figure grinned at him, showing a familiar glint of rakish amusement in his green eyes as he sheathed the swords.

"Christian . . . ?"

Beyond fear now, Arthur gaped at his brother. Despite the passing of forty years, Christian was virtually unchanged, no more than a boy in appearance compared to Arthur's lined and aged face.

"How?" Arthur asked the mystery standing before him.

But Christian only smiled more broadly, crossed over, and offered Arthur his hand.

He took it, gripping his brother's pale fingers, finding them cold and hard, like sculpted marble. As Arthur was pulled to his feet, he saw the old scar on his brother's wrist, a match to his own. Despite the impossible, it was indeed Christian.

"Are you hurt?" his brother asked him.

How did one answer that when one's life was unhinged in a single moment?

Still, he managed to shake his head.

Christian led him back to the kitchen, to the table where the remains of his last meal still sat. He settled Arthur to a seat, then picked up the empty bottle of pinot noir.

"Nice vintage," he said, taking a sniff at the bottle. "Good oak and tobacco notes."

Arthur found his voice again. "Wh . . . what are you?"

Christian cocked an amused eyebrow—a look that ached with the memory of their shared past, as perfectly preserved as the rest of his features. "You know that already, Arthur. You just must let yourself accept it."

Christian reached to his leg and unhooked a leather flask. Branded into its surface were the crossed keys and crown of the papal seal. Christian took Arthur's empty goblet, filled it from the flask, and pushed it back toward him.

Arthur stared warily at the glass. "Wine?"

"*Consecrated* wine," Christian corrected. "Turned by the holy act of transubstantiation into the *blood* of Christ. It is what I've sworn to drink. It's what sustains me and my brothers and sisters."

"The Sanguinist order."

"The blood of Christ allows us to walk in daylight, to do battle with those who haunt the shadowy corners of the world."

"Like the Belial." Arthur remembered Simeon's sharp teeth.

"And others."

His brother found another goblet from the kitchen, filled it, and joined Arthur at the table.

Arthur took a sip from his glass, tasting only wine, none of the supposed miracle it held. But for the moment, he accepted this truth.

Christian lifted his own goblet, drank deeply, then raised his glass. "Seems we're blood brothers yet again."

This earned a shy smile from Arthur.

Christian reached over and clinked his glass against Arthur's.

"To you, my industrious and persistent brother. I told you before that you would make an excellent journalist."

"You knew what I discovered."

"I've never stopped watching you. But your efforts stirred up a hornet's nest. There are those—even in my own order—who need secrets."

Arthur remembered Simeon's words about the Belial.

Our darkness cannot thrive in the light.

It seemed the Sanguinists needed those shadows, too.

"For your safety," Christian said, "I tried to warn you."

Arthur could still smell a slight scent of gardenias. "The orchid."

"I had to be subtle, using a means of communication that only you would understand. I had hoped you'd abandon this line of inquiry on your own, but I should have known better. When you didn't, I couldn't let anyone harm you."

"You saved my life."

Christian grew momentarily pensive. "It was only fitting after you saved my soul."

Arthur frowned at this.

Christian explained. "It was your love, our bond as brothers that finally broke me down enough to seek out the Sanguinists and what they offered, a path to service and redemption for my sins."

Arthur flashed to the burning church, to the priest in the doorway.

Christian brightened again, straightening his spine. "So I saved your life, and you saved my soul . . . let's call it a wash."

Arthur asked other questions, got some answers, but others were denied him.

He slowly accepted this and the need for such secrets.

Finally, Christian stood. "I must go. You should check into a hotel for a couple of days. I'll send someone over—someone I trust—to fix your window, to clean up the place."

In other words, to get rid of the body.

Arthur followed him to the door. "Will I see you again?"

"It's forbidden," Christian said, his eyes a mix of sadness and regret. "I'm not even supposed to be here right now."

Arthur felt a pang that threatened to break his already old heart.

Christian hugged him, gently but firmly. "I'll always be with you, my brother." He broke the embrace, placing his palm over Arthur's heart. "Right here."

Arthur saw that Christian held something under that palm, pressed to his chest. As his brother removed his hand, a square of stiff paper fell and fluttered toward the floor. Arthur scrambled to catch it, nabbing it with his fingertips.

As he straightened, he found the door open and Christian gone.

Arthur stepped into the hallway, but there was no sign of his brother.

He stared down at what he'd caught, a parting gift from Christian.

It was a black-and-white photo, slightly yellowed, crinkled at the corners. In the background was a rainy pane of glass, and in the foreground two grieving boys gazed into the camera together. Christian held the camera high, and Arthur leaned against him for support, two brothers, blood bonded never to part.

Christian must have carried the old photo all these years.

Now, it was Arthur's.

To keep now and forever.

Back to My Roots

I t's a poorly kept secret that early in my career I wrote a series of fantasy novels (under the pen name "James Clemens"). So when I was approached to craft a young-adult fantasy story for an anthology edited by the illustrious master of the genre, R. L. Stine, how could I refuse?

Years prior, while in San Francisco, I had grown enamored of the street art that decorates many of the city's walls and alleyways. I would look at work that was oftentimes as stunning as it was mysterious. It made me wonder about the artist, about his or her motivation, about the meaning behind that splash of spray paint in the night.

In my head, I build this entire world of secret defenders of the city, who used their art to fend off dark forces. But I never had a place to tell such a story—until that request by R. L. Stine.

The result became the next short story, "Tagger."

Tagger

JAMES ROLLINS

With a practiced flip of her wrist, Soo-ling Choi shook the spray can and applied the final trail of red paint against the cement wall of the dark alley. Finished, she took a step back to examine her handiwork, careful not to get any paint on her black silk dress.

She wasn't entirely happy with the result. She'd done better. It was the Chinese symbol known as *fu*, her signature mark. Only sixteen, she continued to be highly critical of herself. She knew she was talented. She'd even been accepted for early enrollment at the L.A. Academy of Design. But this was more important than any scholarship.

She checked her watch. Auntie Loo would already be at the theater. She scowled at the mark.

It'll have to do.

Reaching out, she touched the center of the Chinese glyph. As usual, she felt the familiar tingling that made her joints burn. The warmth spread up her arm and enveloped her in a dizzying wash. The glyph glowed for a breath, pushing back the dark shadows of the alley.

Done.

Before she could break contact with the symbol, an icy cold pain tore at her wrist like talons. It seared deep, down to the bone. With a gasp, she ripped her arm away and stumbled back.

Ow . . . what the heck was that?

She examined her wrist. It was unmarked, but an echo of that cold touch remained. She rubbed her arm, trying to melt the ice away, and studied her work with narrowed eyes.

On the wall, her bright crimson mark had gone black, darker than the shadows of the alley.

She continued to massage her wrist, bending it one way, then the other, struggling to figure out what had happened. The symbolic glyph— her "tag" for the past three years—was exactly like the hundreds she had plastered throughout the greater Los Angeles area.

Did I do something wrong? Did I draw it too fast, too sloppily, make some dreadful mistake?

Worry grew to an ache in her chest. She considered redrawing it, but she had no more time. The curtain for the ballet would be rising in less than five minutes. Auntie Loo would already be in the family's private box. With little patience for frivolity, her aunt would be furious if Soo-ling were late again.

As the pain subsided in her arm, the shadows seemed to drain out of the paint. The crimson richness of the *fu* symbol returned, as if nothing had happened.

Whatever the problem had been, it seemed to be gone now. She shoved the spray can into her messenger bag and hurried down the alley toward the waiting limousine.

She shot one last glance over her shoulder as she reached for the door handle. The symbolic character still shone on the wall like a splash of blood. To most Chinese, it was merely a blessing of good fortune associated with celebrations of the New Year. It represented two hands placing a jar of rice wine on an altar as an offering.

But for Soo-ling, the painted character of *fu* was power, a ward of protection wherever she painted it. There would be no robbery at this location tonight; the proprietor of this 7-Eleven would be safe.

Or so she allowed herself to imagine. It was a small way she honored her dead mother and her ancient superstitions. A way to stay connected to her, to a past that both mother and daughter shared that went back centuries, to villages nestled amid rice paddies, to mornings fragrant with cherry blossoms.

She cast up a silent prayer to her mother and climbed into the back of the limo. A gust of sea breeze from nearby Huntington Beach wafted inside, tinged with just a hint of salt—and an underlying trace of rot. A shiver shook through her.

Just fish and algae, she assured herself.

Behind the wheel, Charles nodded to her. They didn't need words. He had been with her family for as long as she could remember.

Wanting a moment of privacy, she raised the glass partition between them and tried to compose herself. Her reflection hovered in the window before her. Her long black hair had been coiled into a precarious pile atop her head, the cascade held at bay by a pair of emerald-capped hairpins. Her eyes matched the pins in color and shine.

Like a ghost of Mother.

Over the past few years, Soo-ling could not help but notice that she was slowly growing into her mother's image, one generation becoming another. An ache of loneliness and loss hollowed her out.

She went back to that final bedside visit with her mother before the malignant lymphoma stole her away. The hospital room had smelled of bleach and rubbing alcohol, no place for her fragile mother who believed in herbal tea remedies, the healing power of statues and symbols, and ancient superstitions.

"This is passed to you, *si low chai*, my child," her mother had whispered, sliding a sheet of hospital stationery toward her. "It is our family's heritage, passed from mothers to daughters for thirteen generations. You are of the thirteenth generation, and this is the thirteenth year of your birth. This number has power."

"Mother, rest please. The chemotherapy is very taxing. You need your sleep."

Soo-ling had taken the sheet of paper from her mother and turned it over. In a beautiful cursive script, her mother had drawn the Chinese character for good fortune.

Fu.

"My little rose, you are now the guardian of the City of Angels," she said with a mix of pride and sorrow, struggling to breathe each word. "I wish I could have explained earlier. These mysteries can only be revealed after the first blood of womanhood."

"Mother, please . . . rest . . ."

Her mother continued, her eyes glazed by both memory and drugs. She told stories of prophetic dreams and the power to block curses with the proper stroke of paint on a wall or door. Soo-ling had obediently listened, but she also noted the bleat of the heart monitor, the drip of the IV line, the whisper of a television down the hall.

What place did all these ancient stories full of ghosts and gods have in the modern world of electrocardiograms, needle biopsies, and insurance forms?

Finally, a nurse whisked into the room on rubber-soled shoes. "Visiting hours are over, Miss Choi."

Her mother began to protest, but a quick kiss from Soo-ling calmed her. "I'll be back tomorrow . . . after school."

Glad for the excuse, Soo-ling fled the room, relieved to escape not just the stories but the demon named cancer. Still, her mother had called after her. "You must beware the—" But the closing door cut off those last words, silencing her forever.

That night, her mother had slipped into a coma and died.

Soo-ling remembered staring down at the hospital stationery clutched in her hands.

Blessing and luck, she thought. A lot of good it did her mother.

"We've arrived, Ms. Choi," Charles said, drawing her out of the past as he pulled the limo to the curb in front of the theater in Santa Monica.

Soo-ling shook herself out of her reverie and slid across the seat. The driver already had the door open. "Thank you, Charles."

As she climbed out, an anxious teenager in a rented tuxedo tripped down the steps toward her. "Soo! About time you got here!"

A smile filled her at the sight of him, but she did not let it reach her face. It was not proper for a Chinese girl to show strong emotions. Like casting her symbol, it was another way to honor her mother, to adhere to tradition in this small way.

The young man rushed up to her. He stood a head taller than her, gangly in the overlarge tuxedo. His long hair had been pulled back into a ponytail.

Bobby Tomlinson was her age. He'd been her friend since kindergarten. One of her few. Both misfits growing up, they had banded together. He was a computer geek and film buff, and she was the shy student who never spoke above a whisper. Over time they had grown to share a secret love of tagging. He had introduced her to it when she was eleven, and she was instantly hooked. It became an outlet for rebellion against the world as her mother became sick, a sliver of freedom and joy that helped Soo-ling cope with her overwhelming grief and anger. Over the next years, they ran the streets together, dodging police, struggling to leave their mark on the city in multicolored splashes of paint.

The smile trapped inside her grew larger with the memory. Bobby led her up the steps and inside. He babbled on in a rush about his new intern position at Titan Pictures.

"We start shooting tomorrow on that vampire musical I was telling you about. I'll be helping with the gaffing crew!"

She glanced over to him and lifted a questioning eyebrow.

He shrugged. "I know. I don't know what gaffers do either. But that's where I'll be working."

They reached her family's private box as the orchestra was winding

through its first movement. Bobby glanced back to her, his blue eyes spar-
kling with amusement. The private box was empty.

"Where's Auntie Loo?" she asked, expecting to find her aunt already
here.

"She called and said she had a merger to oversee at the bank. It's just
us tonight."

Soo-ling was shocked to find herself alone with Bobby—not that the
two hadn't spent many long nights running the streets with each other.
But this felt somehow different, both of them all dressed up and sharing
this dark private space. She was grateful the lights were dimmed. It hid the
warmth that bloomed in her cheeks.

Still, she hesitated outside the box seats, sensing something out of
place. This was Auntie Loo's passion. Neither of them were fans of the ballet. Plus a small part of her wanted to escape, to keep moving, troubled by
an inexplicable sense of being trapped.

She rubbed her wrist and turned to Bobby. "You know, with Auntie
Loo missing in action, we don't have to stay here. Over at the Grauman's,
there's a movie retrospective of—"

"George Pal!" he finished. "I know! *War of the Worlds*. Those Sinbad
movies."

She knew how much he loved special-effects filmmaking—from the
old-fashioned miniature models and stop-motion photography of yester-
year to the newest computer-generated gadgetry. In many ways, he was
just as trapped between the past and the present as she was, stuck between
the traditional and the modern.

"Then let's go!" she said, catching his enthusiasm.

Laughing, they fled the ballet and escaped in the limo over to Hol-
lywood Boulevard. They were the only patrons of the Grauman's Chinese
Theatre that night decked out in a tuxedo and a formal silk gown. As they
passed under the massive marquee, Bobby took her arm under his as if
they were waltzing down the red carpet of a movie premiere.

Still, as much fun as it was, Soo-ling was all too conscious of the old
theater's ancient Chinese symbolism and architecture. It stirred again the
ghost of her mother.

But once seated, Bobby's enthusiasm sparked through her and pushed back any painful memories. He went on and on about why the director George Pal was the true father of the modern special effect, how stop-motion photography was a lost art. Then the houselights dimmed and the first movie started. A comfortable silence fell between them as they basked in the flickering glow that separated this world from the land of illusion.

At some point, her hand ended up in Bobby's. She could not say who took whose hand. It happened as naturally as the brush of a stroke of paint.

Still, neither dared look at the other, their gazes fixed toward the screen.

As the lights finally rose during the retrospective's intermission, she turned to Bobby, ready to fill the silence with empty words. She wasn't ready yet to discuss where their relationship would go from here. Her hand slipped from his.

"Bobby—"

Pain erupted in her chest, a whirling blast of ice and fire that burned away any words. Gasping, she fell toward the floor. The theater faded to black as she slipped into pure shadow.

As darkness drowned her, laughter accompanied her on the journey. The black amusement coalesced into a voice, hoary with frost. "Next time, my dear. Next time you are mine."

An image briefly flashed in her mind of the proprietor of the 7-Eleven. He lay faceup in a widening spiral of blood, a raw-edged wound gaping in his chest.

Then nothing, darkness again.

Reality snapped back into focus. Bobby's face filled her vision. She watched his lips move, but it took a moment for his words to make sense. "—hurt. Soo-ling, are you all right?"

She struggled to sit up. "Y-y-yes. I think so."

"Should I call a doctor? It looked like you fainted."

"No, Bobby. I just need to go home." The air in the theater seemed thinner, colder.

"I'll go with you."

She didn't have the energy to argue. Leaning on his shoulder, she allowed herself to be half carried out of the theater and down to the limousine.

"We need to get her home," Bobby told Charles.

"Please," she whispered, collapsing into the leathered interior. "Can we pass by that 7-Eleven on the way?"

She had to know for sure.

Bobby climbed in next to her and shared a worried glance with Charles.

Soon they were speeding down the highway, the traffic mercifully thin. She stared out the window, her breathing shallow. She clenched the edge of her seat with white knuckles. As they exited onto Santa Monica Boulevard, the traffic snarled due to a mass of sirens and flashing lights. They were gathered in front of the 7-Eleven store. A traffic cop, illuminated by a flaming red flare, waved them forward. The limousine glided past the store as a paramedic pushed a draped gurney into a waiting ambulance.

"Do you wish to stop, Miss?"

"No."

She'd seen what she needed to see.

"You tagged this store, didn't you?" Bobby asked, touching her hand, sensing her distress.

She nodded.

"But you couldn't finish your tag? Like back in Laguna?"

She remembered. It was early in her new role as protector of the city. She hadn't really fully believed it herself. She'd allowed the police to chase them off before she'd completed her mark. Afterward a fire burned down that store.

Even after that, she hadn't been truly convinced. Still wasn't. She had taken up the *fu* tag in memory of her mother, to honor her, a duty to tradition born out of guilt and loss.

But now this . . .

"No," she answered softly. "I finished it. It's something else." She remembered the icy claw and the black laughter. Words came tumbling out. She felt stupid even saying them, but she knew they were true. "I think something knows about me—and is hunting me."

Bobby remained silent. She knew he couldn't fully comprehend and probably didn't really believe in her powers, even though he had been the one to get her started. Bobby knew how deeply her mother's death had wounded her. One night, she had shared her mother's stories with him, her claims of a mystical maternal bloodline. Intrigued, Bobby had suggested using the symbol as her new tag, to add weight and purpose to their nightly runs together. And so it began.

But down deep—deeper than she cared to acknowledge—Soo-ling had always known it was more than that. She could not explain it. Tragedies drew her, called to her—and with a can of spray paint she could somehow prevent them.

Until now.

"What are you going to do?" Bobby finally asked.

"I don't know."

"Should I call Auntie Loo?"

Soo-ling frowned. Her mother's youngest sister, Auntie Loo, had taken Soo-ling in after her mother had died. Her aunt was a loan officer for Bank of America, practical and serious. She pooh-poohed the ancient traditions her mother held so dear.

"I'm not sure Auntie Loo can help with this."

Or would even want to for that matter.

But she might know something, anything to make sense of all of this. With no choice, Soo-ling fished out her iPhone. Her fingers trembled, making it hard to call up her aunt's number from the phone's contact list.

Bobby reached and covered her hand with his own. He squeezed once, then slipped the phone from her fingers. "Let me."

"Thanks."

She folded her hands in her lap to stop them from shaking. She stared out the window as Bobby called her aunt. His voice dissolved into the background hum of traffic.

She spent the drive home struggling to understand. Someone knew of her work. Or some*thing*—

Her sight suddenly glazed over, narrowing down into darkness. She blindly clawed for Bobby's hand. She clung to him as if she were drowning. But this time, she knew what was happening.

A vision opened inside her. She saw it all.

. . . a sun rising over the ocean . . . a shoreline bucking and tearing . . . cliff-side homes crashing into the sea . . .

Screams filled her ears.

Then a blank masonry wall appears . . . under the highway exit sign for Riverside . . . above a hidden fault line.

She knew what that meant. The blank wall was her next canvas. It called for her work . . . called for her protection against this coming tragedy. As the vision began to fade, she felt both relieved and terrified. Even after three years, these callings spooked her down to the marrow of her bones. She could no longer dismiss them as coincidences or nightmares born out of anxiety and guilt.

As the screams of the dying faded, mocking laughter followed.

Soo-ling recognized that trail of dark amusement. It was the hunter revealing himself, letting his presence be known. It was both a challenge and a warning to her.

Bobby took her in his arms and held her to him. "What's wrong, Soo?"

She hid her face in her hands, not wanting Bobby to see her so distraught and scared. In a corner of her mind, she still heard the jeering laughter over the screams.

"An earthquake. Tomorrow," she finally mumbled into his tuxedo jacket. "I can block it, but he'll try to stop me."

"Who?"

"I don't know, but we need to hurry. I need answers."

". . . only old stories." Auntie Loo paced the red Moroccan rug of the living room. Cigarette smoke traced her path. She was a stocky woman who cut her black hair into a fierce bob, nothing like the slender grace of Soo-ling's mother. "Mumbo jumbo nonsense. All incense and pseudoreligion."

"Auntie, I don't have time for this. You've been keeping secrets all my life." Soo-ling sat straighter on the leather couch next to Bobby. "Mother knew I had the power, and she must have told you."

"Soo-ling, you don't truly believe—"

"Something is coming for me," she said, cutting her off. "I know it."

A cloud of fear passed over her aunt's features.

"It will tear this city apart to get to me," Soo-ling pressed.

Auntie Loo turned away to study the intricacies of a dynasty vase. Her voice became a faint whisper. "If you're right, then he's found you."

Soo-ling's heart skipped a beat. "Who?"

Her aunt refused to turn around, as if afraid to face any of this. It didn't fit into her world of spreadsheets and financial appraisals.

"Please, Auntie, *who*? Tell me."

"*Gui sou*," her aunt finally whispered, seeming to sag under the weight of ancient history. "The demon."

A stirring deep within Soo-ling responded to the quiet syllables: *gui sou*. With the beast named, her body knew it.

"What do you know, Auntie?"

"Just stories. Told to scare children to bed. Nothing but myths."

Soo-ling crossed the room to her aunt and hugged her from behind. Auntie Loo trembled in her embrace. "Not myths, Auntie. They're as real as my flesh."

Her aunt broke their embrace and crossed to the fireplace. "I did not want to believe."

"But why?"

"The family stories tell of dishonor. Cowardice and shame. Our family is a disgraced line. I was supposed to tell you when you came of age. But it seemed like fiction. I thought I could protect you from needless shame by concealing our family secret."

"But I don't understand. Having this power, this ability to protect, should be an honor."

Auntie tapped out her cigarette on a crystal ashtray. "It was. *Once.*

Our clan was one of thirty-five chosen families, one from each province of China. Each family had the responsibility to protect its province. Our family guarded the Shandong Province on the coast of the Yellow Sea. We were a cherished clan in China."

"So what happened?" Bobby asked.

"As the story is told, the gods of order and chaos are always at war. Guardian families grew to be a part of this balance. They were gifted with the ability to interrupt certain strands of chaos and deflect disasters."

"Like I can do," Soo-ling said.

Auntie nodded and sat on the arm of a leather chair. "Yes. But over the passing centuries, the Chaos Lord became enraged at our interferences and forged a hunter from a part of his spleen, the *gui sou*, to destroy the guardian families. This hunter was unleashed, and many were destroyed before the families finally banded together. Each family sent one representative to form a union powerful enough to entrap the hunter. It took thirty-five guardians to encircle the beast and trap him, but before the enchantment was complete, one member—the one representing our family—panicked and fled. With the circle broken, the spell unraveled. The hunter destroyed the remaining thirty-four guardians. Our disgraced family was banished from China. After decades of wandering, we finally settled here."

"But what of the beast?"

"The story told is that the *gui sou* was injured by the failed assault and can only regain its full strength to push back into our world by finishing the destruction of the circle of guardians. He knows the power of the guardian is passed to only one member of each generation." Auntie Loo stared hard at her. "There is only one member left of that direct descendant line."

Soo-ling crossed back to the sofa and plopped down. "And of course that would be me."

Auntie Loo nodded.

Bobby took her hand, a silent promise that she was not alone.

"So how am I supposed to stop such a creature? It took thirty-five experienced guardians to stop him in the past. I am only one. Where am I going to find so many others before the sun rises?"

"I don't know. The stories give no other clue."

Soo-ling closed her eyes. If she did nothing, then L.A. was doomed. But how could she face this demon alone?

From the hallway, an ancient grandfather clock, an heirloom of three generations, chimed once. They were running out of night.

Bobby spoke up. "I have an idea. But it's a long shot."

Soo-ling turned to him doubtfully. "How?"

"Magic."

At two in the morning, the studio lot still bustled. Spotlights and so-dium lamps held back the night. Levi-clad wranglers from a new western mingled with black-robed ninjas from an action film, while propmen and camera crews scurried to and fro.

No one paid attention to Soo-ling and Bobby as they hurried across the lot.

"What if we're caught?" she asked, sticking close to his side.

Bobby pointed to his back. He'd replaced his tuxedo coat with a bomber jacket. The logo for Titan Pictures was stenciled on the back. "Got it with my internship. No one will give us a second glance."

She must have looked little convinced.

"No worries," he assured her. "This is the land of illusion. It's not about who you are—but who you *appear* to be."

He flipped up the collar of his jacket.

Soo-ling glanced around as they left the chaos and headed into a quieter section of the studio. Bobby had never fully explained his plan. "Where are we going?"

Her friend kept walking.

"Bobby . . ."

He stopped and faced her. "If that demon is tracking you, maybe we'd better keep this on a *need-to-know* basis. For now, the less you know the better."

For the first time, she read the fear in his face. He suddenly looked both older and younger at the same time. His eyes shone in the darkness, full of worry—but beneath that something more, something that had always been there, only she'd failed to recognize it. Until now.

"You don't have to do this," he said. "It's not too late. We could call both our families. Get the hell out of Dodge."

His words held their usual bounce, but she knew it was feigned, as much illusion as the rest of this place. He truly wanted her to flee, to run away, to live.

She acknowledged his fear—and what lay beneath it. Both gave her the strength to lean forward and tip up on her toes. *When had Bobby grown so tall?* She gently kissed his cheek, then lowered to her heels.

"I'm not going anywhere," she said firmly. "This is *our* city."

He smiled, blushing high in his cheeks. "Damn right it is."

Turning smartly on a heel, he led her away. And once again, her hand somehow found its way into his. Together, they hurried through the maze of backlots and alleyways until he halted in front of a green door marked F/X.

"Special Effects?" she asked, confused. "I don't understand."

Bobby finally relented. "Seems like we've reached that *need-to-know* moment."

As he explained his plan, her eyes grew huge. "Are you insane?" she gasped and swatted him in the shoulder.

He rubbed his arm while shrugging. "If you have a better plan . . . ?"

She didn't—and they certainly didn't have time to come up with an alternative. She had to trust that Bobby knew what he was doing.

"Fine. Then let's do this."

His smile grew broader. "Who knew you were this easy?"

"Shut up."

Bobby used his studio keycard to unlock the door and enter the special effects studio. She followed him up to a workroom on the second floor. It was full of computer equipment, giant plasma monitors, and a neighboring green-screen studio.

"Do you know how to run all this?"

Bobby gave her a how-stupid-do-I-look glare. "Who grew up on Xbox and could hand-build his own computer from the age of nine? Besides, as an intern, I spent a few weeks here slinging coffee and doughnuts for the postproduction crew. I learned everything I could. You'd be surprised what doors a double-whip mocha latte will open for you here."

She turned in a circle. "What do I have to do?"

"First, you'll need a new outfit." He pointed to a row of black spandex suits hanging on a row of pegs. The bodysuits had Ping-Pong balls glued all over them. "You can change behind that curtain."

She took a deep breath, grabbed the smallest of the suits, and retreated behind the curtain. She quickly stripped to her bra and panties and shimmied into the tight outfit. Once done, she stared down at her body. The spandex clung like a second skin. She felt naked—and stupid.

White Ping-Pong balls marked each joint and curve of her body.

"What's taking you so long?" Bobby called to her. "I'm all set here."

She stepped from behind the curtain and pointed to him. "Not a word!"

His mouth dropped open at the sight of her. He lifted a finger to his chin and closed his mouth, but his grin remained and spoke volumes.

He crossed to her and handed her a pair of goggles that looked like a large black scuba mask. The goggles trailed a set of black cords.

"What now?" she asked.

He pointed to the neighboring studio wrapped all in green. "The motion-capture suit works best against green screen. Put on the goggles and you'll see everything I do on the computer."

Bobby walked her into the empty studio and helped her put on the heavy goggles. The inside of the mask was one big digital screen. A computerized test pattern filled her vision.

"Okay," he said. "Just stand there until I say go."

"Then what?"

"Do what you do best. I'll run the controls while you just paint."

She heard him plug in the goggle's cords, then retreat out of the studio. The door closed. She felt suddenly alone. Over the years she had developed a suspicion of technology, going back to the machines that had failed to keep her mother alive. She had turned instead to what her mother loved: the simplicity of oil on canvas, of spray paint on walls. That was magic enough for her. She had no use for the cold calculating world of computer technology.

That was Bobby's domain.

She had to trust him—did trust him.

Bobby's voice reached her through tiny speakers built into the goggles. "Soo, wave your arms for me. I want to make sure the computer is properly capturing your motion."

She obeyed, feeling silly.

"That's it! Perfect calibration. I'm activating you now."

The test pattern in her goggles dissolved away, and she found herself staring into a new world. It appeared as if she were standing in front of an easel in the middle of a meadow brimming with wildflowers. Butterflies fluttered among the blossoms, while birds spun and twittered. She raised an arm to block out the sunlight—only it wasn't her arm that rose in front of her, but a computer-generated facsimile.

"Is it too bright?" Bobby's voice whispered from tiny speakers in the goggles. "It's hard to judge from the monitor."

"Yes . . . a little too much glare."

"I'll adjust."

Soo-ling squinted into the meadow. The sun suddenly sank toward the horizon, shadows stretching.

"How's that?" he asked.

"Much better," she said. "But what do I do now?"

"Paint your tag, Soo. That attracted the beast before. Call him into the virtual world. I'll record from here."

Steeling herself, she inhaled sharply and reached for the paintbrush and palette of oils. Though nothing was truly in front of her, the motion and response was so perfect that it made her feel like it was. She swore she could almost feel the brush in one hand and the palette in the other.

After a few fumbling attempts, she fell into her usual rhythm. She dabbed her brush into the oil and tentatively drew her first stroke, a slash of crimson on the white canvas. The remaining thirteen strokes completed her characteristic tag in a few breaths.

Clutching her virtual paintbrush, she waited.

Nothing happened.

"Bobby?"

"Did you paint it correctly, Soo?"

She studied her work. It was perfect.

What am I forgetting?

Then it dawned on her. She reached a finger through empty air, while in another world, a computer-generated finger rose and reached for the center of the painted glyph on the canvas. As contact was made, a familiar tingling surged up her arm. Soo-ling tensed, holding her breath. She waited for several heartbeats.

Still nothing.

She started to drop her arm when a stabbing cold seized her wrist. She wanted desperately to pull away like before—but she knew this time she must stand firm, hold fast, not disgrace the family as her ancestor had done so many centuries ago.

Foreign memories suddenly flooded into her consciousness, like dreams long forgotten slipping back into focus again. She remembered Shandong Province with the sun rising over the Yellow Sea; she remembered fishing with her brothers, cherry blossoms floating on the water; she remembered her first love, Wan Lee, turning his back on her after her shame.

"Soo?" Bobby had an uncertain edge to his voice. "What are you doing? There's this old woman dressed in a robe on the screen where you're supposed to be."

Soo-ling barely heard him, floating between past and present. She began to understand as more ancestral memories filled her.

"She's a friend," she finally mumbled, knowing it to be true. "I don't know quite what's happening, but your hunch was right. It's coming. I sense it. Like electricity before a thunderstorm."

The cold crept up her arm, seeking her heart. Dusty laughter, old and cracked, followed and crumbled into words. "I have found you at long last, *siu far*, my little flower."

Distant memories intruded. A foggy glen, surrounded by towering trees, the lowing of cattle from a distant rice paddy, and a creature of nightmares crouching, its voice mocking.

Soo-ling's lips moved, but she did not know who spoke: herself or her ancestor. "*Gui sou.*"

More dark laughter. "Ah, you know my name. You have hidden well over the years, *siu far*. But now it is time to be plucked. I shall wear you as an ornament once I am free. Free to stalk the world of man."

A mist rose from the meadow floor and coalesced into an ancient face, yellow and wrinkled like a dried apricot. The face split into a leer, lined by fangs. The fog continued to encircle her, forming the coils of a snake— along with a reptilian claw that gripped her wrist.

Old fears arose, like smoke from an extinguished fire.

Trapped, must escape, flee!

Her head throbbed, and the world began to tilt, eyes blurring.

"Soo-ling!" Bobby's voice jolted her to the present. "I can see that monster on the monitor. Get out of there!"

The spiked and scaled body of the beast appeared in the mist. She began to yank her arm away when a foreign thought intruded.

No. Stand firm, child. You must resist.

"Soo, I'm ending the program."

"No, Bobby!" she yelled. Understanding dawned in her. "The circle isn't complete. It will follow me out."

"Let it try!" Bobby said. "I'll take care of it."

His words—full of bravura and love—conjured more recent memories. *Running the back alleys with Bobby. Fleeing police and gang members, laughing. Planting tags throughout the city. My city! Our city!*

"Just do as we planned," she said. "Complete the circle."

The *gui sou* leaned closer, suspicious, its breath stale as an open grave. "Who do you speak to, little one? Prayers, perhaps? Do not bother seeking aid from your puny gods. Prayers will not save you."

"Who needs prayers, when you've got friends who love you?" And she knew it to be true. "Now, Bobby!"

"Engaging copies!"

The empty meadow suddenly filled with thirty-four other easels, exact copies of her original. They encircled the field. Disembodied arms, floating free, repeated what she had painted earlier. Thirty-four arms picked up brushes and palettes and painted identical symbols in unison. Then they all reached forward to touch the center of their glyphs.

A flash of confusion swept over the creature's jaundiced features. Its fiery eyes darted everywhere. The claws gripping her hand faded back to mist. Snaking coils dissolved back to fog. The mocking face leaned close. "What trick is this, witch?"

She knew the answer. "A spell broken long ago is woven again."

"Impossible. There are no other guardians. What trickery is this?"

The *gui sou* collected its mists, like a woman gathering her skirts, and glided across the meadow. It tried to break out of the circle but was stopped by an invisible wall of force. It flattened its mists against the barrier, probing for an opening. With a shriek, it thrashed back and forth across the meadow, flinging itself against the sides of its new prison.

After a full minute, it stopped and rushed at her. "Drop your arm, *siu far*, break the circle, and I will let you escape again."

Same old trick.

"Not this century," she sneered.

"You'll never be able to stand there forever," it warned, rearing up in threat and fury. "You'll tire! Then I will devour you!"

She faced the monster with an arched eyebrow. "Really? Then let me welcome you to the new millennium! You're nothing but a ghost of the past. And the past is where you will remain. Locked forever in *memory*." She called more loudly. "Bobby, *hit it*!"

"Saving to disk now!"

The world within the goggles pulled away, shrinking smaller and smaller until the digital window was the size of a postage stamp. As it receded, she saw them appear, standing behind each of the other easels: different Chinese women, of varying ages, the murdered provincial guardians from the ancient past. They bowed to her, acknowledging an ancient debt paid in full.

At the last moment, a whisper reached her, full of love and pride.

Si low chai . . .

She knew that voice, those tender words. Tears welled, bursting from her swollen heart.

". . . Mother . . ."

A warmth filled her as the tenuous connection faded.

Soo-ling struggled to hold it—but it was like grasping smoke. The connection ended, as it must. That was not her world.

Still, the warmth remained inside her.

The true ghost of her mother.

Her everlasting love.

The image of a computer desktop snapped into place inside her goggles. It held frozen the last picture: thirty-five guardians encircling a demon. Then that file dropped away into a computerized folder icon. A symbol of a combination lock overlay the folder. It clicked closed.

"We're locked up!" Bobby called out.

Soo-ling took a long, shuddering breath, then pulled off her goggles. She stood again in the empty studio. Behind her, the door banged open and Bobby rushed inside. His expression grew concerned as he saw her face.

"Soo, are you all right?"

She wiped her tears. "Never better."

And she meant it.

Bobby crossed to her and handed her a recordable DVD. A thin crust of frost caked its surface. "It should be trapped in there, right?"

She nodded and took the DVD. "I hope so."

"So then we've won," Bobby said, blowing out his relief.

"The battle, perhaps, but not the war."

She knew the *gui sou* was only a small part of the Chaos Lord. There was still a wall in Riverside that needed her handiwork—or come dawn, Los Angeles would really rock and roll.

Bobby stood before her. "What now?"

"Time to go to work. Do you have a can of spray paint?"

He raised his eyebrows as if insulted. "Of course."

She leaned and tipped up on her toes again. This time she kissed his lips. "Then let's go save the world."

Something Completely Different

I wanted to impress George R. R. Martin.

That was why I wrote this next story. I was approached to submit a piece for an anthology to be edited by Mr. Martin and the esteemed Gardner Dozois. The title of the collection was Warriors, and the conceit for this volume was for each author to write a story involving any warrior from any place in history, even the future.

I scratched my head, trying to think of what "warrior" to write about. I imagined I was approached because my Sigma novels were chock-full of soldiers who were uniquely disciplined in the sciences, in other words, "scientists with guns." But that seemed too expected and predictable, especially to present to someone as formidable as Mr. Martin.

Now, I had been reading Mr. Martin's books since high school, long before his success with Game of Thrones. I knew he was a bit of a chameleon. In the past, he had written across various genres, from science fiction to fantasy to horror. Knowing this, I challenged myself to do something completely different and unexpected. My warrior was not going to be a human character. Instead, I was going to draw upon my background as veterinarian and craft a story about a unique warrior: a dog in a pit-fighting ring.

I also wanted to tell this story strictly from the dog's point of view, to put my readers into that harrowing world from the eye level of a pit fighter. To accomplish that, I went back and reviewed the work of Jack London. I interviewed people willing to talk about their experiences. I spoke to a behaviorist who specialized in rehabilitating abused dogs.

And all of that became "The Pit," a work that I still consider to be some of my best writing.

Thanks, George!

The Pit

JAMES ROLLINS

The large dog hung from the bottom of the tire swing by his teeth. His back paws swung three feet off the ground. Overhead, the sun remained a red blister in an achingly blue sky. After so long, the muscles of the dog's jaw had cramped to a tight knot. His tongue had turned to a salt-dried piece of leather, lolling out one side. Still, at the back of his throat, he tasted black oil and blood.

But he did not let go.

He knew better.

Two voices spoke behind him. The dog recognized the gravel of the yard trainer. But the second was someone new, squeaky and prone to sniffing between every other word.

"How long he be hangin' there?" the stranger asked.

"Forty-two minutes."

"No shit! That's one badass motherfucker. But he's not pure pit, is he?"

"Pit and boxer."

"True nuff? You know, I got a Staffordshire bitch be ready for him next month. And let me tell you, she puts the mean back in bitch. Cut you in on the pups."

"Stud fee's a thousand."

"Dollars? You cracked or what?"

"Fuck you. Last show he brought down twelve motherfuckin' Gs."

"Twelve? You're shittin' me. For a dogfight?"

The trainer snorted. "And that's after paying the house. He beat that champion out of Central. Should seen that Crip monster. All muscle and scars. Had twenty-two pounds on Brutus here. Pit ref almost shut down the fight at the weigh-in. Called my dog ring bait! But the bastard showed 'em. And those odds paid off like a crazy motherfucker."

Laughter. Raw. No warmth behind it.

The dog watched out of the corner of his eye. The trainer stood to the left, dressed in baggy jeans and a white T-shirt, showing arms decorated with ink, his head shaved to the scalp. The newcomer wore leather and carried a helmet under one arm. His eyes darted around.

"Let's get out of the goddamn sun," the stranger finally said. "Talk numbers. I got a kilo coming in at the end of the week."

As they stepped away, something struck the dog's flank. Hard. But he still didn't let go. Not yet.

"Release!"

With the command, the dog finally unclamped his jaws and dropped to the practice yard. His hind legs were numb, heavy with blood. But he turned to face the two men. Shoulders up, he squinted against the sun. The yard trainer stood with his wooden bat. The newcomer had his fists shoved into the pockets of his jacket and took a step back. The dog smelled the stranger's fear, a bitter dampness, like weeds soaked in old urine.

The trainer showed no such fear. He held his bat with one hand and scowled his dissatisfaction. He reached down and unhooked the plate of iron that hung from the dog collar. The plate dropped to the hard-packed dirt.

"Twenty-pound weight," the trainer told the stranger. "I'll get him up to *thirty* before next week. Helps thicken the neck up."

"Any thicker and he won't be able to turn his head."

"Don't want him to *turn* his head. That'll cost me a mark in the ring."

The bat pointed toward the line of cages. A boot kicked toward the dog's side. "Get your ass back into the kennel, Brutus."

The dog curled a lip, but he swung away, thirsty and exhausted. The fenced runs lined the rear of the yard. The floors were unwashed cement. From the neighboring cages, heads lifted toward him as he approached, then lowered sullenly. At the entrance, he lifted his leg and marked his spot. He fought not to tremble on his numb back leg. He couldn't show weakness.

He'd learned that on the first day.

"Git in there already!"

He was booted from behind as he entered the cage. The only shade came from a scrap of tin nailed over the back half of the run. The fence door clanged shut behind him.

He lumbered across the filthy space to his water dish, lowered his head, and drank.

Voices drifted away as the two headed toward the house. One question hung in the air. "How'd that monster get the name Brutus?"

The dog ignored them. That memory was a shard of yellowed bone buried deep. Over the past two winters, he'd tried to grind it away. But it had remained lodged, a truth that couldn't be forgotten.

He hadn't always been named Brutus.

"C'mere, Benny! That's a good boy!"

It was one of those days that flowed like warm milk, so sweet, so comforting, filling every hollow place with joy. The black pup bounded across the green and endless lawn. Even from across the yard, he smelled the piece of hot dog in the hand hidden behind the skinny boy's back. Behind him, a brick house climbed above a porch encased in vines and purple flowers. Bees buzzed, and frogs croaked a chorus with the approach of twilight.

"Sit! Benny, sit!"

The pup slid to a stop on the dewy grass and dropped to his haunches. He quivered all over. He wanted the hot dog. He wanted to lick the salt

off those fingers. He wanted a scratch behind the ear. He wanted this day
to never end.

"There's a good boy."

The hand came around, and fingers opened. The pup stuffed his cold
nose into the palm, snapped up the piece of meat, then shoved closer. He
waggled his whole hindquarters and wormed tighter to the boy.

Limbs tangled, and they both fell to the grass.

Laughter rang out like sunshine.

"Watch out! Here comes Junebug!" the boy's mother called from the
porch. She rocked in a swing as she watched the boy and pup wrestle. Her
voice was kind, her touch soft, her manner calm.

Much like the pup's own mother.

Benny remembered how his mother used to groom his forehead, nuz-
zle his ear, how she kept them all safe, all ten of them, tangled in a pile of
paws, tails, and mewling complaints. Though even that memory was fading. He could hardly picture her face any longer, only the warmth of her
brown eyes as she'd gazed down at them as they fed, fighting for a teat.
And he'd had to fight, being the smallest of his brothers and sisters. But
he'd never had to fight alone.

"Juneeeee!" the boy squealed.

A new weight leaped into the fray on the lawn. It was Benny's sister,
Junebug. She yipped and barked and tugged on anything loose: shirt
sleeve, pant leg, wagging tail. The last was her specialty. She'd pulled many
of her fellow brothers and sisters off a teat by their tails, so Benny could
have his turn.

Now those same sharp teeth clamped onto the tip of Benny's tail and
tugged hard. He squealed and leaped straight up—not so much in pain,
but in good-hearted play. The three of them rolled and rolled across the
yard, until the boy collapsed on his back in surrender, leaving the brother
and sister free to lick his face from either side.

"That's enough, Jason!" their new mother called from the porch.

"Oh, Mom . . ." The boy pushed up on one elbow, flanked by the two
pups.

The pair stared across the boy's chest, tails wagging, tongues hanging, panting. His sister's eyes shone at him in that frozen moment of time, full of laughter, mischief, and delight. It was like looking at himself.

It was why they'd been picked together.

"Two peas in a pod, those two," the old man had said as he knelt over the litter and lifted brother and sister toward the visitors. "Boy's right ear is a blaze of white. Girl's left ear is the same. Mirror images. Make quite a pair, don't you think? Hate to separate them."

And in the end, he didn't have to. Brother and sister were taken to their new home together.

"Can't I play a little longer?" the boy called to the porch.

"No argument, young man. Your father will be home in a bit. So get cleaned up for dinner."

The boy stood up. Benny read the excitement in his sister's eyes. It matched his own. They'd not understood anything except for the mother's last word.

Dinner.

Bolting from the boy's side, the pair of pups raced toward the porch. Though smaller, Benny made up for his size with blazing speed. He shot across the yard toward the promise of a full dinner bowl and maybe a biscuit to chew afterward. Oh, if only—

—then a familiar tug on his tail. The surprise attack from behind tripped his feet. He sprawled nose-first into the grass and slid with his limbs splayed out.

His sister bounded past him and up the steps.

Benny scrabbled his legs under him and followed. Though outsmarted as usual by his bigger sister, it didn't matter. His tail wagged and wagged.

He hoped these days would never end.

"Shouldn't we pull his ass out of there?"

"Not yet!"

Brutus paddled in the middle of the pool. His back legs churned the water, toes splayed out. His front legs fought to keep his snout above the water. His collar, a weighted steel chain, sought to drag him to the cement bottom. Braided cords of rope trapped him in the middle of the concrete swimming pool. His heart thundered in his throat. Each breath heaved with desperate sprays of water.

"Yo, man! You gonna drown 'im!"

"A little water won't kill him. He got a fight in two days. A big-ass show. I got a lot riding on it."

Paddling and wheeling his legs, water burned his eyes. His vision darkened at the edges. Still he saw the pit trainer off to the side, in trunks, no shirt. On his bare chest were inked two dogs snarling at each other. Two other men held the chains, keeping him from reaching the edge of the pool.

Bone-tired and cold, his back end began to slip deeper. He fought, but his head bobbed under. He took a gulp into his lungs. Choking, he kicked and got his nose above water again. He gagged his lungs clear. A bit of bile followed, oiling the water around his lips. Foam frothed from his nostrils.

"He done in, man. Pull 'im out."

"Let's see what he's got," the trainer said. "Bitch been in there longer than he ever done."

For another stretch of painful eternity, Brutus fought the pull of the chain and the waterlogged weight of his own body. His head sank with every fourth paddle. He breathed in as much stinging water as he did air. He had gone deaf to anything but his own hammering heart. His vision had shrunk to a blinding pinpoint. Then finally, he could no longer fight to the surface. More water flowed into his lungs. He sank—into the depths and into darkness.

But there was no peace.

The dark still terrified him.

The summer storm rattled the shutters and boomed with great claps that sounded like the end of all things. Spats of rain struck the windows, and flashes of lightning split the night sky.

Benny hid under the bed with his sister. He shivered against her side. She crouched, ears up, nose out. Each rumble was echoed in her chest as she growled back at the threatening noise. Benny leaked some of his terror, soaking the carpet under him. He was not as brave as his big sister.

. . . boom, boom, BOOM . . .

Brightness shattered across the room, casting away all shadows.

Benny whined and his sister barked.

A face appeared from atop the bed and leaned down to stare at them. The boy, his head upside down, lifted a finger to his lips. "Shh, Junie, you'll wake Dad."

But his sister would have none of that. She barked and barked, trying to scare off what lurked in the storm. The boy rolled off his bed and sprawled on the floor. Arms reached and scooped them both toward him. Benny went willingly.

"Eww . . . you're all wet."

Junie squirmed loose then ran around the room, barking, tail straight back, ears pricked high.

"Sheesh," the boy said, trying to catch her while cradling Benny.

A door banged open out in the hall. Footsteps echoed. The bedroom door swung open. Large bare legs like tree trunks entered. "Jason, son, I got to get up early."

"Sorry, Dad. The storm's got them spooked."

A long heavy sighed followed. The large man caught Junie and swung her up in his arms. She slathered his face with her tongue, tail beating against his arms. Still, she growled all the time as the sky rumbled back at them.

"They're going to have to get used to these storms," the man said. "These thunder-bumpers will be with us all summer."

"I'll take them downstairs. We can sleep on the sofa on the back porch. If they're with me . . . maybe that'll help 'em get used to it."

Junie was passed to the boy.

"All right, son. But take an extra blanket."

"Thanks, Dad."

A large hand clapped on the boy's shoulder. "You're taking good care of them. I'm proud of you. They're really getting huge."

The boy struggled with the two squirming pups and laughed. "I know!"

A few moments later, all three of them were buried in a nest of blankets atop a musty sofa. Benny smelled mice spoor and bird droppings, brought alive by the wind and dampness. Still, with all of them together, it was the best bed he'd ever slept in. Even the storm had quieted, though a heavy rain continued to pelt from the dark moonless skies. It beat against the shingled roof of the porch.

Just as Benny finally calmed enough to let his eyelids droop closed, his sister sprang to her feet, growling again, hackles up. She slithered out from under the blankets without disturbing the boy. Benny had no choice but to follow.

What is it?

Benny's ears were now up and swiveling. From the top step of the porch, he stared out into the storm-swept yard. Tree limbs waved. Rain chased across the lawn in rippling sheets.

Then Benny heard it, too.

A rattle of the side gate. A few furtive whispers.

Someone was out there!

His sister shot from the porch. Without thinking, Benny ran after her. They raced toward the gate.

Whispers turned into words. "Quiet, asshole. Let me see if the dogs are back there!"

Benny saw the gate swing open. Two shadowy shapes stepped forward. Benny slowed—then caught the smell of meat, bloody and raw.

"What'd I tell ya?"

A tiny light bloomed in the darkness, spearing his sister. Junie slowed enough for Benny to catch up to her. One of the strangers dropped to a knee and held out an open palm. The rich, meaty smell swelled.

"You want it, don't cha? C'mon, you little bitches."

Junie snuck closer, more on her belly, tail twitching in tentative welcome. Benny sniffed and sniffed, nose up. The tantalizing odor drew him along behind his sister.

Once near the gate, the two dark shapes leaped on them. Something heavy dropped over Benny and wrapped tightly around him. He tried to cry out, but fingers clamped over his muzzle and trapped his scream to a muffled whine. He heard the same from his sister.

He was hauled up and carried away.

"Nothing like a stormy night to pick up bait. No one ever suspects. Always blame the thunder. Thinks it scared the little shits into running off."

"How much we gonna make?"

"Fifty a head easy."

"Nice."

Thunder clapped again, marking the end of Benny's old life.

Brutus entered the ring. The dog kept his head lowered, shoulders high, ears pulled flat against his skull. His hackles already bristled. It still hurt to breathe deeply, but the dog hid the pain. Buried in his lungs, a dull fire burned from the pool water, flaring with each breath. Cautiously, he took in all the scents around him.

The sand of the ring was still being raked clean of the blood from the prior fight. Still, the fresh spoor filled the old warehouse, along with the taint of grease and oil, the chalk of cement, and the bite of urine, sweat, and feces from both dog and man.

The fights had been going on from sunset until well into the night.

But no one had left.

Not until this match was over.

The dog had heard his name called over and over: "Brutus . . . man, look at the *cajones* on that *monstruo* . . . he a little-ass bastard, but I saw Brutus take on a dog twice his size . . . tore his throat clean open . . ."

As Brutus had waited in his pen, people had trailed past, many dragging children, to stare at him. Fingers pointed, flashes snapped, blinding him, earning low growls. Finally, the handler had chased them all off with his bat.

"Move on! This ain't no free show. If you like him so goddamned much, go place a fucking bet!"

Now as Brutus passed through the gate in the ring's three-foot-tall wooden fence, shouts and whistles greeted him from the stands, along with raucous laughter and angry outbursts. The noise set Brutus's heart pounding. His claws dug into the sand, his muscles tensed.

They were the first to enter the ring.

Beyond the crowd spread a sea of cages and fenced-in pens. Large shadowy shapes stirred and paced.

There was little barking.

The dogs knew to save their strength for the ring.

"You'd better not lose," the pit handler mumbled and tugged on the chain hooked to the dog's studded collar. Bright lights shone down into the pit. It reflected off the handler's shaved head, revealing the ink on his arms, black and red, like bloody bruises.

The pair kept to the ring's edge and waited. The trainer slapped the dog's flank, then wiped his wet hand on his jeans. Brutus's coat was still damp. Prior to the fight, each dog had been washed by their opponent's handler, to make sure there was no slippery grease or poison oils worked into the coat to give a dog an advantage.

As they waited for their opponent to enter the ring, Brutus smelled the sheen of excitement off the handler. A sneer remained frozen on the man's face, showing a hint of teeth.

Beyond the fence, another man approached the edge of the ring. Brutus recognized him by the way he sniffed between his words and the bitter trace of fear that accompanied him. If the man had been another dog, he would've had his tail tucked to his belly and a whine flowing from his throat.

"I placed a buttload on this bastard," the man said as he stepped to the fence and eyed Brutus.

"So?" his handler answered.

"I just saw Gonzales's dog. Christ, man, are you nuts? That monster's half bullmastiff."

The handler shrugged. "Yeah, but he got only one good eye. Brutus'll take him down. Or at least he'd better." Again the chain jerked.

The man shifted behind the fence and leaned closer. "Is there some sort of fix going on here?"

"Fuck you. I don't need a fix."

"But I heard you once owned that other dog. That one-eyed bastard."

The handler scowled. "Yeah, I did. Sold him to Gonzales a couple years ago. Didn't think the dog would live. After he lost his fuckin' eye and all. Bitch got all infected. Sold him to that spic for a couple bottles of Special K. Stupidest deal I ever made. Dog gone and made that beaner a shitload of money. He's been rubbin' it my face ever since. But today's payback."

The chain yanked and lifted Brutus off his toes.

"You'd better not lose this show. Or we might just have ourselves another barbecue back at the crib."

The dog heard the threat behind the words. Though he didn't fully understand, he sensed the meaning. *Don't lose.* Over the past two winters, he'd seen defeated dogs shot in the head, strangled to death with their own chains, or allowed to be torn to pieces in the ring. Last summer, a bull terrier had bitten Brutus's handler in the calf. The dog had been blood-addled after losing a match and had lashed out. Later, back at the yard, the bull terrier had tried mewling for forgiveness, but the handler had soaked the dog down and set him on fire. The flaming terrier had run circles around the yard, howling, banging blindly into runs and fences. The men in the yard had laughed and laughed, falling down on their sides.

The dogs in their kennels had watched silently.

They all knew the truth of their lives.

Never lose.

Finally, a tall skinny man stepped to the center of the ring. He lifted an arm high. "Dogs to your scratch lines!"

The far gate of the ring opened, and a massive shape bulled into the ring, half dragging his small, beefy handler, a man who wore a big grin and a cowboy hat. But Brutus's attention fixed to the dog. The mastiff was a wall of muscle. His ears had been cropped to nubs. He had no tail. His paws mashed deep into the sand as he fought toward the scratch line.

As the beast pulled forward, he kept his head cocked to the side, allowing his one eye to scan the ring. The other eye was a scarred knot.

The man in the center of the ring pointed to the two lines raked into the sand. "To the scratch! It's the final show of the night, folks! What you've been waiting for! Two champions brought together again! Brutus against Caesar!"

Laughter and cheers rose from the crowd. Feet pounded on the stands boards.

But all Brutus heard was that one name.

Caesar.

He suddenly trembled all over. The shock rocked through him as if his very bones rattled. He fought to hold steady and stared across at his opponent—and remembered.

"Caesar! C'mon, you bastard, you hungry or not?"

Under the midmorning sun, Benny hung from a stranger's hand. Fingers scruffed the pup's neck and dangled him in the center of a strange yard. Benny cried and piddled a stream to the dirt below. He saw other dogs behind fences. Smelled more elsewhere. His sister was clutched in the arms of one of the men who'd nabbed them out of their yard. His sister barked out sharply.

"Shut that bitch up. She's distracting him."

"I don't want to see this," the man said, but he pinched his sister's muzzle shut.

"Oh, grow some damn balls. Whatcha think I paid you a hundred bucks for? Dog's gotta eat, don't he?" The man dug his fingers tighter into Benny's scruff and shook him hard. "And bait is bait."

Another man called from the shadows across the yard. "Hey, Juice! How much weight you want on the sled this time?"

"Go for fifteen bricks?"

"Fifteen?"

"I need Caesar muscled up good for the fight next week."

Benny heard the knock and scrape of something heavy.

"Here he comes!" the shadow man called over. "He must be hungry!"

Out of the darkness, a monster appeared. Benny had never seen a dog so large. The giant heaved against a harness strapped across his chest. Ropes of drool trailed from the corners of his lips. Claws dug into the dark dirt as he hauled forward. Behind him, attached to the harness was a sled on steel runners. It was piled high with blocks of cement.

The man holding Benny laughed deep in his throat. "He be damned hungry! Haven't fed him in two days!"

Benny dribbled out more of his fear. The monster's gaze was latched on to him. Benny read the red, raw hunger in those eyes. The drool flowed thicker.

"Hurry it up, Caesar! If you want your breakfast!"

The man took a step back with Benny.

The large brute pulled harder, shouldering into the harness, his long tongue hanging, frothing with foam. He panted and growled. The sled dragged across the dirt with the grating sound of gnawed bone.

Benny's heart hammered in his small chest. He tried to squirm away, but he couldn't escape the man's iron grip . . . or the unwavering gaze of the monster. It was coming for him. He wailed and cried.

Time stretched to a long sharp line of terror.

Steadily the beast came at him.

Finally, the man burst out a satisfied snort. "Good enough! Unhook him!"

Another man ran out of the shadows and yanked on a leather lead. The harness dropped from the monster's shoulders, and the huge dog bounded across the yard, throwing slather with each step.

The man swung his arm back, then tossed Benny forward. The pup flew high into the air, spinning tail over ear. He was too terrified to scream. As he spun, he caught glimpses below of the monster pounding after him—but he also spotted his sister. The man who held Junie had started to turn away, not wanting to watch. He must have loosened his grip enough to let Junie slip her nose free. She bit hard into his thumb.

Then Benny hit the ground and rolled across the yard. The impact knocked the air from his chest. He lay stunned as the larger dog barreled toward him. Terrified, Benny used the only advantage he had—his speed.

He rolled to his feet and darted to the left. The big dog couldn't turn fast enough and skidded past where he'd landed. Benny fled across the yard, tucking his back legs under his front in his desperation to go faster. He heard the huffing of the monster at his tail.

If he could just get under the low sled, hide there . . .

But he didn't know the yard. One paw hit a broken tile in the scrubby weeds, and he lost his footing. He hit his shoulder and rolled. He came to rest on his side as the huge dog lunged at him.

Benny winced. Desperate, he exposed his belly and piddled on himself, showing his submission. But it didn't matter. Lips rippled back from yellow teeth.

Then the monster suddenly jerked to a stop in midlunge, accompanied by a surprised yelp. The brute spun around. Benny saw something attached to his tail.

It was Junie. Dropped by her captor, she had come at the monster with her usual sneak attack. The monster spun several more times as Junie remained clamped to his tail. This was no playful nip. She must've dug in deep with her sharp teeth. In attempting to throw her off, the large dog only succeeded in stripping more fur and skin from his tail as Junie was tossed about.

Blood sprayed across the dirt.

But finally even Junie couldn't resist the brute's raw strength. She went flying, her muzzle bloody. The monster followed and landed hard on her. Blocked by his bulk, Benny couldn't see—but he heard.

A sharp cry from Junie, followed by the crunch of bone.

No!

Benny leaped to his feet and ran at the monster. There was no plan—only a red, dark anger. He speared straight at the monster. He caught a glimpse of a torn leg, bone showing. The monster gripped his sister and shook her. She flopped limply. Crimson sprayed, then poured from his lips, mixed with drool.

With the sight, Benny plummeted into a dark place, a pit from which he knew he'd never escape. He leaped headlong at the monster and landed on the brute's face. He clawed and bit and gouged, anything to get him to let his sister go.

But he was so much smaller.

A toss of the blocky head, and Benny went flying away—forever lost in blood, fury, and despair.

As Brutus stared at Caesar, it all came back. The past and present overlapped and muddled into a crimson blur. He stood at the scratch line in the ring without remembering walking to it. He could not say who stood at the line.

Brutus or Benny.

After the mutilation of his sister, Benny had been spared a brutal death. The yard trainer had been impressed by his fire. *A real Brutus, this one. Taking on Caesar all alone! Fast, too. See him juke and run. Maybe he's too good for just bait.*

Caesar had not fared as well after their brief fight. During the attack, a back claw had split the large dog's eyelid and sliced across his left eye, blinding that side. Even the tail wound from Junie's bite had festered. The yard trainer had tried cutting off his tail with an ax and burning the stub with a flaming piece of wood. But the eye and tail got worse. For a week, the reek of pus and dying flesh flowed from his kennel. Flies swarmed in black gusts. Finally, a stranger in a cowboy hat arrived with a wheelbarrow, shook hands with the handler, and hauled Caesar away, muzzled, feverish, and moaning.

Everyone thought he'd died.

They'd been wrong.

Both dogs toed the scratch line in the sand. Caesar did not recognize his opponent. No acknowledgment shone out of that one eye, only blood-lust and blind fury. The monster lunged at the end of his chain, digging deep into the sand.

Brutus bunched his back legs under him. Old fury fired through his blood. His muzzle snarled into a long growl, one rising from his very bones.

The tall skinny man lifted both arms. "Dogs ready!" He brought his arms down while stepping back. "Go!"

With a snap, they were loosed from their chains. The dogs leaped upon each other. Bodies slammed together amid savage growls and flying spittle.

Brutus went first for Caesar's blind side. He bit into the nub of ear, seeking a hold. Cartilage ripped. Blood flowed over his tongue. The grip was too small to hold for long.

In turn, Caesar struck hard, using his heavier bulk to roll Brutus. Fangs sank into his shoulder. Brutus lost his hold and found himself pinned under that weight. Caesar bodily lifted him and slammed him into the sand.

But Brutus was still fast. He squirmed and twisted until he was belly to belly with the monster. He jackrabbit-punched up with his back legs and broke Caesar's hold on his shoulder. Loosed, Brutus went for the throat above him. But Caesar snapped down at him at the same time. They ended muzzle to muzzle, tearing at each other. Brutus on bottom, Caesar on top.

Blood spat and flew.

He kicked again and raked claws across the tender belly of his opponent, gouging deep—then lunged up and latched on to Caesar's jowl. Using the hold, he kicked and hauled his way out from under the bulk. He kept to the beast's left, his blind side.

Momentarily losing sight of Brutus, Caesar jagged in the wrong direction. He left his flank open. Brutus lashed out for a hind leg. He bit deep into the thick meat at the back of the thigh and chomped with all the muscles in his jaws. He yanked hard and shook his head.

In that moment of raw fury, Brutus flashed to a small limp form, clamped in bloody jaws, shaken and broken. A blackness fell over his vision. He used his entire body—muscle, bone, and blood—to rip and slash. The thick ligament at the back of the leg tore away from the ankle.

Caesar roared, but Brutus kept his grip and hauled up onto his hind legs. He flipped the other onto his back. Only then did he let go and slam on top of the other. He lunged for the exposed throat and bit deep. Fangs sank into tender flesh. He shook and ripped, snarled and dug.

From beyond the blackness, a whistle blew. It was the signal to break hold and return to their corners. Handlers ran up.

"Release!" his trainer yelled and grabbed the back of his collar.

Brutus heard the cheering, recognized the command. But it was all far away. He was deep in the pit.

Hot blood filled his mouth, flowed into his lungs, soaked into the sand. Caesar writhed under him. Fierce growling turned into mewling. But Brutus was deaf to it. Blood flowed into all the empty places inside him, trying to fill it up, but failing.

Something struck his shoulders. Again and again. The handler's wooden bat. But Brutus kept his grip locked on the other dog's throat. He couldn't let go, trapped forever in the pit.

Wood splintered across his back.

Then a new noise cut through the roaring in his ears. More whistles, sharper and urgent, accompanied by the strident blare of sirens. Flashing lights dazzled through the darkness. Shouts followed, along with commands amplified to a piercing urgency.

"*This is the Police! Everyone on your knees! Hands on heads!*"

Brutus finally lifted his torn muzzle from the throat of the other dog. Caesar lay unmoving on the sand, soaked in a pool of blood. Brutus lifted his eyes to the chaos around him. People fled the stands. Dogs barked and howled. Dark figures in helmets and carrying clear shields closed a circle around the area, forming a larger ring around the sand pit. Through the open doors of the warehouse, cars blazed in the night.

Wary, Brutus stood over the body of the dead dog.

He felt no joy at the killing. Only a dead numbness.

His trainer stood a step away. A string of anger flowed from the man's lips. He threw the broken stub of his bat into the sand. An arm pointed at Brutus.

"When I say release, you *release*, you dumb sack of shit!"

Brutus stared dully at the arm pointed at him, then to the face. From the man's expression, Brutus knew what the handler saw. It shone out of the dog's entire being. Brutus was trapped in a pit deeper than anything covered in sand, a pit from which he could never escape, a hellish place of pain and hot blood.

The man's eyes widened, and he took a step back. The beast stalked after him, no longer dog, only a creature of rage and fury.

Without warning—no growl, no snarl—Brutus lunged at the trainer. He latched on to the man's arm. The same arm that dangled pups as bait, an arm attached to the real monster of the sandy ring, a man who called horrors out of the shadows and set dogs on fire.

Teeth clamped over the pale wrist. Jaws crushed down. Bones ground and crackled under the pressure.

The man screamed.

From the narrow corner of one eye, Brutus watched a helmeted figure rush at them, an arm held up, pointing a black pistol.

A flash from the muzzle.

Then a sizzle of blinding pain.

And at last, darkness again.

Brutus lay on the cold concrete floor of the kennel. He rested his head on his paws and stared out the fenced gate. A wire-framed ceiling lamp shone off the whitewashed cement walls and lines of kennels. He listened with a deaf ear to the shuffle of other dogs, to the occasional bark or howl.

Behind him, a small door led to an outside fenced-in pen. Brutus seldom went out there. He preferred the shadows. His torn muzzle had been knitted together with staples, but it still hurt to drink. He didn't eat. He had been here for five days, noting the rise and fall of sunlight through the doorway.

People came by occasionally to stare at him. To scribble on a wooden chart hanging on his door. Men in white jackets injected him twice a day, using a noose attached to a long steel pole to hold him pinned to the wall. He growled and snapped. Mostly out of irritation than true anger. He just wanted to be left alone.

He had woken here after that night in the pit.

And a part of him still remained back there.

Why am I still breathing?

Brutus knew guns. He recognized their menacing shapes and sizes, the tang of their oils, the bitter reek of their smoke. He'd seen scores of dogs shot, some quickly, some for sport. But the pistol that had fired back at the ring had struck with a sizzle that twisted his muscles and arched his back.

He lived.

That, more than anything, kept him angry and sick of spirit.

A shuffle of rubber shoes drew his attention. He didn't lift his head, only twitched his eyes. It was too early for the pole and needles.

"He's over here," a voice said. "Animal Control just got the judge's order to euthanize all the dogs this morning. This one's on the list, too. Heard they had to tazer him off his own trainer. So I wouldn't hold out much hope."

Brutus watched three people step before his kennel. One wore a gray coverall zippered up the front. He smelled of disinfectant and tobacco.

"Here he is. It was lucky we scanned him and found that old Home-Again microchip. We were able to pull up your address and telephone. So you say someone stole him from your backyard?"

"Two years ago," a taller man said, dressed in black shoes and a suit.

Brutus pulled back one ear. The voice was vaguely familiar.

"They took both him and his littermate," the man continued. "We thought they'd run off during a thunderstorm."

Brutus lifted his head. A boy pushed between the two taller men and stepped toward the gate. Brutus met his eyes. The boy was older, taller, more gangly of limb, but his scent was as familiar as an old sock. As the boy stared into the dark kennel, the initial glaze of hope in his small face crumbled away into horror.

The boy's voice was an appalled squeak. "Benny?"

Shocked and disbelieving, Brutus slunk back on his belly. He let out a low warning growl as he shied away. He didn't want to remember . . . and especially didn't want this. It was too cruel.

The boy glanced over his shoulder to the taller man. "It is Benny, isn't it, Dad?"

"I think so." An arm pointed. "He's got that white blaze over his right ear." The voice grew slick with dread. "But what did they do to him?"

The man in the coveralls shook his head. "Brutalized him. Turned him into a monster."

"Is there any hope for rehabilitation?"

He shook his head and tapped the chart. "We had all the dogs examined by a behaviorist. She signed off that he's unsalvageable."

"But, Dad, it's Benny . . ."

Brutus curled into the back of the run, as deep into the shadows as he could get. The name was like the lash of a whip.

The man pulled a pen from his coverall pocket. "Since you're still legally his owners and had no part in the dog-fighting ring, we can't put him down until you sign off on it."

"Dad . . ."

"Jason, we had Benny for two *months*. They've had him for two *years*."

"But it's still Benny. I know it. Can't we try?"

The coverall man crossed his arms and lowered his voice with warning. "He's unpredictable and damn powerful. A bad combination. He even mauled his trainer. They had to amputate the man's hand."

"Jason . . ."

"I know. I'll be careful, Dad. I promise. But he deserves a chance, doesn't he?"

His father sighed. "I don't know."

The boy knelt down and matched Brutus's gaze. The dog wanted to turn away, but he couldn't. He locked eyes and slipped into a past he'd thought long buried away, of fingers clutching hot dogs, chases across green lawns, and endless sunny days. He pushed it all away. It was too painful, too prickled with guilt. He didn't deserve even the memory. It had no place in the pit.

A low rumble shook through his chest.

Still, the boy clutched the fence and faced the monster inside. He spoke with the effortless authority of innocence and youth.

"It's *still* Benny. Somewhere in there."

Brutus turned away and closed his eyes with an equally firm conviction.

The boy was wrong.

Brutus slept on the back porch. Three months had passed and his sutures and staples were gone. The medicines in his food had faded away. Over the months, he and the family had come to an uneasy truce, a cold stalemate.

Each night they tried to coax him into the house, especially as the leaves were turning brown and drifting up into piles beneath the hardwoods and the lawn turned frosty in the early morning. But Brutus kept to his porch, even avoiding the old sofa covered in a ragged thick comforter. He kept his distance from all things. He still flinched from a touch and growled when he ate, unable to stop himself.

But they no longer used the muzzle.

Perhaps they sensed the defeat that had turned his heart to stone. So he spent his days staring across the yard, only stirring occasionally, pricking up an ear if a stray squirrel should dare bound along the fencerow, its tail fluffed and fearless.

The back door opened, and the boy stepped out onto the porch. Brutus gained his feet and backed away.

"Benny, are you sure you don't want to come inside? I made a bed for you in the kitchen." He pointed toward the open door. "It's warm. And look, I have a treat for you."

The boy held out a hand, but Brutus already smelled the bacon, still smoking with crisply burned fat. He turned away. Back at the training yard, the others had tried to use bait on him, too. But after his sister, Brutus had always refused, no matter how hungry.

The dog crossed to the top step of the porch and lay down.

The boy came and sat with him, keeping his distance.

Brutus let him.

They sat for a long time. The bacon still in his fingers. The boy finally nibbled it away himself. "Okay, Benny, I have some homework."

The boy began to get up, paused, then carefully reached out to touch him on the head. Brutus didn't growl, but his fur bristled. Noting the warning, the boy sagged, pulled back his hand, and stood up.

"Okay. See ya in the morning, Benny boy."

He didn't watch the boy leave, but he listened for the door to clap shut. Satisfied he was alone, he settled his head to his paws. He stared out into the yard.

The moon was already up, full-faced and bright. Lights twinkled. Distantly, he listened as the household settled in for the night. A television whispered from the front room. He heard the boy call down from the upstairs. His mother answered.

Then suddenly Brutus was on his feet, standing stiff, unsure what had drawn him up. He kept dead still. Only his ears swiveled.

A knock sounded on the front door.

In the night.

"I'll get it," the mother called out.

Brutus twisted, bolted for the old sofa on the porch, and climbed half into it, enough to see through the picture window. The view offered a straight shot down the central dark hallway to the lighted front room.

Brutus watched the woman step to the door and pull it open.

Before she'd gotten it more than a foot wide, the door slammed open.

It struck her and knocked her down. Two men charged inside, wearing dark clothes and masks pulled over their heads. Another kept watch by the open door. The first man backed into the hallway and kept a large pistol pointed toward the woman on the floor. The other intruder sidled to the left and aimed a gun toward someone in the dining room.

"DON'T MOVE!" the second gunman shouted.

Brutus tensed. He knew that voice, graveled and merciless. In an instant, his heart hammered in his chest, and his fur flushed up all over his body, quivering with fury.

"Mom? Dad?" The boy called from the top of the stairs.

"Jason!" the father answered from the dining room. "Stay up there!"

The leader stepped farther into the room. He shoved his gun out, holding it crooked. "Old man, sit your ass down!"

"What do you want?"

The gun poked again. "Yo! Where's my dog?"

"Your dog?" the mother asked on the floor, her voice trembling with fear.

"Brutus!" the man hollered. He lifted his other arm and bared the stump of a wrist. "I owe that bitch some payback . . . and that includes anyone taking care of his ass! In fact, we're going to have ourselves an old-fashioned barbecue." He turned to the man in the doorway. "What are you waiting for? Go get the gasoline?"

The man vanished into the night.

Brutus dropped back to the porch and retreated to the railing. He bunched his back legs.

"Yo! Where you keeping my damn dog? I know you got him!"

Brutus sprang forward, shoving out with all the strength in his body. He hit the sofa and vaulted over it. Glass shattered as he struck the window with the crown of his skull. He flew headlong into the room and landed in the kitchen. His front paws struck the floor before the first piece of glass. He bounded away as shards crashed and skittered across the checkerboard linoleum.

Down the hall, the first gunman began to turn, drawn by the noise.

But he was too late. Brutus flew down the hall and dove low. He snatched the gunman by the ankle and ripped the tendon, flipping the man as he ran under him. The man's head hit the corner of a walnut hall table, and he went down hard.

Brutus spotted a man out on the front porch, frozen in midstep, hauling two large red jugs. The man saw Brutus barreling toward him. His eyes got huge. He dropped the jugs, spun around, and fled away.

A pistol fired, deafening in the closed space. Brutus felt a kick in his front leg. It shattered under him, but he was already in midleap toward the one-handed gunman, his old trainer and handler. Brutus hit him like a sack of cement. He head-butted the man in the chest. Weight and momentum knocked the legs out from under the man. They fell backward together.

The pistol blasted a second time.

Something burned past Brutus's ear, and plaster rained down from the ceiling.

Then they both hit the hardwood floor. The man landed flat on his back, Brutus on top. The gun flew from his fingers and skittered under the dining room chair.

His trainer tried to kick Brutus away, but he'd taught the dog too well. Brutus dodged the knee. With a roar, he lunged for the man's throat. The man grabbed one-handed for an ear, but Brutus had lost most of the flap in an old fight. The ear slipped from the man's grip, and Brutus snapped for the tender neck. Fangs sank for the sure kill.

Then a shout barked behind him. "Benny! No!"

From out the corner of an eye, he saw the father crouched by the dining room table. He had recovered the pistol and pointed it at Brutus.

"Benny! Down! Let him go!"

From the darkness of the pit, Brutus growled back at the father. Blood flowed as Brutus clamped harder on his prey. He refused to release. Under him, the trainer screamed and gurgled. One fist punched blindly, but Brutus ground his jaws tighter. Blood flowed more heavily.

"Benny, let him go now!"

Another sharper voice squeaked in fear. It came from the stairs. "No, Dad!"

"Jason, I can't let him kill someone."

"Benny!" the boy screamed. "Please, Benny!"

Brutus ignored them. He wasn't Benny. He knew the pit was where he truly belonged, where he'd always end up. As his vision narrowed and darkness closed over him, he let himself fall deeper into that black, bottomless well, dragging the man with him. Brutus knew he couldn't escape; neither would he let this one go.

It was time to end all this.

But as Brutus sank into the pit, slipping away into the darkness, something stopped him, held him from falling. It made no sense. Though no one was behind him, he felt a distinct tug. On his tail. Holding him steady, then slowly drawing him back from the edge of the pit. Comprehension came slowly, seeping through the despair. He knew that touch. It was familiar as his own heart. Though it had no real strength, it broke him, shattered him into pieces.

He remembered that tug, from long ago, her special ambush.

Done to protect him.

Ever his guardian.

Even now.

And always.

No, Benny . . .

"No, Benny!" the boy echoed.

The dog heard them both, the voices of those who loved him, blurring the line between past and present—not with blood and darkness, but sunlight and warmth.

With a final shake against the horror, the dog turned his back on the pit. He unclamped his jaws and tumbled off the man's body. He stood on shaking limbs.

To the side, the trainer gagged and choked behind his black mask. The father closed in on him with the gun.

The dog limped away, three-legged, one forelimb dangling.

Footsteps approached from behind. The boy appeared at his side and laid a palm on his shoulder. He left his hand resting there. Not afraid.

The dog trembled, then leaned into him, needing reassurance.

And got it.

"Good boy, Benny. Good boy."

The boy sank to his knees and hugged his arms around the dog.

At long last . . . Benny let him.

Gone to the Dogs

All the prior stories had been published in various ways across different venues. I hope having them all in one volume has been both convenient and entertaining, while perhaps offering a bit of "unrestricted access" to the behind-the-scenes origins to these stories.

Still, in all good conscience, I also wanted to offer something unique to this volume, a new story never before published. And not just a "short" story, but a true novella—a work occupying that blurry borderlands between a short story and a full-length novel.

But what would I write about?

I decided to draw upon everything you just read.

The novella—Sun Dogs—has a tie into the Sigma world, while concentrating on a unique pairing. The story has a fantastical element to it, while being grounded in the sand, rock, and dust of the Sonoran Desert. Similar to "The Pit," it also has sections written from the point of view of a dog.

The two main characters—Captain Tucker Wayne and his military war dog, Kane—were featured in the earlier story "Tracker" and appeared in the Sigma novel Bloodline and in their own solo books, The Kill Switch and War Hawk.

Plainly, this dynamic duo holds a special place in my heart.

But where did they come from?

Certainly writing "The Pit" played a role. I enjoyed putting my readers into the paws of that unique warrior in a dog-fighting ring. Back then, I thought that would be the end of it—until I participated in a USO tour to Iraq and Kuwait during the winter of 2010.

It was an honor to meet the men and women out in the field, to see the hardship of their lives, to visit those wounded in hospitals. But I also was able to see war dogs and their handlers training and working—even playing together. They were such a unique fighting unit that I knew I wanted to try to capture that bond as best I could and share it with the world.

Upon returning home, I visited Lackland Air Force Base and was able to interview dog handlers and trainers and to learn more about those four-legged warriors and the men and women who stood beside them.

After that, I practiced writing about this pair—both in novel-length and in short story form. The novella that follows is my attempt to take all that past knowledge and tell one more story about Tucker and Kane, a story of how grief is etched in bone and sacrifice is never forgotten.

That is "Sun Dogs."

Sun Dogs

JAMES ROLLINS

(1)

April 22, 5:50 A.M.
Sonoran Desert, Arizona

Dawn broke with the crack of a pistol.

Tucker Wayne rolled free of his sleeping bag before the sound of the gunshot faded across the desert landscape. Standing in his boxers, he cocked an ear and listened as the blast reverberated off the slabs of red rock thrusting thousands of feet out of the sand and brush. After years with the US Army Rangers—deployed across sandboxes far more hostile than here in the deserts of Arizona—he always slept with one eye open and one ear cocked.

As he shivered in the dawn chill, he struggled to pinpoint the shot's location, straining his senses. He smelled the perfume of desert poppies. He noted the curl of smoke from a lone ember of last night's campfire. He felt the ice in the breezes funneling through the canyons.

His head swiveled as he identified the gunshot's source.

To the northwest . . . maybe a mile or two off.

His heart continued to pound, fueled both by the present danger and echoes out of his past. Prior battles had been indelibly etched into his body, rewiring his nerves so tautly that it took only the barest hint of a threat—real or imagined—to jangle his entire body, sending him into a near-panicked state of alertness.

And he wasn't the only one.

Kane stood at his knee. His teammate's seventy pounds of lean muscle were stone hard, his tail held high, his ears stiff and straight. Kane was a Belgian Malinois, a shepherd breed often used by the military due to their fierce loyalty and intelligence. After surviving multiple deployments in the field, the two had become bound together tighter than any leash, each capable of reading the other, a connection that went beyond any spoken word or hand signal. After leaving the service, Tucker took Kane with him. The two were now an inseparable team.

Tucker reached down and scratched Kane's black-and-tan ruff. His fingers discovered old scars, reminding him of his own wounds: some easy to see, others just as well hidden.

Even now, Tucker had trouble separating past from present. Old memories flooded through him. While Kane had grown to become an extension of himself, his disembodied right hand, Tucker once had a *left* hand, too.

As he stared, another desert overlapped this one. His nostrils suddenly filled with the smell of burning oil, his gaze flashed to the fall of knives, his ears echoed with screams of his wounded teammates. His sight dimmed to a vision of a dark-furred form sprawled on red rock.

Kane's littermate.

Abel . . .

Another gunshot shattered apart that painful memory, calling him back to the present. He crouched lower. These gunshots weren't imagined. They were no figment out of his war-torn past. This was real.

And far too close for comfort.

A third sharp crack confirmed his earlier suspicion that the weapon

was no sport rifle or shotgun. It was a pistol, which was part of the reason
the hairs on his bare arms stood on end.

Who goes hunting in the desert with a handgun?

He tried to rationalize that it might be someone target shooting. But
his camp was forty miles outside of Sedona, well off any road, reachable
only by a four-wheel vehicle, like the Jeep he'd rented. It was a long way to
travel to pop off at beer bottles on boulders.

He closed his eyes, rewinding events to the moment before he had
burst from his bedroll. Had there been a faint scream accompanying the
first shot? Was that what had set his teeth on edge? Or was the scream just
a delusion, a ghost crying out of his past?

Kane growled next to him, though it was done silently so as not to
give themselves away. The only signal of warning was a low reverberation
of the dog's ribs as Kane leaned against his leg.

Then he heard it: a furious crunching of sand, a frantic crashing of
brittle branches. He turned as a small shape hurtled into view on his right,
running low to the ground. It was another dog, with the spotted sleek coat
and brown head of a German shorthaired pointer. The dog raced across
the desert, aiming for their camp. Its sharp nose must have picked out
their location and sent it running toward the only whiff of humanity.

But why?

Tucker dropped to a knee and signaled Kane to sit next to him, to offer a less threatening greeting.

The shorthaired pointer slowed as it neared the camp and maintained
a wary boundary a few yards off. With its stubby tail tucked low, it turned
twice, weaving a nervous S-shaped pattern. It plainly wanted to join them
but needed reassurance.

Tucker gave it.

"It's okay, boy," he encouraged softly. "We're all buddies here."

To reinforce this greeting, he passed a silent command to Kane.
His furry teammate had a working vocabulary of a thousand words and
knowledge of over a hundred hand signals. Tucker extended his pinkie
and circled it once in the air.

BE FRIENDLY.

Obeying immediately, Kane swished his tail with enough vigor to wiggle his hindquarters, accompanying this greeting with a welcoming whine of excitement.

After another few moments of strained hesitation—evidenced from the shorthair's heavy panting and the amount of white showing around those amber eyes—the dog slunk lower. With its short tail still tucked, the pointer sidled across the invisible boundary and entered their camp.

"That's a good boy," Tucker reassured him.

The shorthair approached to within a few feet, paused, then barreled up to them. Once in Tucker's shadow, the dog quickly sat, shivering, trembling, whining softly.

Kane sniffed at the newcomer, while Tucker rubbed the dog's chest and neck, letting him know he was safe. He checked the red collar, the bronze tag.

He read aloud the name inscribed there. "Cooper."

This earned a brief wag of the dog's tail.

Tucker also noted the couple feet of leather dangling from the collar.

Part of a leash.

He followed its short length to the end. No chew marks, only a clean cut. Someone had freed the dog by slicing its leash. As his other hand continued to rough the dog's flank, his fingers discovered a patch of warm dampness. He pulled his arm up and noticed a crimson stain across his palm.

Blood.

A quick inspection revealed no wound.

So not the dog's blood.

The gunshots echoed in his head.

Not good.

As he debated how to proceed, he checked the backside of the dog's tag and found an address in Sedona, a phone number, and another name: JACKSON KEE. He stared out at the desert, now gone ominously silent.

Was the blood from the dog's owner?

Tucker pictured the man cutting his companion loose in a last-ditch effort to fetch help, maybe praying the dog would reach civilization. Tucker didn't bother trying to extend that reach now with his cell phone. Even in downtown Sedona, cell signal was spotty at best. Due to the surrounding red rock peaks and iron-rich soil, it was even worse out here.

But he had another means of communication.

He debated whether or not to use it. Ever a loner, he preferred to lean on his own skills. He trusted few people, a suspicion ingrained into him long before the horrors of war had revealed the true depths of man's inhumanity. During his decade in the army, he proved to be a superb dog handler, testing through the roof in regard to emotional empathy, which helped him bond to his subjects.

Maybe too deeply.

Tucker knew an evaluation by army psychologists attributed this innate affinity to early childhood trauma. Raised in North Dakota, he had been orphaned as a toddler, when his parents had been killed by a drunk driver. He'd been left in the care of his grandfather, who had a heart attack when Tucker was thirteen. From there, he'd been dumped into foster care. During his years in the system, he learned to read others as a way of surviving, to sense the mood of another, and act accordingly. Such a chaotic and unstable upbringing had not only honed his empathic skills, but it impressed on him how little he could count on others.

Still, to Tucker, it all boiled down to something far simpler, a coda summed up by Sigmund Freud: *I prefer the company of animals more than the company of humans. Certainly, a wild animal is cruel. But to be merciless is the privilege of civilized humans.*

That last part had been reinforced tenfold during Tucker's decade in the army. The battlefield often revealed the best and worst in a person, sometimes at the same time. He did not exclude himself from that judgment.

Again, he pictured blades flashing through the air, stealing more and more of the life from Kane's littermate.

He shook away this memory as he reached the Jeep Wrangler. Before leaving the rental agency, he'd had the doors and roof panels removed, leaving the four-by-four stripped down to its essential frame. His gear was stored in the back. He quickly pulled on a pair of dusty jeans and a short-sleeved khaki shirt. As he shoved his feet into a pair of beat-up Timberland boots, he caught a glimpse of himself in one of the side mirrors.

It took him a breath to recognize the stranger in the reflection. The face was too young, a man in his early thirties, with shaggy, disheveled dark blond hair, and a lean muscular physique, more befitting a quarter-back than a linebacker. It was like he was staring at some younger version of himself. He felt far older than the lineless face in the mirror. But the eyes staring back at him from the mirror—those he recognized—the haunted, angry glint to his blue-green eyes. As he dressed, he also noted the crisscross of scars over his body, the puckering of old bullet wounds in his shoulder and upper thigh.

Unbidden, his hand rose and touched the small black paw print tat-tooed on his upper left arm, a permanent reminder of Abel, of the dog's sacrifice. Grimacing, he reached to the back of the Jeep and pulled on a desert-khaki windbreaker over his shirt, as if covering the tattoo would dim that pain.

It didn't.

Now dressed, he turned his attention to the packs stored in the back of the Jeep. From one, he shook out a steel box buried at the bottom. He carried this with him in case of the direst emergencies. He stared at the panting German shorthair, at the blood drying on the dog's fur.

This counts as one of those times.

He flipped the clasp and opened the box. Inside rested a black Des-ert Eagle, and a pair of magazines loaded with .44 Magnum rounds. He slapped one of the magazines into the pistol and shoved the gun into the back of his jeans. He then removed the compact satellite phone from in-side the box. The phone was packed with the latest military tech. The de-vice was a gift from Sigma Force, a covert team of DARPA field operatives whom he had helped in the past.

I could use their backup now . . . if only from a distance.

He placed the battery back into the phone, tapped in a code, then balanced the phone on the Jeep's blocky fender. While an encrypted connection was being made to Sigma's headquarters in D.C., Tucker used a long rope to secure the German shorthair to the trailer hitch. There was enough length to reach a small cool stream running alongside the campsite with shade offered under the Jeep's raised chassis.

As the satellite connection was made, a small voice rose from the phone's speakers. "Captain Wayne?"

Tucker retrieved the phone and brought it to his ear. "Director Crowe."

Painter Crowe was the head of Sigma. Tucker pictured the man seated in his office under the Smithsonian Castle on the National Mall.

"What can I do for you?" the director asked.

Tucker glanced over to Cooper. The German shorthair wandered over to the stream and took two nervous licks. "I need you to dog-sit for me."

"Happy to oblige. But it looks like you're calling from the middle of Arizona. Not sure I can get anyone out there with a bag of kibble anytime soon."

Tucker glanced skyward, knowing the call had revealed his location. It was why he normally kept the phone locked up in its steel case with its battery removed. He preferred to keep his tracks hidden. But considering where he was headed next—and knowing there was a possibility he might not return—he did not want to leave Cooper tied to his Jeep, to slowly starve to death.

I lost one dog on my watch.

He didn't intend to lose another.

"I think I'm about to intrude where I'm not wanted," Tucker explained. "If you don't hear back from me within the next hour, send help to this location."

"If you're in trouble, I can rouse emergency services out of Sedona. Get a chopper out there in half that time."

Tucker stared at Cooper, at the dark crimson patch on the dog's flank.

He feared he could already be too late.

Still, he knew that if anyone was still in danger, held at gunpoint, the noisy intrusion of a helicopter to this remote corner of the desert could result in the immediate execution of any captives.

"Hold off for now." Tucker gave Crowe a thumbnail account of the gunshots, the sudden appearance of a bloody dog. "Give me the hour to investigate quietly before you raise the cavalry."

"Understood, but the name you found on the dog's collar, Jackson Kee."

"What about it?"

"That must be *Dr.* Jackson Kee."

Tucker tried not to roll his eyes. Of course, the director had already tracked down the dog's owner in less than a minute, using Sigma's considerable intelligence resources.

"He's a doctor of holistic ministry, teaching at both the University of Sedona and at Yavapai College. According to his bio, he's lived in the area all his life, with a heritage going back generations and tied to the tribes of the region, both the local Yavapai and Hopi Indians."

So the guy would certainly know these deserts.

"While you check on those gunshots," Painter said, "I'll see what else I can dig up on Dr. Kee."

Tucker ended the call, set the ringer to silent, and slipped the phone into an inside pocket of his jacket. Outfitted and dressed, he assisted his partner in doing the same. From the back of the Jeep, he removed a K9 Storm tactical vest and fitted it over Kane's shoulders. As he strapped the waterproofed and Kevlar-reinforced vest in place, he felt the pounding of Kane's heart, the tremble of excitement in the dog's muscles. Kane knew he was being called to duty, preparing to transform from furry companion to stealthy warrior.

Tucker scuffled and rubbed Kane's ears, physically bonding by touch. As Tucker knelt before him, Kane stared into his eyes, deepening that connection. Tucker leaned closer, touching noses in an ageless ritual, acknowledging what he was asking of the dog, to put himself in harm's way to save others.

"Who's a good boy?" he whispered to his best friend.

Kane licked his nose.

That's right, you are.

Tucker leaned back and reached to the webbing of the vest's collar. He flipped up a camera hidden there and slipped a wireless radio plug into Kane's left ear. The gear allowed the two of them to be in constant visual and audio contact with each other.

To test the equipment, Tucker positioned the camera's lens to peer over Kane's shoulder and turned it on. He then seated a pair of DARPA-designed photosensitive goggles over his own eyes. He tapped a button on the side of the glasses and live feed from Kane's camera appeared on the inside corner of the lens: a low view of pinyon and rock.

Finally, he slipped a wireless radio transmitter into his own mouth, fitting it behind his last tooth. The device—nicknamed a *Molar Mic*—was new tech used by soldiers in Afghanistan. The tiny radio allowed men and women in the field to communicate to each other in whispers, while incoming transmissions reached the receiver's ear directly via bone-induction through the jaw.

"You ready, buddy?" Tucker said softly, testing the communication channel.

Kane glanced back and wagged his tail twice. His partner's eyes glinted with suppressed excitement, knowing what was coming, anxious to get moving.

Tucker stood and stepped over to the path the German shorthair had taken to get here. He pointed to the trail of paw prints in the sand, then out to the open desert. Even before he whispered the command *"TRACK,"* Kane was already moving, anticipating the instruction.

As the dog swept off into the desert, Tucker followed in his wake. As they ran, Tucker studied the terrain both through his eyes and through the image transmitted to his goggles from Kane's camera. It was disjointing for several breaths—then quickly became second nature. The bobbling view of brush and rock from his partner's perspective merged with his own. Kane's panting filled his skull, coming to match his own breath. Even the tread of his boots settled into an easy harmony with the padding of Kane's paws. In that timeless moment, the two became one, a perfect harmony of action and intent.

This bond between them ran deeper than any training, beyond any high-tech communion of senses.

This was a union forged in blood.

They were both survivors, wounded and scarred together into one, bound to each other's heart, through loss and grief, but also joy and companionship. Still, even now, he sensed another's paws running alongside them, a ghost chasing them through the desert, begging them not to forget.

Never, he promised, *never*.

Tucker raced along a path that wound through fields of fading pink fairy dusters and around red-and-purple patches of flowering hedgehog cacti and prickly pear. His eyes continued to discern scuffs in the sand, broken branches of brittlebush, all marking the panicked passage of the German shorthair.

He lost the trail for stretches at a time over bare red rock, but Kane's senses were far keener, never flagging from the invisible track of scent markers.

As bonded as they were, Tucker could almost appreciate this skill.

Almost . . . but not completely.

*   *   *

Kane forges ahead, untangling the weave of scents in the air to follow one thread. What sight fails him, scent fills in, layer upon layer, marking time backward and forward, building a framework of old trails around him. He takes in more smells, drawing them upon his moist tongue, deep into the back of his throat and sinuses.

Bitter musk of spoor . . .

Acrid sting of a rabbit's urine marker . . .

The perfume of pollen . . .

The wisp of moisture from a nearby stream . . .

As he runs, his ears swivel at every hushed whisper: the howl of brief gusts through rock, the slap of his own pads, the rustle of branches.

As he paints the world around him in scents and sounds, he tests a change in the breeze with an upraised nose. It flows toward him from ahead. He lets the fresher scents wash over him. With it comes a rank undercurrent . . . reeking of sweat and ripeness of body.

Men.

Two of them.

His legs slow.

He forces his panting to grow quiet.

His ears track toward the pair as they approach; his nose picks out oil and old smoke amid the musk of these men. The threat buried within that odor sets his hackles on end.

Kane knows guns—by scent, smells, and sound, he knows guns.

He stops and lowers to his belly, nose pointed forward, signaling his pack-mate.

His message is understood.

Trouble is coming.

(2)

6:04 A.M.

Trembling, Abigail Pike kept her eyes fixed on her grandfather, who was seated across the dying embers of their campfire. She fought to keep her gaze away from the dead body sprawled to her left, from the dark pool of blood steaming on the cold desert sand. Her ears still rang from the gunshot. She felt the heat of the same pistol's barrel near her right ear.

"Let's try this again, Dr. Kee," the gunman said next to her, glaring across at her grandfather. "Or Abbie here will be next. *Where* did that old bastard find that rock?"

Despite her best effort, Abbie's eyes flicked toward the body of Brocky Oro, an old prospector from the Yavapai-Prescott tribe. She had known the irascible loner—who she always called "Uncle Oro"—since she was a young girl. For two decades, she had listened to his tales of forgotten silver mines, of the lost city of El Dorado, of his endless searches for treasures hidden in the trackless wilds of the deep desert. It was those campfire stories that had likely inspired her in part to pursue a geology degree from the University of Colorado, to continue Uncle Oro's hunt, only from a more scientific angle.

And look where that's got us.

She sat on a gnarled log, her wrists bound by zip ties behind her back. Her grandfather was tied up in the same manner. So was the other captive, a middle-aged man seated next to him, Dr. Herman Landon, a physicist from the University of Sedona.

Their group's camp had been raided just before dawn. The bandits had ambushed them while they were still in their tents and bedrolls. The only warning came from Cooper, who had barked outside. The shorthair pointer had been tethered by a long lead to a stake screwed into the sand, to keep him from chasing rabbits into the desert. At the time, believing Cooper had spotted one of his long-eared prey, Abbie's grandfather had yelled for the dog to quiet down.

If only we'd listened to the dog . . .

Still, the end result might have been the same. A six-man team of bandits had swept swiftly upon them, armed with black pistols and semiautomatic rifles. After they were subdued, a beige Ford Bronco had rumbled out of the desert and parked next to her grandfather's battered Jeep. From the Bronco, another two men joined them. One was the group's leader, a man the others called Hawk.

It sounded like a Native American name, but none of the bandits looked to share the same ancestry as Abbie and her grandfather. The bandits all wore similar uniforms: dusty jeans, untucked flannel shirts over stained T-shirts, and some manner of trucker's hat or cap. She had seen such lowlifes for years, haunting the shadowy corners of bars and saloons across Arizona, hard men who lived harder lives of desperation and frustrated anger. She had noted the twitchiness of a couple of them, their stained teeth, clear signs that they'd steeled their nerves for this ambush with hits of crystal meth.

As Abbie and the men had been dragged out of their tents, she had sensed the menacing danger of this group. Her grandfather had not—not until it was too late. He had tried to play dumb when Hawk confronted him about the source of the fist-sized fire agate discovered by Uncle Oro last week, a massive gem worth a small fortune. Uncle Oro claimed it was but a pebble from a far larger find, hidden deep in the desert.

But that was not all he claimed to have discovered . . .

Her gaze shifted to Dr. Landon.

Clearly word of Uncle Oro's discovery had reached more ears than theirs—which was not hard to imagine. Uncle Oro had an unfortunate fondness for cheap whiskey and for spinning tales atop barstools. And now it had gotten him killed.

Her grandfather had reacted to the sudden execution of Uncle Oro by slipping out a hidden switchblade from a cargo pocket of his trousers and slicing Cooper's lead, sending the shorthair running. The dog—already panicked by the gunshot, by the splatter of blood—took off into the desert. As punishment, Hawk had pistol-whipped her grandfather and had bound them both more securely with zip ties.

"One last time," Hawk pressed, punctuating his seriousness with the heavy *click* of a pistol's hammer being pulled. "*Where* was that big rock found?"

Her grandfather cringed, his right eye already swelling shut. "I . . . I'll tell you. Just don't hurt Abbie."

"*Tellin'* ain't good enough." Hawk stepped around and waved his pistol. Two of his men yanked her grandfather to his feet. "You'll *show* us."

Her grandfather knew better than to fight, having learned the bloody lesson sprawled on the sand. Still, he resisted long enough to cast a guilty look at her, for dragging her into all of this. Then he was forced at gunpoint toward the Bronco, its engine still ticking and cooling next to their Jeep.

"If you try any funny business," Hawk threatened, following behind, "we'll kill the scientist first. Then we'll have fun with your granddaughter—all of us—before I put a bullet in her skull."

Her grandfather promised to cooperate, while Landon looked terrified. Abbie watched her grandfather as he was shoved into the back seat of
the Bronco.

Hawk turned toward the dying campfire. The man had shoulder-
length auburn hair, half hidden under a Diamondback baseball cap, its
rim curled down into a horseshoe, and a rust of dark stubble on his chin
and cheeks, looking as if his face was perpetually in shadow. He pointed at
the pair of men still at the campfire.

"Randy, Bo, you keep an eye on these two. Wait for Buck and Chet to
come back. Let 'em know where we went. I'll be on radio."

Randy—who was the twitchiest of the bunch—nodded vigorously.
"What if'n they don't find that damn dog?"

Hawk shrugged. "The coyotes will probably take care of the mutt for
us. If not, we'll be long gone before anyone's the wiser."

Bo chuckled, adding a "Damn straight."

Hawk circled to the Bronco's passenger side and climbed into the
front seat. The SUV rumbled to life. The Bronco turned toward the high
desert, ground sand and rock under its four tires, and headed off.

Abbie followed its path for a few breaths, then found Bo eyeing her,
a leer exposing his meth-rotted teeth. She turned away, staring across
the embers of the campfire. She spotted the trail of paw prints vanishing into the pinyon brush—and the heavier tread of the two men who
hunted the dog.

She prayed Cooper escaped, hoped for even more.

Please find someone to help us.

(3)

6:10 A.M.

Tucker crouched in the long shadow of a red rock boulder. His ears noted
the crunch of sand approaching his hiding spot. In a corner of his goggles,
the feed from Kane's camera showed two men picking their way across a

rocky patch decorated with a swath of Mexican gold poppy. One led with a pistol in hand; the other followed with an assault rifle slung over his shoulder.

Moments ago, Kane had warned of the approaching threat, giving Tucker time to set up this ambush. His furry teammate had similarly gone to ground thirty yards ahead, lying low in a gully, awaiting a command. Tucker held off until the two passed Kane's position and approached the red rock boulder where he hid.

Through Kane's camera audio, he heard the two conversing, believing they were alone.

"Did you see the way that guy's skull exploded when Hawk shot him?" one asked with a wheezing laugh.

"Yeah, burst like a ripe pumpkin. Hawk sure taught that old Indian that we mean business. Betcha the guy's spilling the beans now. And did you get a good look at his granddaughter?"

"Sure did. Now that's what I call some ripe pumpkins."

More snickering laughter. "Let's find that damn dog."

They continued past Kane's position. From the brief exchange, Tucker had assessed plenty enough, especially his targets' murderous intent. Whoever they were, they had killed someone and held at least two more hostages. Upon learning this, Tucker felt no compunction against using deadly force. Still, with his heart pounding, he holstered his Desert Eagle. He needed to do this quietly, so as not to alert these bastards' cohorts.

As the second man passed Kane's position, Tucker subvocalized a two-word command into his radio. "*SILENT. TAKEDOWN.*"

Through his goggles, he watched a low view of desert scrub brush sweep past the view of Kane's camera. Even with the acute sensitivity of the camera's audio, Tucker heard no sound as the shepherd rushed to close the distance on the trailing man. He pictured Kane's paws landing on firm rock, his sleek body avoiding any brush of branches that might alert his target.

Then at the last moment, a low growl.

Done on purpose.

Startled by the noise, Kane's target turned—only to find a massive dog leaping at him. Kane barreled into his chest, knocking the man off his feet and onto his back.

Tucker was already moving. He rolled out from behind the boulder, coming to stand only steps away from the man who had been leading the pair. The gunman had his back to Tucker, drawn by the commotion.

Kane's jaws were already clamped to his target's throat, crushing the man's windpipe, his fangs dug deep into the soft flesh. The man thrashed, his rifle trapped under his back. Kane held tight, riding the man like a wild bull.

Tucker's target had momentarily frozen at the sudden ambush, at the savagery of Kane's attack. By the time the man raised his pistol at the dog, Tucker was on him. He hooked an arm around the other's throat. Startled, the man dropped his pistol and grabbed for Tucker's arm. Tucker jerked him off his feet and swung him around, slamming his head into the boulder that he had been hiding behind.

Bone cracked with a satisfying crunch.

Tucker dropped the limp body and rushed over to Kane. He yanked out his Desert Eagle as he reached the struggling pair. The man mewled on his back, his face purpling from the strangling clamp on his throat. Tucker used a boot to press the man's head to the side, grinding a cheek into the sand. Then he raised his pistol and bashed its butt behind the man's right ear, breaking bone with a muffled blow.

Like thumping a ripe pumpkin.

Tucker whispered a command to his partner. "STAND DOWN."

Only then did Kane release his hold on the man's neck. The dog backed a few steps, his gaze steady on Tucker, still at full alert.

Tucker quickly collected the rifle and slung its strap over a shoulder. He then crossed, picked up the pistol—a 9 mm Glock—and tucked it into the back of his pants. He weighed the time it would take to gag and tie up the men here, but they weren't waking anytime soon, and he wagered, even if they did, these two wouldn't be heroes. Unarmed and woozy, they'd more likely slink away into the desert and do their best to vanish.

So he left them in the sand.

Earlier, he had heard the distant grumble of an engine receding into the desert. He didn't know what that meant, but he sensed time was running short for whoever was being held hostage.

That is, if they were still alive.

There was only one way to find out. He set off again, sending Kane scouting ahead. The trail from here was easy to follow. The two men hunting for Cooper had made no effort to hide their tracks.

Tucker and Kane moved swiftly across the desert, traveling in tandem, two becoming one again in the chill morning. Still, despite the present danger and need to focus, he could not escape the ghosts of the past.

Tucker flashed back to that painful moment in Afghanistan. He again felt the pop of his ears as the rescue helicopter had lifted off from the snowy mountaintop of Takur Ghar. Aboard the chopper, he had clung to Kane, both of them bloodied by the firefight, by the exploded ordnance. But as the helicopter rose from that mountaintop, Tucker had never taken his eyes off Abel below. It had been Abel who had knocked Tucker and Kane clear before the buried IED detonated.

Now they had abandoned him.

Abel raced across the cold mountaintop, limping on three legs, searching for an escape. Taliban forces closed in from all directions. Tucker had strained for the door, ready to fling himself out, to go to his friend's aid. But two soldiers pinned him, restraining him inside the helicopter.

Tucker yelled for Abel. Hearing him, the dog had stopped, staring up, panting, his eyes sharp and bright, seeing him. They shared that last moment, locked together.

Until that bond had been severed forever.

Even now, Tucker's grip tightened on his Desert Eagle, using its weight and solidity to anchor him to the present. A few years ago, an army therapist had offered insight, refining the root cause of Tucker's PTSD to a condition known as *moral injury*, where Tucker's fundamental understanding of right and wrong had been violated by his experiences in Afghanistan. He was told this condition manifested as shame, guilt, anxiety, and anger, along with behavioral changes, such as alienation and withdrawal—which certainly described him to a tee. Tucker suspected his recent path through life was an ongoing attempt to find his center again, to make amends—not so much for what he did, but for what he had failed to do, whom he had failed to save.

While he had lost his partner back then, he intended to do his best to right whatever wrongs he could. But to do that here, he needed to focus.

He topped a slight rise and discovered a low, wide wash below, likely worn away by centuries of flash floods during the rainy season. Kane hovered at the arroyo's edge, stopped by a command from Tucker when his partner's camera revealed a campsite on the gully floor. Four tents circled the ember glow of a former campfire. A green Jeep Wrangler was parked nearby.

Movement drew him flat to the wash's rocky edge.

On his belly, Tucker pulled out a slim set of binoculars. Through the lenses, he spotted two figures seated on logs, their arms bound behind them. One was a black-haired woman, maybe midtwenties, her hair in a long ponytail, dressed in jeans and a long-sleeved shirt under a field vest. The other was a gray-haired older man in cowboy boots and a navy-blue windbreaker.

Tucker paid closer attention to the two men guarding the pair with rifles, a dusty match to the two Tucker had already dispatched. He knew there had to be more than just those two. He shifted his binoculars and focused across to the far rim of the arroyo, to the hazy trail of dust hanging in the air. He remembered the earlier grumble of an engine. He followed the dust trail toward a tall rise of broken red rocks and sheer cliffs. He didn't know where those others were headed and left that mystery for now. He returned his attention to the campsite, took full measure, then lowered his binoculars.

He scooted to his knees and turned to Kane. He pointed down and around, issuing a chain of commands he knew Kane could follow. "CIRCLE. HOLD POSITION. GUARD ON MY MARK."

Kane panted, gave a single savage swipe of his tail, and dropped over the edge of the arroyo. Tucker took off in the other direction. He slipped down an old dry streambed that drained into the wash, sticking to the deepest shadows cast by the low-lying morning sun. He held the confiscated rifle—a Bushmaster carbine—to his belly in both hands.

If there were any other gunmen, he imagined they were all aboard the departed vehicle. If he was right, those others would not hear any gunshots here. *Good.* Taking this into account, Tucker knew what he had to do to, what was necessary to safeguard the hostages.

His attack here would have to be swift and brutal.

Tucker glanced off toward where Kane had vanished and corrected this assessment.

Our attack.

(4)

6:20 A.M.

Seated on a juniper log, Abbie watched a scorpion scuttle from one shadow to another. She wished she could do the same, find somewhere to escape, somewhere to hide. But more so, she wished she had a scorpion's sting.

She glared over at one of the two men, the one called Bo, who kept eyeing her up and down as if sizing up a prized heifer. He caught her looking and sneered back at—

His face vanished in a mist of blood and bone, followed a fraction later by the echoing crack of a gun.

The other man, Randy, dropped to a knee and swung his rifle at her, as if she were somehow to blame. The motion saved his life as another gunshot followed the first. The round grazed the top of Randy's head, knocking his cap off.

Startled, Randy fell on his backside, but his rifle remained centered on Abbie. He fired. Expecting as much, she had rolled behind the log as he squeezed the trigger. The round blasted into the wood where she'd been seated.

Randy dropped to one elbow, his rifle at his shoulder, aimed at Abbie. He shouted to the unknown assailant. "Come out or—"

To the left, a form exploded from a dense bramble of pinyon and leaped headlong across the space and hit Randy's arm. Jaws crushed wrist bones. The weapon went flying. Randy screamed as a huge shepherd used its weight and momentum to roll, throwing Randy over like a rag doll. Randy landed on his face in the campfire, scattering red embers far.

Then another figure ran low from the other side, appearing from behind one of the tents. He came with a pistol raised and sped to the dog's side. Once there, he growled a firm, "*RELEASE.*"

As the dog let go, the newcomer coldly shot Randy in the back of the head, a single pop that made the man's body bounce, then his form lay still, smoldering atop the fire.

The stranger stayed crouched, weapon raised, his dog panting at his side. Only now did Abbie note the shepherd's dark camouflaged vest, sprouting what looked like a camera on a stalk.

"Are you both okay?" the man asked.

Abbie had no idea who their rescuer was, but from the viciousness of his attack, he scared her, left her breathless. It was Dr. Landon who spoke first. Like her, the physicist had flung himself off the log and huddled behind it.

"I . . . I think so," Landon said and glanced toward Abbie.

She simply nodded, still on her side in the sand.

"Where are the others who attacked you?" the stranger asked.

Abbie sat up, finally finding her voice. "Gone. They took my grandfather."

The man turned to her. His eyes were hard diamonds, his dark blond hair disheveled. "Dr. Jackson Kee?"

She nodded again. *How did he know my grandfather?* And more importantly— "Who are you?"

"Tucker Wayne," he said. He removed a dagger from a sheath on his belt and quickly set about cutting them free. He ended by pointing the knife tip at his companion. "And this big boy is Kane."

At the mention of his name, the shepherd wagged his tail twice.

Landon rubbed his wrists and glanced off to the open desert. "How . . . how did you find us?"

"Kane made a new friend," Tucker said and related a thumbnail sketch of the gunshot, the sudden arrival of Cooper, and his and Kane's overland hunt for the parties involved. "Before setting out, I alerted outside authorities, someone I trust. But until I knew what was going on, I had him hold off sending in the cavalry. As open as these lands are, I feared any approach by police helicopters or trucks with flashing lights could have . . . well . . ."

He trailed off, so Abbie finished, "The bandits would've shot us and run off."

Tucker stared at her for an extra breath. "What about you all?" he asked. "Why are you out here? Why did they come after you?"

"For this." Abbie crossed to her backpack. She opened it and removed a fist-sized chunk of fire agate. She held it up to the sun, where the light refracted brilliantly off its surface, polishing it to a fiery opalescence. "It's worth tens of thousands of dollars, if not far more."

"And according to Brocky, that stone is but the tip of the iceberg." Landon waved at Uncle Oro's body, which Randy had covered with a sleeping bag, as if that would somehow absolve him of the murder—or maybe it was just to keep the blood from drawing flies. "The old prospector claimed there was a whole treasure trove of such rocks out there."

Abbie shook her head. "They must have heard Uncle Oro's story. Ambushed us. Demanded to know where that mother lode is located."

Tucker nodded, staring correctly at the distant ridge of broken scarp. "And they kidnapped your grandfather to lead them there, holding you here to keep him properly motivated."

"Those bastards needed him as a guide," Abbie admitted. "We're in the most remote corner of the Sonoran national forest, two million acres of desert, rock, and cliffs. That ridgeline marks the gateway into a hundred square miles of gorges, ravines, and towering slabs of red rock. My tribe, the Yavapai, call this area—when they speak of it at all—*Ingaya Hala*, or

Black Moon. Though the older connotation is simply the *Land of Night-mares*, which is appropriate considering how easy it is to get lost there, not to mention the dangers from flash floods, sudden rockfalls, treacherous drops."

"And it's *there* that your dead friend claims to have found that rock's mother lode?" Tucker asked.

"And maybe something more amazing," Abbie mumbled, earning a warning look from Landon.

Tucker seemed not to have heard as he bent down to search Bo's body. He stood back up with a confiscated radio in hand and pointed it toward those badlands. "I assume, as treacherous as that terrain sounds, that the ones who took your grandfather would need to continue on foot once they reached that ridgeline."

Abbie nodded.

"Then there's a chance to catch up with them." Tucker turned and pointed to the Jeep. "It that yours?"

"My grandfather's."

"Do you have the keys?"

She frowned. "He leaves them in the visor."

Tucker headed over, drawing Kane with him. "I'll let the authorities know where you are," he said. "But the best chance to save your grand-father is not to wait for them here. Once your grandfather has taken them to the mother lode's site—"

"They'll kill him," Abbie said, following at his heels. "I'm going with you."

Tucker reached the Jeep and turned to her. "I can track them." Then motioned to his dog. "*We* can track them on our own."

He opened the door, but she slammed it back closed with a palm. "You—" She pointed to the shepherd. "And *you*, too. Neither of you know these deserts like I do. And I'm not about to risk my grandfather's life on your inexperience."

Tucker stared silently for a breath, then reached to the small of his back and removed a pistol. He held it out. "Do you know how to handle this?"

She scowled and took the weapon. "This is Arizona."

Landon rushed over and grabbed the rifle near Randy's body, then joined them.

Tucker eyed the weapon, then the man.

Landon hefted the rifle higher. "Native Arizonian. Going back three generations. Also put myself through school on an ROTC scholarship."

Tucker simply shrugged, opened the back door, and whistled his shepherd into the rear. "Then let's go."

(5)

6:32 A.M.

Tucker drove the Jeep roughshod over the rocky terrain. The elevation climbed steadily toward the towering broken cliffs. They sped across an open land of cacti, prickly pear, and blooming spreads of wild heliotrope and lupine.

He held his satellite phone cradled to his ear with his shoulder, needing both hands on the wheel to keep control of the bucking Jeep. He had already updated Painter Crowe on all that had happened. "You've still got my GPS?" Tucker asked.

"We've been tracking you since you left your campsite," Painter confirmed.

Of course, you've been.

"Then go ahead," Tucker said. "Rouse the local authorities in Sedona. Get them moving. But don't dispatch anything by air. Not until we've secured Dr. Kee."

Stealth still remained their best chance to safely recover Abigail's grandfather. As murderous as these bastards were, at the first thump of a police helicopter's rotors, they would put a bullet in the old man's skull and vanish deep into those badlands. Speed was also essential. Tucker did not have the time to wait for the authorities to arrive overland, and even if forces did come by air, they'd likely still get here too late. Instead, Tucker needed to quickly close on those bandits—led by a man named Hawk—before that mother lode was found. After that, Jackson Kee's life would be forfeit.

Still, it wasn't only Tucker at risk now. He glanced over at Abigail, who was seated up front with him. She nodded. He got the same confirming nod from Landon in the back with Kane.

They both understood the situation.

For now, we're on our own.

"I'll set everything in motion," Painter promised. "Including air support."

"But I said—"

"I'll have helicopters dispatched with instructions to maintain a ten-mile perimeter from your position. Once we hear word that you've secured Dr. Kee, they'll swoop down on your signal."

Tucker appreciated the director's strategy. Painter was right. Before this was over, they might very well need a fast evacuation.

"Okay," he agreed.

Tucker ended the call and concentrated on maneuvering the Jeep as the terrain climbed out of the high desert into a scraggly forest of junipers. Through the open window, the crisp air smelled of wet clay and sandstone, all scented by fresh pine.

They were still five or six miles from the cliffs that marked the boundary into the labyrinth of badlands, a territory that the local Yavapai tribe considered both sacred and cursed. Tucker used the time to address one question nagging at him.

He turned to Abbie. "Back at your camp, you said something. That it wasn't just the mother lode that had been discovered up there, but *something more amazing.* What did you mean by that?"

Abbie's eyes widened, obviously surprised he had heard her. She glanced back to Landon. In the rearview mirror, Tucker noted the man's deep, scolding frown.

Landon gave a small shake of his head. "Probably just a fever dream of old Uncle Oro. Maybe from too much sun, too much whiskey."

Abbie looked unconvinced. "Maybe. But even your tests confirmed the anomaly in the stone."

Tucker had enough. "I'm risking my life," he pressed. "Kane's life. If there's anything I ought to know, something you're not telling me . . ."

Landon sighed and leaned forward. He gripped Abbie's headrest to keep his seat in the rocking Jeep. "What do you know about Sedona's vortexes?"

Tucker was momentarily taken aback by the question. He fought the Jeep up a slope of loose shale and sand, tires spinning for traction. "Not much," he finally admitted. "Just that landmarks around Sedona are said to be the focal points for some strange earthly energies."

In fact, all he knew about the subject came from a Sedona resident, a former biker who Tucker had met at a breakfast counter along the town's touristy main drag. The beefy, tattooed man had not struck Tucker as someone who would be prone to swallowing any mystical mumbo jumbo. The biker had declared as much. When the man had landed in Sedona twenty years ago, he had dismissed such claims as *the hogwash of crystal munchers*. Then a couple of years ago, the guy had been out four-wheeling with buddies in the deep desert and stopped at a cluster of tall rocks for a pit stop, when suddenly, to a man, they all got heated up, covered with goose bumps, and light-headed. *Never felt anything like it before*, the biker had said with a shrug. *No doubt about it. I'm dang sure there's something strange going on out there.*

Landon continued. "As a physicist, I'm not supposed to believe in such energies. Certainly not the claims that Sedona's vortex sites—like at Airport Mesa, Bell Rock, or Boyton Canyon—mark some intersections of mysterious energies of the earth. Still, after living here most my life, it's hard to dismiss the myriad accounts of strange experiences at those sites. Tingling of the hands, buzzing in the head, even recorded rises in body temperature. So, I began to study those sites, to see if there's any scientific basis for these reported phenomena."

"Sounds like it could all just be psychosomatic," Tucker said. "You want to believe it, so you feel it."

"That's certainly a possibility, but even skeptics have felt it."

Tucker remembered the biker's account. That guy certainly hadn't wanted to jump on the bandwagon of those crystal munchers.

Abbie offered a counterpoint. "Maybe you simply have to be sensitive to it. Or just emotionally vulnerable. Besides the physical effects, many experience a shift in consciousness. You're warned to keep your mind calm when near a vortex. If you're angry, anxious, or depressed, the energies could amplify those feelings, magnifying them to the point of leaving one stuck in a waking dream."

"A hypnagogic state," Landon explained. "That transitional point between sleep and wakefulness, often accompanied by a strange paralysis."

"Which some people also report at vortex sites," Abbie added. "An inability to move, trapped in a dreamlike state."

Tucker wanted to dismiss this—like the biker had—but he remembered how acutely he had felt the loss of Abel while camping here, the overwhelming guilt, even the vivid flashbacks to that mountaintop in Afghanistan. Even now, he had to swallow back that rising heat in his belly, that mix of bile and regret.

He wanted to change the subject, *needed* to. "That's all well and good, but what does any of that have to do with the mother lode in those badlands?"

Landon nodded to Abbie, who removed the giant fire agate from her pack. "It's because of that," he said.

Abbie explained. "Like Dr. Landon, my field of research centers on the area's vortexes, but I study the geology of the region in an effort to explain those local legends. In fact, the high Sonoran Desert is tectonically peculiar, with dozens of fault lines crisscrossing the region. Here limestone caps basalt, which sits atop the sandstone of ancient oceans. The different rates at which those varying strata erode is what created Sedona's towering pinnacles, mesas, and canyons. From a compositional standpoint, the rust-red rocks are colored by all the iron oxide they contain. In addition, the soil is rich in volcanic crystals, which have been forged by titanic forces into all manner of precious stones. Turquoise, malachite, amethyst, topaz, garnet, even diamonds. Elsewhere, labyrinthine veins of magnetic lodestones wreak havoc on compasses. There's nowhere else like this on the planet. It's why it's only here—and a few places in Mexico—that you can even find deposits of fire agates."

She lifted the stone. "And *nowhere* can you find specimens like this."

"Why's that?" Tucker asked.

"Fire agates were formed during the hottest period of local vulcanism, back in the Tertiary Period, when sheets of silica and iron oxide were compressed into stone. It's those alternating layers of the gem's microstructure that diffract the light into its unique fiery appearance. Such stones were valued by the local tribes for their ability to calm those who are troubled. By staring deep into the gem's mother-of-pearl–like luminescence, it was said to soothe anger, to relieve tension, to create a sense of inner peace."

"But that's not why *that* stone is so rare," Landon said. "If what I suspect is true, the scientific value of that gem far exceeds its monetary worth. It could rewrite all we know about physics."

Tucker sensed these two were finally getting to the crux of the matter. "What's so unique about it?"

"Because that's not just a fire agate." Landon pointed at the fist-sized rock. "That's a *time crystal.*"

(6)

6:48 A.M.

"I know how that sounds," Abbie said, noting Tucker's look of disbelief, hearing the scoff in his exasperated breath. "I didn't believe him either. But hear him out."

Tucker grudgingly waved at the agate in her hand. "A time crystal? Really?"

Landon explained. "Back in 2012, an MIT physicist proposed a unique theory. He noted that many crystals formed by repeating the same pattern of crystallization. Like you see in table salt or in the formation of snowflakes. It's a repetition of structure in *three* dimensions. He speculated if it might be possible to create crystals that repeated in a *fourth* dimension, too, namely time."

"What does that even mean?" Tucker asked.

"I wondered the same," Abbie admitted.

"The MIT physicist theorized a crystal whose atomic structure would repeatedly rotate—a *tick* to the left, a *tick* to the right—forever marking time. Perhaps moving on its own as electrons flowed endlessly through a closed loop, like some perpetual-motion machine. Or perhaps rotating under the influence of an outside electromagnetic force."

"Sounds preposterous," Tucker mumbled.

"Many thought the same, until time crystals were successfully created in several labs, including at Harvard and Yale. Even the military—specifically DARPA—is looking into them as a means of refining atomic clocks."

"DARPA?" Tucker asked, looking quizzically back at Landon, as if this had some significance to their rescuer.

Landon nodded. "That's right."

Tucker looked incrementally less skeptical. "Go on then. Are you saying that agate stone is like one of those time crystals grown in a lab?"

"Except it could be the first *naturally* occurring one ever discovered." Landon explained his theory. "When Oro first brought the large gem to Dr. Kee and Abigail, the prospector told of a cave full of such stones. He also spoke of losing time, an entire day, of seeing terrifying visions. He finally escaped as night fell and only felt better once he carried the gem far enough away. After hearing all of this, Abigail analyzed the stone in her lab, identifying a unique microstructure of the iron oxide in the gem."

"Unique in what way?" Tucker asked.

"The oxide in the agate," Abbie said, "it's all chemically of one type—Fe_3O_4—better known as magnetite."

"Or lodestone," Landon added.

"I discovered that the agate's iron oxide is configured into microcrystalline ferrimagnetic layers." Abbie rolled the stone in her hand. "I'd never seen anything like it before, so I consulted with Dr. Landon."

"Normally iron atoms in magnetite are fixed in alignment," Landon said. "Creating a north and south pole, like in any magnet, but the atoms in this specimen are suspended in an octahedral microcrystalline structure, capable of flipping in the presence of an electromagnetic pulse."

"Like the *ticking* you mentioned before, marking time."

"Exactly."

Abbie shared a look with Landon, who gave her the okay to reveal what they had theorized together. "We think that fire agate—maybe the *entire* mother lode—was doing that in the cave Uncle Oro found. Spinning and ticking away for untold ages."

"Possibly powered by an unmapped vortex out there," Landon said.

"And when Uncle Oro carried his stone away from that site, his gem stopped spinning, stopped affecting him."

"But affecting him how?" Tucker asked.

Landon offered one possibility. "Magnetite isn't just found in rocks, but in biological systems. It's believed magnetite particles in migrating birds' brains allows those species to navigate vast distances by attuning themselves to the earth's magnetic field."

"And magnetite isn't just found in birds," Abbie said. "We have the same particles in *our* brains. They can be found throughout our frontal, occipital, parietal, and temporal lobes—all areas of the brain where we process outside stimuli, turning electrical impulses from our sensory nerves into the world we see, feel, hear, and smell. Even our brainstems and basal ganglia—regions that control our most basic emotions—are loaded with magnetite particles."

Tucker glanced at her. "You're thinking that when your uncle Oro entered that cavern, that those magnetic particles in his brain got scrambled."

"Making him hear, see, and feel strange things. Maybe even short-circuiting him enough to temporarily paralyze him, to trap him in a hypnagogic state, and lose his sense of time."

"The effect inside that cave could be quite intense," Landon warned. "Over time, maybe the two forces—time crystal and vortex—formed some paleomagnetic feedback loop, fueling off each other to make them both stronger."

"It also made me wonder," Abbie said and turned to Tucker, "could this explain why some people are more sensitive to the vortexes of this region? Perhaps their brains are richer in magnetite particles, making them more attuned to those forces emanating from the earth."

"But keep in mind," Landon warned, grounding them back to reality, "this could all just be a fever dream, like I said, from too much sun and whiskey."

Tucker pointed ahead. "One way or the other, looks like we're about to find out."

Abbie faced fully forward. She spotted the beige Bronco parked at the top of the next slope, nearly lost in the deep shadows of cliffs that climbed hundreds of feet into the sky. The vehicle looked abandoned. No one came running into view, drawn by the Jeep's rumbling.

Still, Tucker parked their vehicle under the cover of a juniper tree. "We'll go on foot from here."

(7)

7:17 A.M.

With his Desert Eagle clutched in one hand, Tucker ran low toward the Bronco. He left Abbie and Landon hidden in a copse of junipers.

Kane had already scouted the perimeter of the parked SUV, circling it fully. Afterward, Tucker had sent his partner over to the narrow canyon cut into the cliff face to stand guard. Even now, through the camera feed streaming to his goggles, Tucker had a view down the shadowy gorge, where a thin spring-fed stream trickled, bordered on one side by loose shale and patches of bunchgrasses, and the other by a mix of scrubby junipers and a scatter of broader oaks.

Tucker reached the Bronco and did a quick search through the open windows to make sure it was truly unoccupied, that there was no guard napping inside, someone who Kane could not spot from his low vantage point. It was indeed empty. In the back, he saw a wooden crate, cracked open. It held the last few sticks of a load of dynamite. A neighboring cardboard box had been overturned, spilling blasting caps coiled with fuses.

Tucker had hoped to find extra ammunition, maybe a spare magazine for his Bushmaster rifle. He did spot a box of 9 mm shells that should fit Abbie's confiscated Glock. He raided what he could, then stabbed his KA-BAR combat knife into all four tires of the Bronco to immobilize the vehicle.

Satisfied, he waved Abbie and Landon up to the SUV.

Once they joined him, he kept his voice to a whisper, not trusting the acoustics among all the towering red rocks. "Stay quiet once we enter the canyons. Move silently. Step where I step." He glanced to the cut into the cliff. "From the lack of a guard posted here, the thieves must be feeling full of themselves, sure they have the upper hand. Let's keep it that way."

Tucker turned to lead the way when his pocket chirped brightly. He pulled out the radio that he had taken from one of the dead men. A burst of static became a voice. *"Bo, Randy, report in. Have you heard anything from Buck and Chet?"*

Tucker searched the others' faces. If Tucker failed to answer the call, suspicions would be raised. Men could be sent back here to check on the status of the others.

Abbie waved for him to answer. Landon simply shrugged.

Tucker lifted the radio. He closed his eyes, recalling the voices he had heard through Kane's audio feed. He did his best to imitate a slight twang, but he kept his voice low, his words clipped, and played with the radio's squelch button to frazzle his call even further.

"Say again," Tucker radioed. "You're cutting out there, Hawk."

"Any word from Buck or Chet about that damn dog?"

Tucker laughed. "Oh, yeah. They caught the lil' bastard. Shot 'em up good. Didn't you hear the gunfire?"

Tucker didn't know if Hawk's team had heard any of the firefight at the campsite, but if so, he hoped his lie helped cover things up.

"*Fan-fucking-tastic. We're almost to the mother lode. Hang tight.*"

"Will do." Tucker lowered the radio and faced the others. "That worked for now, but from the sounds of it, we're running out of time."

He led the others to the steep-sided ravine where Kane waited. He dropped to a knee next to his partner and rubbed the dog's thick ruff.

Here we go, buddy.

Kane turned and gave him a quick lick on his nose. Tucker felt the trembling tension in the dog. Kane was clearly anxious to get moving, excited at the prospect of the hunt.

Tucker pointed to the scuffle of boot treads in the sand, then up the ravine's trickling stream. He ended by clenching his fist twice, once with his pinkie extended, then with the finger tucked. He reinforced the signal with a whispered command. "*TRACK. QUIET. HIDDEN.*"

He lifted his hand from Kane's ruff, and like a wolf after a rabbit, the dog bolted forward. In three bounds, Kane vanished into the dark bower of the juniper forest to the stream's left. Tucker straightened, having already lost sight of his partner. His ears strained to hear him. But he could not detect any crack of branches, any crunch of sand. It was as if Kane had melted into those shadows, becoming one with them.

He glanced over to Abbie, who mouthed a silent *wow*.

Tucker tapped the side of his goggles to bring up Kane's camera feed. He slipped his radio earpiece in place. Still, he heard nothing, just the barest hint of his partner's breath. As Tucker watched the camera view sweep through and around the gnarled boles of trees, he felt the familiar division of his brain. A part of him still saw the view up the canyon from his position. The other half settled into his partner's paws, his eyes, his breath.

With his Desert Eagle in hand and the Bushmaster rifle over his shoulder, he set off, calling back to the other two. "Stay close."

Tucker kept to the same side of the stream as Kane, but only at the edge of the forest, knowing he could never move as silently as his partner through the dense brush and trees. With one eye, he picked the quietest path, sticking to rock, avoiding sand where he could. With the other, he ran through the forest with Kane.

He heard the others behind him, doing a decent job of staying silent. Still, their breaths sounded harsh and loud. Their footfalls heavy and hurried. He waited for them to settle into his rhythm, then slowly increased his pace.

Still, they could never match Kane's agility and speed.

Afraid his partner was getting too far ahead, Tucker whispered a command. "SLOW. HALF-SPEED."

* * *

Kane wants to ignore those words.

His heart pounds in his throat. Instinct fires his blood, driving him to run faster. His nose remains on the trail of sweaty musk, on gun oil. But he trusts his packmate. Each syllable of that command sinks into him, reins in his pace, cools that fire to a hot glow.

His flowing swiftness becomes stealth.

He angles around bushes as he runs through the forest. His senses extend outward. Whiskers detect which branches are the most brittle and need to be avoided. Guard hairs on his body warn him when to shy away, when to bend. His sensitive pads inform him how best to shift his weight between his four legs to avoid any crinkle of dry leaf or rustle of pine needles. His eyes note the gradations of darkness ahead of him, guiding his path to the deepest shadows. His nose is even more sensitive, his nostrils flare, taking in every scent, painting the world in a kaleidoscope of trails, both past and present. They fill him and extend outward, tangling all into a whole, making him one with the forest, with the damp limestone, with the breeze blowing through the canyon.

In such moments, he is freed from his flesh and bones, from his panting breath and pounding heart. He senses a wider world beckoning him. It calls to him in the scrambling passage of a squirrel, in the bitter marker of a bobcat's urine, in the flash of bright feathers as a warbler takes wing.

*But he keeps his ears pricked high, swiveling one way, then the other. He
hears those behind him, tracks their noisy passage, slows his pace to match. He
ignores that call to race away into the larger world that tempts him, that calls
to him. Instead, he feels something stronger tethering him here. It trails back
to that well of warmth, that familiar tang of sweat and breath, to the promise
buried there, of pack and home.*

So he runs onward—but never too far.

(8)

7:42 A.M.

After only twenty minutes into the badlands, Abbie was already lost.

Sweat covered her body, less from the exertion and fast pace than from
the sense that time was running short for her grandfather. Her disorientation was compounded by the need to hurry through the maze of ravines,
canyons, and gorges, while also trying to match her steps to Tucker's, to
place her boot where he set his.

A tension headache pounded between her eyes. Her panting had
grown into a dry-mouthed gasping. She clutched the Glock between both
palms, letting its solid weight and heft anchor her, like a tightrope walker
using a heavy pole for balance.

The group turned into a pinched crevasse, so narrow she could probably reach out with both arms and brush her fingertips along the sandstone
walls to either side. Tucker did not slow, rushing along as the passage cut
ever deeper into the land. She still caught no sight of his shepherd, but she
knew the dog was somewhere ahead, guiding them unerringly along the
bandits' trail.

She swallowed and tried to distract herself with the unique geology
of these badlands, what her people called *Ingaya Hala*, or Black Moon.
Legends of this territory spoke of spirits who led trespassers to their doom.

But, ghosts or not, she knew it would be easy to get lost in this labyrinth. She also read the danger in the rocks all around her. The tumble of boulders and scree from old collapses, the broken stump of arches overhead that they hurried under, the stained erosion of lower strata marking the riotous passage of countless flash floods.

This treacherous maze put the *bad* in badlands.

She knew from her study of this region that one of the major fault lines of the Sonoran Desert passed under this area. It was likely that fault's instability that had shattered this rampart of raised bedrock into its current form, then centuries of rain had eroded those cracks and crevices even deeper.

She also recognized that their current twisted path was leading them steadily downward. She could feel the change in elevation in her ears, noted it as the cliffs rose higher and higher around them, squeezing ever tighter.

Ahead, Tucker lifted a hand, warning them to stop.

She obeyed, casting a glance back to Landon whose face was pasted with dust, lined by rivulets of sweat. His eyes pinched with tension.

Tucker ran ahead, to where the narrow crevice ended. He took a swift look, waved them to follow, and vanished out of sight. She hurried after him.

The crevice ended at a steep-walled bowl, like a giant's well. She craned her neck at the sheer cliffs. She could not see any exit. It appeared to be a dead end.

Had the dog led them astray?

Across the way, Tucker crouched next to Kane, who paced the wall there, sniffing along the bottom edge. She heard a soft whine coming from the normally quiet dog. She crossed the bowl of sandstone to join them.

"Look at this," Tucker whispered.

He pointed low, to a passage no higher than her knees. She bent down and placed a palm on the sand and the oddly smooth pebbles along the bottom. She twisted back around and examined the sandstone bowl, noting the snow-white band of strata halfway up the cliffs, where scale and minerals scarred the red rock, marking the level of an old water table.

She turned back to the wall and realized it was actually a slab of red rock that must have fallen across the gorge millennia ago, closing the place off and damming it up. Over the passing centuries, winter rains must have flooded down here, filling this bowl with water—until pressure and erosion had worn a channel under the slab, finally breaking through and draining the ancient lake and exposing this passageway.

"They went through here," Tucker whispered. "You can see a few handprints and boot scuffs. The tunnel's not long, maybe thirty yards. I can see sunlight on the far side. I'll go first with Kane. You hang back until I give the all-clear."

She nodded.

Tucker signaled Kane, and the dog lowered his head and shimmied under the slab's edge and into the passageway. The shepherd no longer whined, but before he vanished, she noted the hackles raised along the dog's exposed neck and shoulders.

Tucker followed on his hands and knees, leaving her alone with Landon. They both crouched at the tunnel's mouth, watching the others' passage.

"Can you feel it?" Landon asked, sticking close, his words a breathless whisper.

She frowned at him.

Landon had his rifle slung over his shoulder and rubbed his fingers, cracking his knuckles. He shook his hands. "The tingling? Like ants crawling under your skin?"

She shook her head, feeling nothing but her headache, her pounding heart. But she understood his meaning, remembering Kane's whining and shivering hackles.

The dog had felt it, too.

"A vortex," she whispered, both excited at the prospect and disappointed that she felt nothing. She waved behind her. "I bet this bowl had been sealed up for centuries. Remember that hellacious wet winter two years back? Those storms might have overflooded this place, enough to finally break open this natural dam."

"If you're right, then it's no wonder no one ever found this site."

"Until Uncle Oro stumbled upon it."

They both watched as Tucker and Kane cleared the passage and disappeared. After several breaths, Tucker popped back into view. Limned against the sunlight on the far side, Tucker waved them over.

Abbie went first. She shoved the Glock into her waistband, dropped to her hands and knees, and crawled under the heavy slab. Landon huffed behind her, urging her faster.

She finally exited the far side—into a larger version of the bowl behind her. This valley stretched two hundred yards across. The cliffs were even taller here and sheltered a dark juniper forest. The shadowy trees were massive, clearly centuries old. The torrent, when the red-rock dam burst, had cut a swath through the forest, uprooting trees and digging a wide shallow trench in the sand. But the waters were long gone, having seeped into the depths of the sandy bowl or evaporated away.

Before she could discern more, Tucker motioned her to stay low and rushed her to the left, into the forest's edge. They were followed by Landon and met up with Kane in those deeper shadows.

Kane's eyes shone in the darkness. The dog panted, pacing a few steps back and forth, tail swishing in plain agitation. His hackles were still raised.

Even Abbie felt it now. Her scalp tingled; her hearing felt dulled as if she were underwater. In the past, she had felt similar inklings at vortex sites around Sedona, but never this strong.

"What do you make of this?" Landon said, his voice hushed with awe.

The physicist stood to the side, examining the bole of a huge, gnarled juniper. Its thick trunk was savagely twisted, the branches, too, even the bark. It was as if the old tree had been caught in a tornado and frozen in place. Just staring at its tortured shape, Abbie could almost hear the howl of that storm, feel that wind pressing against her.

Abbie ran her fingers along the bark. "You often see this type of effect around vortexes. Trees unusually twisted, supposedly swirled by the site's energies."

"And it's not just the one tree," Tucker said. He stood at the edge of the flood-ravaged wash. He lowered a pair of binoculars and passed them to Abbie. "Look."

She lifted the scopes to her eyes and panned the enclosed valley. She didn't see it at first, then the larger pattern snapped clear. She finally saw the forest through the trees. The encircling grove of ancient junipers—while all twisted—were bowed in the same direction, frozen in a perpetual spiral around the valley, a woodland version of a whirlpool.

"Check out the center," Tucker said.

She followed the eddy of twisted trees to the sandy bottom of the bowl, where the forest ended. A tall black mound rose there, its top high enough to reach the morning sunlight angling over the edge of the cliffs. Crystals in that black rock refracted the light, creating a fiery crown at the summit.

"A cinder dome," Abbie said.

"From an old volcano?" Tucker asked.

She shook her head. "Likely just a pimple on a far larger face hidden below." She lowered the binoculars, picturing the depression down which they had traveled. "I'd wager we're standing within a collapsed caldera, maybe miles across."

Landon pointed to the right, where there was movement near the cinder slope. "And that must be the entrance down into it."

Tucker took back the binoculars and studied the spot. "There's a stone archway. Looks like they posted a single guard at that opening." He turned to them. "You two work through the forest and get positioned directly across from there."

"What're you going to do?" Landon asked.

"Kane and I'll take that guard out. As silently as we can. Then we'll see about rescuing Dr. Kee." He pointed across the washed-out gully to the forest on the other side. "If anything goes wrong, stay hidden."

They both nodded and set off across the gap, using the root balls of upended trees to mask their passage. Halfway across, Abbie glanced back, but Tucker and Kane had already vanished. She hurried after Landon. For a moment, she got a full-on view of the dark cinder dome. It was hemispherical in shape, as if a giant black ball had crashed here and jammed halfway into the sand.

No, she realized, *not a ball.*

She shuddered as she recognized its shape, its dark crystalline color.

Here was the true heart of *Ingaya Hala.*

The Black Moon of legend.

She tore her gaze away and rushed after Landon. She remembered what else was said about that place, what those legends claimed that black moon hid.

The land of nightmares.

(9)

7:58 A.M.

Crouched at the forest's edge, Tucker waited for Kane to get into position. He stared at the giant cinder dome. Its slopes sparked with crystals; its crown blazed with the first touch of the morning sun. A moment ago, he had sent Kane circling around the back of the dome, to close in on the archway from the other side. Once his partner was in place, Tucker would approach from this side.

Through his goggles, he watched from Kane's point of view as the dog slinked along the edge of the dome. As he waited in the forest, Tucker's skin crawled and itched. He wanted to dismiss the feeling as nerves, tension, or maybe the power of suggestion from all that talk about vortexes. Still, the hairs on his arms and his neck shivered. He found it harder to breathe, as if his chest were being squeezed in a vice.

He knew this wasn't all in his head.

Kane had clearly felt it, too.

Tucker had never seen the dog so edgy. Besides the ridge of raised fur, Tucker read the subtler signs in his partner: the way his ears lay flatter, his tail held stiff and straight, the twitch in the big fella's eyes, as if forever searching for a hidden enemy.

I get it.

Tucker also felt as if he were being watched. Finally, Kane's camera feed revealed the edge of the stone doorway on the far side. The stone arch stuck out slightly from the cinder slope.

"HOLD," he radioed to Kane.

The shepherd lowered to his belly, his nose pointed forward, the camera fixed on the opening.

Tucker left the forest and rushed low across the ten yards of open ground to the hill. As he ran, Tucker felt that unnerving effect grow. His vision blurred at the edges. His skin felt hot, like after a sunburn. With every step, the vise on his chest squeezed tighter. Even Kane's camera feed had begun to cut in and out.

Finally, Tucker reached the black slope and crouched lower, less from the need to keep hidden as much as to duck away from that pressure, as if he could somehow hide from it. He edged along the hill until he spotted the opening, then stopped. He noted movement at the arch's threshold. He caught a glimpse of a shoulder, an elbow, as a guard paced, likely as nervous and affected as they all were.

Tucker needed to draw him out into the open.

He started to signal Kane to bark, to lure the man out—but instead, the guard stepped fully into view on his own, a radio at his lips, a pistol in his other hand.

"Hawk, what's going on in there?" the guard demanded. "I've got the detonator all wired up out here. One through six. Let me know when to blow the first charge."

Tucker pictured the near-empty box of dynamite in the back of the Bronco. Hawk's team must be planning to do a little controlled blasting to speed up the extraction process. The mining equivalent of a smash and grab. It was risky, but Hawk's team must know their time was limited and had to take the chance.

"Hawk!" the guard yelled. "Why aren't you—?"

A piercing scream, full of terror, echoed out of the tunnel.

Startled, the guard jumped and turned—too fast for Tucker to retreat out of sight. The gunman did a double take in his direction. With a small cry, the man jerked his pistol up.

So much for stealth.

Tucker had already centered his Desert Eagle's sights on the guard and fired two quick shots. Both .44 Mag rounds struck center mass, blowing clean through the man, knocking him backward.

As the sharp blasts echoed off the cliffs, he ran forward. According to Abbie, Hawk had another two men with him, somewhere down in that hill. Along with Jackson Kee, hopefully still alive.

He reached the opening, bridged by an arch of sandstone. Its surface had been etched with ancient petroglyphs: writhing figures of men and women, dancing amid flames, a sunburst at the very top. He stepped toward the mouth—only to be hit by an even stronger wave of energy. He gasped, his body burning. He stumbled back, momentarily losing his sight until he adjusted to that pressure.

He lifted an arm against it until he could see.

Kane ran up to him, whining deeply.

I'm okay, buddy.

He lowered his arm and patted the dog's side. Behind him, Abbie and Landon came running out of the forest toward him. He tried to warn them back with a raised palm. They ignored him and rushed to his side. They clearly felt the energy, too, their faces tight, eyes wincing—but neither of them seemed as deeply debilitated as him. Even now, that energy felt like a physical wind blowing out of the hill, trying to keep him away.

He remembered Abbie's story about how some people were more sensitive to vortexes. He glanced down to Kane, knowing his partner—and his littermate Abel—were assigned to him because of his unusually empathic nature, a trait that allowed him to bond with his dogs at a deeper level than most handlers.

Was that trait somehow tied to his sensitivity now?

He didn't know.

He didn't care.

Instead, Tucker faced that harsh wind and ordered the others—even Kane.

"Stay here. Guard this exit."

(10)

8:01 A.M.

As Tucker vanished down the dark tunnel, Abbie paced on one side of the opening. Tension kept her breathless. Her bones vibrated like a tuning fork, making it impossible to stand still. She kept a firm grip on her Glock. Her ears strained for any indication of what was happening, but this close to the cinder dome, her hearing was further dampened, like a wet towel had been wrapped around her head.

Still, she was certain the scream a moment ago had not been her grandfather's.

Please, still be alive.

She was not the only one worried. Kane stood under the arch, his nose pointed down the tunnel, his ears stuck up high, his tail low. His back legs were slightly bunched under him, ready to leap to his partner's defense.

"I should be down there," Abbie moaned. "We all should."

Sheltered on the far side of the archway, Landon disagreed. He pointed his rifle at the tunnel. "That passage looks narrow. We'd just get in each other's way. Tucker is right. This is the only way out. If anyone but Tucker or your grandfather shows their face, we take them out. We may be the last line of defense out here."

She nodded and swallowed. To distract herself, she stared up at the arch of sandstone, at the ancient pictographs carved into its surface. Stick-like men and women danced and writhed within rust-red flames. She felt her skin continuing to burn, her nerves on fire. She reached out her free hand and touched one of the tortured figures.

Is this a representation of the vortex energies here?

She craned her neck and stared up at the giant sunburst inscribed at the top of the arch. The beams struck the nearest figures and shattered their forms into broken pieces.

If so, what did that represent?

She stepped back and stared higher, to the top of the cinder dome, to where sunlight set the crystals up there on fire. A cold sense of dread settled through her.

To her side, Kane began a long, low whine.

She turned to the dog.

His tail was now tucked between his back legs. His body trembled, in tune with that whine. His neck was bowed, his head low, his nails dug into the sand—as if his entire body were trying to bottle up a howl from bursting out.

She stared down into the dark tunnel.

What's going on down there?

(11)

8:03 A.M.

Tucker headed blindly along the tunnel, which descended steeply. He dared not use his penlight. His pistol blasts surely had alerted those down below, but if anyone came up to investigate those shots, he didn't want his flashlight to give away his presence in the tunnel. He needed every advantage he could muster, especially with the odds being three against one.

As he continued deeper, he held his Desert Eagle pointed forward, running the fingertips of his other hand along one wall to keep his bearings, testing each step ahead of him. He sensed the path was not only descending, but also curving ever clockwise, spiraling toward the heart of the black hill.

Finally, an eerie green glow flowed around the bend ahead.

He stopped, his ears straining for any threat. But by now, the unearthly pressure had dampened his hearing to the point of deafness. His body burned like a torch, making it harder to feel the cold stone under his fingertips. As he moved through the darkness, his vision had begun to dance with flames at the edges, growing ever narrower. It was as if all his senses were being overwhelmed, being shut down as they were overloaded.

Before he lost everything, he continued forward.

He rounded the curve and discovered the source of the eerie emerald sheen. It was simply a dozen plastic glowsticks scattered across the floor of a cave ahead. He paused and stared at the strange tableau illuminated inside.

The cavern walls reflected the wan light and cast it back in brilliant rainbows of fire. The entire chamber, even the curve of the floor, was covered in fire agates, from pebble-sized stones to huge boulders. In a breath, he understood what he was seeing.

It's a giant geode, lined by opalescent fire agates.

As soon as he thought it, he knew it was wrong.

He felt his assaulted senses spin.

These were not ordinary fire agates.

He remembered Abbie's description of the ferrimagnetic iron oxide layered throughout those stones, and Landon's explanation of the true nature of these agates. He gaped out at the expanse of the cave.

This was a geode made up of *time crystals.*

He feared entering the space, especially considering the state of the bodies inside. Two figures stood upright, visibly shaking, facing a quarter turn to the right, their features frozen and aghast. Tucker recognized the auburn-haired one with the scruff of dark beard from Abbie's description.

Hawk.

Neither of the men sensed Tucker's presence, their gazes fixed to the right.

Between them, a third man—gray-haired and ponytailed—knelt on the floor. His back was to whatever the other two men were transfixed by. One of the man's legs stuck out askew, bent wrong. A pool of blood doused the fires in the stones around him. From the looks of it, he had been shot. Still, the man kept his forehead pressed to the pebbled floor, his arms bound behind him.

It was Jackson Kee.

Tucker edged into the cavern, staying low. "Dr. Kee . . ."

The man looked up, his eyes wild, confused. "Who—?"

Tucker had no time to explain. He didn't know why the other two men remained frozen, but he recalled the old prospector's story of being trapped here, held in a hypnagogic state until nightfall, stuck in a waking dream. If the same was going on here now, Tucker intended to take advantage of it. He considered executing the two men as they stood, but that seemed even too cold-blooded for him.

Still, he gripped his pistol.

If anything changes . . .

Breathing hard, still struggling with his senses, he hurried low toward Jackson, judging if he could be moved. Tucker reached the old man, dropped to a knee, and cut the zip ties binding the guy's wrists.

"Abbie sent me," Tucker said, hoping that using his granddaughter's name would help reassure the old man of his intent.

Once free, Jackson grabbed Tucker's shirt and tugged him lower. "Don't look."

He might not have, except for that warning.

He glanced past the old man's bowed back. Across the way, another arch of sandstone framed a passageway. Tucker had a hard time focusing on it. The fiery refracted light dazzled across the opening. He shook his head, which only stoked his headache. He blinked, trying to clear his pinched vision, only to have it narrow further.

Still, he spotted a body sprawled halfway into the tunnel.

As addled as he was, he had forgotten Hawk had a *another* teammate. The man lay facedown on the agate floor, his legs still in the cavern, his upper body across the threshold. Only there was no *body* on that other side—just bones.

As Tucker stared, the skull crumbled to dust as if it were centuries old.

"I tried to stop him," Jackson said, drawing back Tucker's attention. The old man waved at his broken leg, shattered by a bullet.

Over by the arch, Tucker spotted an abandoned pistol on the floor, the barrel still smoking. Tucker pictured the gunman diving at that arch, falling across it, his upper body either burning—or maybe *aging*—to ash and bone, leaving only his legs intact on this side.

"I . . . I think it started when the sunlight struck the hilltop," Jackson said as Tucker scooped an arm under his shoulders, ready to haul him up. "It felt like a thunderclap inside here, only noiseless but still powerful."

Tucker didn't care. Though he suspected Jackson was right. The old prospector had only escaped at nightfall, possibly when the hypnagogic spell broke. Tucker glanced at the two men standing stiffly with horrified expressions. He intended to be long gone before they woke. Once outside, he would call Painter, have the director summon the choppers, and bring Hawk and his teammate to justice.

That was the plan.

He straightened, lifting Jackson who gasped in pain, but didn't struggle.

"This . . . place," Jackson panted, perhaps talking to keep from screaming. "It amplifies your fears. Wakes what's buried deepest."

Tucker remembered Abbie's description of the emotion-magnifying effect of Sedona's vortexes, of her belief that the electromagnetic energies could play havoc with magnetic particles in the brain, addling one's senses, stoking that lizard part of one's brain, where the basest emotions were rooted.

"Maybe the Yavapai found this place," Jackson said. "Used it as a test. To make you face your fears, to control your emotions—or die." He glanced to the archway, then back again. "You mustn't go near that portal. Nothing living can survive its energies."

Wasn't planning on it.

Tucker turned Jackson toward the exit. Even supported, the old man stumbled, swinging out an arm. He ended up striking the guy next to him, Hawk's teammate. The man yelled, as if bitten by a snake.

Tucker crouched and lifted his Desert Eagle at the man, fearing Jackson had woken him. But the guy still stared toward the archway, began shambling toward it, moaning.

"*Mama, no, wait, Mama . . .*"

"You have to stop him," Jackson said.

But before Tucker could move, the man darted toward the archway, which now shimmered with refracted light, like a poorly tuned television.

As the man neared it, traceries of energy played across his limbs, atop the crown of his head. Then the radio at his hip exploded, violently enough to spin the man, to break the spell. The man's arms flailed—but it was too late. Momentum cast his form backward across the arch's threshold. Fiery energies burst around him, consuming him. On the far side, a cloud of dust burst into the far tunnel, along with the rattling cascade of bone.

"Go," Jackson urged. "It gets worse just after—"

Tucker had stared too long.

The pressure on his ears popped, his tunnel vision expanded into full technicolor. He heard the thumping of a helicopter. Men screaming. He smelled the sulfur of gun smoke, the reek of burning flesh. His cheeks were frozen, traced by hot tears. He stared at the mountaintop below. Men lay broken on the rock; blood steamed on patches of snow. A pit smoked from where the IED bomb had exploded, ambushing the team. He heard the scream of Taliban soldiers, rallying and triumphant. He watched them run to the top of the slope, heads swaddled in black, shaking rifles, several firing at the retreating helicopter.

Others chased down a limping dog, who scrambled one way, then the other, seeking a way to escape.

"Abel," he screamed, then and now.

The dog stopped and stared up at him, gazes locking.

Abel . . .

The dog lifted its head and howled forlornly, begging for help, to not be left behind, to not be abandoned. Abel howled again, shattering Tucker's heart into pieces.

But another heard it, too.

* * *

Kane's ears prick higher.

A breath ago, he heard a name cried out, one that woke old pain. Still, he held his position, following his packmate's last command: Stay on Guard.

He obeys.

Still, he listens, less with his ears than with his heart. Here in this strange place, where the air buzzes with unseen wasps, where his fur shivers from hidden winds, the long tether that binds him to another has grown far stronger.

He feels another's anguish, he tastes fear, he smells fire and smoke.

Then faint, but as real as the rock under his pads, a howl echoes to him— reaching not his ears, but some place far deeper, to bonds and memories buried in his bones, in each breath, in every beat of his heart. He remembers nestling with his brother in the greater warmth of their mother, bellies full of milk. He again romps, chasing the other's tail. Shoulder to shoulder, they sit stiffly in training, ready to prove themselves, to be rewarded. They sometimes fight, more often lick each other's wounds. Then two become three, and all was even better. Three run courses together, race across deserts, through forests. They hunt and play and feast. They pile together in a rucksack, each warming the other, breaths shared—until three became one.

Now, another howl.

It can no longer be ignored.

It shatters the command that binds Kane to this spot.

With every fiber of muscle, he leaps to bring them all together again.

For three to become one once more.

(12)

8:08 A.M.

Abbie gasped as Kane burst from his tense crouch and lunged into the tunnel. Startled, she fell back a step. There had been no warning. She had never suspected the dog could move so fast—there one second, gone the next.

A moment ago, she had heard some faint yelling, maybe a name being called out. She had shared a look with Landon across the archway, unsure what to do. There had been no gunshots. Still, fearing the worst, they had retreated a few steps from the opening. Landon had lifted his rifle to his shoulder; she had raised her Glock.

Then the dog had burst away.

Abbie stared where Kane had been steadfastly posted. "He must've heard something," she said to Landon. "If he broke command, then something's seriously wrong."

"What do you want to do?"

"I'm going to trust Kane." She shifted forward. "If the dog thinks Tucker, maybe my grandfather, are in danger, I believe him."

"What's the plan then?"

"I'm done waiting." She headed into the tunnel. "I'm backing Kane up."

(13)

8:09 A.M.

Inside the helicopter, arms held Tucker and restrained him from leaping out of the chopper. He fought to be free, to go to Abel's aid.

"*Don't get any closer,*" someone warned, sounding distant and faint, but familiar.

Tucker's shoulders were strangely weighted down. He heard pained gasps in his ear. He shoved it all away. A body crashed heavily to the side with a cry of agony, then another warning.

"*Stay back . . . please . . .*"

He ignored this.

I can't leave. I won't. Not again.

With this thought, he was suddenly out of the helicopter, standing on the mountaintop. His boots crunched through snow. Frigid winds whipped and snapped at his uniform. Across the way, Abel fought to escape the gunfire. A knife flashed. The dog dodged at the last second, limping, getting weaker.

Hold on, Abel. I'm coming.

He took another step, then another.

He lifted the pistol in his hand, momentarily confused.

Where's my rifle?

Then his pant leg was grabbed. He was tugged back, nearly losing his footing. He batted at what held him. But his fingers found a cold nose, soft fur. He heard a sharp whine. *Here* was a warning he could never ignore.

Kane . . .

Still, he kept his gaze fixed on Abel's struggle to reach the two of them. Tucker continued forward, dragging Kane with him—but Kane held tight. The dog braced all four paws, becoming an anchor.

Again a whine, more urgent, full of warning.

Tucker finally glanced down to his leg, to his partner, and the world fractured around him.

He saw Kane clamped hard to his pant leg, but Tucker was no longer in uniform. He wore jeans and a khaki jacket. To the side, he spotted a form crumpled in agony on the floor, a leg broken under him, an arm reaching toward him.

Jackson . . .

Still, he heard the screams of dying men, the ululating cries of savage triumph, the beat of rotors. He smelled smoke and blood and bodies. He turned enough to see Abel fighting to escape, to reach him, every step agony, every movement desperate.

Tucker turned to face that which wounded him most.

Abel stared back at him, barking, yelping, his gaze mournful.

Kane tugged at his leg. As Tucker took another step, Kane refused to let go, ready to be dragged wherever Tucker went.

For a moment, trapped in this hypnagogic state, Tucker saw both worlds, past and present, real and not. It was like when he ran with Kane, seeing simultaneously through both his eyes and his partner's.

Tucker had been trained for this, his brain wired for it.

He knew what he had to do.

He could not doom Kane, but he could not abandon Abel.

So, he stood his ground.

Jackson had said nothing *living* could pass through that portal, that view into a past that his fevered brain had conjured. He remembered the radio exploding earlier, casting that other man through the fiery curtain. It wasn't just the living, anything *powered* could not withstand the maelstrom of energies focused there, which pretty much encompassed all living things.

What are we but biological machines, as electrical as any radio.

No, Tucker knew what he had to do.

Toss a rock, something inert.

Only with a lot more force.

He aimed his pistol at the portal, toward where Abel struggled. He fired again and again and again. He watched one Taliban soldier drop, then another. A black-clothed figure came at Abel with a raised dagger, a shout on his lips. Tucker cut it off with a round through his throat. By now, the other Taliban soldiers froze and looked around, unsure where the hidden sniper was shooting from. Spooked, they fled in all directions.

Until only Abel stood there, panting, hurt, but alive.

The dog stared at Tucker, still begging to be reunited.

Kane let go of his pant leg and came around to Tucker's side. A whine flowed from the dog—not in warning now, but in the excited whimper of a wolf greeting a long-lost member of the pack.

Kane stepped toward his brother, but Tucker dropped to a knee and hugged Kane, holding him fast.

"He's free," Tucker whispered in Kane's ear.

We all are.

Tucker held tight to Kane, feeling the heat of his partner's body. He stared at Abel, the dog's form already turning ghostly. He stared one last time into Abel's eyes.

"Run, my good boy . . . run until you're home again."

Abel acknowledged his words with a toss of his head, then turned and hobbled away. He slowly gained speed with each step, until he was racing—and vanished over the mountain's edge and was gone.

Tucker stood up, staring after him.

Kane barked after Abel, as if cheering his brother onward.

The loud bark finally broke the spell's hold over Tucker. The glamour vanished all around him until there was only the radiant cavern and a sandstone arch framing a dark and empty tunnel.

Unfortunately, the spell did not only break for Tucker.

A gasp rose to his left.

He turned.

Hawk stumbled away from him, his eyes still haunted and wild. The bastard swung his assault rifle toward Tucker and Kane. Tucker lifted his Desert Eagle, but the weapon's breach had sprung. He had emptied his pistol defending Abel.

Tucker didn't regret it.

Hawk leveled the rifle and fired.

Tucker twisted around. He had failed to save Abel years ago. He refused to lose Kane now. He swept down and covered Kane with his own body. Gunfire blasted, deafening in the cavern.

But he felt no impact, no fiery pain.

Instead, rounds strafed over him, sparking and ricocheting off the agate on the far side. He glanced back—in time to see Hawk crashing backward, half his face gone.

Tucker turned fully around.

Abbie stood at the threshold to the cavern, a smoking pistol in her hand.

(14)

8:11 A.M.

"That's for Uncle Oro," Abbie said.

She lowered her Glock and stepped into the cavern.

Landon came up from behind and joined her. He took in the room, then stiffened, and rushed past her. He dashed over to where her grandfather lay on his side on the floor, propped up on one arm.

Landon waved to Tucker. "Help me with Jackson. Hurry!"

Tucker responded to the urgency and joined the physicist. They each grabbed an arm. Her grandfather's left leg was bleeding heavily, soaking through his pants, the bone clearly broken. His eyes were glassy with shock. But that wasn't the reason for Landon's urgency.

Over Landon's shoulder, Abbie saw something flashing and buzzing swiftly along the far wall. *A fuse.* One of Hawk's wild rounds must have sparked it to life. It led to a stick of dynamite poking out of a crack in the far wall. Below was a stack of more red sticks. As a geologist, she knew dynamite was sensitive to concussion. Struck with enough force—a nearby blast, a pelting of rocks—it could all blow.

Tucker must have realized it, too. He yanked her grandfather into his arms and hauled him in a fireman's carry. "Run!"

Abbie turned and led the way back up the tunnel. She barely made it a few yards when the world exploded behind her. The blast tossed her forward, sprawling her headlong. Crystalline dust rolled over her. She quickly regained her feet, knowing it wasn't over.

She tossed aside her Glock, fumbled out a flashlight, and clicked it on. "Keep going!" she hollered to the others.

She ran faster up the tunnel's spiral.

Another boom—muffled by the distance, but far stronger. The entire hill quaked from the explosion. She stumbled and fought to keep her footing. Cracks skittered across the walls and roof. She lifted an arm to protect her head as sections broke, spilling rock and cinders.

Finally, the end came into view, the exit brightly lit by sunshine after the gloom of the tunnel. She raced to it and out into the open air. Once free, she slowed, panting, heart pounding.

"Don't stop!" Tucker shouted, still carrying her grandfather's limp form.

Landon and Kane followed.

The ground trembled ominously. Behind them, the cinder dome shook, slowly disintegrating, sending down avalanches of rocks. Abbie fled into the forest and angled toward the flood-washed path up to the rock dam. She glanced back through the twisted tree trunks and saw a huge black boulder crash down the cinder hillside and smash through the archway. Silt and sand flowed after it, covering the opening, until there was no sign of the tunnel ever being there.

Finally, she reached the open wash and climbed past uprooted trees. At the top, she turned around. She leaned her back against the red-rock slab that had sealed this valley for centuries.

The ground continued to quake in a worrisome manner.

She pictured the fault line running through the center of this ancient caldera.

None of them felt confident enough to crawl through the tunnel under the slab. Not with the earth still shaking. Especially since the tunnel here had already shrunk to half its size, as the slab settled earthward.

And maybe they wouldn't have to risk it.

Tucker joined her. He had left her grandfather to Landon's care. He lowered his satellite phone. "Help's on the way. Med-evac will be here in a couple of minutes."

"Thank you," she mumbled, then turned to Kane. "Thanks to *both* of you."

"Considering you just saved *our* lives back there," Tucker said, "I'd say that debt is paid in full."

She wasn't so sure that was true.

Still, she stared back to the center of the valley. A wide fissure had opened down there. As she watched, the broken remains of the dark cinder dome sifted down into that crack, slowly sinking and vanishing away.

She felt both relieved and saddened.

At long last, that Black Moon was setting.

(15)

April 26, 6:50 P.M.

Four days later, Tucker sat atop a tall arch of stone. As sunset neared, he dangled his feet over the fifty-foot drop. Devil's Bridge was a Sedona landmark, one of its largest natural stone arches.

And nowhere near a vortex.

Kane sat next to him, his tail idly swishing, his tongue lolling happily. They had enjoyed the short, easy hike from the trailhead. Kane had chased a few jackrabbits, gave a roadrunner a good race. The trail was a popular one, but this late on a cold day, they had this singular attraction all to themselves.

Which is the way Tucker preferred.

The past few days had been hectic, full of noise and bluster. Then again, he had left a trail of dead bodies across the desert. Director Crowe had helped grease wheels here, so Tucker and Kane wouldn't have to stick around these parts for long. It also helped that Abigail Pike, Jackson Kee, and Dr. Landon—who were all well respected locally—readily vouched for him. He did his best to avoid the press, which was like trying to escape a buzzing cloud of mosquitoes.

But matters were already quieting down.

Especially as much of their story remained untold.

Who would believe any of it?

Tucker even wondered how much was real and how much was some fevered dream stirred up by vortex energies. They had all agreed to keep silent, to stick to a story of claim jumpers and lost treasure, which fitted these lands perfectly.

Tucker had visited Jackson Kee at the hospital. The old guy seemed to be recuperating well, especially as he was attended to by a furry and devoted nurse. Cooper had been ecstatic to be reunited with Jackson and refused to leave his bedside.

Now that's loyalty I can understand.

Tucker reached over and scratched Kane's ear, earning a heavy thump of a tail.

Over at the University of Sedona, Abbie and Landon planned to continue their study of the huge agate that the old prospector had discovered. It was all that was left of the vast mother lode. The giant geode had broken apart and fallen deep into the earth, along with a good chunk of the valley. Even if any pieces were recoverable, the land was part of Yavapai sacred grounds, where mining was prohibited.

And just as well.

As the sun sank on this day, Tucker tried to remember what had happened. Like most dreams, he had a harder and harder time remembering the details of his vision.

After the group had been airlifted to safety, they had all compared notes. Tucker had shared what he'd experienced. Jackson claimed not to have seen any of that war-ravaged mountaintop, only that Tucker had been transfixed and started walking toward the arch, despite the old man's best efforts to stop him.

Tucker glanced over to Kane.

But you saw something, didn't you, buddy?

He remembered his partner's reaction, the way Kane seemed equally focused on Abel, calling out to his brother. Maybe it was some testament to their bonds, not just Tucker and Kane's, but all *three* of them.

Tucker shook his head.

Landon had tried to offer various hypotheses for Tucker's experience, going on about alternate dimensions, quantum entanglement, string theory. Abbie offered a more clinical opinion, repeating her idea of vortexes stimulating magnetite particles in the brain, reawakening emotional trauma buried deep in the basal ganglia.

All Tucker knew was that he felt better.

Lighter in spirit.

For now, he let it all go, enjoying this moment with Kane. As he did so, a huge halo formed around the setting sun. Tucker shaded his eyes against the glare. To the right and left, smaller suns appeared at the edges of the halo, ghostly mirages of the sun in the center. Tucker had witnessed this atmospheric effect in the past. It was rare, but not unheard of.

Still, he took it as a sign.

The two smaller patches of brightness were called *sun dogs*.

The phenomenon was ephemeral, a brief moment in time when these twin suns would accompany their larger brother. They burned brightly, but only for a short time. While the sun would always shine, the time it shared with its smaller companions was destined to be fleeting.

Tucker reached out and pulled Kane closer.

He remembered his last view of Abel, standing on that mountaintop.

He would treasure them both—no matter how long or how brief they shone beside him. He pictured Abel turning away and vanishing.

What did any of it truly mean?

He gazed at the sun dogs in the sky.

Who knows?

Maybe in some other place, in some other time—there was an answer waiting to be found.

* * *

The dog runs across the cold desert under colder stars. A bright moon casts the sand and scrub into shades of silver. He has been running for eight days, hiding where he could: a stone barn, a hollow log, a deep gully.

He knows his destination, but not the distance.

He follows what guides his heart, the tether that leads him unerringly toward his goal. He heads ever onward. He drinks from icy streams, eats carrion, anything to keep moving. As he runs, his left forelimb hangs uselessly, but he holds it up and forges on.

He was given an order, a command he refuses to forsake.

As night brightens toward morning, he sees a cluster of tents, a circle of sandbag fences, topped by razor wire. He limps toward it, near exhaustion, his ribs sticking out, his paw dragging, no longer able to hold it up.

He smells cookfires, sizzling meat.

He hears voices, both bright and dark.

He forces himself the last of the way to the fence. He circles until he stands shakily before the gates. A bright light blinds him. The gate creaks. Boots rush toward him.

He finally sits, balancing his front half on his good leg.

Hands rub him, breaths bathe him, excited voices echo.

Then he feels it, deep inside him.

The tether grows shorter.

Someone speaks. "Is that really him?"

A form drops in front of him, kneeling there.

He feels another come forward and nose him, whining, whimpering.

He knows his brother.

But he gives all his attention, all his heart to the one before him.

He wags his tail, knowing he has not failed. He was given an order on a mountaintop: Run until you're home again.

He feels his snout gently lifted, and a nose touches his.

"Who's the best boy?"

Abel licks Tucker's nose.

I am.

Author's Note to the Reader

Truth or Fiction

As with my past Sigma novels, I thought I'd spend these final few pages discussing how much of this novella is based on fact and how much is born of my own imagination. So please bear with me:

Sedona and the Sonoran Desert. I had a chance to vacation in Sedona. I was not planning to write a story about the town or the surrounding desert. I had touched upon this area in my novel *The Devil Colony*, so I hadn't thought there was another story to tell here. Then, like Tucker, I met a former biker at a breakfast counter (do eat at the Wildflower Bread Company). We got to talking, and he told me his story of his skeptical nature, how when he had first come to Sedona, he hadn't believed any of that "hogwash from those crystal munchers" (his words) about the area's vortexes. Then years later, he had the encounter described in the novella and became a believer. He was so adamant, so convincing, that I had to look more deeply into the subject manner, which meant traveling to many of Sedona's famous—

Vortexes. Now, I have to admit I did not experience any of those effects. Maybe I was too skeptical, too analytical, that I failed to settle into the right frame of mind. But I did interview several people—both locals and scientists like Abbie and Landon—who firmly believe these sites to be nexuses for earthly energies. I listened to their theories and included several in this novella. I took copious notes about their experiences, which also appear here, including their warning about keeping firm control over your emotions when visiting a vortex, as those energies were believed to magnify feelings, especially bad ones. So, if you're curious, I'd encourage you go out there and explore those sites for yourself. If nothing else, you might get a good story out of it. I know I did.

Time Crystals. This novella explores the scientific anomaly of time crystals. Surprisingly, such time-sensitive crystals are real. I find it fascinating that they were first *theorized* by an MIT physicist and Nobel laureate, Frank Wilczek—then eventually made *real*, created in labs at Harvard and Yale by following a recipe designed by Norman Yao at the University of California, Berkeley. And yes, DARPA is indeed exploring the military use of time crystals. So, of course, Sigma (i.e., Tucker and Kane) had to get involved.

Mysterious Arizona Portals. You may believe the portal described in this novel is purely of my own imagination. Nope. There is an archway seated atop a mesa in southeastern Arizona that is tied to legends going back to the 1800s, stories of people vanishing, of time-altering effects. If you'd like to read more about it, check out: *Searching for Arizona's Buried Treasures* by Ron Quinn, Mary Bingham, and Robert Zucker (specifically the chapter "Doorways to the Gods").

Military War Dogs and Their Handlers. Tucker and Kane first appeared in the Sigma Force novel *Bloodline*, but even then, I knew their journey wasn't over. Their adventures continued in *Kill Switch* and *War Hawk*—and I still have plenty more trouble for them to get into, including a return to Sigma. How did this dynamic duo come to life? I first encountered this heroic pairing of soldier and war dog while on a USO tour to Iraq and Kuwait in the winter of 2010. Seeing these pairs' capabilities and recognizing their unique bonds, I wanted to try to capture and honor those relationships.

To accomplish that, I spoke to veterinarians in the US Veterinary Corps, interviewed handlers, met their dogs, and saw how these duos grew together to become a single fighting unit. Some may read this account of Tucker and Kane and wonder how much is truly possible. Can a dog and his handler truly do so much? I vetted these past stories (including this novella) with handlers, who told me that not only are such actions plausible, if anything these dogs could do so much more. What about Kane's ability to understand over a thousand words and to follow a chain of commands? Besides confirming such an astounding ability with those same handlers, I'd be remiss not to mention another inspiration: an intrepid border collie named Chaser, who had a tested vocabulary of 1,022 words. Sadly, Chaser passed away at the age of fifteen in July of 2019—about the same time I finished this story. Thanks, Chaser, for helping me bring Kane to life!

Now, if you'd like to know more about war dogs and their handlers, I highly recommend two books by the author Maria Goodavage: *Soldier Dogs: The Untold Story of America's Canine Heroes* and *Top Dog: The Story of Marine Hero Lucca*.

Post-Traumatic Stress Disorder. Another topic raised in this story is a new understanding of one aspect of PTSD. It goes by the name of *moral injury* and is explored in this novella as Tucker struggles to deal with his loss of Abel, a death that haunts him. According to the US Department of Veteran Affairs, moral injury can manifest as shame, guilt, anxiety, and anger, along with behavioral changes, such as alienation, withdrawal, and self-harming (including suicide). We see shades of this in Tucker in this novella, and as with most veterans, there is no quick fix. For those afflicted, it's an ongoing process to find their center again, and tremendous resources can be found at www.nvf.org (hotline: 888-777-4443).

*   *   *

Unfortunately, though Tucker has made some significant progress toward that center, he and his partner, Kane, will find their newfound sense of peace sorely tested as their adventures continue. For now, I'll let them rest, recuperate, and recharge their batteries—because Sigma will soon need all their skill, cunning, and most of all, their unbreakable bond.

Acknowledgments

This collection spans from the start of my career straight through to present day. But I'd be remiss to not mention one collection of first readers, who served both as critics and as great friends. They're collectively known as the Warped Spacers. I joined this critique group about four years *before* my first publication. They've stuck with me through all the various incarnations of my storytelling, from stuff that's safely buried in my backyard to my latest novel. While some members have come and gone, the current roster has helped with these stories, either from the very beginning or more recently. They include Chris Crowe, Lee Garrett, Matt Bishop, Denny Grayson, Matt Orr, Leonard Little, Judy Prey, Steve Prey, Caroline Williams, Sadie Davenport, Sally Ann Barnes, Lisa Goldkuhl, and Amy Rogers. But I also have to single out David Sylvian for sticking with me from the first short story to this current book's novella. Of course, none of this would happen without an astounding team of industry professionals who I defy anyone to surpass. To everyone at William Morrow, thank you for always having my back, especially Liate Stehlik, Danielle Bartlett, Kaitlin Harri, Josh Marwell, Richard Aquan, and Ana Maria Allessi. Last, of course, a special acknowledgment to the people instrumental to all levels of production: my esteemed editor, Lyssa Keusch, and her industrious colleague Mireya Chiriboga; and for all their hard work, my agents, Russ Galen and Danny Baror (along with his daughter Heather Baror). And as always, I must stress that any and all errors of fact or detail in this book, of which hopefully there are not too many, fall squarely on my own shoulders.

Credits

With the exception of Rembrandt's *The Raising of Lazarus,* all art courtesy of the respective authors.

About the Author

James Rollins is the #1 *New York Times* bestselling author of international thrillers that have been translated into more than forty languages. His Sigma series has been lauded as one of the "top crowd-pleasers" (*New York Times*) and one of the "hottest summer reads" (*People* magazine). In each novel, acclaimed for its originality, Rollins unveils unseen worlds, scientific breakthroughs, and historical secrets—and he does it all at breakneck speed and with stunning insight. He lives in the Sierra Nevada.